PARTY
OF
LIARS

PARTY
OF
LIARS

A NOVEL

KELSEY COX

MINOTAUR BOOKS
NEW YORK

First published in the United States by Minotaur Books, an imprint of St. Martin's Publishing Group

PARTY OF LIARS. Copyright © 2025 by Kelsey Cox Writer, Inc. All rights reserved. Printed in the United States of America. For information, address St. Martin's Publishing Group, 120 Broadway, New York, NY 10271.

www.minotaurbooks.com

Design by Meryl Sussman Levavi

The Library of Congress Cataloging-in-Publication Data is available upon request.

ISBN 978-1-250-37881-1 (hardcover)
ISBN 978-1-250-37882-8 (ebook)

Our books may be purchased in bulk for promotional, educational, or business use. Please contact your local bookseller or the Macmillan Corporate and Premium Sales Department at 1-800-221-7945, extension 5442, or by email at MacmillanSpecialMarkets@macmillan.com.

First Edition: 2025

1   3   5   7   9   10   8   6   4   2

For Mom and Dad, who made me feel brave enough to try,
safe enough to fail, and strong enough to try again

When Death first enters a house, he throws so long a shadow—it seems to touch everyone.

—Fanny Longfellow, in a letter following the death of her seventeen-month-old daughter, 1848

PARTY
OF
LIARS

1

The Night of the Party

The house has always belonged to *The Mother*.

Perched atop the highest cliff in Comal County, Texas, the Queen Anne–style Victorian was built in the late nineteenth century by Wilhelm Vogel. Wilhelm had fallen in love with young Ada Müller, a debutante, notorious for declining suitors, turning away their trinkets, poems, and various attempts to charm her. What she wanted was a castle. So Wilhelm, a notable businessman and stone carver, set his sails for the Texas Hill Country, like so many German immigrants before him. There he purchased the land. He brought an architect by train from New York City to draw the grand plans, and construction began. Limestone was quarried locally. Stained-glass windows and handcrafted woodwork were shipped from Europe. Finally, with calloused hands, Wilhelm planted tulips—Ada's favorite flower—in the gardens along the latticework. Then he sent for her. Some months later, upon her arrival, she saw it from her carriage, so high up—asymmetrical facade, turrets and dormers, two-story wraparound porch—imposing against the backdrop of an endless Texas sky. Ada was pleased.

The ranchers who lived in the house's shadow saw Mrs. Vogel often, tall and slender, with pale skin and pale hair—combing out her curls in the upstairs window, tending to delicate blooms of yellow, cream, and pink that stood sentry around the estate. Later, they watched her pushing the baby's pram through the grounds, and at sunset, standing on the balcony, face to the wind.

Then came Ada's death. So very soon after the magnificent house was completed. A story in and of itself. *A fall,* people repeated. *An accident?* they questioned. And some wondered and might have even whispered behind closed doors but never in polite company about whether it was proper to bury her in consecrated ground.

And after—after Wilhelm moved away, after the windows were shuttered and the house fell into disrepair, after the town grew beneath it like so much switchgrass and wild rye—the stories took a different shape.

Haunted, they said.

———

For more than a century, the house lay dormant. Until one summer day in 2010 it was purchased by someone new, and ever since the townsfolk have waited to get inside.

They watched the renovations from below. First, the exterior was painstakingly restored—limestone bricks scrubbed clean, the stained-glass windows releaded, the intricate gingerbread trim repaired and repainted in bright sugarplum colors. A basement and wine cellar were excavated from the limestone. Then, inside, walls were knocked down, floors peeled away, ceilings stretched to soaring. Claustrophobic woodwork was removed, along with tufted, claw-foot furniture and moldy Victorian tapestries. Until everything glowed bright, all white, Calacatta marble tiger-striped with veins of gold, modern chandeliers like soap bubbles.

The whole town could see the changes clearly. Because last and most shockingly, the entire back wall of the home was removed, sliced away, replaced with a floor-to-ceiling wall of glass, exposing the interior. Even the balcony—glass, extending the entire back of the top floor, hovering over the infinity pool, three stories below.

The house opened like a lidless eye.

A life-sized dollhouse.

———

Tonight is an unveiling of sorts—a party. The iron gates are open. The doors are unlocked. They have finally been invited in.

The house is a beehive cracked open, buzzing, buzzing.

It's elaborate for a Sweet Sixteen—catered canapés, a three-tiered cake, a DJ turning the bluestone patio into a dance floor. They've rented tuxedos and polished their boots, teased their hair and purchased

Badgley Mischka and Halston gowns at the Nordstrom in the La Cantera mall.

By 8 P.M., everyone gathers from their distant corners to sing "Happy Birthday." Lights off. Sixteen candles are reflected in the blackened wall of windows. The birthday girl makes a wish, blows them out, plunges them all into fleeting darkness. They can see the small lights of their own houses far below, can see the town the way the house sees them. For this moment, they feel a part of it, of this house. But it doesn't belong to them. To any of them.

It belongs to *The Mother.*

The lights come back on. The cake is torn apart. The dark windows are like mirrors in the night, reflecting the party guests back to themselves. They can't see outside anymore.

But they can hear it.

The scream. Just long enough for a body to fall through air.

Then. The sickening thud.

Echoes—sounds this house has heard before.

2

Dani

The Evening Before the Party

Charlotte makes a little sound. Not quite a cry, but I recognize it for what it is: a warning. She is tiring of her ExerSaucer. I have . . . maybe forty seconds before she completely loses her shit.

I've been working on the cake all day in the small pockets of time the baby has graced me with. "One second, sweetie." I'm finishing a row of hot pink buttercream petals. The cake is a riot of neon colors— somehow the '90s have come back around in fashion. But really, I need more than a second. I need hours of undivided time.

Charlotte arches her back and lets out an earsplitting wail. Of course, it's that exact moment when Ethan enters the kitchen.

A few months ago, he would have made a joke—*Poor thing. Is Mama torturing you?* Not anymore, though. Now, he tosses his briefcase on the island, rescues Charlotte from her ExerSaucer prison. Her crying stops as suddenly as it started.

"Where's Órlaith?" he asks, looking around the huge, open room for our nanny.

This kitchen is a dream, better than any feature spread from *Bon Appétit* magazine that I have ever drooled over, dog-eared, clipped, and tacked to the vision board in my apartment closet. Twelve-foot ceilings, two islands, all solid white marble, Gaggenau appliances, Sub-Zero refrigerator, custom brass hardware to match the one-of-a-kind geo-metric pendant lights. I should be deliriously happy.

"I'm sorry." I set the piping bag down, wipe my hands on my apron. "I sent Órlaith upstairs to fold laundry. I swear, Charlotte was fine a second ag—"

"Dani, relax. I know." He has Charlotte on his hip now. She is pulling at the collar of his shirt. He looks sexy. The way he always does after a long day at work. White button-up a little rumpled, the top two buttons undone. It makes me think of getting drinks on a weeknight in some dim bar, my legs tilted toward him, knees touching, hungry. It feels like a lifetime ago.

"How did today go?" he asks. "The cake looks incredible."

I pick up the piping bag, twist the open end, apply even pressure as I form the next petal. "My session with Curtis went great," I answer, because I know that's what he's really asking. Our conversations lately are like a game of Taboo—no one is allowed to say what they really mean. "He was really supportive of me making the cake. Said I needed to start reestablishing old routines." This is a bit of a fib. Curtis, like everyone, wants me to take it easy. But taking it easy is driving me crazy.

I steal a glance at Ethan, to see if he bought my little white lie. He claims that he and Curtis don't discuss my sessions, but I don't know. I mean, if the tables were turned? I'd have my ear pressed to the door. He's giving Charlotte attention, though, keeping his own cards close.

"My mom called," I say.

Charlotte is fascinated by a button on the cuff of his shirt. "Oh, yeah? How's Pam?"

I didn't have time for the call. Frankly, it came at the worst possible moment. I was changing Charlotte's diaper. There were three minutes left on the oven timer. But, with everyone so worried about me, I don't have the luxury of letting a call go to voicemail right now.

Oh, honey, I forgot to tell you yesterday. Remember that armadillo that's been digging up my azaleas? Well, Tom finally caught him.

Really? I thought he kept getting out of those traps you bought.

Another round of Taboo. Mom didn't care about the armadillo story and neither did I. But we had to pretend, because what Mom really needed was to judge the cadence of my words, the pitch of my voice, to hear Charlotte babbling in the background. Finally, as the timer beeped and I single-arm-wrestled Charlotte back into her bouncy chair, we skimmed close to the real point:

Honey, are you sure you don't need us there tomorrow? Because I can pack an overnight bag. It's no big deal.

No, Mom, really. It's fine.

Translation: *I am fine.*

"They caught that armadillo," I tell Ethan.

"Pam must be thrilled." He's pinching Charlotte's squishy bare leg.

I set down the piping bag again. "Let me see her." I take my daughter into my arms.

Charlotte tips her head back. Her smile is always so quick, so generous, eyes squinted to slits, cheeks round and red as apples. She has recently sprouted two bottom teeth, which has somehow changed her whole face and also made her look more like herself. I grab my phone off the island, stretch out my arm, press my cheek to hers. We both smile in the selfie beside the cake.

Then she reaches out a chubby arm and swipes her hand through the frosting.

"Shit." I yank her away, but the damage is done.

Charlotte is startled by my response, eyes wide and mouth trembling. She's gauging whether or not to cry. Like, really cry. "It's okay. That's okay." I sing the words, bouncing her to an unknown rhythm.

I'm soothing myself as much as her. Now I'll have to redo the whole layer, scrape the frosting off and start again. I can't express any of this frustration, because it will only confirm to Ethan what he already thinks: that this is all too much for me.

Ethan wanted to buy a cake. A "professional one." I wanted to say *I am a professional. Or, at least, I used to be.*

Instead, I said, *I miss baking.*

There was a time in my life when I baked every day, multiple times a day. Before the baby, before Ethan, I could spend a week trying to perfect a recipe—mango vanilla bean tart, perhaps—make it and remake it twenty times until it was Instagram-worthy, the shortbread crust thin and flaky, the filling melt-in-your-mouth, the uniform slices of perfectly ripe mango spiraling into a rose.

Ethan takes Charlotte back from me. "Órlaith," he calls out.

Órlaith is quick to appear. Like she'd been hovering just past the doorframe this whole time. I still haven't gotten used to having someone in my home. Órlaith is a short Irish woman in her late sixties with a practical haircut and orthopedic shoes. She's genuinely Irish, accent and all. She just immigrated here recently, after her husband died.

The woman is death-obsessed in that way that old people get some-times. Everything loops somehow back to someone she knows who died in some awful, tragic way. *Oh no, you won't be seeing me drinking one of those diet fizzy drinks,* she'll tell me. *They have that what's-it-called in it, that only causes cancer, like. I had a friend, Mary O'Connor, drank one diet fizzy drink every day of her life, and wouldn't you know what happened? Sure, brain tumor. She died terribly slow. Used to be full-faced and only gorgeous. The line of boys wrapped around the street back in our day. But by the end she hardly looked herself, cheeks sunken and no joy in her eyes.*

I'm left standing stupid in front of the open fridge with a can of Diet Coke, like I offered her a glass of antifreeze. Seriously, she finds death in everything. No topic of conversation is safe.

And she's always just *there,* right in the next room folding endless burp cloths, or picking up toys behind the sofa, or beside me when I turn to reach for the diaper cream. It's like having a mopey, morbid shadow.

"I know you're about to clock out," my husband says, "but would you mind getting Charlotte down for bed before you go?"

"I'd be delighted." She takes Charlotte from his outstretched arms. "It's lovely," Órlaith says of the cake. The bottom two tiers are assembled—multicolored and multishaped sprinkles applied by hand, fondant rain-bows with marshmallow clouds, neon-colored macaroons.

I don't answer, concentrate on scraping the top tier clean to be redec-orated. I don't mean to be bitchy. It isn't Órlaith's fault I don't like her. Not really.

Once they are gone, Ethan is behind me, rubbing my shoulders. I force them to relax. "How much longer?" he asks.

All night. I want to get it perfect. I'm nervous about tomorrow—the Sweet Sixteen for Sophie, Ethan's daughter from his first marriage—and focusing those nerves on a cake is more therapeutic than any session with Curtis could ever be.

"It shouldn't take long." I smooth a base layer of lime green butter-cream.

His lips are on my neck now, his breath warm, the prickle of his chin just the right amount of rough. His hands wander down my body, to my waist, to my hips. He leans closer, leans into me, his front flush against my back, and I can feel the need of him. "What if I can't wait that long?" His voice comes from deep in his throat.

My skin goose-bumps, involuntary and primal. I set the spatula on the marble, twist to face him. When I kiss him, his tongue dives into my mouth. We've been together over three years now, but he still kisses me like it's the first time, like he is desperate to taste me, to have me. It's intoxicating. I succumb—my restless thoughts eclipsed by physical sensation, the pressure of his fingers, the smell of his skin, and in this carnal moment, I feel, rather than think, *Maybe everything really can go back to normal.*

He presses, pinning my hips between his body and the hard marble countertop.

"What if Órlaith comes back down?" I ask, a little breathless.

"I don't care." His lips are back on my neck, teeth scraping that tender spot just below my jaw. Over his head, through the open doorway, through the great room, I can see the sweep of the staircase, the underside of the loft above. Suddenly, I imagine Órlaith, not in the nursery, but perched silent on the landing, her shapeless form like a gargoyle, observing.

I snake my hands to his shoulders, push him gently away. "I need to finish the cake."

He lets out a groan of disappointment, then kisses my forehead and lets me go.

"Let's have drinks by the pool tonight." He goes into the butler's pantry between the kitchen and the dining room, where we have a wet bar. The pantry is about the same size as the entire galley kitchen of my old apartment, but with much nicer fixtures—hammered copper sink, mirrored backsplash, mullioned cabinet windows to display every kind of wine and cocktail glass. Choice whiskeys and scotches line a shelf, alongside sipping tequila and Tito's vodka, made just an hour away in Austin. A slim, glass-doored wine fridge holds a handful of bottles for easy access—Ethan's full collection is downstairs in the cellar. I can hear him taking down glasses. "The weather is perfect."

I turn to glance at the wall of glass. The view still takes my breath away. The depth of so much open sky beneath me somersaults my organs. Dusk gives the air a solid quality from way up here, gray and compressed, like lint pulled from the dryer, like if you fell, you might land softly. Cars snake along the highway down below, and ranches on the other side are a patchwork quilt. Spring has started, and here in Texas, that means wildflowers like streaks of paint, splashes of yellow, the bright orange of Indian paintbrushes, and large swaths of bluebonnets.

"I hope it stays that way," I say. "I know Sophie and her friends are looking forward to using the pool tomorrow."

He comes back into the kitchen, whiskey glass in one hand, checking his phone in the other. "Supposed to be a little windy."

I'm working on the rows of hot pink buttercream petals again. It's going faster now. "Speaking of Órlaith," I say. I don't look at him. "Do you really think we still need a nanny?" I don't want to see his face during this conversation. It's my turn to play Taboo. I brace myself for his response. What I'm really asking: *Do you trust me yet?*

He surprises me. "You do seem to be getting better."

I look up. He leans against the opposite counter, one foot crossed over the other, the crystal glass of amber liquid in his hand. The hint of a smile on his face.

The tension melts from my shoulders, genuine this time. His words are a validation, a light at the end of the darkest tunnel I've ever clawed my way through.

I smile back at him, start on the next row of petals.

But the sense of relief is short-lived.

Because he doesn't know the whole truth.

3

Kim

I lean against the doorframe, wineglass in hand, watching Sophie try on her dress for the party tomorrow. How is it possible that my daughter is turning sixteen? How did I get this old? I swallow more wine. Sweetie, my favorite cat, a black and orange tortoiseshell with golden eyes, weaves figure eights around my ankles.

Somehow, I have three cats and two dogs, none of whom I specifically sought out—friends who find a litter of kittens by a dumpster or have a stray mutt show up during a storm know I'm a sucker for a sweet face (or a one-eyed face, like my gray tabby, Mad-Eye Moody).

I took Sophie shopping a month ago. She must have tried on thirty dresses before falling head over heels for this sparkly, powder blue, off-the-shoulder gown. It surpassed my budget by more than a little. But it's hard for me to say no. Raising a child after divorce means being in constant competition with the one person you loathe.

The extra expense was worth it. The look on her face. I wish anything as simple as a dress could make me that happy. She's sixteen—with the slim waist and long legs that used to be mine. The dress laces up the back, exposing a bit more skin than I'd like. But, overall, it has a sweet, Cinderella feel.

"Who's dropping off Mikayla?"

Mikayla is Sophie's oldest friend. She lives in our old neighborhood. They met shortly after we moved in, became inseparable in that way little girls can. It's tradition that they celebrate their birthdays with a sleepover, pizza in bed, and movies late into the night. Now, of course, Ethan is throwing Sophie a sinfully over-the-top party to show off what an awesome dad he is. It's also his chance to show off our old house, the renovations. He's invited as many of his friends, neighbors, and colleagues as Sophie's own guests. He's so sure they're all salivating to get in. The pathetic thing is he's right.

I was glad the girls still wanted their sleepover here tonight. Maybe because it makes me feel like I still have one up on Ethan. He gets the facade of the party. I get the real deal. Or maybe I'm just not ready for my baby to grow up.

Sophie made the cheer squad last year, which came with a slew of new high school friends that I don't really like. Girls whose daddies are real estate developers, whose mamas run the booster clubs, girls who kiss each other on the cheeks and exchange thinly veiled backhanded compliments.

Mikayla is the opposite. Red hair and a smattering of freckles, she always looks like she just stepped off the farm, because she did. Her family is old Bulverde—they've owned land and raised cattle here since it was a rural area way outside San Antonio, before the city spread like an inkblot and brought McMansions and, even more recently, overpriced tract homes.

I'm glad Sophie has a solid friendship like that. I might be a colossal fuckup, but I must have done something right in raising her.

Sophie shrugs. "Probably Caleb."

Since I'm not driving, I take another sip of wine. "So, are we doing hand-tossed or thin-crust?"

Sophie scoffs like I said something offensive. "I had some veggies and hummus. Mikayla's eating with her family."

She is turned to the side, looking into the floor-length mirror, smoothing her hands down a nonexistent belly. I don't say anything. If she changes her mind, I have some "emergency chocolate" tucked up on the top shelf of the pantry.

"You look gorgeous, Soph," I say. In some ways she still looks—still is—so much a child. Face plump, limbs awkwardly long, as though they sprouted overnight. But I can see the hints and curves of womanhood like warning signs.

"Yeah?" she asks. Then, "Yeah," like an affirmative. She turns to check out her backside. "Yeah. Okay." She tries on a different pair of shoes.

"I just want you to have fun, babe."

I can see the smallest of eye rolls in the mirror, as if I just don't get it. Sophie's first-ever boyfriend—a kid named Mason, quarterback on the football team, with floppy dark hair and nice yes ma'am, no ma'am manners—broke up with her a few weeks ago. She has spent almost every night since crying on the phone with Mikayla. She'll bite my head off if I bring it up, but I understand more than she thinks.

Sophie invited Mason to the party. Mason, being the polite boy that he is, gullibly accepted. She told her friends she did it to show him how much she doesn't care. I know better. She wants more than Mom's approval. She wants to light up the room, wants to set it aflame, to burn Mason to a crisp.

"I need this party to be perfect," she says.

I set the wineglass on her dresser. I stand behind her, hands on her shoulders, and we are both reflected in the mirror. "It will be perfect. I promise." Though I can make no such promise, I double down. "Absolutely nothing will go wrong tomorrow."

4

Mikayla

"Caleb James, why on earth can't you leave your boots by the door? I've only told you a thousand times. You've traipsed grass all through my clean living room."

Mom is doing a circle around the table, scooping green beans onto everyone's plate.

It's like white noise. She's said it all a million times. Grass is her enemy. She has literally used those words—*You know that grass is my enemy*—whenever one of us inevitably forgets to take off our shoes before coming in the house. But if it wasn't grass, it would be something else. I don't think I've ever seen Mom sit down. Even now, she'll flutter between the table and kitchen like a hummingbird because Dad needs salt for his mashed potatoes or because Kylie dropped her fork or because Mom oh-for-heaven's-sake forgot the rolls in the oven like she always does. In between these errands, her butt might kiss the seat. She might even raise her fork to her mouth, but then something else will need doing and she'll be off again.

"For God's sake, Alice, sit down," Dad says sometimes, but I think at this point it's just habit.

When Mom slings a "No cell phones, young lady" at me, Dad perks up.

"Hey." He snaps his fingers toward my phone, which I tuck into my lap. Dad doesn't give a crap about grass in the living room or water around the sink. But he hates "teenage bull" like cell phones and jeans with holes in them. *You want holes in your jeans*, he likes to say, *you can come work the stables with me for the day.*

"It's Sophie," I say, pushing potatoes around with my fork. "She needs my help with her outfit." She's been texting me selfies in her dress—*Hair up or down? Heavy eye or a softer look? What about shoes?* She looks drop-dead, of course. Sophie couldn't look bad if she tried.

"Aren't you spending the night over there?" Caleb asks.

"You're driving her," my father says. "I need you to pick up some corn for the feeder from Tractor Supply on the way back. I'll give you my card."

"She wants me to see how it looks on camera," I explain. "You know, for Snapchat."

Caleb rolls his eyes.

"She's dating the Fuller kid, right?"

Sophie and Mason broke up a few weeks ago, but Dad doesn't actually care about that. He just wants to talk football.

"Scouts from all over Texas and out of state were after him. He's smart to stay in Texas. A&M is a heck of a school."

"Her Sweet Sixteen," my mother says in a dreamy swoon, sinking into her chair. "You're both so grown-up now."

My own Sweet Sixteen was nothing special, no different from basically every other birthday party I'd ever had. Aunts and uncles and cousins, a handful of friends, Dad smoking a brisket, and Mom making a cake and her famous banana pudding, Memaw giving me two hundred-dollar bills in a card, which was more than she'd ever given me before, so I guess that was kind of special.

"Don't you remember when they were tiny things, George? Oh—" Mom hops up. "The tea. Did I really? I could have sworn . . . ?" Her eyes scan the table before she flies back to the kitchen and returns with a pitcher of sweet tea. "You two were just the cutest. When did they move in up there? Y'all couldn't have been older than three. Do you remember her riding the pony for the first time, George? She was such a little doll." She's making her way around the table as she talks, filling up everyone's glass. "You better stay my baby forever," she says to Kylie, kissing her on the cheek. Kylie's only six.

I do remember Sophie on the pony, actually. Even as a little kid, Sophie was pretty—long blond hair that rippled like water, outfits that all matched, shiny shoes without a single scuff. She was golden, and I couldn't believe my luck that she wanted to be *my* friend, sleep over at *my* house, sit next to *me* on the story-time rug, claimed *me* as her partner when Mrs. Whitaker told us to buddy up for our field trip to Natural Bridge Caverns, letting all the other kids know I was hers. She could have picked anyone. Every other girl wanted to touch her hair, try on her necklace, be near her. She had that kind of radiance—like just being in her general vicinity gave you some of her shine. She still does.

"You aren't eating," Mom says. "Everything okay?"

I lift my shoulder. "I'm fine."

"You better not be on some wacky diet," Dad says. "Guys don't like a skinny girl, right, Caleb?"

Caleb shrugs.

This isn't true. Guys love a skinny girl.

Spring of eighth grade, Sophie made the cheer squad. Which meant she was busy most of the summer with camp and then in the fall with practice and games, things I wasn't a part of, a whole new set of friends. It was the first time there was this silent tug between us, like trying to hold hands during red rover. Plus I'm an FFA girl—a Future Farmer of America—raising and showing my goat, Ed, for the Comal County Junior Livestock Show. By anyone's account, Soph and I shouldn't be friends.

But our grips on each other are strong, our childhoods threaded tightly together like two necklaces tangled in the back of an old jewelry box. I can't conjure a memory without her. *My sister from another mister,* Sophie says sometimes, slipping her hands around my waist and kissing my cheek when she drags me to a party that she was invited to and I wasn't.

She didn't leave me behind. Wouldn't.

If they wanted Sophie there, they had to accept me as well. I was like a free gift with purchase—a makeup pouch you may or may not use after you spend seventy-five dollars on a pot of blush and brow filler at Ulta.

So I go to the parties, I sit with the cool kids at lunch, I laugh at their inside jokes, even when I don't understand them, and I link arms with Sophie, who links arms with Gabby and Emma and Ava. We walk through the halls like a force.

But I'm not one of those girls. They're hard to look at, as glossy as magazine covers. That's how I've started to think of them—*the glossy girls.* Their thin legs like glossy stems, their cheeks and the straight line of their noses highlighted with shimmer, their high ponytails with a literal shine, tied up with enormous Ranger blue bows, so they look like the porcelain baby dolls my memaw collects.

It seems girls like this are always trying to be smaller—crawling into the guys' laps, tucking their legs up in a chair, shrieking *No, no, don't pick me up,* when all they clearly want is to be picked up. Maybe it's a trade-off, some unwritten rule of the universe, that the smaller a girl's body is, the bigger her personality is allowed to be.

Dad and Caleb are talking about trimming Buck's hooves for the upcoming rodeo.

I sneak a look at my phone under the table, text Sophie—*Love the sparkly heels! You look freakin amazing!*

I wish I could enjoy this moment with her, be the girls we used to be. The girl I used to be. Things used to go unspoken because we understood each other so fully that we didn't need words. We could have a whole conversation with just a sideways glance, cause each other to burst into giggles with a raised eyebrow.

Now, it hurts to even look at her. There are things that simply can't be communicated, can't be spoken, words that can never be said, because I know, deep down in my bones, that it would mean the end of us. The end of everything.

I want to yank the tablecloth, upturn everyone's plates and glasses of tea, send it all crashing to the floor.

Sophie responds with a GIF of Beyoncé booty-shaking in a gold dress.

"Oh, for heaven's sake, the rolls," Mom says, and leaps from her seat to the kitchen. There is the slight smell of burning.

5

Órlaith

Is there anything sweeter than rocking a baby to sleep? Half past seven at this time of year, the sun is still setting. The blackout curtains darken the nursery, but enough light seeps around the edges that I can see the curve of her cheek, the pretty bow of her mouth.

I sing softly in rhythm with the sway of the chair—*Sleep, sleep, gran mo chree. Here on your mamma's knee*—the same lullaby I sang to my own gorgeous girl. It's been decades since my daughter was this age. But when I hold Charlotte, I can almost imagine that she *is* mine. *Angels are guarding. And they watch o'er thee.*

Though I'd be in heaven snuggling her all night, I lay her down. I shuffle from the room and hold the knob as I close the door so that it doesn't even make a click.

Mr. Matthews waits on the landing. "Thanks for getting her down." He chats for a bit, asks whether Charlotte gave me any trouble, if I have plans for the evening. But it's clear he has something specific on his mind. He checks behind him more than once. Mrs. Matthews must still be downstairs in the kitchen, working on that elaborate cake of hers. "How is she?" he finally asks.

"Oh, she's a gem, she is. She'll be crawling soon, I'd say."

He shakes his head. "No. Dani. How's my wife? She's thrown herself into this cake. And, I don't know, maybe that's a good thing. I just don't want her to get overwhelmed and—"

I interrupt him. "She's grand, sure. She's a new mam. I remember when I first had mine. All she did was cry, and so all I did was cry too. You get through it."

His expression relaxes a bit, the crease between his eyebrows uncreasing. "How many kids do you have?"

"Just the one. My Colm and I, we had plans for a right litter. Six kids, my Colm wanted. But you know what they say: If you want to make God laugh, tell Him your plans. And He did laugh, so He did. But isn't He always right in the end? Because our girl turned out to be the picture of perfection."

His lips curve politely. "Any grandkids?"

"No, sure."

"Well, I bet you're looking forward to that."

I smile.

"You're amazing with Charlotte. We're lucky to have you. I worry about leaving Dani alone . . ." He trails off.

"With the baby?" I ask. I know he has his reasons.

"No, no." He is quick to backpedal. "Well, yes. I feel guilty leaving them both alone, I mean. It's nice knowing she has a little help when I'm not here."

———

I say goodbye to Mrs. Matthews on my way out. She mumbles a response without looking up from her cake. She is manically using a pair of tweezers to apply sprinkles one by one.

Outside the sun has set and the sky is blue-gray with twilight. The house is like a big cake itself, outlined against the wide blank sky. It sits on the edge of an honest-to-God cliff, a sheer straight drop hundreds of feet down. Three big black birds circle in line with the cellar. Buzzards, they call them here, a type of little vulture. There is something dead down below.

I am getting in my car, but I can feel it. Every night, at the end of my shift, I feel it. Like a hand tugging me back. I turn the ignition, start around the circular drive toward the black iron gates. I want to go back inside. I want to gather the baby in my arms and bring her with me.

I don't, of course. Every night I ignore the tug. But I know—

Solid as a prayer, I know—

There is evil in that house.

6

Dani

Poolside is picturesque. *It's like a resort,* I told my sister the first time I stayed over at Ethan's. The gauzy curtains of the cabana billowing, the warm glow of the underwater lights, the sharp edge of the infinity pool, a mirror to the black Hill Country sky, stars like a cast handful of salt. The house looms large, every light on except the nursery. It's like a diorama, like a castle flayed open. I relax into the plush lounge. Ethan has mixed me a cocktail—fruit, vodka, not too sweet—while he sips another whiskey. The baby monitor sits on a metal table between our two chairs. A staticky version of the white noise machine plays at a low volume.

The monitor is a good one—Ethan always spends top dollar—but it has a glitch. Sometimes, when you first turn it on, for a moment it shows an old image from just before it was turned off. It's given me a jolt more than once, usually because it shows an empty crib. My mind can't catch up fast enough, can't outrun the panic. Once I nearly jumped out of my skin when I saw a woman standing over my child, her long, stringy hair dangling down into the bed. Until I realized I was looking at a vestige of myself.

On the screen now, Charlotte sleeps peacefully.

The night is gorgeous. Too dark to see much beyond the glow of the pool, the lights of other houses dotted far below, a track of headlights. There is a cool breeze, just enough to ripple the water, to flutter the hairs on my neck. The sounds of leaves rustling, of ice in our glasses, of unseen frogs and insects chirping. We live far enough outside San Antonio to see the stars on a clear night like this, far enough to see jackrabbits and wild turkeys during the day. But close enough that we can pop into town for dinner on the River Walk, drinks at the Pearl, or a play at the Majestic.

He is holding my hand, our fingers intertwined.

When I first met Ethan I was working at a coffee shop within walking distance of his practice. I noticed him right away. Dark hair, peppered with gray at the temples. A smile that dimpled his cheeks. Jeans and a blazer—I've always been a sucker for that look. He stopped by every day, ordered a black coffee and whatever pastry I recommended. He hung his jacket on the chair, looked over papers while he finished his coffee, then left me a generous tip. After a few weeks, he asked me out. "I'd like to take you on a date," he said. It was so direct. No games. I liked that.

He picked me up at my door, took me to Bohanan's downtown. I wore a red dress. Over a bottle of wine and steaks, we talked, and he listened. Really listened.

It was so different from dates with men my age. I had tried all the apps—Plenty of Fish and Tinder and Match.com—but the men my age were Peter Pans, eternally on the cusp of getting their shit together, wanting to meet for happy hour, split the bill, then take me back to the apartment they shared with two roommates. I didn't have the time. I was too busy building my own career. I had gained a following on Instagram—nearly 300k after one of my videos was featured by BuzzFeed—posting artsy photographs of latticeworked pies or intricately piped sugar cookies, decorating videos sped up and set to pop music.

I became addicted to growing my following, and soon I was baking more consistently and elaborately than ever before. A hobby that I started long ago to spend time with my grandfather had turned into pretty pictures on the internet, which were turning into local orders. I had never thought of cooking as a career before, but the idea of opening my own bakery became a goal.

Ethan was fascinated by all of it. And I was fascinated by him—a psychiatrist who owned his own successful practice with his best friend, Curtis.

At the end of the night, he dropped me off at my doorstep. I was debating inviting him inside. I didn't want the night to end. I was the perfect amount of tipsy—we had shared a bottle of wine—but also the evening had been exquisite, I had a buzz just from smiling. I swayed onto my toes, leaned toward him ever so slightly, willed him to kiss me. He did. His hand cupped my jaw, the pads of his fingers on my neck, his thumb on my cheek. I was on tiptoes.

When he broke the kiss, my internal debate was over. I was about to ask him inside, but he said, "I'd like to call you tomorrow."

I couldn't do anything but nod. He left me there, tingling from head to toe.

The rest was a whirlwind. Expensive dinners and tickets to the ballet, an out-of-town trip—a quaint bed-and-breakfast on the river in Gruene—and then, when he found out I'd never left the country, a trip to Paris, where we sampled wine and pastries until we collapsed on our hotel bed, bellies full and laughing. Another trip, later that same year, to Spain, where he proposed at the Park Güell in Barcelona, before the mosaic tile bench that winds its way along the terrace.

Ethan sets his empty whiskey on the table beside the monitor and gets up. He takes my glass from me and sets it aside as well. He sits on the edge of my lounge chair. He leans down to kiss me—my lips, my jaw, my ear, and down my neck, making me gasp. His hands travel me, and soon he is tugging down my yoga pants, climbing on top of me, finishing what we started in the kitchen. He reads me absolutely—responding to each arch of my back, inhalation of breath—and there is such freedom in being understood. I watch the stars while we make love.

It's all so perfect. My life. How did I get so lucky?

Yet, there is a weight like a stone in my belly. I feel it more in these perfect moments than ever.

Earlier today, in the library upstairs, Curtis asked about my *tendencies.*

I put on my prettiest smile. *I check the locks before bed.* I tucked a strand of hair behind my ear. *Probably too many times,* with a breath of a laugh.

That's fine, he said. *That's normal. What about sleep? Have you noticed a decreased need for sleep?*

Are you kidding? I'm exhausted all the time. Whether or not I'm getting the sleep I need is another question, but not the one he asked. My foot jiggled up and down, up and down. I stilled it when I noticed him noticing, his almond-slivered eyes cut under his brow, pen poised over his notes. *Purposeless movements,* they call them sometimes, another warning sign. I smiled.

Do you ever see, hear, or feel things that others can't? Have you noticed sounds or visuals that occur without any external source? Worries that aren't based entirely in reality?

A variety of ways to ask whether I've been imagining things. How would I know, though, if I was? I shook my head.

He closed his notebook. Our session was coming to an end. I knew the question he would ask next, my chest tightening in anticipation.

You know I have to ask this. A sympathetic lift to his lips. *Have you had any thoughts about hurting yourself or others?*

Not at all. I made my face serene. *I feel completely like myself again.*

Wonderful, he said.

I'm pretty sure he believed me.

He clicked the pen closed, tossed it and the notebook onto the end table. He removed his bifocals and relaxed into the chair, arms crossed behind his head. *Tell Ethan I'm expecting that Cuban tomorrow. Oh, and Gemma was wondering if she needs to bring anything?* It was always strange, the way he shape-shifted roles, from therapist to friend. But Curtis is a friend. Ethan's oldest friend, in fact, going back way before the practice. Ethan got his first job at fourteen doing clerical work for Curtis's father. The Barkers—Curtis and Gemma—are our go-to couple.

At first, I thought it would be nice, talking to a friend, that it would feel casual instead of clinical. But now the lines are blurry. Between my sessions with Curtis, Órlaith's spying from every corner of this sprawling manor, my mother with her nearly daily check-ins, and Ethan's constant words of reassurance—I am a bug under glass.

That's why I've kept it a secret from all their prying eyes.

Because none of them would believe me.

A few days ago, I found a note on our front step. I didn't imagine it. I didn't imagine the nasty words or the slanting hand. Didn't imagine the threat folded inside that piece of paper.

7

Kim

I'm standing in my kitchen, empty wineglass in hand, debating whether to rinse it and go off to bed or to pour another. I told myself only two glasses tonight. To be fair, I say that most nights.

Fuck it. I give myself a healthy pour, then eye the package of Milano cookies on top of the fridge, but think better of the latter impulse. I have some self-control, no matter what anyone says.

The dress I plan on wearing tomorrow is hanging on my closet door. I bought it a few months ago, two sizes too small, with big plans. I still have friends who rave about the keto diet—the pounds melting away like all that butter they slather on bacon and broccoli. Then I realized the strict carb counting basically nixed my wine, which basically nixed that diet. I bought a pair of heavy-duty Spanx instead, started skipping dinners, popping diet pills.

Ginger, my Pomeranian, tip-tap-tips behind me. When I plop down on the sofa, she jumps up as well. I turn up my television. There's a true crime documentary playing on Netflix—the torso of an unidentified woman is found floating in a lake—but I open my phone and click on Instagram.

I'm not sure why I feel the dress matters all that much. Ethan has a twenty-seven-year-old wife, for Chrissake. That's how old we were when we had Sophie. I can't compete with that. And I don't want to.

It's just . . . our old house, our old friends, this party—once upon a time, Ethan promised me a party like this one. I guess I don't want to be the sad sack everyone thinks I am.

I scroll for a bit, but I can't help myself. I take a long swallow of wine and click on Dani's account.

I watched Dani's Instagram obsessively in those early days. Between images of opulent cakes and rainbow bagels and videos of her rolling dough in a tank top, a dusting of flour on her cute little cheekbone, there were pictures of him, of them, of their growing life together. A stroll by the Alamo, a B and B on the Guadalupe River, a profile shot of Ethan looking handsome at some patio bar, whiskey in hand, #ManCrushMonday.

One post had really set me off: Ethan and Dani in front of a winery in Fredericksburg with Curtis and Gemma Barker, sunglasses and smiles and cabernet.

Curtis is good-looking in a way that implies he is well-bred like a horse—tall and slender, close-cropped blond hair, long and delicate fingers. His family drips Texas oil money, back generations. Gemma is his compact, travel-sized trophy wife, bleached hair bumped high on her head, a former Dallas Cowboys Cheerleader. By the look of her, I never would have expected to like her. Turned out, it was impossible not to.

What ticked me off was that, buried in my own Instagram account, existed nearly the exact same photograph, except it was the four of us— the Barkers and Ethan and me, standing in front of that same winery. That had been a fun trip. Ethan had booked it for my thirty-seventh birthday. A steak dinner at Crossroads, antiques shopping and baskets of peaches from a roadside stand, Gemma and I laughing in the shuttle from one winery to the next, her legs draped over mine.

When we separated, my life fell to shit. Not Ethan's, though. No, I'm convinced the universe is stacked entirely against me, because Ethan's luck only multiplied.

Three weeks after our divorce was finalized, Curtis's father, "Big Roy" Barker, suffered a massive heart attack while dove hunting with only his black Lab for company. The death was unexpected, but an even bigger shock came during probate. It wasn't surprising that Roy left something to Ethan—they'd always been close. Ethan had worked for Big Roy from the time he was fourteen years old, and they shared a mutual admiration for each other. Roy had supported Ethan in countless ways over the years, so it was easy to assume he'd get a mention in the will. Still, I don't think anyone expected what Roy had hidden up his sleeve. Trust me when I say that the timing of our divorce was real shit for me. Along with a staggering inheritance, Big Roy gifted Ethan half his practice, the one meant solely for Curtis. Barker & Matthews was formed.

The son my father never had, Curtis used to joke.

There was the bite of truth to it.

When Curtis and Ethan graduated med school together, Roy paid for a party at Houston's River Oaks Country Club. He was *proud of both his boys,* he said in his toast. But Curtis owed his degree to Daddy's money—lawyers that got Curtis out of trouble in undergrad, donations that scrubbed his record clean, favors that swayed the admissions board—and everyone knew it. Curtis had no love or aptitude for psychiatry. He'd taken the easy path of following his father.

But Ethan reminded Roy of himself. In Ethan he saw someone who wouldn't rest on the achievements handed down to him. A man who sought to make a name for himself, just like he'd done.

Ethan used a large portion of the inheritance to finish the last of the plans for the house that we had laid out together. He stripped off the entire back wall, replaced it with panels of glass the size of aquarium exhibits. I'd always wanted to see that view. Our dream home was finally complete, and I wasn't in it.

For nine years, I sacrificed for that house—put aside plans, went into debt, broke fingernails to build that goddamn house brick by brick. If only I'd known then that I'd been building it for Dani all along.

The worst part of it all was that Sophie was smitten with Dani as well. Sophie was only twelve when she met Dani, and little girls always look up to slightly older girls, don't they? Dani let Sophie help her decorate a dozen unicorn cupcakes once. The post garnered thousands of likes. For days, Sophie bounded into the room to show me every new comment.

I was well-behaved, feigning delight and telling her *Wonderful, sweetheart* instead of what I wanted to say, which was *Don't get too attached, baby. Daddy's bound to find a new twentysomething plaything soon.* And thank God I didn't, because I would have been wrong. Instead, he married her.

Sophie had been excited to be in their wedding—Dani made her a junior bridesmaid—and was even more thrilled to have a little sister. But Sophie has spent exactly one night at the old house since the baby was born, dragging along Mikayla and a big bag of gifts. They haven't invited her over since. Not once in the past four months.

I always thought, if nothing else, that Ethan was a devoted father. But, I guess, now that he has his new wife and new baby, he has no need for his old baggage.

As soon as I refresh the page, a brand-new post appears.

Dani has made my daughter's sixteenth-birthday cake, and it's objectively gorgeous. She smiles beside it, pretty as ever, with her cherub-cheeked baby.

I think suddenly of Sophie's first birthday cake—white cake from a box with white frosting from a can, *Happy Birthday* spelled out in crunchy candy letters. Ethan and I singing, laughing when she grabbed a handful, tasted it, then squealed with sugar-rushed pleasure.

Just thinking about those two cakes, about the fifteen years in between, about the me then and the me now, I am more than pissed. I am livid.

I want to shove Dani's perfect, stupid cake off that shiny marble island—that's *my* marble. I chose it. It's only available from one quarry in Italy. Bright white with dramatic gold bands. I should have taken it with me, pried it from the cabinets with a crowbar, or just smashed it to pieces.

I toss the phone onto the couch, unfold my legs from beneath me. *Get a fucking grip.* No one should get this angry about a countertop.

I down the rest of my wine, which helps a little, and get up for a refill. *I won't drink at the party,* I promise myself. Just like the promise I made my daughter—hopeful and hollow—that *absolutely nothing will go wrong tomorrow.*

8

Mikayla

We're on Sophie's bed, under the salmon pink covers—me in navy blue athletic shorts and an oversized *Comal County Junior Livestock Show* T-shirt, the logo faded from endless wear, Sophie in a pale blue cami and sleep short set. Her bare legs, smooth as silk, slide against mine whenever she reaches for the junk food spread over the comforter on our laps. We are bingeing classic romance movies that we've seen a hundred times before—like that old-school *Romeo + Juliet* with Leonardo DiCaprio, from when he looked like a cute boy who might go to our school instead of like someone's hot dad.

Sophie pops a "fun size" 3 Musketeers into her mouth, then nestles down into the covers, resting her head on my shoulder. Her golden hair tickles my neck. "It hurts to watch these," she says, "now that I know what it really means to fall in love."

Her breath smells of chocolate. I murmur some kind of agreement. She thinks I don't share her pain, that I don't know. But I do. The heartache is so sharp it's almost delicious. Like hot chocolate that burns your tongue. Like when we were nine and Sophie's parents took us halfway across the country for a three-day Disneyland vacation. I had never been on a plane before. We sat together, in matching *Minnie Mouse* T-shirts, hands held tight, squealing as the plane lifted from the ground. My stomach dropped and I felt so happy that it made me sad, because soon I'd be on another plane, heading back, and before I knew it, I was. Now I can only look at pictures from that trip. It's been almost seven years.

On the screen, Leo repeats Shakespeare's lines. We read the play in Mrs. Garcia's English class just this year: "Beautiful things muddled together into an ugly mess! Love is heavy and light, bright and dark, hot and cold, sick and healthy, asleep and awake—it's everything except what it is!"

I feel the words chime against my bones like a tuning fork. How beautifully tragic, how tragically beautiful:

To love someone you shouldn't.

9

Dani

Three A.M. A scream.

I sit bolt upright in the dark nursery. Charlotte, who has been sucking lazily at my breast, is jolted wide awake.

I strain to make out the familiar shapes of furniture from the room's shadows. The changing table, the dresser, the bookshelf, the bin of toys. I listen for any unfamiliar sounds. The wind moans against the windows. The sound machine whirs. The glider click-click-clicks.

I heard a woman scream.

Didn't I?

Do you ever see, hear, or feel things that others can't?

Since Charlotte's birth, my imagination has been bombarded with intrusive thoughts. Sudden infant death, tipping bookcases, deadly fevers, choking hazards.

All new moms worry. I know that. Newborns are impossibly small, heads bobbing on their useless necks, heartbeats visible in the pulse of their soft spots.

On the first day Charlotte was home, I took her out onto the balcony to show her the view. I had a sudden flash of her tipped over the railing, of Charlotte's fragile head cracked against the bluestone patio below like an egg. It made me ill. Made me clutch Charlotte tight in my arms. But I didn't trust myself. I could drop her. No, I could throw her. I could throw my baby over the edge.

These aren't normal thoughts.

I didn't go out on the balcony again.

I breathe. I feel the sensations of my surroundings. The weight of my baby in my arms, the pull of the milk, the click-click-click of the glider, the whir of the sound machine, the moaning of the wind.

Just as I've convinced myself the scream was only a dream, it comes again. A sound of pure agony.

I don't give myself the chance to second-guess. I am up from the chair. Charlotte twists herself painfully from my nipple as I hurry with her down the hall. I swing the bedroom door open. I flip on the light, blinding after so much darkness.

Ethan's eyes squeeze tight, and he pulls up the duvet to shield himself. "What the hell?" He peels open one eye to check the digital numbers of the clock.

I sit on the edge of the bed. "Ethan." I can hear the fear in my voice, and he must too, because he sits up. "I heard a woman scream."

"What?"

"Twice."

We wait. But this house lies.

It is quieter than ever, and with the lights on, it appears entirely benign—decorative pillows stacked on an armchair, my glass of water on the nightstand, Ethan's watch atop the dresser.

He lays a hand on top of mine. Concern is plain on his face. Concern for me. For Charlotte. This is all too familiar. We don't say it, but we're both thinking of that horrible night four months ago. We are thinking about the way a mind can play tricks on itself.

But I didn't imagine it.

Did I?

Charlotte is looking from her daddy to me, and her face spreads into a grin, displaying those two prominent bottom teeth—she's happy and wide awake. We'll never get her back to sleep now, and we have such a big day ahead.

Ethan says nothing. Shame, heavy and solid, slides down my esophagus.

Then—another scream.

Ethan hears it too this time, his eyes going wide for a moment.

He smiles, tired eyes creasing into crescents. "It's a fox," he says.

"What?"

He squeezes my hand. "Sometimes foxes make that noise. It's horrific."

"Oh my God." A laugh of relief bubbles up my chest.

He takes Charlotte from me.

I rub hard circles into my eyes with the heels of my hands. "What an idiot."

"Look, you lie down, get some sleep. I'll take a shift."

"No. No." I start to stand.

He puts a hand to my shoulder, presses me back to the bed. "Babe, come on. Curtis says we need to watch your sleep." His thumb circles my bare shoulder. "It's my turn anyway."

So I sink into the bed. I let him take Charlotte from the room. I curl into the sinfully luxurious bedsheets as he turns off the light.

The heavy weight of exhaustion pulls me under quickly, and as I fall, I hear it one more time—the scream. I'm already half asleep. In my dreams, I see *her*, white dress and long ivory hair snatched into the night air, mouth open, the sounds of her wails indistinguishable from the wind.

10

Kim

I wake to a panicked "Mom!" Sophie leaning over me, shaking my shoulders.

I sit up. The room spins. It takes me a moment to orient myself, especially when the walls and the furniture refuse to stay in one place. I close one eye, and that helps. I passed out on the couch. My contacts are glued to my eyes like drying starfish. My head is pounding.

Sophie must have been trying to wake me for some time.

I grab her hand. "I'm sorry, sweetheart. I was just asleep."

My head is clearing, the room solidifying around me. The lamp on the end table is switched on. The TV as well, Netflix paused and asking if I'd like to continue. Mikayla hangs back by the doorway in her baggy pajamas. "We heard a noise." She worries the hem of her T-shirt between her fingers.

"It sounded . . ." Sophie trails off, looks to Mikayla, shrugs, as if she doesn't want to say what it sounded like.

"I think it was a fox," Mikayla says.

I nod. A mating female fox can sound terrifying, like a woman screaming bloody murder.

"Should we check on the dogs?" Sophie asks, unconvinced.

I hear them barking now. I'm so used to the sound, it might as well be static.

"What time is it?" I rub the sore spot in the middle of my forehead, where all the wine has gathered to punch a hole straight through my skull.

"Three," Mikayla says.

I give Sophie's hand one more squeeze, then heave myself to standing. "Go back to bed. I'll check on the dogs."

The girls disappear down the hallway.

I slide into a pair of worn house slippers tucked under the armchair and shuffle to the kitchen. I pick up the box of wine from the counter to feel the weight, to judge how much I drank. *Fuck.* A lot more than my optimistic two glasses. Earlier in the night, I checked down the hall. The gap beneath Sophie's door was dark. I've always liked that quiet, safe part of the night, when I belong entirely to myself. It's hard to give that up, go to bed, start all over with the next day. I remember looking at my empty glass, feeling that light, giddy sway, and thinking, *I'm not going to drink tomorrow at the party, and that will be miserable, so why not live it up tonight?*

One half of me is insidiously manipulative. The other half is dumb enough to fall for it every time.

I take my keys from the hook and pull in the side door off the kitchen, which creaks loudly, then swing out the screen door, which creaks louder. I live in a three-bedroom ranch-style built in the eighties with beige brick and a roof that needs replacing.

But I used to live in a castle at the very top of a cliff with a view of the world.

———

The house was 115 years old when the real estate agent showed it to us, sagging under the weight of countless Texas thunderstorms, cedar trees reaching branches out through broken windows.

Get a load of this view, Ethan said, wrapping his arms around me, resting his chin on the top of my head. I leaned back into the firm, warm weight of him as Sophie toddled through overgrown grass. *It's the highest point in the whole county. Can you believe that?*

That's what he liked about it. The way it stood tall. Stood over.

We can bulldoze the house, if you want. Build something new.

I couldn't stand the thought. I imagined that scene in *It's a Wonderful Life* when George and Mary throw rocks through the windows of the old mansion.

I, too, wanted the moon, back when I knew how to want things, and when wanting seemed the same as having.

It has good bones, I said.

It's a steal. Ethan dug two fingers between my ribs so that I squirmed with breathless laughter in his arms.

Why is it so cheap? I asked, because even if the house was falling apart, the land alone must have been worth the asking price.

It's haunted, Ethan said.

And we laughed. I still remember that. How we laughed.

—————

The sky is dark and full of stars, glittering between the branches of live oaks that twist and spread into a canopy. The night is loud with the constant, raspy percussion of cicadas. But no screaming foxes, not right now anyway.

I step onto the porch, activating the floodlight. Whatever woke the girls and riled the dogs either wasn't big enough or wasn't close enough to trip the motion sensor.

I used to work at a sleek veterinary practice in Stone Oak, between here and the heart of downtown. Now, I run a business out of my home—well, out of the red barn beside my home which I converted, doing most of the labor myself: pouring a concrete floor, transforming horse stalls into dog kennels, laying sod for the fenced runs.

The space between the house and the kennels is a parking lot of crushed limestone. It crunches beneath my feet, and I can feel every jagged edge of rock through my soft-soled shoes. The woods beyond my spotlight look even darker in contrast. Under the floodlight's glare, I feel on display as I cross to the kennels, where the barks sound frantic now.

A movement in the trees catches my peripheral vision. Something white. A screech owl? A possum? I turn, peer into the darkness, but whatever it was, it's gone now.

Or, at least, out of sight.

I hurry to the kennel door and unlock it. "Shh, shh, it's me." At the sound of my voice, the dogs quiet. It's dark in here. I don't want to turn on the light and make them think it's time to start the day. Enough moonlight shines in through the windows for me to check that all dogs are accounted for and unharmed. There is a strip of concrete down the center of the barn, kennels lining either side.

"Here, girl," I call. I let my own gentle giant, a Great Pyrenees mix named Molly, roam free, like the RA of a dorm. She paces up and down this center aisle, checking on everyone throughout the night. Usually she would be the first to greet me, chucking her big soft head beneath my hand. "Molly?"

All is silent.

There is a lump in my throat that I can't swallow down. What is wrong with me?

It was the panic in Sophie's voice, bringing me back to a dark place.

It was the flash of white between branches that looked almost for a second like the pale hair of a woman. A woman I once knew.

But I left *her* behind at the old house. In my old life.

It is Molly not coming when I call her, because she always comes when I call. I walk about halfway down the aisle. Then I see her. My shoulders relax. "There you are, girl."

She faces away from me. She stares into an empty kennel in the back corner.

"Molly." I pat my leg, but she doesn't move. I have never seen her stand so still, stare so intently.

The kennel where she is looking is dark. It's empty, but the longer I look, the more the shadows seem to take shape, form into something crouched.

I fish my cell from the pocket of my sweatpants, turn on the flashlight, and shine it into the corner. The light trembles in my shaky hand. It illuminates nothing. A clean kennel, an empty dog bed, a dry bowl.

Molly snaps out of her trance. She's animated again and turns to me, chucks her head beneath my hand. "It's time to go to bed," I say as she nuzzles my leg. "We have a big day tomorrow."

As I make my way back to the house, I can't help searching the dark tree branches for glimpses of a woman in white, the woman who once haunted me.

The Night of the Party

Outside on the bluestone patio, the bloodstained sheet covering the body flaps in the wind.

Lights from cop cars and the ambulance pulse, flooding the glass house and painting the guests detained within its walls in intervals of red and blue, red and blue. They have been assembled in the expansive living room, under strict orders not to leave. They've been told to stay off their phones as well. They are trapped inside a house they were warned never to come into. Their minds race, recounting the events of the day. Innocent exchanges now seem sinister. Talking too much draws suspicion and staying silent does the same. They can't help but wonder which of them are suspects. Wonder if they themselves might be sitting beside a killer.

"It wasn't a fox they heard last night," the nanny says in her soft Irish lilt to a young officer, who pauses his scribbling in a yellow notepad. "It was the banshee's keening. Terrible omen, that one. It foretells a death, you know? In Ireland, we talk of thin places, where the veil between this world and the next is so sheer that one can walk in both at once. I fear this house is such a place."

12

Órlaith

The Day of the Party

I arrive to find the black iron gates already open. I drive through, pull around the wide cobbled drive that encircles the bigtooth maple, shaded by the grand silhouette of the house. I look up at it as I pass, seat scooted as close as it will go to the dash, neck craned over the steering wheel—my Colm used to tease me so, but I like to see over the whole of the hood. High up on the pointed top of the tower, those three buzzards perch, wings spread wide, backs to the morning sun. Light filters through their silver-feather tips like fingers.

My car is only just now cooling, the poor air conditioner whining, as I drive around the side of the house, down to the gravel on the lowest level. The vinyl seats are still sticky with heat, as is the wheel in my sweaty palms. I park beside one of three Chloe's Catering vans. There is also a dark blue Lexus, a black SUV decorated with a cartoon man spinning records, a half dozen other sedans I do not recognize.

I hear the commotion before I even round the corner.

The back garden sits atop a jutting ledge beneath the main house, before the final sheer plummet of the cliff. The grass is trim as a billiard table, green as anything in Ireland. One long edge of the pool falls off to nowhere, while a continuous waterfall trickles lovely over a natural formation of limestone at a narrow end.

It might be tranquil, except there's a whole team of people setting up. They say everything is bigger in Texas. If this party is anything to go by, that's the God's honest. A DJ booth, outdoor games, three margarita machines. Round cocktail tables dot the grass, clear beach balls filled with multicolored glow sticks float atop the water's surface, and a massive garland of balloons arches up and over the cabana tent—neon pink and electric green and translucent white filled with metallic confetti like disco balls.

"Jaysus, but isn't this a bit much, like?" I say to a woman standing at the corner of the garden, just on the edge of the patio, surveying the work. She holds a clipboard in the crook of her arm, wears smart black trousers, a cream-colored blouse tucked in, hair coiled into a neat bun.

She turns to me. Her lips are a hot pink, much too bright for her age. She glances at my plain cotton T-shirt and elastic-waisted jeans—a clear sign that I'm no one of importance. "Hi. You must be . . ." She flips a page on her clipboard, scans a list.

"The nanny."

"The party planner," she says, holding out a hand, slick nails painted the same color as her lips.

"Your man there, is he a bartender?" The outdoor kitchen island is covered in shoulders of spirits and neat rows of glasses that glimmer in the sun. "Drinking's not legal for American teenagers, is it?"

"Don't worry. He'll be checking IDs."

"Back in my day, a child's birthday party meant a few friends over for a homemade sponge."

She breathes a laugh through her nose. Sure, she's made an entire business out of the ridiculous whims of spoiled children. "No," she suddenly barks across the garden. "No table there. Keep that area clear. That'll be the dance floor." Two young men holding the offending cocktail table side-shuffle it into the grass, spacing it equidistant from the others.

I touch the woman gently on the elbow. "You'll be wanting to be careful there, won't you? That stonework will be getting a bit slippery when wet. With the kids in the pool and everyone going in and out of the house."

She clears her throat.

"Oh, heaven forbid. Of course you know what you're doing. Look at the state of you. Not a hair out of place. No, you're grand. Sure, anyone can tell that. I'm just pointing out that the patio might not be the best idea for a dance floor. People think, ah, you slip, no harm done. But my brother-in-law, the one married to my littlest sister, Moira, he had a wife before. Married young, so they were. I want to say her name was . . . Well, let me think. It's just there on the edge of my mind. Give me a moment."

Her eyes drift toward the staff carrying crates of dinnerware from the vans to the house. This younger generation, so used to the constant input from their televisions and computers and cell phones that they don't even have the attention span to finish a conversation.

"Oh, yes," I forge on. "It was Maeve. How could I forget that? I had a best friend in primary school named Maeve. Cute as a button but had a bit of a lazy eye, the poor pet. Anyway, this other Maeve, the one married to my brother-in-law, she was the picture of health, that one, maybe nineteen, whole life ahead of her. They were just messing about, kicking a ball on the footpath. She went to kick and missed, fell flat on her back, hit her head against the pavement." I touch the back of my own head to demonstrate. "You think it would just be a laugh. That's what Kevin, my brother-in-law, thought as she lay there. He did, actually—laugh, I mean. But then she didn't get up, like. They took her to hospital, but it was too late. Bleeding on the brain, they said. She was dead that night."

The party planner blinks. "I'm sorry, who?"

"Maeve. My brother-in-law's first wife."

She nods. There is a pause. "You're the nanny?" she asks again.

"Yes."

"All right. Well, so nice chatting. I think Mrs. Matthews is waiting for you upstairs."

"Ah, yeah. Lovely meeting you."

I cross the garden toward the house. Here on the lowest floor of the estate, a walk-out basement, rough-carved from the limestone, contains a poolside lounge, currently being decorated with vibrant fresh blossoms. The wind is strong today. Balloons jumble into one another in a cacophony of latex. One pink balloon rips suddenly from a bunch tied to a lounge chair. I watch it float, battered higgledy-piggledy by the breeze.

The covered patio is framed by two staircases. They sweep up and around, mirrors of each other, to the next level of patio. There, on the ground floor of the house, the wall of glass exposes the kitchen and the great room. Now, in direct sunlight, the glass mostly acts as a mirror, reflects a cornflower blue sky void of clouds, but I can also see beyond, see the shadowed shapes of waiters milling about like ghosts.

I crane my neck, watch the balloon soar higher still, bump against the glass balustrade of the balcony, then disappear over the roof.

I am almost to one of the staircases now. I'm not watching where I place my feet, and I almost step on it. Lying on the stone steps is a bright red cardinal, on its back, one wing spread open, head twisted in an unnatural angle, beak open. I watch its breast for a rise and fall that doesn't come.

"And what happened to you, love?"

I take another look at the balcony, turn my head this way and that so the sleek surface catches the light. And, yes, there it is, where the poor dear must have made impact—a hairline fracture. A weakness in the glass.

I'll have to warn the party planner. Could be dangerous, sure.

I look back at the creature. A dead bird is a sign of change to come. That's what my mam used to say.

But it won't do to leave him here for the party guests to stumble upon. People don't like reminders of death.

I take a tissue from the pocket of my jeans, unfold it, drape it over the bird and lift the body. He deserves a proper burial. With the edge of the tissue, I fold the wing back in. I pinch the beak closed. I wrap the tissue around him like a swaddle.

From inside, I hear the doorbell ring. The first of the guests has arrived.

13

Mikayla

We're still at Kim's house. Sophie sits on the carpet in front of the floor-length mirror, leaned against the wall, long legs folded beneath her. She does her makeup as I swipe through my phone.

"Nothing," I report.

Her cheeks are sucked in as she applies blush, sweeps it up into her hairline. "Are you sure?"

I flick my finger upward across the screen, scroll through more pictures on Mason's Insta. "Football practice. His truck."

"He's not seeing someone new?"

I shrug. "No evidence here."

She tilts her head in the mirror. My eyes trace the smooth column of her throat, the line of her jaw, the perfect point of her chin—all the features of her face flawlessly balanced.

There is a list as long as my arm of boys who would run across broken glass at the chance to date Sophie Matthews.

But Mason dumped her without a solid reason. We speculated for weeks. Was it because she was a terrible kisser? (*No way*, I assured her.) Was it because his feelings were so strong they scared him? (*Yeah right.* Sophie rolled her eyes.) Was it because she wouldn't put out? Or, at least, hadn't yet?

I watch her lips part as she slides the mascara wand down her lashes, from root to tip. When her eyes shift to me in the mirror, I dart mine away like I've been caught.

I lock eyes with my own reflection instead, just for a moment: my red hair crimped from last night's braids, my face washed out and featureless, my body hidden in a shapeless dress—the same one I wore to homecoming, because there was no way Mom was going to buy me a whole new dress just for a birthday party. Dad would have literally flipped.

Though the whole exchange was a matter of seconds, Sophie has seen the emotions flicker across my face and understood them. We are still that close, can still communicate without words, the way cells send chemical signals between each other in one body.

Her lips curve into a devilish half-smile, and she begins to crawl toward me on hands and knees.

I laugh. "No way."

"You always say that."

I hold my hands up to fend her off, but it's half-hearted and she can sense my weakness.

"It's my birthday."

I drop my hands, roll my eyes. "Fine," I say, like I'm only humoring her.

Sophie sits back on her heels and claps. She grabs her makeup bag and gets to work.

I'm not into all that stuff, I usually say. *It's just not me.* But the truth is I'm afraid. It would be so embarrassing for anyone to think I'd put in a ton of effort. Because what if the result was still unimpressive? Better for people to think, *Maybe she could be pretty if she'd just . . .*

Today, I let Sophie give me a makeover, because—well, to admit it makes me feel oily with shame, but—in this moment I desperately want to be beautiful.

The edge of her pinky rests on the top of my cheek so she can apply my eyeliner. I can feel her breath on my face. I swallow, and she tells me to keep still. I look up at the ceiling, try not to blink when the pencil touches my bottom lashes, try not to let the big storm cloud of emotions rise to my throat, make my eyes tear up. But if they do, I can blame it on the eyeliner.

Sophie leans back to assess her work, liner poised in the air. Her face cracks into a grin.

"Girl," she says. "Today, you're gonna slay."

14

Dani

The doorbell rings. The party has begun.

Ethan's arm encircles my waist as he opens the door. I'm wearing a red dress, stiletto heels, and a swipe of deep berry red lipstick, and I feel a little like my old self again. It's the first time I've worn a real bra in months.

"First ones here. We get a prize?" The man on the other side of the door is bigger than Ethan, taller and broader, older too, veins spiderwebbing across a bulbous nose, deep lines beside his eyes when he smiles big. He wears a dark suit with cowboy boots and an oversized silver and turquoise belt buckle, coordinating with the silver and turquoise cross hanging around his wife's neck.

"How about a Shiner?" Ethan claps the man on the shoulder, steers him in the door. "You remember Dale and Eileen Landry?" he says to me. "Dale serves with me on the board of the Bulverde Landowners Association."

Dale grasps my offered hand in two of his. His grip is firm, his skin dry and rough as butcher paper.

"That's right," I say. "We met at the fundraiser."

"The one on the square," Eileen confirms, following her husband inside. I see her eyes take in the house: the grand spiral staircase, the modern chandelier, and, of course, the wall of glass and that view—rolling Texas hills, the grid of pastures below, the vast blue of the sky. "Fixing to do it again in June, and we'll be needing volunteers. Ethan tells us you are something of a magician in the kitchen."

"Speaking of the BLA, we need to talk about this Cypress Creek Ranch business," Dale says.

"Drinks first."

I glance at the open door, and see that another car is already pulling through the iron gates, the valet rushing to meet them. Soon, people will crowd around me like a swarm of hornets. The thought makes my scalp prickle with unease.

I'm thinking of that threatening note, the one I found on our front porch a few days ago, the one I hid in a black high-heeled shoe on a bottom shelf of my closet. I don't know who wrote it or what they want from me. I only know our house is open now. To friends. To strangers.

I push the thought away. I dial up my smile, compliment Eileen on her necklace.

"Two Shiners," Ethan says to a tuxedoed waiter. "Eileen? Pick your poison."

The older woman shakes her head. "I'm driving. Dale can do the sinning for both of us today."

I watch two women step out of a white Lexus. I recognize them from Bulverde Methodist—Miss Marjorie and Miss Jo Ellen. I've only ever seen those two women together. They both wear exquisitely tailored pantsuits, big pearl earrings. Their hair is big as well, just like my grandmother styles hers, hot rollers back and up, teased to the heavens—*The bigger the hair, the closer to God.*

A black Mercedes circles the drive, followed by a silver pickup.

———

It doesn't take long before the house is alive with conversation—two dozen guests already.

"Five hundred and thirteen acres right off of Highway 46," Dale explains to me. He's talking about Cypress Creek Ranch. A favorite topic of conversation in Bulverde, especially among the older crowd, is the way it's changing, the way San Antonio is spreading out, swallowing Bulverde up. "One of these faceless, heartless developers is trying to buy the ranch," Dale goes on. "They're planning to put twenty-four hundred of their Cracker Jack houses there."

Marjorie tsks beside me. "Did you read the mayor's letter in the latest *Front Porch News*? The wells are going dry. Bulverde doesn't have the infrastructure for this population boom."

We circle a cocktail table. Waiters crisscross the room, filling drink orders, though it's barely noon. They bring trays of hors d'oeuvres—

gourmet spins on Texas classics: brisket sliders on brioche buns with habanero jam, jalapeño poppers stuffed with Brie and wrapped in prosciutto, maple bourbon pecan tarts.

"We want Raymond Fischer to sell Cypress Creek Ranch to the state of Texas instead, so it can be preserved. We've secured grant money, but we need private donations as well. That's where your husband comes in."

"I'm with you, Dale," Ethan agrees.

"Now, Raymond is good people. He cares about legacy. He said when he sells this land, it's going to be like walking his daughter down the aisle. He wants to know she's in good hands."

My phone chirps inside my black satin clutch. "Excuse me," I say, pulling the phone out to see a text from Gemma Barker—*On our way!* I send back a party popper emoji, but my stomach sours. I take a sip of white wine.

I've always loved Gemma. She is big-hearted and warm. When Ethan and I first started dating, I was nervous to meet his friends, a kid who'd just been invited to the grown-up table, but Gemma never made me feel out of place. After Charlotte was born, while other friends sent well-meaning *Just let me know if there's anything I can do* messages, Gemma showed up with a stack of casseroles, which she slid into the fridge before taking Charlotte from my arms, ordering me to take a shower while she watched the baby. *We'll be fine*, she promised. *Go, and make it a long one.*

I feel guilty because I haven't seen her since.

I'm sure she's aware that I've been seeing her husband for therapy sessions. What all has he told her? Does she know about the time I was dancing with Charlotte in the kitchen and had a vision of swinging her too hard, of crashing her soft-boned skull against the corner of the marble? Does she know I still cup the top of my daughter's head in my palm when I pass the island?

Did he tell her what happened four months ago? What I did?

"This sure is some party," Marjorie says, biting into a pecan tart.

"This sure is some *house*," Jo Ellen says beside her, turning to look up at the vaulted ceilings. "This is the first I've ever set foot in here. Did you know that? Lived in Bulverde my whole life."

"Not me." Marjorie smiles bashfully at me. "When I was a kid, a group of us used to dare each other to come inside this house. It didn't look like this, mind you. It was downright spooky. One of the boys, Del-ray Becker, stole Coach Miller's stopwatch from his desk. We'd time how long each of us could stand it in this house alone. I never did win. We all thought this place was haunted in those days." She whispers this last part, eyes flicking up to the corners of the ceiling, as though she doesn't want to be overheard. As if she still believes it.

"Oh, hush, you! You'll scare the poor girl," Jo Ellen says, smacking Marjorie on the arm, waving away her superstitions. She swivels her head in my direction. "Besides, we're all far more interested in that sweet new baby. Where is your gorgeous girl today? I've only ever seen her pictures."

"She's taking a nap, but she'll be up soon."

"And why haven't you brought her by the church? We haven't seen hide or hair of you in months."

I apologize. The women are having none of it.

"New mamas are not supposed to be alone," Marjorie assures me. "It's true what they say: It takes a village. Honey, you'll go crazy trying to do it all by yourself."

Go crazy. She doesn't mean anything by it. They're already moving on to talk about the new pews at Bulverde Methodist, how the old ones will be auctioned off, how a church pew would look just perfect in Jo Ellen's entryway.

But I'm thinking again of a session I had with Curtis early on.

Shadow-mother syndrome, Curtis told me. *It's a term found in a few medical journals from the late nineteenth century to describe the puerperal period, what we might now call the baby blues or, if prolonged, postpartum depression.*

He meant the term to be clinical, to validate my descriptions of "going through the motions," of feeling disconnected from my baby, from myself, like I was watching it all from a slight distance, from just over my own shoulder.

But it made me think of other shadows.

This house—all white and bright, wall open to the open sky— somehow still harbors darkness in its corners. I sometimes catch movement on the edges of my vision, but when I turn to look, nothing is there.

A waiter offers us a tray of appetizers—bite-sized chicken-fried steak with truffle-infused gravy, mini lobster tacos, apple-smoked pork belly burnt ends.

The party planner discreetly slides beside me when there is a break in the conversation.

"Should we bring out the cake?" she asks. "Now that the guests have arrived?"

"Let's wait for the birthday girl," I say, but my eyes are drawn up, over her head, to the second floor, by a movement among the shadows.

It's Órlaith. I watch her shuffle across the landing, slow and silent as a ghost.

15

Kim

I enter the neighborhood and take the road that winds around and up the hill to the highest house. Sophie and Mikayla are in the backseat, their two heads bent together over one phone, whispers and giggles. I check the rearview mirror, make eye contact for a moment with Mikayla, who smiles her shy smile and darts her eyes back down. She looks different today. She's wearing makeup, her pale lashes darkened with mascara, her green eyes rimmed with black liner. It changes her whole face, turns her features striking.

Sophie's gift is in a silver bag on the passenger seat. I maxed out my last credit card to buy the damn thing—the newest iPhone. When did phones get so expensive? Ethan told me not to worry about it, that he could buy the phone, that I could still say it was from me. I told him to fuck off. *Well, that's nice,* he said. I hung up after that. I hate when he gets all high-and-mighty like he's never said anything harsher than *Golly gee.* Mr. Unflappable.

I avoid this drive as much as possible. I make Ethan do pickups and drop-offs, or I insist we meet somewhere neutral.

There are more homes now than when I lived here. I pass a McMansion, two horses grazing in the front lawn, corralled by a high metal fence. But the twists and turns of the road, the pressure needed on the gas to make the incline—these things are muscle memory.

"'Last night I dreamt I went to Manderley again,'" I say in my best slow, British drawl.

"What?" Sophie asks.

"It's the first line of *Rebecca*."

Silence from the backseat.

"The book. Daphne du Maurier?" Still no response. "What are they teaching you in school?"

"We're reading *Catcher in the Rye* in Mrs. Garcia's class," Mikayla offers helpfully.

In the rearview mirror, I see the girls exchange a look, their mouths curving in twin smiles, as if I'm ridiculous.

I guess I am. I was able to squeeze myself into the two-sizes-too-small dress, and I'm feeling pretty proud of that. I don't look twenty-seven, but I do look good, the dress hugging my curves in all the right ways.

I have to brake to allow a few deer to cross in front of us. Even with all the new construction, a wildness remains.

It didn't take long after we moved in before I heard the story from some of the locals, about the first mistress of the grand house on the cliff. She had lost her baby to one of those terrible diseases—scarlet fever or diphtheria—and, driven crazy by grief and guilt, she threw herself from the second-story balcony. According to local legend, she can still be heard wailing, wandering the woods on windy days and stormy nights.

The Mother, they call her.

At first, I thought maybe the ranchers were just pulling my leg, sick of yuppies like me and Ethan swooping in to pick apart their dying rural lifestyle like buzzards.

I didn't believe in ghosts. But I had felt emotions that were too big for my body, that clawed at the insides of my rib cage, swelled up my throat and into my mouth. Who knows if people can live on past death. But maybe pain can.

Today is one of those windy days. The trees shivering, occasionally bending. And the wind gets stronger the higher we climb. Until we are at the very top. I pull through the yawning iron gates. The house comes into view, as imposing as ever. The steepled silhouette stark against the blank canvas of an empty skyline.

Most of my nights are dreamless. The wine helps with that.

But when I dream, I do return to this house. The dimensions of each room, the length of each hall, the steps of each staircase, the way light slopes through windows, measures hours across the floor— these are also muscle memory. In my dreams, the house never lets me go.

16

Dani

I've excused myself from the party to sneak upstairs. I stand just outside the nursery. The door is ajar a finger's width.

I can hear the murmur of conversation down below, like the buzzing of cicadas in the trees, hear a shout of welcome as yet another guest arrives.

Through the crack in the doorway, I can see that the curtains are all thrown open. The nursery is filled with sunlight. The balcony is exposed. The crib is empty. Out of sight, at the changing table, most likely, I hear them. Órlaith humming, Charlotte giggling.

An hour ago, I had left my daughter napping in her crib. The floor-to-ceiling blackout curtains had been drawn along the entire wall, the lights off, the sound machine whirring.

———

In those early days after Charlotte's birth, before we had a nanny, Ethan was at work and I was left alone all day with a newborn, the hours like an ever-turning pinwheel of nursings and mustard-colored diaper changes and snatches of sleep. I began to find rooms different from how I'd left them.

It was small at first. The pantry door open when I knew I'd shut it. The light on in Ethan's office, though I knew I'd passed it dark just that morning.

Things moved as well. A photograph of me and Ethan on the River Walk turned face down on the console table by the front door. A bottle of scented hand lotion I kept on my nightstand suddenly missing.

Where did you put my cuff links? Ethan asked one night as he was packing for a weekend conference. It was my first solo mission with the baby. A few days without backup, and I was feeling more than a little tense at the prospect.

I set them on your dresser like you asked.

Well, they aren't here, he said.

I put them there. I know I put them there. I went to look, but of course he was right. The dresser top was empty. I looked behind the dresser. I dropped to the floor, ran my hand over the wood, checked under the bed.

Ethan chuckled, dropped to a knee beside me. *It's fine.* He kissed my forehead. *Just a little case of mom-brain.*

Though hot tears of frustration pricked my eyes, I figured he was right.

But I continued to feel a presence in the house.

I came home from taking Charlotte on a short walk around the neighborhood and, in my closet, I smelled perfume as though it had just been spritzed around the room. I recognized the scent—Electric Cherry by Tom Ford. Ethan had given it to me for our first Christmas together, and I kept the nearly empty bottle buried in my panty drawer. It was still there, but I had the feeling that someone had moved my things. That a stranger had pushed aside the few lacy pieces I hadn't reached for in ages, burrowed beneath dozens of haphazardly folded cotton briefs, found the bottle, sprayed it once, maybe twice, and replaced it.

But that was ridiculous. Wasn't it? Who would do that? And why?

It kept happening, though—lights turned on or off, doors opened or closed. The house is a labyrinth—three floors, a separate wing, a main staircase in the foyer, an old servants' staircase behind the kitchen, and a narrow set of metal spiral steps up to the top of the tower. With so much space, how could I be sure I was alone? And that wall of gaping glass. Ethan says we're too high up for anyone to really see inside—but everywhere I went, I felt watched.

I became obsessed with noting the details of the house: the exact placement of objects on shelves, the angle of shoes by the door, the position of a blanket laid over the arm of the couch.

I needed to pull it together. Drink more water, try some yoga, or actually sleep when the baby slept.

I knock on the nursery door as I nudge it open. Outside, the DJ starts the music, the first notes of a Waylon Jennings song drifting up.

Órlaith looks up from beside Charlotte, who sits atop the changing table. "Oh, doesn't Mammy look pretty?" Her words are kind, but the way she holds her hand like a protective claw to Charlotte's shoulder makes me feel like I'm an intruder. "Was this the dress you were wanting her to wear?"

I nod. Charlotte looks beyond precious in her party dress, pink gingham with matching bloomers. "It's even cuter on," I say. I'm taking a step closer, lifting my hands, about to reach for Charlotte, but Órlaith turns back to her in that same moment, blocks me slightly with her body.

"Sure, she's a living doll." Órlaith fluffs the skirt, runs one finger down my daughter's cheek. "Which reminds me." Órlaith reaches for her purse, which she usually holds high up on her shoulder, the bag as big as her torso. "I have a gift for my girl." She digs around, sets the purse up on the changing table beside Charlotte, burrows through crumpled receipts and napkins. Finally, she pulls out a cloth doll, off-white with a few faded stains blotching an arm, a leg. The hair is brown yarn, twisted into two plaits. The dress is white, or was, edged in lace and browning with age.

Órlaith turns the doll over so I can see her embroidered face. The eyes are half-moons on a slightly downward slope, not quite perfect matches, and the irises are done with a blue thread so light it nearly fades into the skin, so that her expression appears vacant. Her red mouth is a little O, as if she's been caught off guard. There is something sweet about her, but also off-putting. She gives me the creeps.

"Oh, Órlaith, you didn't need to . . ."

But she's already handing the doll to my daughter. Charlotte's eyes are big with wonder as she reaches for the doll, and as soon as she takes hold of it, she pulls it to her mouth to chew on one of the yarn braids.

Órlaith laughs. "Look at the pet. I knew she'd love it, sure. If you can believe it, my mam made her when I was expecting my own girl."

I feel a sudden panic. "Your mother made it?" I ask, just to be sure I heard right. Charlotte has already drenched the one braid with drool.

It's only a matter of time until she pulls strands of hair out, tears a seam, unravels the hem of the delicate lace dress. "Let's give the dolly back to Miss Órlaith, baby," I say to Charlotte, reaching for the toy.

"Ah, no, she's grand. Isn't she enjoying it? I knew she would, sure. My own girl used to carry that doll around with her everywhere, sleep with her every night. Polly was her name. Polly the Dolly. Once, we took a family trip to the seashore. Watched the boats, did a bit of fishing off the pier, had lunch at a chippy down there right on the water. Now what was that place called? Oh, but it escapes me. I think it was a woman's name, like."

Órlaith stops to think, as though the detail matters, as though I care about the name of a restaurant where she had lunch forty years ago.

"Oh, for heaven's, it'll come to me," Órlaith says. "It was a lovely lunch and a lovely day and we made it all the way home for the night, time to put the girl to bed, and wouldn't you know it, we had left poor Polly somewhere. Oh, the crying and the wailing, let me tell you. There would be no peace in that house until Polly was found, like. And didn't my Colm drive back to the shore and retrace our every step until he came home, triumphant? He did, sure. That's the kind of father he was."

I try again to pry the doll from Charlotte's destructive little grip, but as soon as I loosen her fingers and pull the toy away, she lets out a scream as if in pain.

"I told you," Órlaith says, a hint of humor in her voice as she pushes the doll back into Charlotte's greedy fingers. "Let her play with it."

"I'm just worried she'll damage it."

"Let her," she says, scooping Charlotte into her arms. "I'm giving it to her. It's hers now. Toys are for playing, aren't they? No use sitting pristine on a shelf, collecting dust." Charlotte clutches the doll with both hands.

"Órlaith, that's too generous. I don't even know how long . . ." I trail off.

"How long what, love?"

How long we'll need a nanny, is what I want to say. *How long you'll even be in our lives.* But, though I'd been anticipating this conversation, it suddenly feels like a rude thing to say. Especially as Órlaith squeezes my daughter tightly, nuzzling their faces together and kissing her plump cheek.

"When we hired you . . ." I hesitate. "I mean, obviously, it's been such a blessing to have the help. But I think, well, *we* think that I've been getting better." My chest tightens.

"Aw, pet." She pats my cheek with her free hand. Her palm is cool to the touch, her skin soft and thin like the skin around your eyes. "You are, sure. You've got color in your cheeks again. Don't I love to see it? You know I say a prayer to Saint Anne every day for you."

"Thank you. What I mean, though, is that I'm not sure how much longer I'll need the help."

Órlaith's brows snap together. "Oh," is all she says.

"Anyway," I say, my voice falsely bright to break the awkwardness, "I just think this doll is so special. She should stay in your family. Your daughter must want her. If it were me—"

"Oh, but," she cuts me off, "my daughter has passed, love. I could have sworn I'd mentioned it before. Though I know I'm always going on about one thing or another."

She says it without frills, just a statement of fact, and it takes a moment for the words to unscramble in my brain, to form a meaning. When they do, when I realize what she has just said—that her daughter, her only child, is dead—it's as though the air in the room has been vacuum-sucked.

"I can't even imagine. I'm so sorry . . ."

"It's all right." She pats my arm as if *she* is comforting *me*. "She was very young. It was a long time ago."

I don't know what to say. My mind races through all its favorite horrors. Illness? Accident? And that little voice inside whispers: *See? You were right. Right to worry and check. The worst really can happen.*

"So, you see," Órlaith says, "I don't want Polly to go to waste. Not when my gorgeous girl here loves her so. What do you say we head down?"

I'm shaken, but I don't want that to show. "You can take Charlotte. Thank you, Órlaith. I'll be there in a moment."

Once they have gone, I cross to the library and look out the window to watch the cars pulling up. From downstairs I can hear the sounds of people talking over one another, of clinking glasses and country music.

———

The presence was more than a feeling—more than shifting objects and flipped lights.

When Charlotte turned one month old, I came into this library to look for an old photo album—I wanted to post a collage of baby pictures, Charlotte's and mine and Ethan's. I looked down from this upstairs window, which overlooks the driveway and the front lawn, and I saw someone standing completely still in the shadows of the trees.

———

From that window now, I watch Kim's silver sedan pull up. The birthday girl has arrived. Sophie climbs out the back, then Mikayla, and finally Kim steps from the driver's side.

Sophie looks up at the house. She must see me standing in the window, because she waves. I raise a hand to wave back and force a smile onto my face.

17

Kim

Sophie is unbuckling her seat belt before I've even put the car in park. There's a balloon archway over the front door, threatening to be ripped away by the wind. A valet appears, opening my door, taking my keys. Sophie is waving toward the second floor, so I look up and see Dani standing in the window. Queen of the castle. Bitch.

I tug the waistband of my Spanx, do a little shimmy to make sure everything is in place. Then I put on my biggest, fakest smile, and make my way toward the front door.

Inside, Ethan has pulled out all the stops. More balloons, cocktail tables draped in metallic iridescent fabric, strands of fairy lights hanging from the vaulted ceilings, a photo booth with a giant light-up marquee one and six.

There are already guests—forty or so of them—grouped into clusters of conversation. I was right: Ethan has invited more of his friends than Sophie's. There isn't a single teenager in sight. I catch eyes with Marjorie and Jo Ellen, who are sharing a plate of bite-sized food. Jo Ellen's hand shoots up and she waggles her fingers at me, the frenetic movement bobbing the impressive heights of her hair. "Hi, honey," she calls across the room.

"Well, hello, ladies," I say, waggling my fingers right back. We're all big smiles and big hospitality, but those judgmental biddies will be dragging my name through the mud before I even look away.

I can't care right now. I'm more concerned with my house.

For the first time, I see the finished renovations in their entirety. The entryway has been joined with the great room, giving the house a more modern open-concept layout. The marble staircase we'd always planned spirals up to the second story. And the backdrop to it all—that wall of glass—has a view every bit as breathtaking as I ever imagined it would be.

This house was mine. We came up with the plan together. For nine years, we did the work, at first by hand, before we could afford the contractors and the laborers and the white porcelain tile floor so polished that it is a mirror. Back then, we scraped wallpaper, sledgehammered walls, filled a rented dumpster with rotted wood, moldy carpets, rain-soaked books. We salvaged and restored some original features—decorative crown molding and trim, ceiling medallions, the walnut banister with its hand-carved spindles. We painted the walls a white as bright as a wedding veil, knocked down walls and even ceilings to create an open space for entertaining. Now I'm just an unwanted guest at the first big party.

And there is Ethan himself, near the bottom of his marble staircase, looking like James Bond—Ethan loves a good reason to put on a suit, even if he has to fabricate that reason. He excuses himself from a conversation with Dale Landry—that old blowhard—to greet us. Sophie runs to him, throws her arms around him, and he picks her up and into a big, twirly hug.

"You like it, baby?" he asks.

She giggles, seeming five years old again. I think of when he used to play Big Bear, stomping into the room all booming voice and growls, sending a tiny Sophie squealing with equal parts delight and terror into the nearest hiding place—under a blanket, behind the sofa. He would feign searching for her, knocking throw pillows onto the floor, while she trembled in anticipation. When he eventually "found" her, he would spin her around and around this big open room just like he's doing now.

I want to roll my eyes at all his demonstration, but I am glad to see Sophie so happy. She's been pretty down since her breakup, and I really do want today to be perfect for her. I know it's just a birthday party, that this is all too much, but it matters to her. And that matters to me.

"Oh my God, Dad," she says, when he sets her back on her feet. "My friends are going to literally die. Like, seriously. Mikayla, right, that photo booth? Snapchat is going to be flooded."

Ethan looks to me. "You look good, Kim."

I want to punch him. I'd rather he said I looked like a fat cow. He is using his doctor voice, as in *You look well, healthy. It's nice to see you on your feet.*

When we were married, Ethan said I had a special talent for finding criticism where there wasn't any. I prefer to think I had just gotten good at reading between the lines.

"You look like you're getting a lot of sleep," I say, mimicking his oh-so-calm demeanor. "For a man with a new baby."

There is the slightest crease between his brows, but he otherwise doesn't respond. Ethan is good at maintaining composure.

I'm not. I needle just a bit more. "Speaking of"—I throw my purse onto the nearest armchair—"where is your new family?"

"Mom," Sophie says, her voice half-reprimand, half-plea. *Don't embarrass me. Not today.* I try to squelch the flame that's ignited in my chest. I can feel Eileen Landry, just a few feet away, eavesdropping. No doubt she'll be joining Marjorie and Jo Ellen soon so they can shit-talk me under the guise of concern—*Bless her heart, I love her to death, but I'm worried. Did you hear about . . .*

I make a promise to myself. *Don't poke. Don't antagonize. Don't make a scene. Do it for your daughter. And for Chrissakes, don't drink.* "Where is my baby sister?" Sophie asks. "Dani sent me a video the other day of her stacking those little cups I sent. Oh my God! She is so dang smart."

"Charlotte's around here somewhere." He looks around the big room. "The nanny has her."

I can't help raising my eyebrows. "You have a nanny?" I think of when Sophie was a baby and Ethan was in residency and taking extra shifts at the state hospital so that we could make ends meet. I think of days that I cried alone because Sophie refused her naps, because her schedule was all out of whack, because she woke at 2 A.M., so that I was eternally behind on everything—dishes and laundry and schoolwork and, most of all, sleep. I think of Ethan suggesting I put off veterinary school, just for a year or so, or maybe until Sophie was in kindergarten. I refused. I was scared that if I stopped, I'd never start again. I'd dreamt of being a veterinarian from the time I was six years old and my grandfather took me horseback riding for the first time. I already felt I'd lost so much of myself in motherhood. My dreams were the only things that belonged entirely to me anymore.

So I pushed through. I didn't get a nanny. We could barely even afford day care for the hours I was in class.

"She just comes to help out during the day," he says.

I put a hand to my chest in mock horror. "You have to take care of your own baby all night? Just the two of you?"

I think I see Eileen tilting her ear in this direction. Ethan's jaw tightens. That's the only reaction I'm going to get from him, but I have to celebrate the small victories. I'm like a splinter. Not a deep enough wound to kill him, but he knows I'm there, and he's annoyed.

He's saved from having to respond anyway because Dani appears at the top of the stairs. "Oh, Sophie, honey, happy birthday."

She looks incredible. Chestnut hair in big bouncy curls, face fresh but for a little mascara and deep red lipstick, her skin unlined. She is wearing the most ridiculously sexy red dress. Marilyn Monroe with a cinched waist and plunging neckline, her breasts weightless as she hurries down the stairs. I can't believe this bitch had a baby six months ago. I can't believe she would wear that to a kid's birthday party.

Once at the bottom of the stairs, she reaches for my daughter, pulls her into a warm hug. Then she pulls back and looks Sophie over. "You look absolutely gorg. Oh my God, you both do."

Mikayla's ears flame red as she looks at the floor.

Sophie beams. "Yeah?" She looks down at her Cinderella gown, her sparkly heels. "Mason is coming to the party." She says it in a low tone meant only for Dani.

The words are a knife in my chest. I had no idea Dani knew about the breakup. It only happened a few weeks ago. It means Sophie and Dani have been chatting like girlfriends. When she's in her room, crying on the phone? When she's texting in the car beside me? Do they Snapchat each other cute little selfies with sparkly eyes and koala bear ears?

Dani waves the mere idea of Mason away like he's a gnat. "One, he's going to die of regret the moment he sees you. Two, who cares about him? You are going to break a million hearts, believe me. Today is about you."

When I tell Sophie she's beautiful, she rolls her eyes. But I can see that she believes Dani, that she's soaking in the words like sunshine.

Because, in Sophie's opinion, Dani would know a thing or two about breaking hearts.

"Have you had a chance to see everything?" Dani asks. When she turns, I see that her dress is jaw-droppingly backless as well. The hussy. "The bartender is out back and has a whole list of mocktails. He let me taste . . . What was it, honey?" she asks of Ethan. "Oh yeah. A watermelon *no*jito. Isn't that adorable?"

"We haven't seen the baby yet," I chime in. "I guess she's with the nanny? That must be nice."

"We're very lucky." She looks to Ethan, her knight in shining armor, the perfect man who can give her anything her silly little heart desires—a house on the hill, a baby, someone to take care of that baby. Aren't they just so blessed?

"You know," I say, "I really underestimated how hard it must be to be an influencer."

Dani just smiles. Is there even a thought in that pretty head? She probably thinks I'm serious. She's probably mentally patting herself on the back right now, thinking about how she is setting such an inspiring example for young women, like my daughter—women really *can* have it all. They can be mothers and business owners, and look damn hot while doing it too. It's not even hard. All you need is good genes, a little luck, and a rich guy.

Ethan knows that I wasn't giving Dani a compliment, so he rushes in with, "The cake," placing an arm around his new wife's shoulders. "Soph, you have got to see this cake Dani has cooked up for you. It's unbelievable."

Everyone at the party gathers around the long table parallel to the glass wall, and the caterers bring out the cake. It's monstrous, taking four people to carry it. It is even more spectacular than the Instagram photo. Pillowy frosting in vibrant colors and minuscule handcrafted decorations. Sophie is awestruck, hands clasped over her mouth. Everyone oohs and aahs. I want to vomit.

"Dani, you seriously have to open your own bakery," Sophie says. "Maybe that could be my first job. Right, Mom? You've been saying you want me to get a job this summer. I could run the cash register or clean the tables, and you could teach me everything." When Sophie was little, she wanted to be a veterinarian.

"I've been saying Bulverde is due for a sweets shop," an old man offers. I can't remember his name. He's a rancher, from one of the families that has been here for generations. "We've got the donuts and kolache place over on 46, plenty of coffee shops, but we don't have a real sweets bakery—cakes, cookies, pies."

"Well, that was the plan," Dani says. "Opening my own bakery, I mean. But, I don't know. Maybe when Charlotte's a little older . . ."

"Don't shortchange yourself," I say. "I was able to finish veterinary school and get my ass to work all while caring for Sophie. And I didn't even have a nanny."

Why do I have to be such a miserable bitch? I don't want this life, this house, Ethan. I'm glad to be free of it all. I just hate seeing him happy. The injustice of it nearly burns my skin clean off.

I want to see him broken like me. Is that so unreasonable? That I want to see him hurt, to see everything he loves ripped away?

18

Órlaith

The whole lot of them are standing near the cake when I enter the great room, holding Charlotte. It's the birthday girl who notices us first, squealing and running to snatch the baby from my arms. Based on this lavish party, I expected a spoiled brat, but she seems genuinely excited to see her baby sister. It's sweet. I've always loved to watch siblings interact.

The only thing I ever wanted in life was a home brimming with laughter and arguments and always someone's socks to pick up off the floor and someone's plate to clean.

Little Charlotte. Dani. This house. It's the closest I've felt to a family in a long while now.

I am pulled from memories to the here and now as Sophie lets out a disgusted howl. Charlotte has spit up on her. Not a small bit, either. It's the waterfall variety, like she's lost her whole lunch, milk mixed with sweet potato puree dripping down the poor girl's pretty party dress.

"Oh my gosh." Mrs. Matthews grabs Charlotte.

For a moment, we all just stare at the girl, who herself is staring down at the ruined dress.

"Someone get a napkin," the ex-wife snaps. The party planner is quick to supply a tea towel, handing it to the girl, but we all know it's hopeless. Poor pet. I can see tears welling in her eyes as she grinds the stain farther into the fabric.

"Maybe some club soda will help?" a nearby partygoer offers.

"I'm so sorry," Mrs. Matthews keeps repeating.

The girl isn't saying anything, like, trying to keep her composure. My heart goes out to her. It's just a dress, but this is the kind of molehill that becomes a mountain to a young one.

"I could try to soak it," I suggest.

"This is so typical." The ex-wife directs this comment at Mr. Matthews, though I can't see how any of this could be typical. "I'll go home. I'll find something else for you to wear. What about your homecoming dress?" She barges toward the front door, grabbing her purse from an armchair on the way.

"There's no time," the girl says. "Gabby texted me. She's already on her way." Her voice is wobbly.

"Hey." Mr. Matthews comes around the table to put his hands on his daughter's shoulders. His voice is soothing. "Hey, look at me." She does. "It's going to be okay."

"How?" she says, but it's not a challenge, it's a plea for her da to make everything better.

"Dani will take you upstairs to find a new dress. Won't you?" He looks to Mrs. Matthews. She is holding Charlotte on her hip. Charlotte is resting her head on Dani's shoulder, perfectly content and unaware of the chaos she's caused.

"Of course," Mrs. Matthews says. "Yeah, of course."

"Crisis averted." A gentleman wearing a dark jacket and a bolo tie pats Mr. Matthews on the back like he's done a good day's work.

I step forward, offering to take the baby, and Mrs. Matthews hands her over.

"You two are about the same size, right?" Mr. Matthews asks.

"Oh, Soph, I have a ton of cute options." Mrs. Matthews heads toward the stairs. "Come on."

The partygoers are already spreading back out, conversations starting back up. Mr. Matthews is already engaged in talk of the local high school football team, of their chances of making the playoffs again in the upcoming year, now that they'll be relying on a new starting quarterback.

The ex-wife still hovers near the door, purse tucked beneath her arm, keys at the ready. She scoffs. No one else is paying her any mind now as

Mrs. Matthews leads both teenage girls up the stairs. But I'm tempted to reach for the rosary beads, because the look that ex-wife is giving Mrs. Matthews, sure, it's pure snake's venom, I'd say. Dani best steer clear of that one, if she knows what's good for her.

19

Dani

The girls spill into my closet.

My closet is beautiful, bigger than the entire bedroom of my old apartment. A four-tiered chandelier hangs from the center of the ceiling, sparkly as a diamond. Two white armchairs face the fireplace, double-sided, so I can see through to the bathroom—a luxury all on its own, with heated floors, a stand-alone slipper tub, a doorless wet room with rain showerheads and multiple body jets. The closet has a full vanity, a round tufted ottoman where I can sit to buckle the straps of my shoes. Shelves line the wall, with undermount lights to display pumps and wedges and sandals like pieces of art, folded jeans and sweaters, handbags and scarves. Dresses hang in every color like jewels.

Sophie caresses the hem of a raw silk blouse that cost more than I used to make from a week of shifts at the coffee shop, walks her fingers up a stack of cashmere sweaters. Mikayla spots a pair of nude Louboutins and mouths an *OMG* to Sophie.

I keep my eye on the plain black pumps where the note left at my door lies hidden.

Kim's words irritate like gnats on my brain. She was going out of her way to be mean. She doesn't like me, and that's fine. I get it.

It reminds me of online trolls, only I can't just delete her comments. Once I posted a process video, the camera set on a tripod on the counter as I spun and frosted a cake for a friend's twenty-fifth birthday. Most of the comments focused on the cake itself—handclap emojis with *#inspo*, heart eyes and *This is absolutely stunning* and *I am literally obsessed.* Aspiring bakers asking questions about products or techniques. I have a handful of devoted fans as well, people who never fail to like and comment and share, the screen names of these strangers as familiar as friends by now. And of course, there were a few compliments aimed at me personally—*You are so pretty! Share your skin care routine?*

In the video I wore a solid black tank top, and one random guy felt the need to add *Meh. Small tits* to the conversation.

I thought about that comment for weeks. Still think of it from time to time.

Kim's words cut much deeper than a comment about the size of my breasts, though. Even the word *influencer* makes my stomach turn. But I can't really call myself a professional baker either. I'm a stay-at-home mom . . . with a nanny. I'm a half-assed, fake version of everything I appear to be.

Then, of course, my darling baby went and threw up all over poor Sophie.

And then, even worse, my supportive but oblivious husband said, *You two are about the same size, right?* in reference to me and his teenage daughter. Why, for the love of God, did he have to say that? Because when he did, I felt myself melt under the heat of Kim's utter hatred. And, really, can I blame her?

I've done the math. I'm closer in age to Sophie and Mikayla than I am to Ethan and Kim. By five years. I'm not stupid. I know what people think.

And now—though he didn't mean anything by it, didn't think anything of it at all—he has sent me up here to giggle and play dress-up with the kids while the adults wait for us downstairs.

Not a good start to the day.

But, hey, if this is the worst thing that happens today, we can work with that. I can salvage this situation. I can put a dress and a smile on Sophie. I can make nice with Kim, let her insults roll off me, or at least appear to. I'm good at crafting the perfect image. It's what us *influencers* do, right?

Sophie is standing before the full-length mirror now, arms at her sides, staring at the orange-pureed puke stain splashed across her chest, dribbling down her waist and onto her skirt.

"It's totally ruined, isn't it?" she says. "Mom must be so pissed right now. We spent all day trying on dresses, this one was crazy expensive, and—"

"Hey." I stop her mid-spiral with a hand to her shoulder, turn her gently to face me. "I will get it dry-cleaned. It'll be as good as new, and you can wear it to prom next year. Okay? That'll be even more special."

"She's going to be in a bad mood all day. My party totally died before my friends even showed up."

"Your mom just wants you to be happy," I say. Sophie does a half-hearted eye roll, but I press on. "Today is about you. Now let's find you something killer to wear."

She looks to Mikayla for reassurance, and Mikayla delivers. "You would look good in anything, Soph," she says, and she casts wistful eyes over my clothes.

"You want to borrow a dress too?" I ask. Why not lean into this makeover montage moment?

Mikayla's eyes go wide.

But before she even answers, Sophie jumps up and down in excitement. "Oh my God, yes, please."

"I don't know. Maybe," Mikayla says.

Sophie squeals and claps her hands like Mikayla has just given her a definite yes. "This'll be fun." Sophie looks at me, hands clasped under her chin, brilliant smile back on her face. She reminds me suddenly of the twelve-year-old girl she was when Ethan and I first started dating, even if she's almost as tall as I am now. "I missed you," she says.

My heart clenches with guilt.

Sophie used to spend every Wednesday night after school and every other weekend at our house, and more often than not, Mikayla was in tow. I made it a whole to-do: rom-coms on Netflix, high-end Korean face masks and gel nail polish, homemade pizza with goat cheese and sun-dried tomatoes, a new dessert recipe to try together—mermaid cupcakes with teal and purple swirled batter, buttercream frosting, fondant scales, a candy fin, silver sparkles. We'd upload our creations on Insta and Snapchat, post a video of us doing a TikTok dance in the kitchen while we cleaned up.

But we haven't seen much of the girls lately, and that's my fault.

"I'm sorry it's been so long," I say.

Sophie and Mikayla have only spent one night here since Charlotte was born.

Don't go back there. Focus on the future.

Sophie shakes her head, turns to the rack, and starts flipping through dresses. "Oh my God, no, Dani, don't even. It's fine."

Ethan tries, of course, takes Sophie out for lunch on Saturdays, makes it to football games when he can to see her cheer on the sidelines, but it isn't the same. He wants her here, wants his family together. He doesn't talk about it, but I know he sees his divorce as the biggest failure of his life.

Early in our relationship, I had to learn to ignore my jealousy, put it into a teeny-tiny box, seal it tightly, and shove it in the back of my mind. I had to learn that there was a difference between wishing his marriage had worked and missing his ex-wife.

Ethan's parents divorced when he was eight years old, and he never wanted his own kids to be raised in a broken home. It's Sophie that he misses. It's Sophie that he wishes the marriage had worked out for.

"Besides," Sophie continues, "Dad explained everything. You're busy with Charlotte, and you've been getting, like, no sleep. I know it's not the same, but, Mikayla? Remember when we stayed up all night for that European history final? Like, for real, we didn't sleep the whole night, just mainlined Red Bulls and Skittles. Lack of sleep can seriously make you cra—" She stops short, looks to Mikayla, who starts to fidget with the makeup strewn across the top of my vanity.

"Totally," I say, my voice as casual, as breezy as possible. "But Charlotte is getting so much better about sleeping through the night. And we miss you. I'll talk to your mom today. We'll figure out a day in the next week or two to have you stay the night again. Both of you. Now let's find you two something to wear and get this party started."

The girls focus on excitedly rummaging my wardrobe.

I flip through a few long dresses. *Crazy,* I think. That's what she was going to say, what she stopped herself from saying. With my foot I discreetly tuck the plain black pumps out of sight.

But the words from the note scrawl themselves across my mind anyway.

Charlotte was six weeks old, and I had felt the presence for a few weeks. It was evening. I had just put Charlotte down for bed. She wasn't sleeping through the night yet, but she usually gave me a longer stretch at that time of day. On a good night, it was enough to unwind for a bit with Ethan on the couch and maybe even catch an hour or two of sleep. It was six thirty, maybe seven, but late November the sun sets so early that it was dark outside. I was in Ethan's office downstairs, checking the window locks.

I pushed the curtain aside, lifted the blinds. And there, just beyond the glass, was a face, eyes level with my own. My heart fell through the empty column of my body. My blood roared in my ears, so loudly that I didn't even hear myself scream. I stumbled backward, dropping the curtain back over the window.

Ethan was immediately at my side.

Someone was there, I said. My voice trembled so much that it didn't sound like my own. Ethan looked around the room. I raised my arm, pointed a shaky finger at the window. *Outside. There was someone at the window. They were pressed against the window, Ethan. They were looking inside.*

What the hell? He tore back the curtain, but of course the face was gone. *Stay here,* he said, rushing from the room. *Stay right there.*

I tried to steady my breath. I pulled at the strap of my nursing tank, pressed my fingers to the rapid pulse in my neck. I closed my eyes and took deep breaths.

After a few minutes, Ethan returned, slightly out of breath. He shook his head. *They're gone,* he said. *I looked everywhere.* He had his phone in his hand. *Are you all right?*

I nodded.

He tapped the screen, then lifted the phone to his ear.

What are you doing? I asked.

Calling the cops.

I felt a wave of relief. This sense of dread that had been hanging over me like a dense fog, this feeling that someone was watching me, that someone was watching us, me and my newborn daughter—it felt more real than ever in this moment, and somehow that felt better. Like someone had turned on the light, exposed the boogeyman, pulled him from the closet to say, *Look, here he is.*

Ethan rattled off our address. *Yes,* he said. *We've had a suspicious person lurking around our home.* He gave a few more details, then tilted the phone away from his mouth. *What did he look like?*

What? I don't, I don't know, I said.

Anything you can remember. Clothing would be helpful.

I shook my head.

Height? Age? Eye color? Facial features? Skin color?

Um. I closed my eyes, replayed the moment in my mind, pulling up the blinds, the well-lit room reflected in the dark glass, the realization of a face beyond, eyes matching mine, eyebrows raised in equal surprise. *White?* I said.

Ethan's brows drew together. *Is that a question?*

No, I snapped. *He was white. Or she . . .*

The crease between his brows deepened.

I didn't get a good look. It was dark outside. My own reflection was . . .

I could see him thinking behind his eyes. *One moment,* he said into the phone. Then he stepped from the room. I followed him as far as the open doorway. I stood there, hand on the frame, head tilted to catch random snatches—*New mother. A little on edge lately. Sorry.* His voice was smooth as butter again, his composure returned, his charm. I even heard his deep, throaty chuckle.

I sat back in the chair when I heard him coming.

Are the cops on their way? I asked.

I think I might have been a little rash in calling them.

There was someone creeping around outside our house, Ethan. We have a baby. We can't take chances.

I looked everywhere. I promise. If he was here, he's gone now.

If? Heat rose up my chest.

Look. He sat in a nearby chair, pulling it closer to mine. *I've been thinking that I need to help out more. You're such a great mom that I take for granted that you've got this, you know? Do you have any milk in the freezer? How about tonight I take the first shift with Charlotte? You sleep in a little.*

I stood. *There was someone outside,* I said again, my voice sure, even as my confidence slipped and doubt needled its way into the back of my mind.

You haven't been yourself lately.

I had a baby six weeks ago. I wasn't sure if I wanted to scream or cry, and there he sat, his posture, his face relaxed. I had the sudden urge to slap him.

That's what I'm saying. And again with the hormones and the blah, blah, blah.

There was someone outside. I wanted to sound firm, but it came out petulant instead, frustration swelling into my throat. My eyes began to water. *Not just tonight.*

He reached out and took my hand.

And suddenly I was spilling everything—the figure I had seen on the front lawn, the lights turned on or off, the doors opened or shut, the sounds and the shifting, missing items. But the more I listed my evidence out loud, the flimsier my case seemed.

Ethan stood and pulled me into him. I laid my cheek on his chest as his arms wrapped tightly around me. I closed my eyes, inhaled the scent of him. I felt myself melt, my legs going weak as the adrenaline of the last half hour or so flooded from my body.

I want you to talk to someone, he said. *I have some colleagues who specialize in postpartum anxiety.*

You think I'm crazy.

He kissed the top of my head. *No.* His voice was a husky whisper.

I was hesitant to go to therapy. It felt like admitting something was really wrong. Ethan mentioned this to Curtis. That's when Curtis suggested that I see him. Because they were partners, I could see Curtis more discreetly—he had even agreed to come see me at the house, meet with me in the upstairs library. At the time, it had seemed the perfect compromise.

———

I pull a canary yellow column dress from the rack. "This would be a pretty color on you, Soph."

When I turn, Sophie is already holding up a dress in front of her body before the mirror. The smile on her face stretches from ear to ear. "Please, please, please," she begs.

My stomach sinks, and all I can think is, *Oh shit.*

20

Kim

Oh dear God.

Sophie descends the spiral staircase, her lithe teenage body Saran Wrapped in a champagne sequined tube dress that nearly matches her skin color. The stretchy fabric clings to every curve, making them look like more than they are. The top is low and the skirt is short, barely covering her butt, her skinny legs a million miles long.

Behind her, Mikayla has transformed as well. She wears a Kelly green halter dress, the color gorgeous against her pale skin and copper hair. The silhouette skims over her hips, cinches her waist, and leaves plenty of cleavage on display, cleavage that I, quite frankly, didn't realize had been hiding beneath her baggy dresses and *FFA* T-shirts.

We—Ethan and I and anyone nearby with eyeballs in their heads—have been stunned into silence. When Sophie gets to the bottom of the steps, she does a spin, presenting the full illusion of her nude body. "Well?" she says.

Ethan opens his mouth to respond but seems to have swallowed his tongue. His eyes flick to me, then to Dani, who is coming slowly down the stairs, a smile plastered on her dumb face. Her own sexy red dress looks tame now in comparison.

"You look beautiful, obviously, sweetheart," Ethan says, finally finding his voice. "But are you sure . . ." He trails off.

Sophie looks down at herself, smooths her hands over her hips.

Ethan is trapped, I realize, and suddenly this whole situation is a little more fun. What can he say? This shocking, risqué . . . hell, this *slutty* dress belongs to his wife. Marjorie and Jo Ellen, standing together just off to the side, are quite literally clutching at their pearls. I see them exchanging glances, scandalized by just being in the same room as *that dress.*

I lift my fist to my nose to cover the smile tugging at my lips. "Wow, Dani."

Dani's smile doesn't move. She's such a ditz. Ethan's jaw looks tensed enough to break a tooth.

We are saved by the party planner, who appears with a tray of champagne flutes and fruity drinks. Waiters weave about with even more glasses of champagne. "For the girls," the party planner says, presenting Sophie and Mikayla with sugar-rimmed glasses filled with a pretty pink drink garnished with mint and a triangle of watermelon.

Ethan takes two of the champagne flutes, hands one to Dani. He lifts his glass in a toast to Sophie.

"Actually," I say to the party planner, though I'm keeping my eye on Ethan. "Could I have one of those virgin cocktails instead?"

"Of course. They are absolutely refreshing." She scurries off to retrieve my drink.

Suck it, Ethan.

The girls twirl away with their fancy drinks and their provocative dresses to take pictures in the photo booth. Which means that photos of our teenage daughter wearing *that* dress will be uploaded to every social media platform on the internet. And it's all his fault.

No one will see that, though, will they? Of course not. Look at him. He's a *good dad.*

Everyone knows that if something goes wrong, the mother is to blame.

21

Mikayla

We're in the photo booth, just Sophie and me. Her cheek is pressed against mine so hard that I can feel her smile. We can see ourselves in the screen as we pose. It's weird to be wearing Dani's dress. I look nothing like myself, but also it feels like this dress was made for me.

Sophie glances toward her parents, still gathered by the bottom of the staircase, drinks in hand. The atmosphere between them all is suffocating.

"Dani seems good, right?" she says.

"Mmmhmm," I murmur. "Let's do kind of a silly one."

Sophie cocks a hip, throws up a peace sign, and makes a duck-lipped face. I put my hands on my hips, push my cleavage toward the screen—like, for real, my boobs look crazy good in this dress—and stick out my tongue.

"I mean, we text, like, all the time, obviously, and Dad told me she was getting better. But I haven't actually seen her since . . . well, you know . . . *that* night."

"Yeah, me either," I say. This isn't quite true, though. The other day, I was getting out of the car after school, slinging my backpack over my shoulder, and I turned and saw Dani across the street, pushing the stroller. I didn't know what to do. But then Dani smiled and waved, and I felt my hand lifting to wave back, and she kept walking, and that was it.

"She seems good," Sophie repeats, as if convincing herself one final time. "I think everything is going to be fine." She wraps her arms around me from behind, clasping her hands near my sternum. She rests her chin on my shoulder and stares at the image of us on the screen.

"You look so freakin' sexy, Mik." I feel the breath of her words on my collarbone.

I am hit hard again with the urge to break something, to shove the expensive photo booth screen to the floor.

I am always fading into the background. *My shrinking violet,* my me-maw calls me, like it's some kind of cute pet name. Because everyone assumes that if you are quiet, then you are sweet, you are docile, you are following the rules.

But there is a blackness inside me, roiling and bubbling, and I'm afraid I can't keep it bottled up. I'm afraid it'll erupt, uncontrollable and ugly.

The camera snaps one last time. The doorbell rings again, and the door swings open. Enter the glossy girls.

22

Dani

I open the door to three shrieking teenage girls—Sophie's fellow cheer-leaders, I think—who flutter straight past me like a flock of colorful birds, all long hair and vibrant dresses and multicolored tissue paper sprouting from gift bags. They descend upon Sophie in a flurry of hugs and squeals.

"Well, there go our eardrums." The woman on the porch shifts her Kate Spade clutch into one hand, sticks out the other in introduction. She is wearing a one-shouldered, floor-length fuchsia gown. "Isabel," she says. "I'm Gabriela's mom." She points toward a miniature version of herself with the same shiny black hair.

"Dani," I say, taking her hand.

But she isn't looking at me. She's looking over my shoulder, into the house, her eyes going up and down in astonishment.

"Wow," she says. "I mean, I've looked up into the windows, I don't even know how many times." She smiles—perfectly straight teeth a few shades too white. "My husband jokes that he's going to get me a pair of binoculars."

I let out a breath of laugh, but for a moment I don't know what to say. It's a weird joke, isn't it? The back wall of glass exposes my kitchen, my living room, my bedroom, the nursery.

Luckily, I don't have to say anything at all, because Ethan comes up behind me. "We met at a football game, didn't we?" he says to the woman. "The home game against Reagan. Isabel, right?"

"Good memory," she says, smile dialing up a notch as she tucks a strand of hair behind her ear. My husband has a talent for remembering names, little details too, has a way of making each person feel special, feel like the only one in the room.

"Honey," he says to me, "Isabel is the cheer team's booster club president."

"Right again," Isabel says, unable to contain her utter delight. "I heard from a little birdie that there was going to be a former Dallas Cowboys Cheerleader at this party. Is that true?"

Ethan nods. "My partner's wife, in fact."

Isabel's eyebrows raise. Her forehead remains impressively still. "I may just need to pick her brain, maybe even convince her to give a little talk to our girls."

Ethan ushers her inside. "Let's get you a drink." A member of the catering staff appears, asking if she'd like to check her bag. Another brings a tray of cocktail options. They both grab drinks, and Ethan leads her away on a tour of the house.

I am about to close the door when I see another car pulling around the circular drive. The valets rush forward. Another car is coming up the road, followed by yet another. More guests I don't recognize. I stretch my smile wide and wave, but I can't help wondering who, exactly, I'm inviting into my home.

———

Three days ago I came out here to check the porch for a package—new cake decorating supplies—and tucked just under the doormat was a plain white envelope with my name handwritten across the front— *Dani.* No last name. No address. No stamp.

I glanced down our long private road—empty—before sliding my finger beneath the flap. I pulled out the single sheet of white paper, unfolded it.

Things had been going so good lately—Charlotte was growing; I was feeling stronger; I even caught Ethan relaxing from time to time, *really* relaxing, instead of keeping his vigilant watch; and I was baking again: shopping for cake supplies, sketching designs, firing up the oven for test bakes that filled the house with warmth and the smell of vanilla— that I had almost let myself slip, like sinking beneath the surface of a warm bath, let myself slip back into the comfort of who I was before. As though none of it had ever happened at all.

Then I read the words. An angry scrawl—

You don't deserve your perfect life, you crazy bitch.

And it all came slamming back. The terror. The paranoia. But beneath all that, something bloomed. A feeling that said: *You were right. You were right the whole time.* Because this . . . this was real. This was undeniable. Physical. Proof.

I'm not crazy. I'm not imagining things. And maybe I never was.

23

Kim

The house is packed now, alive with moving bodies and vibrating conversation. Ethan promised me parties like this. We designed our renovations with entertaining in mind—the open floor plan, the cathedral ceiling, the pièce de résistance of this panoramic view, unencumbered by the floor-to-ceiling glass along the back. We were saving to have the doors custom-built before everything fell apart. It was the final piece to our dream home. Ethan didn't want anything obstructing the dollhouse effect. Twenty-foot-tall panels slide open, a moving wall of glass, blurring the boundary between the indoors and the outdoors. Open now, they let in a breeze that shivers the sequined tablecloths, swirls long skirts around women's ankles.

I'm talking to a guy named Ted. He lives in the neighborhood, but clearly must have moved in within the last four years, because he didn't live here when I did. He's a stranger to me. Which is a big, fat point in his favor. Let's put it this way: I'm not talking to Ted for his sparkling conversation.

I know almost everyone here—old neighbors, Ethan's coworkers, the parents of kids who have shared a classroom with Sophie since pre-K. That group of guys near the double-sided fireplace split a deer lease with Ethan for years. The other wives and I would pack up the kids and stay long weekends at the lease's eight-bedroom lodge, assembly-lining sandwiches, playing cards, and sipping wine, while our husbands hunted and our children explored the scrubby brush and shallow creek beds like feral animals. I still remember when the kids brought us a scorpion in a pickle jar, asked if they could keep it as a pet. That couple—the Davidsons—spent a week with us at the Gaylord

Texan Resort, outside Dallas, when Sophie was ten and their boys were nine and eleven. The bottle-blonde over there in a blue metallic high-low dress, Sheryl Quinn, is my old spin-class partner. I used to save her a back-row bike beside mine. Now she averts her eyes when she sees me. They all do.

Sophie used to love to play Mario Kart. *Mommy, race me, race me. Mommy, I want to be the princess. Mommy, do you like the mushroom guy?* As you raced, your customized character drove alongside a transparent phantom version of itself, a shadow version replaying your best run through the track. *Ghost cars,* that's what Sophie told me they're called.

I feel that now, moving through my old house, my old friends, my old life, catching glimpses of phantom versions of myself.

Anyway, that's why I'm talking to Ted.

He is also semi-handsome. Another point for Ted. He's tall, at least—over six feet—and his shoulders are broad, which makes up for his belly. He's going bald, but it kind of works for him. He's got a bit of a Bruce Willis thing going on. There's a gold ring on his finger, but he doesn't seem to mind when I put a hand on his wrist, when I throw my head back to laugh, let my thick mane of curly blond hair cascade down my back, expose the deep V of my neckline.

"You're going to have to slow down, Ted," I say. "The most I know to do with a computer is shop online."

He's been explaining his job to me. Ex-military, he works in the private sector now. An engineer. Something to do with tech security.

I'm perfectly capable with a computer. But men like a woman who is a little befuddled, and it saves me the pain of hearing every boring detail about servers and coding.

"And what do you do?" he asks.

"I'm a veterinarian." I've always liked saying it, seeing the impressed reaction, the reassessment of me. And he does—reassess me, I mean; looks me up and down, lingering on the curves of my hips, the swell of my breasts. He isn't trying to hide it.

"Your drink is empty," he says.

I shake the ice in the glass. "I like a man with keen observation skills."

"What are you drinking?"

I'm actually on my second watermelon nojito. That's another reason I'm flirting with dull and married but slightly sexy Ted here: a zero-proof kind of buzz.

Waiters weave through the clustered groups with trays of cocktails—a layer of jewel-toned grenadine along the bottom of a tequila sunrise, slivers of fresh pineapple on the rim of a frozen piña colada, a purple orchid floating atop a margarita on the rocks.

There are probably a lot of reasons I shouldn't drink today. I know what they all think of me now. What they say about me. *Poor Kim, bless her heart.* They *worry* about me.

At least, that's what Ethan says when he calls me at 9 P.M. and thinks he detects a slur in my voice. *I just worry about you, Kim.* I mean, really, why is he calling so late? He always has an excuse, of course—he needs to touch base about Sophie's cheer schedule, which of us will be picking her up from which out-of-town football game—and he works all day, so sometimes 9 P.M. is the first chance he has. I don't buy it. He *wants* to catch me drunk. Wants to click his tongue, shake his head, offer his help. Ethan and his hero complex.

Ethan's first love, his first fiancée, suffered from mental health issues. She was nineteen when she died. He was twenty-one and completely devastated. It solidified his decision to follow Roy Barker into the field of psychiatry. If I'm being generous, which, quite frankly, I'd rather not be—that is obviously why he worries so much. About the people he loves. About me.

Still—surprising me with random phone calls, even after our divorce, like he's my parole officer or something? It feels more controlling than caring. And it's just wine, for Chrissakes. Just a few glasses at the end of the day. Everyone drinks wine. I mean, come on, look at all the drinking-mom memes, the fuzzy socks with *Wine O'clock* printed along the bottom, the *Mommy Juice*-etched wineglasses. Just look at this room. There isn't an adult at this party without a drink in their hand.

However, I think of the panic in Sophie's voice last night when she couldn't wake me. That's really why I'm not drinking today. For Sophie. Because when I promised her that nothing would go wrong today, the implication of that promise was that I wouldn't drink.

I'll reward myself tonight instead. I'll swipe a bottle or two from

Ethan's stash in the cellar. My shoulders melt just thinking of ripping off these Spanx, pulling on my soft black joggers and oversized gray T-shirt, no bra, curling up on the sofa with my favorite worn quilt, Sweetie the cat in my lap, firing up my true crime marathon, and letting that first sip of wine coat my tongue.

I focus instead on poor pathetic Gwyneth Porter—across the room, standing around a cocktail table among a cluster of women. Gwyneth is Ethan's assistant, has been since he started working under Roy Barker before it became Barker & Matthews. That's how long she's been in love with him too. To be fair, he's hard not to love, so long as you aren't married to him. She is younger than me, but not by much, health-obsessed, constantly posting yoga poses and MapMyRun accomplishments, one of those angular, hollowed-clavicle, sharp-elbows-and-knees types. Right now, she is wearing a simple spaghetti strap dress that hangs off her, accentuates the almost-not-there quality of her, her shoulders pointy and tanned. Gwyneth has never liked me, blinded by her puppy-dog devotion to my husband.

So I can't help but smile now—watching Gwyneth chat politely with Ethan's new wife, whose soft, youthful glow just makes Gwyneth's sharp thinness look haggard in comparison.

"Club soda with lime," I tell Ted, handing him my empty glass.

"You sure? Open bar."

I turn my head to glance toward the bar through the sliding glass door. But in the midst of my swivel, I spot them instead—Curtis and Gemma Barker.

Shit.

Curtis is wearing a western tux with cowboy hat and boots. He isn't the only man at this party wearing either, but most are legitimate ranchers, shining their work boots with mink oil for the party. Curtis is wearing alligator Luccheses. Gemma looks like a Miss Texas pageant contestant—platinum hair teased high and dress glittering.

———

My own mother had five sisters. When I was growing up, whenever any of my aunts (or all five) would come to town, my mother would pack a suitcase for me, my brother, and herself, we would kiss my father goodbye, and we'd go stay at my grandparents' for days at a time. We lived ten minutes from their house. We could have much more easily gone back and forth each day to visit. But my mother's time with her sisters was sacred, and it was the nights she craved.

Sometimes, I would lie awake on my pallet on the floor in the sunroom (because every bed and couch in the house was taken by one family member or another) and listen to their laughter around the kitchen table. Sometimes, I would sneak to sit just outside the kitchen door so that I could hear their conversations. My mother never seemed more herself than during those night talks. And throughout my childhood, I desperately wished for a sister of my own.

The closest I ever came to a sister was Gemma Barker. We'd call to make sure the other one would be at the party of a mutual friend. *I can't stand her without you. Please tell me you're bringing the Riesling.* Text each other pictures of our outfits. Drink wine on the porch and laugh until we cried. When her mother died, it was me she called first, nothing but sobs on the other end. *Are you home? I'll be there.* I had known her mother was sick. Pancreatic cancer.

It took me fifteen minutes to get to her house, toting a bottle of wine and a chunk of some smelly cheese I'd found in my fridge, still in the sweatpants I'd been wearing to clean the house. She answered the door with bloodshot eyes, her nose raw from the tissues. I hugged her, and she melted in my arms. I stayed over that night. We stretched out on the sectional sofa, toes touching, soft blankets piled on top of us, and Gemma told me story after story about her mother until the sky outside was gray with morning.

———

Now, Gemma's eyes scan the room and she catches sight of me. Her smile fades. Her expression is so cold I feel a literal chill.

"Vodka," I tell Ted. Because, really? Who was I kidding? Ethan started this party so goddamn early because he wanted it to be an event, an all-day affair. It was just a matter of time before I ordered a drink. I might as well get it over with.

He smiles. "I like a woman who knows how to have a little fun." He grazes his knuckles along my forearm, and I will myself to feel a crackle of electricity between us.

I'll cut myself off after two. I just want that warm blanket on my brain. A little distance from the ghosts that haunt this party.

I try not to look back toward the front of the house while I wait for Ted to fetch my drink. It's been almost four years since I saw Gemma Barker, and the last time was in the red and blue glow of the ambulance lights.

24

Mikayla

I'm in the inner circle, amid the glossy girls.

"That's her," Gabby says, leaning into the group. We all turn to see Mrs. Gemma Barker enter the party, hand on the crook of her husband's arm. She used to be a Dallas Cowboys Cheerleader. That's what they say. She seems to glide, her silver dress sweeping the floor, her back straight as a board, big teeth bright white in a big smile. Gabby is going to be a Dallas Cowboys Cheerleader. That's what she says, and, despite the odds, I can't help but think it'll be a cakewalk for a girl like her.

"My mom is going to get her to come to one of our practices," Gabby says. Her mom is president of the booster club, and, just like Gabby, she tends to get what she wants. "Maybe she can help you with your jump splits." She says this to Ava, who nods, then crinkles her forehead.

"What's wrong with my jump splits?"

"This house is straight fire," Emma says. Her hair is twisted into space buns, which bob on her head as she takes in the height of the room, the windowed wall open to an unobstructed horizon, making the space appear endless, everything sparkly as a diamond today, crystal chandeliers and crystal cocktail glasses and twinkling lights and sequined tablecloths and satin-sheened dresses.

I would feel way too silly to even try pulling off space buns in real life, but of course she's killing it, looking like she's going to Coachella or something. "We always talk about this house—my family," Emma goes on. "My little brother calls it the Dollhouse, because, well, you know, you're driving down 1863, and you come around that bend, and bam, there's this big mansion up on the cliff with, like, the whole back taken off, so you can see into all the rooms, like freakin' Barbie's Dreamhouse or something. I didn't know you lived here. You should totally get a pink convertible to match the vibe. It's giving main character energy."

Sophie shrugs. "It's my dad's house. I mostly live with my mom now."

"It's haunted, you know?" Gabby says, leaning into the center of the group, one thick, sculpted eyebrow raised.

We all know the story, of course—it's a Bulverde legend—well, all of us except Emma, whose family moved here from California, just in time for Emma to try out for the cheer squad at the end of eighth grade and slide straight into the cool crowd before high school even started. There are a lot of people moving from California these days. *It's fine if they want to drive the property values up,* my dad says, *as long as they keep their wacky politics back in California.*

Emma's eyes are wide now and she's looking to each of us, like she's checking whether or not Gabby is just messing with her. Gabby likes messing with people.

"My mom used to hear her all the time, back when she lived here," Sophie says. "My dad always said it was just the wind, but Mom swore it was her, moaning while she looked for her child."

People hear her all over town. *She wanders,* they say. *She searches.*

"We should do a séance or something," Ava says, even though her daddy is the preacher at First Baptist and would most certainly pitch a fit if he heard her talking that way.

"Mom saw her a few times too," Sophie continues. "Dad said it was probably just a deer. Mom said it was a white dress weaving through the trees in the dark."

"What happened? I mean, who is this woman?" Emma asks. She's still holding her birthday present for Sophie, and I bet it's some supercool, expensive crop top or nail polish kit. I made Sophie a scrapbook, which was really, really stupid, and now I'm praying she doesn't open her gifts in front of everyone.

"They call her *The Mother,*" Gabby says. "My abuela used to tell us about *The Mother* all the time, like a bedtime story. So this was, like, a hundred fifty years ago or something. Some rich German family built this big castle house up here on the cliff. They had everything—a cook, a butler, a scullery maid, whatever—like, full-on *Downton Abbey,* you know? And they had an infant daughter. Well, one day the mother and the baby both came down with a terrible fever. It went on for weeks. The mother was delirious—pouring sweat, hallucinations, the whole thing—and when her fever finally broke, her husband had to tell her that the baby didn't survive. They had already buried her in a tiny wooden casket in the church cemetery."

"That's awful," Emma says in a whisper.

"Just wait," Ava says.

Gabby goes on, "But *The Mother* kept hearing her baby's cries—in the other room, up in the tower, outside in the carriage house, in the neighbor's house, in the church. *My baby is still alive,* she started to tell people, *I just can't find her.* Finally, a year after the baby's death, they exhumed her coffin to prove to *The Mother* that she really was dead."

Emma looks to the rest of us. Ava wrinkles her nose, but doesn't dispute the facts.

"The husband warned her that it would be a gruesome sight, that the baby would be nothing but bone and shapeless flesh. They pried open the lid, and there she was, still and perfect as a doll, the little white dress untouched, tucked beneath her feet, a sheer white cloth covering her face, and through the cloth, *The Mother* could see her daughter's precious features: closed eyelids, round cheeks, button nose. She began to cry with joy. She reached out to lift the cloth, only to find it wasn't cloth at all—it was a thin layer of white mold."

Emma gasps.

"She went mad after that. Jumped to her death from the balcony." Gabby tips her head to the window. The bottom edge of the balcony can be seen above. So much free air spirals below. "People say they can still hear her, especially on windy nights. Tonight looks like it's going to be pretty windy." A gust whistles against the glass.

Ava exaggerates a shiver. "I used to be so afraid of *The Mother.*"

"My abuela used to warn us never to whine," Gabby says. "If you whine, *The Mother* will assume you aren't happy with your own parents, and she'll come to steal you away for herself."

My family gave the same warning. *Mikayla Jane, you better not be talking back to me, young lady. Do you want* The Mother *to hear?*

"Wow, thanks for the nightmares, guys," Emma says.

"Anytime," Gabby says, flipping her hair. "OMG, is that a photo booth? Come on, girls." Then she adds, for literally no reason at all, "Mikayla, you should come too."

I trail behind them, until Sophie slips her arm through mine and propels me forward.

When I was a little kid, I used to lie awake at night, convinced that any sound outside my window was *The Mother*. The thought that a monster could come from the shadows and take a person was terrifying.

But, as I've gotten older, I think maybe it's scarier that a regular person can so easily become a monster.

25

Dani

The house is so crowded that I've had to lean in multiple times to hear the person I'm talking to, have to just laugh because I only caught half of what they said. A line has formed at the bar outside, and a mountain of gifts has appeared on top of the grand piano beneath the spiral sweep of the stairway.

Despite everything, I'm enjoying myself. I'd forgotten that I like having conversations with other adults, not that I have much to contribute to an adult conversation these days. *Do you prefer Gerber puffs or Happy Baby? Because, no matter what the packaging says about melting in your baby's mouth, I've had nightmares about Charlotte choking on both.*

A group of us circle a cocktail table with our plates of hors d'oeuvres. Charlotte is on my hip, and I'm talking with Gwyneth, Ethan's assistant, and a few women from the neighborhood, Kristin, Jaci, and Liz . . . or is it Lisa? I went to their book club twice before I had Charlotte. They've invited me to their next one in a few weeks. I doubt I'll make it this month, but maybe soon, and it's fun to imagine having a social life again.

And everyone is talking about my cake. Isabel, the booster club mom, has already exchanged numbers with me to see if we could talk cake designs for Gabby's Sweet Sixteen, which led to two other moms saving my number to their phones.

Ethan was right. I did need this. A spark of hope flickers.

I look over at Ethan across the room, standing before a semicircle of men and women, in the midst of some story, gesturing with the drink in his hand. Everyone laughs.

I forgot this too about parties, about socializing: I like watching my

husband hold court, put people under his spell. Because I know everything he's overcome.

He catches me staring. He winks. Without even a pause to his conversation. It sends a flutter of butterflies through my stomach.

It was one of those early days, the ones we spent lying in bed like
cats, lounging in sunlight-streaked sheets. His hands on every inch of
my skin, making me feel things I hadn't even known I'd been missing.
And between sessions, while we caught our breath and interwove our
fingers, we talked, and the talking was just as good as the sex.

I stuttered as a kid, he told me.

I rolled myself to face him, wrapped in the creamy luxury of his
high-thread-count sheets, rested my forearms on his chest. *You?* It didn't
sound true. His voice was like honey. He spoke slowly, almost melodi-
cally in the way he connected his words. It's one of the things that makes
him seem so confident. He's never in a rush to get out his ideas.

It's a speech therapy technique, he explained. *Smooth speech.*

He described the blocks he'd experienced—how in his mind, his
words were perfectly fluent, his ideas whole, but as they came from his
mouth, he would anticipate the block, know before he got to a word that
he was going to have trouble. An "s" or a "t" or the dreaded combination
of them both—to *stop,* to *start,* to *stumble.* And he would freeze.

I was terrified, he said, *to move forward, to keep speaking.*

I trailed a finger through his chest hair, watched his face as he spoke.
I felt a shift in our relationship. This wasn't a part of himself he shared
with many people. I knew that without him having to tell me.

I was a quiet kid, he said.

I breathed a laugh. *I can't imagine you quiet.*

He grinned. *When you don't talk, you spend a lot of time listening. It
might be one of the things that led me to psychiatry. Everyone—teachers,
aunts, uncles, other kids—thought I was shy. People make all these as-
sumptions about you. That you're shy, that you're nervous, that you're
slow.*

I could see by the set of his jaw, by the way he stared into the middle
distance, that this was the worst part for him. This thing that he couldn't
control, that wasn't his fault—it determined how others saw him, how
they judged him.

I imagined him as the boy from one of the photographs on his desk—maybe six years old, sitting beside his mother on a bench next to Lake Travis, wind blowing their hair, matching smiles and eye squints into the sun. My heart hurt for that little boy. For the man in front of me. I realized that it would hurt, too, if I lost him. This wasn't a fling anymore.

And that hurt and that happiness squeezed the breath from me. That's when I realized I loved Ethan Matthews.

Jaci must have caught our little exchange, his wink in my direction. "I wish my husband still looked at me that way," she says in a low murmur, inching over to me. "Hell, I wish anyone did." Gwyneth, standing beside Jaci, catches our side conversation, looks between me and Ethan, and I'm feeling a little embarrassed, feeling heat pink my cheeks, as if we were caught in some crude display of PDA.

I smile, bury my face in my wineglass. I deflect from the comment by bouncing Charlotte. But I can't help glancing back at my husband.

They see the flirtation, but I know what the wink really means: *Don't worry, babe. I got this.*

Proper nouns are the worst, he has told me. People's names. It's because you can't replace them with a synonym last-minute. I can only imagine the prep-work he's done for a party this size. When he meets someone new, he commits their name to memory, practices the combination of vowels and consonants again and again.

That's a big reason Ethan is so successful: He doesn't shy away from a challenge. He commits, he rehearses, he has an obsession with getting things exactly right. That's how he gained control of his stutter—by forcing himself into situations that could embarrass him, situations that terrified him, then plowing through. Choosing to give an oral book report in the third grade after a teacher pulled him aside and offered to let him submit a written alternative, auditioning for a middle school play when he had no hope of landing the part, applying for a job at fourteen to help out his single father when he was out of work. It was that job, Ethan has told me, that changed his life. Curtis's father—Big Roy Barker—was larger-than-life, came from big Texas oil money going back generations, but made a name for himself in psychiatry.

He was the type of man who commanded every room he entered. Ethan admired him, and the feeling was mutual. Big Roy noticed the quiet kid with the strong work ethic. It was actually Roy who put Ethan into speech therapy, who wrote letters of recommendation that got him scholarships to the University of Texas.

In the library upstairs is a photo in a pewter frame. A young Ethan, in his early twenties, and Big Roy, a barrel-chested man, broad cowboy hat on his head, white mustache. They're at the rodeo. Roy leans his elbow on the fence, a horse in the background. He's laughing at something Ethan has said. I've seen Curtis glance at it more than once during our sessions.

"You need business cards," Kristin tells me. "You are seriously talented. Have you thought about starting your own business?"

"That's the goal. I'm just . . ."—I gesture at Charlotte, who is yanking on my necklace—"short on time lately."

Kristin waggles her fingers at Charlotte. She has kids of her own— older, I want to say middle school–ish, though I can't remember if it's a boy and a girl or two boys. "That's why you have a nanny," she says. "Listen, I get it, you've got mom guilt. You feel bad if you enjoy even a second to yourself."

"God, I remember those days," Liz or Lisa says. "I'd get that tight-chest feeling just taking a shower."

"You get over it." Jaci tips back her glass to drain what little liquid she has left around her ice cubes. The other women laugh.

"I don't know how long we plan to keep Órlaith on," I say. "It was kind of just a temporary . . ." I let myself trail off.

"Well, why not?" Kristin says. "Look. A happy mama is a good mama. You need something that is just for you."

Gwyneth leans in. "Do you even get any work done with her around? Or does she just talk your ear off?"

I have to chuckle. "Did she corner you already?"

I can see Órlaith, near the open sliding glass door, in conversation with one of our other neighbors, Vera, a lady in her mid-seventies who lives near the entrance of the neighborhood and serves as president of the homeowners' association. She walks every day, carrying a big stick for support and stopping anyone she passes to chat about the weather and the neighborhood gossip and the status of the deer. It is actually Vera that we have to thank for finding Órlaith. Ethan had mentioned to her that we were looking for a nanny, and Vera recommended her friend, just moved from Ireland and looking for a job.

Gwyneth rolls her eyes elaborately. "I am keeping my distance from her today. I mean, not to be rude or anything. She came into the practice once. I actually thought she was coming in to make an appointment. That's how bad she is at getting to the point. Curtis was on vacation, so we weren't taking on any new clients, which I explained to her, and really, I was like *Thank God*, because I could not handle that woman in my office on a regular basis. I don't know how you have her in your home all day every day."

She must have the timing confused, because Curtis was last on vacation back when I was pregnant, long before we hired Órlaith, before we ever planned on having a nanny.

I'm about to say so, but Kristin adds, "So get a space outside the house to work. You don't have to be best friends with your nanny. You just have to trust your kid with her."

"What about that spot near Smokey Mo's?" Liz or Lisa asks. "It used to be a taco shop, so it must have a kitchen. It's been available for, what? A year now?"

"I bet you'd kill," Jaci says.

"Y'all have seen her Instagram, haven't you?" I don't know this woman's name. She sidled up to the group a while ago, slipped her plate of food and her glass of Coke onto the table between us. She feels vaguely familiar, but I can't place her, so I don't want to introduce myself or ask her name, in case we've met before. She is short, a little on the plump side, with a round sweet face and peaches and cream complexion, like a kindergarten teacher I once loved.

Do you live here in the neighborhood? Kristin asked her earlier in the conversation. The woman shook her head, covered her mouth to swallow a bite of the brisket slider. *River Crossing*, she said, which is another neighborhood along Highway 46, more multiple-acre lots and custom-built homes. She's young, though, maybe late twenties or early thirties, which is nice. Pretty much all of my friends, the friends my age, live in San Antonio proper. Which I get. Out here in Bulverde, some kind of cross between the suburbs and rural farm life, there's nothing to do and no way to meet anyone.

My stepdaughter is around here somewhere, she said, twisting her head and indicating the patio. *I'm like you,* she said to me with a giggle. She seemed to giggle at everything.

"Instagram?" Kristin says now, raising an eyebrow at me.

Jaci is already pulling her phone out of a crossbody bag. "What's your what-do-you-call-it? Your screen name?"

I tell her, trying not to let the heat creep up my cheeks. Lisa or Liz is looking over Jaci's shoulder as she types it in. Jaci gasps, shows the phone to Kristin, who slaps my arm. "Girl, you're famous."

I laugh, shake my head, and set my glass down so I can shift Charlotte onto my other hip.

"This is kind of embarrassing," the sweet-faced woman says. "We've never met—I'm MaryBeth, by the way—but I've actually followed you on Instagram for, like, forever. I love baking. I don't do anything like you, not even close. But I love looking at all your cakes, and oh my gosh, the pies, and you're just always so positive. Sorry, I'm gushing. I'm such a weirdo."

"Oh my God," I say, that vague familiarity clicking into place. I can imagine her profile picture now, that same round sweet face, that same kind smile. "You're MB95."

She covers her face to laugh, her cheeks flushing a bright pink. "I can't believe you remember."

"Are you kidding?" MaryBeth really has been following me since the beginning. She's one of my regular fans, commenting on nearly every post. We've been exchanging sweet messages for years. "How? What? This is unreal." I pull her into a hug, Charlotte crushed between us. MaryBeth is giggling so hard her whole body shakes as if she's trembling.

"Isn't that so funny?" Gwyneth says. "I knew you had a following, or whatever. Ethan's mentioned it. But I guess I hadn't thought about you having, like, fans."

MaryBeth is still pink in the face. She grabs her plate off the table and picks at the cubes of cheese. "About a year ago, you posted a picture from one of Sophie's football games. And I was like, hey, I recognize that stadium. I mean, I guess I knew you were in Texas, maybe even the San Antonio area, because I think you've posted the River Walk or something, but I didn't realize you were here in Bulverde until then. What are the chances?"

"Want me to take a picture?" Kristin asks. "Of the two of y'all?"

"Is that weird?" MaryBeth asks.

"Of course not." I hand Kristin my phone, throw an arm around MaryBeth. She's still shaking. We smile while Kristin takes a few shots. When she hands the phone back, I swipe through them, pick the best one of both of us. I hoist Charlotte more securely onto my hip, set the phone on the cocktail table so I can crop and edit with one hand.

Liz or Lisa glances over as I flip through filters, adjust the brightness and the saturation, ever so slightly lighten the shadows beneath our eyes, whiten our teeth just a shade or two, nothing overtly noticeable. "Holy crap, can you do that to all my pictures?" Liz or Lisa says.

I show the pic to MaryBeth. "Mind if I post it?"

"Of course not." She giggles again.

I make a post, *Finally getting to meet this bestie IRL!*, tag MB95. Before I close the app, I see a few hearts already floating by.

Then, a loud familiar voice sails over the crowd: "I need to squeeze that sweet baby."

I turn to see Gemma walking toward me. Despite her sky-high nude pumps and gymnast-like posture, she's a head shorter than the people around her. When she catches sight of me, her smile is big enough for two women. She sweeps me into her arms, reaching up on tiptoes to hug my neck.

"It's been too, too long." She squeezes tight, lets me go, but keeps a hand on my arm. "I missed you."

"I know. I'm sorry."

"Oh, honey, don't you apologize for anything." She holds my eyes for a moment. "You understand me?" She doesn't wait for a response, doesn't linger on the moment. Her attention slides to Charlotte, and she beams. "I forget how itty-bitty they are. Can I hold her?"

I hand Charlotte over and Gemma makes a show of inhaling her head. "Don't you love that baby smell?"

How could I have ever thought this would be awkward, have ever thought Gemma would be anything other than warm and reassuring?

"I'm so glad you're here," I say.

Curtis appears. "Looking lovely, ladies," he says, bending down to kiss both my cheeks. He looks sharp in his black suit and boots. I can feel the other women in our circle assessing him, shifting slightly.

"Where'd you disappear to?" Gemma asks.

"Called to check on the boys. The sitter is doing great."

"How old?" Kristin asks.

"Eight," Gemma says. "Twins."

"Aw, my youngest is eight," Jaci says. "Fun age."

"And where is that worthless husband of yours?" Curtis asks me.

But Ethan is already walking toward us with two drinks. He hands Curtis a beer, Gemma a glass of white wine. "Glad y'all could make it." He is quick to make the introductions, which I had forgotten to do, even remembering Liz's name (not Lisa) and that she and Gemma share the same alma mater (A&M).

Ethan's arm is around me again, his thumb rubbing the top of my bare shoulder. I lean into him. This feels nice.

"Oooh, look," MaryBeth says, holding her phone out to me. "We're getting comments already."

I take the phone. The message is from an anonymous profile, the name just a random series of letters and numbers, the profile picture just a gray icon of a person. The comment: *Must be nice to have such a perfect life.*

The words echo too closely to the handwritten note—*You don't deserve your perfect life, you crazy bitch.*

I look up. The house is a kaleidoscope—men in identical suits gliding past women in colorful dresses, the opalescent chandelier, the crystal cocktail glasses casting prismatic patterns, a lurid mosaic of neon balloons and gift bags and open mouths, laughter overlapping, all of it tumbling in my vision, swirling and sinking to the pit of my stomach.

Whoever has been tormenting me is here. I know it.

AFTER

The Night of the Party

Forty-five minutes after the first responders arrive, a mustached man in a gray suit and round brim hat enters the grand ballroom of the Vogel mansion.

Vera Weber notices him instantly, and her curiosity is piqued because she's never seen him before. She wonders if the hat he wears is standard for a detective brought in from Bexar County or if he had perhaps been pulled from bed with no time to comb his hair. Vera is seventy-six years old. She notices everything. Both as president of the HOA and as an active member on the City Council. She is a Rolodex of information on Bulverde. She sees the importance in being aware of one's neighbors, of being engaged in the concerns of her community. She could tell the detective a lot about the people in this room, about the events of the day, a lot more than the local police department could.

He is speaking to a young, uniformed officer now, Timothy Price. Vera was the organizer and lead sponsor of Timothy's Little League baseball team when he was in the sixth grade. She brings them both coffee and introduces herself. Sure, the whole town might see her as a busybody, but unlike the other guests in the room, she's watched enough *Columbo* to know one thing for certain: If the cops have called in a detective from the big city, it can only mean one thing—they suspect foul play.

Mikayla

The Day of the Party

We're waiting at the bar, Emma and Ava perusing the mocktail menu. Gabby, first to get her drink, of course, is now over at the DJ booth. When her song comes on, the beat low and seductive, she sways her hips toward the center of the dance floor. She slides both hands up the side of her body in a way that would make me feel ridiculous, but she moves perfectly in sync with the music. She lifts her hands into her hair, tilts her head back, eyes closed, and shakes her shiny mane of thick dark hair. She lowers her chin, looks straight at Sophie, and crooks a beckoning finger. Sophie joins Gabby on the dance floor. I hang back on the edge, watching with a mixture of awe and jealousy. Why can I never be that fluid? That confident? Gabby holds Sophie's hand above both their heads, and Sophie twists herself close to the floor, sticks her butt out, and rolls her body back up.

"Come on, Mikayla," Emma says, suddenly at my side, shoving another fancy watermelon drink into my hand. Ava loops her arm through mine and together they drag me onto the dance floor.

Just a few minutes ago, when we were all crammed into the photo booth, bodies turned at a 45-degree angle so that all five of us could fit into the screen, with my hair smoothed and curled, black liner winging my eyes, this borrowed green dress, and my cleavage spilling out, I almost felt like I was one of them—one of these glossy girls.

But my makeover is a coat of paint, and that's painfully clear now on the dance floor. I've never understood what makes someone a good dancer, how people let go, *feel* the music. I never know what to do with myself—my feet, my hands. But I try now, because I want so much to be a part of this.

"Looking for Mason?" Gabby asks. Sophie must have been scanning the party, but her answer is quick and confident.

She makes a snort of derision. "I'm so over him." The way she says it, I'd almost believe her, if I didn't know better.

"Yeah?" Gabby asks.

"Definitely."

"Good," Gabby says, then she reaches out and tucks a strand of Sophie's hair behind her ear, finger trailing along her jawline.

I close my eyes, try to sync up to the beat, move my body side to side. I remember how good I looked in the mirror upstairs, in Dani's closet, in Dani's dress.

"OMG, look at Mikayla," Gabby says with a giggle. My eyes snap open. "You're so cute with your little dance moves." To my complete horror, she puts her hands to her hips and mimics my movements. She looks stilted and awkward for, probably, like, the first time ever in her life. I want to die right here and now. "Aw," she says, pouting her bottom lip. "I'm just kidding. You're precious. Here." She hooks an arm around my waist, presses her body against mine, and starts to rock us both in rhythm. I'm smiling so hard that my cheeks hurt. I am super pissed, but I can't be pissed, because *Come on, it was just a joke.* Or maybe I'm going to cry, but I cannot, please, oh please, I cannot cry. I don't care. I absolutely do not care at all.

A new song comes on. Gabby lets me go and turns to the others. All four of them—Gabby, Emma, Ava, and even Sophie—squeal in unison. I don't know the song. I've never even heard it on Spotify. But, on cue, as soon as the chorus hits, they break into a choreographed number, just for a few steps, before they collapse into each other, laughing. Then I understand. It's one of their cheer routines.

Again, I'm on the outside. I thought today might be different, but it feels painfully similar to every other party, where Sophie would inevitably be pulled away by one drama or another, leaving me by the food table, pretending to be totally engrossed in something on my phone.

Sophie skips over to me, throws her arms around me. I think maybe she's sensing that I feel left out. Instead, her breath is in my ear. "Oh my God, Mik, he actually came."

Without being obvious, I glance over my shoulder. On the upper patio, a group of guys emerges from the back of the house. Leading the pack is Mason.

"How do I look?"

Her expression is bare, her voice low and only meant for me. She might be friends with Gabby and Emma and Ava, might share inside jokes and cheer routines and a text message chain filled with gossip. But it's me that she can be vulnerable with.

"You look incredible," I say, and she squeezes my hand.

"Hey, y'all," Gabby sings out across the party.

The pack of boys, already making their way down one of the sweeping sets of stone steps, hoot back a response.

Sophie spins away from me, swaying her body in the middle of the dance floor alone. She doesn't look toward Mason or the other boys, acts as if she doesn't notice or doesn't care. But they all notice her. She is a siren, her body a long column of shimmer and sex.

I'd kill to be hungered for like that.

28

Órlaith

Vera and I stroll the perimeter of the garden, arms looped to support one another. She has arthritis in one foot, so she can't be sitting down in one spot for too long, and I'm glad for the chance to drift from that loud teenage music, to feel the spongy grass beneath our shoes and breathe in the fresh air.

And, sure, Vera is always lovely to chat with. We have a lot in common. She's a bit older—seventy-five or six—but a widow as well. She has two sons in their middle age, around the age my own girl would be. The sons sound lovely. One lives far away—Cincinnati, I think—but he sends his mam a big box of chocolate-covered strawberries on the first Sunday of each month, and his children FaceTime her often. Her younger son is local, and he stops by multiple times a week to change Vera's lightbulbs and her air filter, to cut her grass and fix that bathroom faucet that's been dripping. He's single, but only because he's busy. He's a lawyer and has only just now got his footing in a big firm.

Still, Vera would like to see him settled. No surprise there. She has pestered Mrs. Matthews to see if she has any single friends who might be interested in a lawyer or if maybe she could set him up with one of those online dating profiles.

"He best be careful with those, like," I warn her. "The stories you hear. Don't they make your hair curl? Beautiful young women getting drugged and sold into some kind of sex slavery. Young men showing up on a doorstep, flowers in hand, only to be robbed and stabbed and left for dead."

"Well, that's true," Vera agrees.

I think again of my own girl. Who would she be now? Would she be living in Cork or Cincinnati or Timbuktu? Would she be a lawyer who was too busy for a family but always had time to help her mam unload the groceries or teach her how to FaceTime? Or would she have a husband who loved her and a houseful of babies, my grandbabies?

If she were still alive. If that car hadn't veered over the double yellow lines one night.

Beside me, Vera tsks, and I follow her gaze back toward the party to Mr. Matthews' ex-wife—Kim—tossing back a drink and leaning against a tall balding gentleman, her cleavage pressed along his arm.

"Earlier," I say to Vera, "I overheard Mr. Matthews asking Sophie after her mother. I gathered he was concerned about her drinking. Now I didn't mean to be earwigging, mind you. I got myself caught in the pantry, snagging a teething biscuit for the little one, and they just so happened to be chatting beside the door."

Vera nods and says, "I knew them when they were married, you know? I've lived here a long time. Used to be you could walk a mile without seeing a single soul. He came to my door once at ten o'clock in the evening. Gave me such a scare. Who knocks on an old lady's door at that time of night? I was fixing to go to sleep, had to put on my robe and my house slippers, my hair an ungodly mess, and there was handsome Ethan Matthews on my doorstep. Bless his heart. He was clearly horrified to be waking me. He was wanting to know if I'd seen Kim, thought maybe she'd come over to my house. Evidently, she'd had one too many to drink that night and gotten upset at Ethan over something or other. And she had just gone and stormed out of that house. Pajamas and everything. He couldn't even tell me for certain she had shoes on her feet. I mean, good Lord."

"Heavens, was she driving, like?" I ask.

"That is exactly what I asked. But Ethan had already taken to hiding the car keys. Apparently, it had become a habit of hers, storming off when she was drunk and angry. Dangerous habit for a woman, if you ask me, even in these parts. She was just on foot. Ethan figured she'd be back after she let off all that steam. But by then, she'd been gone over an hour. He'd driven up and down the neighborhood with no sign of her. I never seen a man so distraught."

"And what about the girl?" I ask. "Sophie?"

"That was my first thought too, Órlaith, because I asked that man point-blank, where is Sophie? He told me she was sleeping. Home. Alone. This big scary house? She couldn't have been more than eight years old. I said to him, honey, do you need me to go watch that sweet child? But, well, anyway. I guess it all turned out, because I ran into Kim at the mailboxes the very next morning, and they were just all Howdy Doody again. All I know is, that man put up with more than his fair share."

I nod in agreement, take another look at the ex-wife. The story paints an ugly picture—there is nothing worse than an irresponsible mother.

We circumvent the pool, nearly completing our circle of the garden now, catching snips of conversation. "I heard there is a full gym in the other wing," one woman says, a glass of wine in one hand, another on the arm of her friend as she leans in.

"I saw it," the other woman says, her floral shift dress dragging along the patio stones. "Ethan gave us a tour. There's a steam room and a sauna. Can you imagine?"

"My God."

Vera and I make it to the back fence—a cable railing so as not to impede the view. We stand on the cliff's edge, just thin metal wire between us and the fall.

"What a view," Vera says.

The garden's limestone bluff protrudes from the cliffside, so nothing but air and a lone buzzard hangs between us and the landscape. Wind sweeps clouds across the blue sky and shadows across the ranchlands below. Breathtaking—quite literally, the shock of that razor-sharp descent sucks the breath right from your lungs, leaves you dizzy and oxygen-deprived.

My knees buckle, legs collapsing beneath me like a broken umbrella.

"Whoopsie," Vera says, as she leans into me to avoid us both toppling over. "Did you roll an ankle?"

"I'm just feeling a bit weak, to be honest." Blood pounds in my ears and my vision darkens on the edges.

"Low blood sugar," Vera says, helping me over to a nearby pool lounge. "Happens to me all the time. Sit tight, dear, and I'll get you an orange juice from the bar."

She's gone, and I'm left alone.

With my senses dimmed, I am slightly separated from the party, like a curtain dropped. It isn't low blood sugar, or a rolled ankle, or even vertigo.

Sure, I am here now, but I'm also not. The wind flutters the sleeves of my T-shirt, tickles my hair against my ears and the back of my neck.

Then a pressure on my shoulder, like a hand resting there. A hand pressing, fingers curling. The wind begins to sound like whispers. I strain but can't make out the words.

Then, nearly as suddenly as it came, it goes. The shadowed tunnel of my vision brightens, and it is as though someone turns the volume back up, the music blaring and the pulse of the bass and the teenage girls laughing on the dance floor and the adults crowded at the bar ordering drinks. Vera stands near the back of a long line. She catches my eye, waves happily.

I am near the dance floor and the thudding speakers. I sit no more than ten feet from Mr. Matthews and his colleague, Curtis Barker—a man I've met before, another psychiatrist. He's been to the house quite a few times—has his own key, I believe—to have drinks with Mr. Matthews by the pool, to meet with Dani in the library. They seem not to notice me.

I place a hand on my shoulder where the pressure was, but there is nothing. No one. I pull a tissue from my pocket and dab at the sweat on my brow, as if a fever has broken.

A thin place, where the barrier between Heaven and Earth is porous, is usually a place of unspeakable natural beauty—people talk of Skellig Michael, Croagh Patrick, the Hill of Tara. In such a place, you are just as likely to encounter a red fox as you are the face of God.

I have yearned for my own thin place. Just to peek behind the curtain, just to check, as a mother checks for the rise and fall of her sleeping baby's breath.

I'd thought only of myself. I'd thought only of my own reaching toward the other side. I hadn't thought about how a doorway allows people in as easily as it allows them out. I hadn't thought about what might reach back.

29

Kim

We've moved outside—closer to the bar and far from Gemma Barker and all the memories she brings to the surface. I'm on my second drink, second *real* drink, one of those margaritas with a floating purple orchid, because it's so damn pretty—nearly finished, actually, and I can feel it happening. Have you ever had a scalp massage? Rivulets of pleasure trickling to the core of you? That's how being tipsy feels to me. The tension melts from my shoulders. Edges are softened. Who wants to live in an HD world? Give me some Vaseline on the lens. Conversations are easier, people's jokes are funnier, *I* am funnier.

I'm with Ted and some woman named Jaci that we met at the bar, who is wearing my same exact Kendra Scott pendant necklace—it's how we got to talking. (Ethan bought the necklace, but Sophie was the one who picked it out as a Mother's Day gift, so I still wear it.) I'm telling them about the time I had to operate on a golden retriever who had devoured the entire contents of his owner's underwear drawer. The dog was fine. I'm hamming the story up, miming pulling the tangled chain of eleven lacy panties from the dog's stomach like a magician's scarf trick.

Jaci is laughing so hard, she's having trouble catching her breath.

I like being the life of the party. I'm good at it. *God, I love drunk Kim,* my friends used to say once my volume increased and my wit dialed up a notch. And, honestly, I love drunk Kim too. Well, I love tipsy Kim. I love being two drinks in.

Two drinks always sounds so reasonable when I make the silent promise to myself. Just two. How hard is that? Hard—as it turns out, as it *always* turns out. The problem is I never want this feeling to fade, which is where drink number three comes in, and four. My eyes are already wandering to the bar, assessing the length of the line.

Jaci pulls her cell phone from her purse. "What's the name of your practice? I have a friend, Tonya, do you know her? She breeds border collies. She's looking for a new vet."

"Looks like you could both use a refill," Ted chimes in, taking our empty glasses.

"You're amazing," Jaci says. "Sauvignon blanc."

"Club soda," I say, "splash of lime."

"Don't make me drink alone," Jaci says with a play pout.

I laugh. "Just pacing myself. It's a long party." *Maybe a water in between each alcoholic drink,* I think, as if this is the first time I've ever had this brilliant idea.

Ted obediently wanders off to the bar.

"You know what," Jaci says. "Just give me your number. I'll send you an invite to the next bunco. You can meet Tonya there. The girls will absolutely love you." She unlocks her phone. "Why have we never hung out before? Do you live in the neighborhood?"

"I used to. I'm Sophie's mom."

"Sophie?" she says, a bit taken aback. "Like the birthday girl?"

I smile.

"Wait, so you're . . . Oh my gosh, you're *that* Kim."

I smile again. "I am *that* Kim."

She breathes a laugh. Her polite smile stays intact, but I can see the wheels turning in her mind, the pieces clicking into place. The screen on her phone goes dark. *That Kim,* she's thinking. *Ethan's crazy ex-wife Kim.* She's cataloguing the stories she's heard about me.

It isn't long before her eyes slide past me, over my shoulder, and catch on someone else. Her hand shoots up to wave. "Oh my gosh, I need to go say hello. But it has been so nice to meet you, Kim."

"Of course," I say. And before we get the chance to do that little phone number exchange, she's off, embraced by a cluster of women waiting for drinks. I watch Jaci grab the nearest friend, another woman I don't know with a dark bob, and whisper in her ear. The woman raises her eyebrows. She tries to covertly glance in my direction, then leans in to whisper to the next woman in the cluster and so on.

————

I went to an AA meeting once. It was a total waste of time, just like I knew it would be. I sat in the back and declined to share my name and "story." A man with stringy gray-brown hair, pulled back into a low ponytail, missing a bottom front tooth, told about his rock bottom, about the time he pushed his own grandmother down when she caught him stealing from her purse, fractured her forearm, how his sister convinced Grandma to press charges, how it ended up being the best thing that ever happened to him because he got sober in jail, and now he was collecting his one-year chip.

I felt for him, and for the woman who was trying to get custody of her kids even though it was pretty clear she was a few drinks in right there at the meeting, and for the young girl with a Tinker Bell tattoo behind her ear who was proud of herself for her promotion to shift manager at the Chicken Express.

I felt for them, but I wasn't one of them.

They're losers, I told my mom that evening at her kitchen table.

Oh, Kimberly, my mom said in an exasperated breath.

My brother, standing cross-armed in the doorway, rolled his eyes and walked away. The AA meeting had been his idea. He had been the one to look it up, to drive me there and back, hands in the perfect ten and two position, an audiobook droning about something quantum that I didn't understand. Michael works for NASA. He's a literal rocket scientist. He doesn't like problems he can't solve.

You're enabling her, Ma. That's what he had said after I'd been living in Houston with my parents for two months following the complete decimation of my marriage, the implosion of my entire life. I had spent the majority of those two months barricaded in my childhood bedroom with a few boxes of wine and a marathon of *Snapped,* a true crime show about women who, well, snapped. Their husbands were usually the victims. It felt apt.

You'd think everyone would cut me a fucking break, given the circumstances. You'd think my only brother would be driving me to a bar instead, ordering shots, taping a photograph of Ethan over the dartboard.

But my mother was teary-eyed, and my dad was outside in the darkening dusk on his hands and knees weeding a lawn that didn't need weeding just so he wouldn't have to be part of this conversation. So I reached across the table and took my mom's hand. *All right, Ma,* I said, *no more drinking.*

I employed my 6 P.M. rule after that. No drinking before 6 P.M.

If you wake up early every day, take a shower, put on makeup, people mainly stay off your back. If you get your kid to school on time and pay your bills, then how the hell is it anyone's business if you enjoy a nightcap?

I moved back to Bulverde, into my own place with Sophie. Ethan had promised if I moved back close to him, he wouldn't fight for custody. With me in my current state and Big Roy keeling over, he had more than enough reasons and money to do so. But he wanted things to be easy for Sophie. No matter how much I hate him, I'll always be grateful for that.

My brother Michael had originally refused to cosign on the loan. *You know I can't take that risk,* he said, which stung. But then he lent me the cash for the down payment, and he's never so much as asked for a dime of it back. I am going to repay him, obviously, eventually, once I get the new business in the black.

Once I got settled, Mom and Dad came to visit, to stay in my new guest bedroom. Dad spent most of the time making trips to Home Depot and fixing little things around my new house. Mom took me to lunch.

I want you to meet someone, she said.

Who do you know here?

Anita Lewis was in her mid-fifties, professionally highlighted hair swept into a classy chignon, uncreased linen pants, and a matching shell and sweater set.

Anita is like you, Mom said, after we'd ordered iced teas and a caprese salad appetizer.

Anita was an alcoholic, it turned out. Once a corporate lawyer with a thriving practice, who had found herself disbarred and homeless. Now, ten years sober, she had been reinstated and represented nonprofits, focusing her skills and efforts on underserved populations.

Mom wanted Anita to be my *sponsor*. My mother needs help ordering shoes from Amazon. How on earth had she navigated the research it took to find this woman? I imagined her googling, reading through pages about alcoholism, writing down phone numbers on the ASPCA notepad she keeps by her computer, calling this Anita woman, pleading for her help. It broke my heart. So I exchanged numbers with Anita.

Then I ignored her texts and phone calls until she stopped texting and calling, evaded Ma's questions until she stopped asking.

———

Ted returns, balancing another beer for himself between the glass of club soda and the glass of white wine.

"Where's Jaci?" he asks.

I wave toward a general direction, take both glasses from him. I sip the soda, then set it on the nearest table. "I think I'm ready for that next drink anyway." I down half the wine in one swallow. It hits my veins like stardust.

"Wow," Ted says, though I'm not sure whether his tone is impressed or apprehensive, and I'm not sure I care. I snake my free arm around his neck, lean my body into his, let him feel the full curve of me. Screw Jaci. Screw her cluster of gossipy friends. Screw all the faces I can feel turning my way, the whispers on my back. Because this is a party, isn't it? So let's have a little fun.

30

Mikayla

Sophie tugs me from the dance floor toward the covered cabana where people have piled their things—purses and cell phones and beach towels. Gabby is there with that catlike grin, like she's up to something. The guys are hanging around too—Mason and his friends.

When they first arrived, Sophie had kept dancing until the guys were right next to her, until they got her attention with a *Happy birthday*! She turned then and smiled like she was so surprised to see them all. *Thanks for coming, y'all.* She hugged each of the guys in the group with equal vigor. It was perfectly played. I saw Mason drink in the sight of her body. How could he not? How could anyone not?

"Well." Gabby shimmies her shoulders, arches an eyebrow at Braydon.

He pulls back one of the beach towels, exposing two big bottles of alcohol.

"Yaas!" Gabby thrusts out her glass, still half full of Shirley Temple.

Braydon takes a quick scan of the yard before kneeling between the lounge chairs. He starts topping off glasses as quickly as they're handed to him. I catch Sophie's eyes. I've only ever had the few sips of champagne my mom gives me on New Year's Eve. Sophie's tried beer a few times—says it tastes so nasty she can't finish one before it goes warm.

Sophie hands Braydon her glass.

"Atta girl," Gabby coos.

"Mikayla?" Braydon holds out his hand. My glass is empty. I hesitate, but only barely, half a heartbeat, maybe, before Gabby chimes in to answer for me.

"Don't corrupt sweet Mikayla. She's a good girl." She flashes me a smile, like she's just speaking up on my behalf because I'm too shy to do it myself. Braydon shrugs and starts screwing the cap back on the bottle.

"Want to try it?" Mason asks. He offers his own drink out to me across the circle. "This thing is so sweet, you can barely taste the vodka."

I take the glass and sip. The first taste on the tip of my tongue is bright and sugary, but as I swallow, the sudden gasoline fumes make me cough. Everyone laughs.

Except Mason. "How is it?"

I wipe my lips with my thumb. "Not bad. Just surprised me." I hand it back, but he shakes his head.

"You can have it."

I can feel Sophie's eyes on us, so I turn to her. I smile, raise the glass. "Happy birthday, Soph."

"Happy birthday," everyone repeats, and we all take a drink together.

I drain it too fast. When Braydon ducks down for another round, he grabs my glass this time without asking, and I don't say anything in protest.

———

Last year, Sophie dragged me to their big pasture party following the homecoming football game.

I'm not going to know anyone.

You'll know me, Sophie said, which was kind of like a promise that she'd stick by my side.

But as soon as we got there, seriously, the second we climbed off my four-wheeler, Gabby shot toward us, linked an arm through Sophie's, and tugged her away, babbling about some fight between Emma and Ava. Emma had gotten pissed at her boyfriend about something and had thrown her homecoming mum in the dirt. That pissed Ava off because it's her mama who owns the spirit store, who spends hours upon hours making the mums, and she'd given all the cheerleaders a discount.

Emma didn't understand the whole mum thing. Since she wasn't raised in Texas, this was her first experience with them, but they're a pretty big deal. My mom and I make mine together, but some girls spend three or four hundred dollars on one. My memaw said they used to wear real chrysanthemums pinned to their homecoming dresses, but as the years went on, the tradition grew. Nowadays, all through spirit week leading up to homecoming, we walk the halls with enormous mums hanging from our necks—they have to hang from our necks now, because of the sheer weight of them—artificial flowers made from looped ribbon, decorated to fit our personalities with teddy bears and piñatas, feather boas and military-braided ribbons and strings of battery-powered lights streaming to the floor, ringing and clanking with sleigh bells and cowbells.

Emma's mum was discarded like trash, face down in the mud, trampled and torn.

Emma said it was a ridiculous tradition anyway. Ava said Emma was a dumb bitch. Now, Emma had locked herself in some upperclassman's crew cab, and apparently it was Sophie's job to untangle the mess.

My dad likes to say that, nowadays, people *manufacture problems.* I usually think he's being unfair. People can't help how they feel, you know? Just because you might think what they're crying about is stupid doesn't mean they made it up. It just means they're different from you. He's one to talk, anyway. From the moment he wakes up at the crack of dawn, it's like, *Well, shit, Alice, I just got a call from Art down the road who said he saw a few of our cows out on 1863 when he was heading into work. There must be another hole in that goddamn fence.* Then it's an all-day emergency—wrangling the cows back in, fixing the fence—even though he knows, everyone knows, it's just a matter of time before that fence needs patching again. And if it's not the fence, then it's one of the cows calving, and if it's not the cows, then the sheep have pneumonia. And it's like, hey, Dad, did you know you could have just worked at a bank?

But, also, I kind of knew what he meant, because here it was Friday night and Gabby and Emma and Ava and now Sophie, who are all gorgeous and popular, still in their cheerleader uniforms, were standing around some stranger's truck, crying and yelling over each other about nothing at all. What was even the point? I'd rather have been home in my pajamas on the couch with my mom, bingeing old episodes of *Friday Night Lights.*

The moon was so white and bright that the trees cast shadows. The party was packed, people circled around the bonfire or dancing to the music blaring from someone's truck. We'd won the game, and everyone was high on Ranger pride, finger guns in the air, chanting *Guns out!* But when I looked around, not a single one of my friends was there.

I sat myself in the bed of someone's pickup, beside a cooler of beer and cokes. I sipped from a can of 7UP and smiled at anyone I happened to make accidental eye contact with, just praying Sophie would appear from between the trees.

That's when Mason showed up. *There any Dr Pepper in there?* he asked, tipping his head at the cooler.

I pushed up the sleeve of my sweatshirt and sank my arm into the melted ice, felt around for a can.

This was months before he started dating Sophie, before he was anywhere near my social orbit. I knew *of* him, of course—quarterback and the cutest guy in school, at least according to a group of us girls who had flipped through last year's yearbook at a sleepover and ranked the upperclassmen.

His parents were cattle ranchers too. As kids, our paths crossed often—both our families at a livestock auction, our dads talking for what seemed like hours whenever they'd run into each other at the Tractor Supply, my dad buying an old riding mower from his dad, his mom coming to our house to pick out one of the puppies when our sweet Sadie had a litter.

I handed him a cold can.

Thanks, he said while I wiped my forearm on my jeans.

We heard a shriek. Emma, or maybe it was Ava, yelling something that sounded like, *I'm not going to fucking calm down.*

Mason cracked open the Dr Pepper. *There's always some girl crying about something. It's, like, the unwritten rule of parties.* Then he added, *Sorry. Are those your friends? I thought I saw you with them earlier. Gabby and those girls?*

It's fine. But there was something snap-crackle-and-popping beneath my ribs, because he had kind of just said he'd noticed me. Hadn't he? Mason had thrown the game-winning touchdown. He was practically the town hero, and here he was, talking to me. *That's why I'm hiding out over here. I was up at 4 A.M. to help feed the cows. I'm too tired for all that drama.*

Exactly. He smiled. Mason has a great smile, wide and white, mouth open, like he's always just about to laugh, like you're in on the joke with him. *Your family raises cattle?*

My dad's George Donovan. He's friends with your dad, I think. Y'all got a puppy from us once.

His brow creased for a moment, and I could see his eyes do a quick down and back up. *No kidding?* Then it was back to that hundred-watt smile. *No, yeah, I remember you. You're uh . . . um . . .* He snapped his fingers a few times. *Kaylee, right?*

Mikayla.

Yeah, Mikayla. Wow. You were just a kid. I guess we both were. He looked me up and down again, openly this time, and I could feel the heat blooming up my neck to my cheeks. I blush easily. I'm so pale and such a stereotypical redhead. I swear the space between my freckles connects, turns me into one giant freckle. He laughed, rubbed the back of his neck. *I mean, wow.* The way he said it. Was it possible he was flirting with me? He set his elbow on the truck, leaned in. He was so close to me, I could smell the sweat off him, smell the wet grass from the football field. *We still have that dog, you know. My dad named him William Munny. Like that Clint Eastwood western?*

My dad likes that movie too, I said.

I guess they all do. Anyway. We call him Munny, for short. But everyone always thinks it's Money, like, you know, dollar bills. Drives Dad crazy.

You should get another dog. Name him Johnny Cash.

Cash and Munny? He laughed. *That's funny. You're funny.* His eyes were on my face. They creased to happy half-moons when he smiled. His eyes drifted down to my lips, lingered.

Then Sophie appeared, breaking the shimmer of whatever had been sparkling between us. *Mik, I am so, so sorry.* She grabbed my hand and pulled me from the truck.

See you later, Kaylee, Mason said just to make me laugh, and I turned to look over my shoulder to see him watching me leave.

———

Everyone has had two drinks now, at least. We're back on the dance floor. Mason was right: The vodka doesn't taste bad mixed into the watermelon mocktail. You hardly notice the burning after a few sips. I was thinking I didn't feel any different. I didn't see what the big deal was. Maybe alcohol didn't work on me.

But there's something about the music, about the cluster of us laughing, swaying our bodies.

I'm dancing with Sophie, our fingers intertwined. I press the back of her hand to my cheek. "I love you, Soph," I say, and the smile she gives me in response makes my heart ache.

———

I think I just had a moment back there, I whispered into Sophie's hair once we were safely out of earshot of Mason, buried in the crowd of people dancing in the field, muddy from a week of rain, with the heartbeat of music swallowing everyone's words. There was a balloon swell in my chest, expanding my ribs, reaching up to my throat. I couldn't stop thinking about the way Mason had looked at my lips. Had he thought about kissing me? Was he thinking about it now?

Sophie pulled back. She had an eyebrow raised.

I tipped my head toward the pickup we'd just left behind. She reached on tiptoes to look over dancing heads.

With Mason Fuller. We got to talking, and, I don't know. I can't explain it. It just felt like, I don't know, something. But I did know. It felt like electricity, like stars crossing, comets colliding.

I've heard he kind of flirts with everyone, Sophie said.

The words were a stab between the ribs, the balloon sliced open, my organs all sinking back into their stupid, normal positions.

I must have made a face.

Ugh. I'm sorry. That was bitchy. I didn't mean it like that.

No. It's fine. You're right. He does seem like kind of a player now that I think about it.

She cupped my face in her hands. *Exactly. You're too good for him. I don't want some douchebag breaking my best friend's heart.*

Tell me all about the Emma drama, I said.

Her face broke into a smile. *Oh my God, they're so dang stupid sometimes. This is why you'll always be my best friend.*

Somehow Gabby is on me again, but this time, I'm dancing back, my head and limbs loose now. My hands are on her waist, slide onto her hips.

Gabby's whisper is in my ear. "The boys are watching. They love when we dance together. Come on. Tell me who you like." She turns away from me, but keeps her backside pressed against me. She raises her arms to hook them around my neck. She slides her body along mine. I take a look around. More people have arrived, the entire town, it seems, grown-ups in fancy dresses and suits scattered around the pool, clustered around cocktail tables, moving in and out of the poolside lounge, lining up at the bar, up and down both sets of stairs, the upper patio packed, and Gabby is right, the boys are sneaking glances at the dance floor, elbowing each other in the ribs and laughing.

That's when I notice Mr. Matthews by the bar, and I grow hot with embarrassment as Gabby continues writhing against me like a stripper. But he isn't looking at us. He's facing the other direction, out over the cliff, talking to his partner, Mr. Barker.

Mr. Barker is looking in our direction. He's watching, his eyes lingering over Emma, then Ava, and down the line of us. He takes a sip of his beer, gaze never breaking. I can feel his eyes on me like hands, slide up my legs, hips, waist, breasts. He looks me right in the eyes. One side of his mouth curls in a slow smile.

31

Órlaith

I'm still waiting for Vera to return with my orange juice, enjoying the sit-down and watching the young ones dance. Much too sexually suggestive, if you ask me, but I suppose I'm an old fogey.

"Good Lord," Curtis Barker says, jabbing an elbow into Mr. Matthews.

He's looking straight at the pretty girl with the tiny figure and the shiny black hair. She's been dancing with her friends—if that's what passes for dancing these days. She's a bit of a performer—in this, and, I'd be willing to guess, in most things—hands on her own body, hands on her friends' bodies. Now, she has one leg hiked up to her friend's hip, shaking her rear, the already high slit of her skirt bunched up nearly to her waist. Making her friend blush and giggle. Making the boys salivate.

But not just the boys, it seems.

Mr. Matthews follows his friend's gaze, probably catches himself a good eyeful of bum, and looks back at Curtis. I can't see his expression, but I'm assuming he gives the other man a disapproving look, because Curtis says, "What?" hands up and defensive.

"Jesus," Mr. Matthews says. It's a reprimand. Fair play to him. Because the girl might be putting on a show, but she's still a child, and these grown men have no business ogling her rear.

"Oh, come on, there's no harm in looking."

"These are my daughter's friends, Curtis. I've watched some of them grow up."

"Mmm." Curtis takes a sip of beer, still watching the dance floor. "And grow up they have."

My stomach sours, at his lecherous leering, at his total lack of shame, at his words—their repulsiveness, but also their dishonesty. The girls are pretty, no doubt. But they are children. Legs like tulip stems and hips straight as book spines.

He keeps going—"Everyone has fantasies," and how Mr. Matthews should be well-aware of that, all the dark shite they hear from their patients, day in and day out. How it's only natural for a man to lust after a young girl. It's biological.

"St—" Mr. Matthews starts, loud and firm, but comes to an abrupt halt. Again, "St—" Then a sound like he's choking on the word. He pauses, takes a sip of his beer. "Cut it out."

I've seen this once before. When I first started working for the Matthewses, Dani was bedridden. I didn't see her for the first few days of my employment. Just me and the baby and the big airy house with sunlight through wide windows, and Mr. Matthews coming from the master bedroom with bottles of expressed milk to store in the fridge, and the noises from behind that door—the moaning something awful and the soft, sad sounds of weeping.

How is she? I asked him in a whisper, even if we were on another floor. *The poor pet.*

I think she's get—get— It was then that I witnessed it: Mr. Matthews' staccato speech, like a hand gripping his throat mid-word. *She's improving.*

Now, Mr. Matthews turns his back on his friend and walks off toward the bar. He leans over and says something to the bartender, who hands him a spoon. He clangs the spoon against his pint glass.

"Excuse me." He is smiling that white-toothed grin. "Excuse me." His voice has the edge of a laugh. Slowly, the chatter dies down. Slowly, the guests turn his way. The DJ turns down the music. The party planner rushes to Mr. Matthews with a microphone. The girls stop dancing. "Sorry to interrupt everyone's fun," he says, his voice now projected from the DJ's speakers. The people on the upper balcony quiet now as well, turn, begin to fold in closer. "It looks to me like most people have had a chance to arrive and get a drink. So, I thought now would be the perfect time to raise a toast."

32

Dani

It's just me, MaryBeth, and Gemma. The rest of our group has been absorbed back into the mass of the party.

Gemma still holds Charlotte, while MaryBeth fawns over her leg rolls.

"Do you plan on having any of your own?" Gemma asks.

"We've been trying," MaryBeth says. "No luck yet." She giggles, even at this.

Gemma starts to share her own in vitro journey that led to the twins.

I want to be here in this conversation, but I keep noticing the people around.

Like that woman near the grand piano, who walks the neighborhood every day, who always waves to me and Charlotte but has never stopped to chat. She keeps looking over here. We've made eye contact three times.

All the people here, every time I connect eyes with someone, my innocent history with them is now tainted with suspicion.

Gemma says something. MaryBeth giggles again.

I can't focus. The noise of the party is overwhelming.

A waiter appears. "I'm sorry, ma'am," he says to Gemma. "We've run out of Riesling. Can I get you something else?"

"Oh, sure, any white is fine. Pinot Grigio?"

I jump at the chance to escape. "We have plenty of Riesling downstairs," I say.

"No, Dani. It's no big deal."

I'm already heading that way, fleeing. "Just watch Charlotte, will you?" I say over my shoulder. "I'll be right back." I weave through guests toward the kitchen and the back staircase that leads directly into the wine cellar. The crush of bodies surrounds me, conversations blending, fragments of words and fleeting faces.

If things get to be too much, step away. Those were Curtis's instructions. *Don't overdo it right now.*

"Dani," Gemma calls.

I'm almost free, close to the kitchen, almost through the throng of people.

But she calls again, MaryBeth joining her, a chorus of my name.

I turn. Gemma tips her head toward the back patio. The party is moving slowly in that direction, bottlenecking at the open door. I follow, looking over the sea of heads. The party planner catches sight of me and waves me forward. When I reach her, she puts a hand to my shoulder, steering me out onto the upper patio. "Ethan is making a toast," she says.

"Thank you all for coming." I can hear Ethan's voice now over the speakers. A few people in front of me move aside, and now I see him, down by the dance floor, shading his eyes. "There she is," he says when he sees me. I slip between guests, down one of the staircases. I go to Ethan. He holds out a full champagne flute, and I take it.

The caterers maneuver through the crowd with bottles of Veuve Clicquot, filling every empty glass. Everyone is quiet now.

All eyes on us.

Ethan holds out his glass toward Sophie, who stands in the middle of the dance floor. "We are here to celebrate my lit—" he begins. But that is where he stops. "Excuse me," he says, after a long pause. "She isn't my little girl anymore. Is she?"

I see women put a hand to their chest, exchange looks with each other. They think he's getting choked up, that it is absolutely adorable to see such a strong man brought nearly to tears for his daughter, #girldad. But I heard the guttural halt of his speech, felt the tension of his body.

Ethan would have practiced this toast a dozen times. He gives toasts. He speaks at conferences. Public speaking does not make him stutter.

I've only witnessed it a handful of times. When some asshole in a lifted pickup blew through a red light and nearly T-boned me and Sophie on the passenger side. When the hospital called to say his mother had a stroke. When some guy grabbed my ass in a crowded Sixth Street bar in Austin.

Moments when he scrambled to regain control.

What has him so shaken here?

Ethan is speaking smoothly now, talking about how proud he is of the woman Sophie is becoming. I see women dabbing the corners of their eyes with cocktail napkins.

"If I could," he says, "I'd give you the world." He reaches into his pocket, pulls out a card in a pale pink envelope. "A little something from Dad." He squeezes me into him. "And Dani, of course."

Sophie skips over to us. "Da-a-d," she singsongs. "This party is enough." She takes the envelope and slides her finger beneath the flap. She peeks inside, looks at Ethan, and smiles. "What is this?" She opens the birthday card—a gold-glittered *16* flashing on the front—pulls out and unfolds a single sheet of paper. Her brow furrows.

The teenagers try peering over Sophie's shoulder.

Her jaw drops wide. She clutches the paper to her chest. "Oh my God," she says. She reads the paper again. Clutches it again. "Is this for real?" She looks to Ethan, and he nods.

I glance up at Ethan, a question mark on my face, but he is watching Sophie intently.

She squeals, crumpling the paper against her chest as she does a dance on tiptoes.

"What is it?" people are asking.

I look up to Ethan again, his arm still around me. This time I wait until he finally looks at me. *What?* I mouth. He just keeps grinning. He rubs my arm briskly.

"OMG, Soph, spill the tea," Gabby says.

Drawing out each word for emphasis, Sophie says, "A monthlong trip through Europe!"

Her friends huddle around her, chirping and squealing like seagulls.

I'm trying to process what she just said when Ethan adds, "It'll be a family trip. The four of us." He's looking at me now, and the smile on his face is so brilliant it hurts, so brilliant that I can't do anything but smile back and hope that everyone watching can't see the absolute horror that I feel. What the hell was he thinking? How could he have planned this without talking to me? I imagine a twelve-hour flight with Charlotte, bouncing her up and down the aisles as she screams.

Sophie spins off with her friends, chattering and squawking. She's reading the travel itinerary—"Barcelona, Paris, London, Prague? I don't even know where that is."

Conversations have started again, people drifting back inside or into the line for the bar, back to their cocktail tables or their lounge chairs around the pool.

Ethan pulls me tightly to him, kisses the top of my head, whispers, "Surprise, baby."

"Dani, you look a little green around the gills," Curtis says as he comes around, a beer in his hand. "Let me guess. That was one of Ethan's bombshells?"

I press a hand to my cheek, feeling claustrophobic. "No. I was just . . . I can't quite believe it."

"So exciting," Gemma says as she joins us.

"Where is Charlotte?" I ask.

"Your nanny came and got her. Said it was time for her second nap."

"Is it that late already?"

Ethan claps Curtis on the back. "I promised you that cigar, didn't I? It's upstairs in the library. Let me get it. I'll meet you in the man cave."

"Oh my gosh," I say to Gemma. "The Riesling."

"I told you, don't worry about it."

But I beeline this time, ignore every face I pass. I need a moment to breathe.

33

Kim

The fucking nerve of him.

My flirty, tipsy shimmer has popped, and I'm left feeling heavy-limbed and sweaty.

Ted is droning on about Europe, but he's found a way to make it boring, listing the countries he's been to like he's reading the ingredient list on a box of cereal.

Ethan never told me about this trip. He never asked me if it was okay to take my daughter to another country, another continent for an entire month. Is this his idea of . . . what the hell is he always going on about . . . *cooperative co-parenting*? Sophie is in her crowd of friends, her smile as luminous as a flash in the dark. It's the same smile she gave Ethan when she was a toddler, when he spun her around the room.

She's that same girl—for him, at least. I watch Ethan excuse himself, head into the house.

"I need to use the ladies' room," I tell Ted.

"I'll have fresh drinks for us when you get back."

I toss my hair over my shoulder, send him a wink as I walk away. Once inside the house, I grab a glass of champagne from a passing waiter, sip it as I scan the room for Ethan. I catch sight of him at the top of the spiral staircase, just as he disappears onto the second floor.

I follow after him, pause at the bottom of the stairs to down the rest of my drink in one swallow, fizz tickling the end of my nose. I set the empty glass on the round foyer table, beside a crystal globe vase bursting with pink cabbage roses.

I take the stairs quickly, heels clicking on the marble, but at the top step the toe of my shoe catches, and I stumble. For a horrible second, I think I might lose my balance completely, might tumble backward down and down and down. But I catch hold of the banister, pull myself up. I lean over the railing for a moment, contemplate the long drop down to that shining tile floor.

I've had more than my promised two, but I haven't had *that* much to drink.

It's this house. It's always been this fucking house. There's something wrong with it—an energy that throws everything off balance.

Things were good before we moved in here. Life was small and cramped, bills piled on the countertop, linoleum floors in the kitchen, downstairs neighbors whose pot smoke wafted through the shared ventilation. But it was good. It was sweet. It was Ethan rubbing my shoulders as I studied from a textbook at the kitchen table. Frozen pizza and microwave popcorn on a Friday night. Grocery store bouquets for no reason at all.

Then we moved into this house, started renovating, tearing down the walls, and our lives unraveled with it.

———

When we first bought the home, it was like we were kids at a buffet, eyes bigger than our stomachs. Or, more accurately, our wallets. I was so caught up in the romance of it—Mr. Darcy's Pemberley, Heathcliff's Wuthering Heights. With Ethan and I both working now, we could afford the house, but we quickly realized that we couldn't afford to renovate it, not professionally.

I threw myself into the work. There was something satisfying in the physical labor, in shoveling debris, sledgehammering walls.

The house was in a perpetual state of repair—or disrepair, depending on how you looked at it—tattered plastic sheeting peeling from the walls like a sunburn. There were noises too—creaks and groans, that screeching wind, scratching behind the walls. We carved out a suitable living space in the center of the home. But the estate's extremities were half wild, windows broken by storms and teenagers, creeping vines covering graffiti.

Once, when I was home with Sophie—she was five or six, out of school for Spring Break, Ethan at work—I heard a tap-tap-tap. I set down the kitchen knife—I'd been chopping something for lunch—and listened. The sound came again, the same rhythm. Tap-tap-tap. Like the gentle rapping of fingers on the wall. It grew louder, more insistent with each repetition, building to a steady knocking. I left Sophie coloring at the table and went to investigate.

We hadn't refinished the kitchen cabinets yet, so we were using what is now the butler's pantry as our storage room. I expected to find something there, a raccoon digging into our cereal, maybe. There was nothing, aside from dry groceries and a box of still unpacked cookware. The sound persisted. But now it was in the next room over. The townspeople said this house was haunted, and I didn't believe them. I've never been afraid of the creak of settling wood or a mouse rustling behind a wall.

But this sound was different. It was purposeful.

And it seemed always just around the corner, leading me through the maze of pocket doors and half-demolished walls, support beams exposed like open ribs. It was a heartbeat that vibrated my sternum, soft as raindrops at first, then growing loud as a drumroll.

I ended up in the room that is now the home theater. Only there were no rows of fully reclining leather chairs, sixteen-foot projector screen, or popcorn machine. Then it was the gutted bones of a hundred-year-old second sitting room in the east wing.

The room was unnaturally dark, smelling of dirt and dank wood, dusty fingers of light reaching between the cracks of the boarded-up windows. A heavy sheet of plastic hung from the ceiling, and as I watched, it clung to a shape, a figure, the opaque plastic smoothing around the form of a head, of a face, mouth open wide.

For an instant, my body was nothing but a flash of adrenaline, a spark of fear, but then the wind released its tension. The plastic fell flat again. The room was empty and ordinary.

The tension in my own body spilled out just as quickly, and I was weak with relief, hands shaky and heart pounding. Jesus Christ, how silly, how idiotic. Still. I didn't pull back the sheeting. I didn't check the darkest corner. I turned and walked away.

When I got back to the kitchen—Sophie still coloring, *Mommy, do you like my rainbow?*—and started chopping again, I heard it faint as moth wings, that soft fluttering call. I flipped on the little radio we kept on the counter, turned the volume up.

I began to wonder then whether or not we should have disturbed the house at all. I wonder it still, particularly on those nights when my dreams bring me back to this place. Because I'm afraid that when we tore open these walls, we released something better left buried.

———

Now, I turn to face the empty hallway. I take a few steps toward the master bedroom door, which is open just a crack. I stand outside it, listen for sounds of Ethan. I nudge the door a few inches more, so I can see a sliver of the room now. She's changed the bedding—I suppose I would have too. Gone is my ornately patterned comforter in rich reds and browns, replaced with a plush cream-colored duvet, a sage throw blanket draped decoratively over a corner.

But it's still my heavy cherrywood bedroom set, my crystal chandelier.

I'm assaulted by a sudden wave of sensory images—memories, shuffled like a deck of cards: the sound of Sophie sobbing just out of reach; the smell of vomit, the bitter taste of it on my tongue; Gemma's hands on my shoulders, soft at first like a caress, then rough, painful, almost violent.

I pull the door shut.

"Hey." Ethan's voice from down the hall makes me jump. "What are you doing up here?"

"Jesus," I say, "I didn't hear you."

He's strolling toward me, holding a leather cigar case in his hand. I got him the case for his thirty-eighth birthday. Had it monogrammed too.

"What the hell was that?" I fling an arm out to vaguely gesture downstairs.

He raises an eyebrow.

"A European vacation?" I say.

He still looks a little blank.

"Are you kidding me?"

His brow furrows. "Sophie seems really excited. She's been dying to go to Europe, ever since Spain fell through."

"Oh, for fu—" I cut myself off.

A few years ago, I begrudgingly agreed to let Sophie go to Spain with Ethan and Dani. He'd just gotten Sophie's passport when I slipped off the edge of the porch trying to stop Sweetie from darting outside and sprained my ankle. It was bad—there was a complete rupture of the ligament. The doctor said I had to wear a boot for eight weeks, which meant I needed Sophie to stay home to help me around the house with the animals.

Ethan had acted as if I'd done it on purpose, like I'd put myself in a cast just to ruin his plans. He didn't say that, of course. All he asked, flatly, over the phone, was, *Were you drinking?*

No, I'd told him, annoyed at the question. I'd only had a glass after dinner, maybe two. That wasn't why I fell. It was just that damn cat and the porch, the concrete cracked and unlevel, the patio light burnt out.

Ethan proposed to Dani on that trip, and this one feels like a way to get back at me.

I don't even know why I'm entertaining this line of thought. That's what he wants—to tangle my mind in knots.

That trip has nothing to do with *this* one now. Nothing to do with the simple fact that he is way out of line. "You can't just spring something like this on me. I'm her mother."

"What are you talking about?" He looks genuinely confused.

"You know what I'm talking about. This trip. This monthlong trip through Europe." Am I going crazy? This is what he does. He talks in riddles until I'm so worked up I could just spit in his face.

"I'm supposed to get Sophie for the summer," he says.

"Not in fucking Europe!"

He tilts his head. "We've talked about this."

I let out a sound, something almost like a growl. Ethan hates when I curse. Like he's a goddamn preacher or something. It's a *boundary* he has set up with me. *No degrading language.* It's one of the *rules of fair fighting,* from some bullshit worksheet he hands out in his pathetic couples therapy sessions.

Really, it's just a way for him to get the upper hand, so the conversation becomes all about my vulgar language, my raised voice, my emotions. Instead of what it should be about. What it's really about: He has no right to plan this trip without my consent.

He pushes my buttons. Pushes. Pushes. Pushes. Until I do go too far, until I *am* the one in the wrong, no matter how or why the argument started.

It works. Because before I even have the chance to think better of my words, I'm spitting, "Oh, p-p-poor Ethan." It isn't the first time I've mocked his stutter, either. God, I really am a bitch.

He isn't hurt, of course. It's worse. He's looking at me with utter pity.

"Let's just cool down, okay? This isn't the time or the place. We can talk about this later. Tomorrow, huh?" He goes to put a hand on my shoulder, but I jerk away, almost lose my balance on my high heels.

"You have no right," I say, and my hands are in fists.

"How much have you had to drink?" There is a hint of exasperation in his voice, like he should have expected as much from me.

"Oh, fuck you."

"Real nice, Kim. Lower your voice." He takes a step toward the stairs, peers down as if making sure no one can overhear us.

"Fuck your guests too," I say, and it feels good to say it.

"I said lower your voice." His own is stern now. "Órlaith is trying to get the baby down for a nap."

"Don't pretend like this is about the baby. You don't want me to make a scene."

"Correct."

"You want your precious neighbors and your coworkers to think you have everything under control. Perfect Ethan Matthews."

He puts a finger to the spot between his eyebrows and takes a breath. "Kim, please."

"And your poor, pretty little teenage wife. She'll be so scared if she hears the big bad ex-wife throwing a tantrum." But the thing is, I *am* throwing a tantrum, aren't I? Why did I have to say *fuck you*? Why did I have to drink all those cocktails? My head is swimming. My body is pulsing with rage. How did I let this conversation get out of control so quickly?

"I'm sorry that you are unhappy," he says. "I really am. But you act like I took fifteen years of marriage and flushed it down the toilet. I'm not the one who left. That was you. You left me. You threw our marriage away."

I try to swallow, but my mouth is dry. How did we get here? How does every conversation end up here? "You can't just take Sophie—"

"We did talk about it."

I blink. I try not to have any expression on my face.

"About a month ago. You don't remember?" He shakes his head. "I called you after work. So I guess that means you were already drinking. Figures. You know, I will say one thing for you, Kim. You've gotten a lot better at holding your alcohol. I didn't even know you were drunk during that conversation."

I don't break eye contact, but I feel a trickle of dread beginning on my scalp, sending goose bumps along my limbs. I hate this the most. Being told about something I've done, something I've said that I don't remember.

Did we have this conversation?

The worst thing is: I don't know.

"Sophie is going on this trip." The way he says it, it's like there is no room for discussion. "And when we get back, we're going to have to talk about what's best for her."

"What the hell does that mean?" The outrage hits me fast and hard enough that I taste it, metallic as blood on my tongue.

He towers over me. I don't know if he leaned in or took a step forward, but somehow I am bent at the neck to look at him. "I've been thinking about it for a while," he says. "But with Dani and the baby and the practice growing, I've let myself get distracted. I told myself Sophie was happy. I know you love her, Kim, but I can't ignore your self-destructive habits any longer."

"What the fuck are you getting at, Ethan?"

"After our trip, we should think about Sophie moving back here for a while."

"Fuck you." The words come out between teeth clenched so hard my jaw aches. He's only saying this to be mean. He wants me to react, to prove him right.

"This isn't the place." He steps suddenly away. "We'll discuss it later." Then he turns and heads back down the hallway toward the stairs, leaving me breathless and shaking.

I want to run at him, to lunge at him, to fling him over the banister, watch his head split against the tile.

I don't know how far he would go to hurt me. But I can't just wait around to find out. I can't lose my daughter. He can't have her.

I have to make sure of that.

34

Dani

The cellar is a cave. Quite literally. The original house had a small basement, the "milk room," they called it, a dark, cool space for milk and
food storage in the days before refrigeration. When Ethan and Kim
went to expand, to create a wine cellar, they dug into the limestone and
found an open cavern under the house.

The Hill Country is full of caves and caverns. The most famous is just
ten minutes away, Natural Bridge Caverns, a whole underground net-
work of open chambers decorated with stalagmites and stalactites, col-
umns and draperies, glittering chandeliers of stone. Something about
millions-of-years-old fault lines and water dripping between fissures to
form underground rivers.

Ethan decided to incorporate the cavern into the architecture. The
interior walls are ordinary—drywall, painted rich, dark colors, burgundy and emerald, velvet-textured wallpaper—but all the exterior
walls, the ceilings, are natural limestone, layered and rough-textured
and sparkling, smelling of damp minerals, of cool earth.

I find it unsettling that just beneath our beautiful home, the world is
still eroding.

Down here in the caves, there is a poolside lounge with a sunken
sofa, a bar, two full bathrooms for changing into swimsuits or rinsing
off the chlorine. In the showers a nook is carved straight into the limestone to create a shelf for soaps and shampoos, the arabesque tile on
one wall cut to fit the jagged natural edge of the other. And in the back
of the basement, directly below the kitchen, where the old "milk room"
was, there is a wine cellar, two rooms deep.

I am in the back, where the whites are stored. An onyx island sits in the middle of this room, backlit with an LED panel so it glows like bioluminescence, an undermount sink, hanging wineglasses beneath, drawers for wine openers, vacuum sealers, and cheese boards. In the corner is a cluster of leather club chairs. The room is designed for intimate entertainment, for quiet evenings, the two of us and a bottle of red.

I am squatting, balancing on my stilettos, wine bottle in one hand, phone in the other, trying to look up the label, make sure it isn't some five-hundred-dollar vintage, but my phone always has trouble connecting down here. As I wait for the page to load, I hear the cellar door creak on its hinges.

"Hello?" I call out, but no answer. I put a hand to the shelf in front of me, hold my breath, listen hard.

I hear the heavy door fall closed.

"Hello?" I say again. Still no answer. I hear footsteps, muffled on the oak floor, but definitely there. I stand, clutching the bottle and the phone to my chest. Goose bumps rise on my arms. I adjust my grip on the neck of the bottle, tighten my fist. It's a weapon in my hand. My heart hammers, and I think of the note. Of the Instagram comment. Of the unlocked front door and the steady stream of people coming and going. I came down here without thinking. I am a mouse trapped in the dead end of a maze. There is nothing beyond these walls but solid rock.

The footsteps are clicking closer, taking the two steps up into the cellar's back room. I see the shadow first, cast larger than life onto the floor, stretching up onto the uneven stone wall.

Then Kim rounds the corner.

"Oh, hi," I say, with a breath of relief, which is funny—being relieved to see Kim. "More wine." I readjust my grip on the bottle quickly, hope she doesn't notice. I hold it up and give it a little shake. "We ran out of Riesling, but I don't really know what I'm doing."

"Let me see." Kim comes close enough that I can smell her perfume. She takes the bottle from me, reads the label. "No," she says, putting it back. She bends at the waist and starts inspecting the lower shelves.

It occurs to me that Kim might choose the priciest bottles out of spite. But I don't care. I'm glad not to be responsible. And I'm waiting for the steady pace of my pulse to return. "Thanks," I say.

She hands me a bottle. "This is Gemma's favorite," she says. I look at it, vaguely recognize the label. Kim scans the racks, pulls another. Crouches down for the bottom row. "Already dipping into the private reserves, huh? This is one hell of a Sweet Sixteen."

As she passes the bottles back, I set them atop the onyx. "Well, we all know this is really Ethan's party."

She looks up at me. A manicured eyebrow arches. "Aren't they all?"

"Total diva. I tell him that all the time."

She laughs, turns back to the wines and pulls one out, studies the label. "This is a good one. Let's have a glass. What do you say?" She doesn't wait for an answer, though. She stands, goes to the island, opens a drawer and pulls out a hinged corkscrew. She unfolds the knife from one end, uses it to slice through the foil around the neck of the bottle. The blade cuts smoothly, sharp as a scalpel.

I grab two glasses from beneath and set them in front of her.

She pours generously, lifts her glass, holds it out to me, and I clink mine with hers. The wine is crisp, like a green apple. This is nice, this moment with Kim. I know it's too much to ask that we be friends. But we'll be in each other's lives forever. Our daughters are sisters. This party is just one of many life events that we'll have to share. Wouldn't it be so much nicer if that meant exchanging a few jokes at Ethan's expense and sharing a glass of wine?

"Can I talk to you about something?" she says.

"Of course."

Now that I think about it, this may be the first time Kim has ever talked to me at all. She talks in front of me, she talks around me, and about me. But I don't know that she's ever directly addressed me before.

"It's about this trip." She slides her fingers up and down the stem of her glass. "I'm not comfortable with Sophie being gone that long. And so far away. You're a mom now. You get that, right?"

"Oh my gosh. Yes. I get anxious when I'm not in the same room as Charlotte. I promise you, Kim, I will watch her like a hawk."

"I'm sure you will."

"And you know Ethan. It'll be all five-star hotels and the safe parts of town."

"That's all fine, but—"

"I can make sure she calls you every night. Or whatever would make you feel—"

"I don't want her to go," she says, point-blank, cutting me off. "At all." Recessed canister lights in the floor wash the cave walls in a dramatic glow. They illuminate Kim's face in odd angles, all pits and hollows, like holding a flashlight under your chin while you tell a ghost story.

"Oh." I don't know what to say. "She seems really excited."

"Of course she's excited. It's Europe. She's sixteen." Kim tops off both of our glasses, though I'd only taken a sip. She drinks more. "Charlotte is five months now?"

"Six."

"She sleeping through the night yet?"

"Sometimes."

"Teething?"

"Just got her bottom two."

Kim nods. "When Sophie was that age, no way in hell I'd trek through Europe. Have you really thought about it? How hard it will be?"

I've barely had the chance. Right now, all I can imagine is bouncing Charlotte up and down the hotel hallways at night, nursing beneath a cover or in tucked-away corners, making sure my bag is stocked with diapers and wipes and snacks and a change of clothes and an assortment of teething toys and books, checking for fevers, studying foreign menus and tearing hot food into bite-sized pieces, always looking for a place to change a diaper, always soothing, entertaining, caring. It sounds endless and exhausting. Not a vacation, but a triathlon.

"He didn't tell me about this trip," Kim says. "Do you know that? I never agreed to it."

That can't be true. Ethan wouldn't do that. All he ever wants is for things to go smoothly with Kim, for Sophie's sake. But I don't want to contradict Kim directly. "You know Ethan. He gets carried away sometimes."

"Bullshit," Kim says. The word is venomous, echoes off the stone. It shifts the tone of our conversation. She's tipsy, I think. There is an energy about her, like a coiled snake. Suddenly, I don't want to be here anymore—here in this cellar with Kim, the walls so thick we can barely hear the bass thumping outside. "Did he tell you that I agreed to this?"

"Ethan would never want you to feel uncomfortable."

"But did he tell you?" She presses. "Did he say that I agreed?"

She is waiting for a response. "Well, I mean, I assume—"

"Oh my God," Kim says. She laughs dryly. "Oh, of course. He didn't tell *you* about this trip either. Did he? You were just as blindsided as me out there. Oh, I remember that. Ethan is good at surprises, isn't he?"

It's true. He is. When we were dating, he surprised me all the time— flowers, tickets to *Hamilton,* even, yes, our Paris trip was a surprise. Back then, it was magical.

"It's romantic at first," she says, as if reading my mind. She tosses back a long swallow, refills her glass again at the halfway mark. "God, it was romantic." The way she says it, sliding the pendant of her necklace along its chain, like she's reminiscing, tugs my gut with jealousy. She's leaning against the island, cleavage spilling onto the counter, hip jutting out. Kim has that kind of sex appeal I've always admired—big curls and big curves, a quick wit and a loud laugh.

She leans in closer. I can smell the alcohol coming off her like steam. She raises that eyebrow of hers. "But it's kind of manipulative, you know? Like he just gets to do whatever he wants without your input, and then you feel like an ungrateful bitch if you question it. Look, learn from my mistake. Speak up now. Otherwise, you'll end up consumed with resentment. If you don't want to go on this trip, just tell him." She leans back, takes another drink. "You're a brand-new mom. He'll understand."

Surprise, baby, Ethan had said. That kiss to the top of my head. Had he really thought what I needed right now was a surprise? Maybe he did keep it a secret because he knew I would have said no. Does Ethan always get his way?

Why am I even playing into this? The one being manipulative here isn't my husband. It's Kim.

I lift my glass carefully. It is filled precariously to the brim. I take a sip. I remain a neutral party, restoring my placid smile, giving Kim an airy shrug. "I really don't know much about it. You're going to have to talk to Ethan."

Her face darkens. She is holding the corkscrew, flicking the blade at the end open and closed, open and closed. She asks me in slow, deliberate words: "What would you do if someone tried to take your daughter?"

I breathe out an awkward laugh. "It's just a trip."

"Bullshit," she says again, jabbing the little knife like punctuation, and this time her vitriol is targeted directly at me. Her eyes bore into mine, hazel with flecks of gold around the edge of the iris, pupils huge and wild. She is definitely drunk. And I've heard that she can be a mean drunk. It is clear to me in this moment that Kim feels that her daughter is being stolen from her.

And there is nothing more dangerous than a desperate mother.

35

Mikayla

I probably would have forgotten about the whole encounter with Mason. Okay, not *forgotten,* necessarily, because, come on, you don't forget a moment that gives you butterflies. But I would have just chalked it up to what Sophie said—he's a flirty guy, and I was reading too much into it.

The next time I saw him at school, in the hallway between bell rings, textbooks held to my chest, he was walking with a group of guys, midstory as we passed. We made eye contact, and he smiled, did that guy chuck-of-the-head thing that means *Hey.*

But, still, right? That could just be more of the same—a flirty nature.

It kept happening, though, over weeks, all of these little things—a smile here, a wink there. Once in the cafeteria, I glanced over at him because I heard his booming voice telling some joke, entertaining his table of friends, and he was already looking my way. He elbowed the friend beside him, leaned over to say something, and the friend looked over at me, so that I could have sworn he was talking about me. He had to be.

Or another time, I was passing the football field with Jane, my friend from FFA. It was after school, and we were walking toward the car pickup line. The football team was out practicing, so of course, I was sneaking glances toward the field, low-key looking for his number—18—in the crowd. Then I heard him yell, *This one's for my girl, Kaylee,* before tossing the football down the field. He pointed straight at me. *Oh my God,* Jane said. *Is Mason Fuller talking about you?* I shrugged and we hurried away, giggling.

Each moment was nothing by itself, but they added up to a feeling that I couldn't ignore.

I found myself thinking about him all the time. Like, without realizing it, while I was washing my hair I'd be rehearsing some imaginary conversation I might have with him. Or when I got dressed in the morning, I'd just kind of wonder what he'd think of my outfit, just in case I happened to run into him.

I was running into him more and more. I didn't really mean to—like, I didn't do it consciously—but I'd sort of figured out his class schedule, and I'd started taking different routes so I'd bump into him. Every time I did, he would do some little thing that made me feel good, feel seen, and all day, I would just float.

I never said any of this to Sophie. She had no idea I was nursing this crush, that we had something fragile but blooming.

———

Everyone is talking about Sophie's European vacation. It's still windy, but the sun has broken free from the clouds. The pool glitters like a disco ball.

"I don't care what you losers think," Gabby says. "I'm getting in." She pulls a swimsuit from her bag, dangles it from her fingers—just a few strips of red fabric. One of the guys hoots the response she's looking for. She slinks off toward the poolside lounge to change.

Everyone will follow her lead. They always do.

"That balcony is insane," Braydon says. "What would you pay me to jump from there to the pool?"

We all took a shot to celebrate Sophie's big trip. People aren't thinking clearly anymore.

"No way, man," Tyler says.

"Y'all are morons." Mason gets up, grabs his swim trunks from the pile of things, and starts to head toward the house. As he passes, though, his eyes slide over, catch mine.

He holds my gaze for one long beat.

I'm not sure why I kept my crush on Mason a secret. I guess because I didn't want Sophie to think I was stupid. I didn't want her to tell me I was stupid.

Sometimes I still wish I had told her.

Because then maybe none of the rest would have happened.

But how can I wish that? I can't. Not with my full heart. No matter how bad this all goes down in the end. For the good parts, it was worth it. Wasn't it?

Sophie plops down on the lounge chair beside me and her knee touches mine, only the sheer chiffon fabric of my long gown between us. "What do you think? It'll be fun to get in the pool." She knocks me in the shoulder.

"I brought two suits," Emma says, sitting down across from us and digging in her bag. "Help me decide."

"Oooh, the purple," Ava says. She is tipping back her glass, but it's empty.

I jump up before they find out I didn't bring a swimsuit and attempt to squeeze me into Emma's extra one. The alcohol makes my head spin. Makes me feel a little sick and a little brave. "I'll get more drinks," I say so that I can hurry away while they're all distracted. I have other things on my mind.

36

Dani

"I should get back," I say.

"You haven't finished your wine," Kim says. She holds the corkscrew, balancing the tip of the blade against the tip of her pointer finger, as she spins it in her hands.

She is waiting for me to say something. A test I can't possibly pass.

But I'm saved, because the big cellar door swings open, and someone calls out, "Yoo-hoo. Is anyone down here?"

Kim and I both turn. MaryBeth, sweet-faced and smiling, steps up and through the second doorway. "There you are, girlie. Your friend Gemma said you disappeared down here, so I came to drag you back to the party. Oh, hi, I don't think we've met." She is balancing too many things in her arms—a shawl, a phone, a handbag—and she shuffles them all to stick out her hand for Kim. "MaryBeth." Her smile is sunshine. I want to kiss her.

"Nice to meet you," Kim says flatly, though she doesn't bother shaking MaryBeth's hand. She drains her glass, sets it upside down in the sink. She shoves the cork back into the bottle and tucks it under her arm. "Just talk to Ethan. Okay?"

"Of course," I say, but she's already walking away.

When we hear the cellar door close behind her, MaryBeth shoots me a grimace. "Sorry. Did I interrupt something?"

"Actually, yes. And I'm glad you did. Thank you." I fold the blade away, replace the corkscrew in the drawer.

MaryBeth is nodding. "I had a feeling. I saw her follow you down here. That's the ex-wife, right? I have one of those too. I mean," she giggles, "Ernesto has an ex-wife. She hates me. I've never had someone hate me, you know?"

"Yeah, actually. It's weird to be hated just because you exist."

MaryBeth has slid up close beside me and she bumps me with her elbow, looking up and smiling. "See? We have so much in common."

I laugh, gather the wine bottles in my arms. "Let's go back." Mary-Beth follows me as I flip off the lights, open the door, head up the rough stone stairs, eager for sunlight and fresh air on my face.

37

Órlaith

Charlotte has been asleep for a while now. Ten, twenty, thirty minutes. It's hard to keep track of the time. Even harder to put her down.

Her tiny hand is curled in a fist. I place a finger just there at the center, marvel at the way her fingers tighten on instinct. When you're a new mam, it's hard to really soak in the beauty of these moments. It's all sleep deprivation and raging hormones and just wishing you could get a shower, like, just wishing you could have a moment without somebody pulling at your hair or your necklace, screaming in your ear, needing everything you don't have to give, and wondering if maybe you're just total shite at this whole thing.

But, sure, I could stay here all day, memorize the dimpled knuckles of her pudgy fingers.

That's why God blessed humanity with the gift of grandparenthood. It's supposed to be our chance to enjoy the things we were too tired, too anxious to enjoy the first go-round. Our chance to correct the mistakes we made.

I'm not sure how much longer I'll need the help, Mrs. Matthews said earlier. I heard her say it again to a group of ladies, implying that she won't be needing a nanny in the near future.

I hear a lot of things. People don't notice someone like me.

I heard the teenage girls talking spirits and screams in the night. Stories to give each other goose bumps, make each other squeal with fear. It's a game to them. But they best be careful what they play with. The veil is thin here, thin as gossamer.

I hold sweet baby Charlotte. I keep rocking and rocking. I wait for it to pass—the urge. The urge to steal her far, far away from here, to keep her safe.

To correct my mistakes.

38

Dani

I find Ethan in the carriage house, a separate structure originally used to house the horses and the carriage with a second-floor living space for the caretaker. Now, a wood-beamed cathedral ceiling tops a pub of sorts—a wet bar with a built-in tap, a poker table, leather recliners, flat screens mounted to the walls—making it the perfect man cave for Ethan to host Super Bowl parties and poker games. That's what they're doing now, Curtis and a few other guys, playing cards around the table. The air is thick with cigar smoke.

The men are laughing, ribbing one another in that way men do, showing they care by cutting each other down.

Ethan comes up behind Curtis, squeezes his shoulders. "You know, star quarterback Mason Fuller is just outside," Ethan says, a grin spread across his face. The guy beside Curtis sniffs a laugh and looks back to his cards, shaking his head.

Curtis turns to look up at Ethan, eyebrow raised. "That so?"

"We should go get you his autograph, Curtis, and the fellas and I can thank him personally. Thanks to the kid's exploits, now we'll never have to hear about"—Ethan pauses for a beat and stretches his hands in the air, like he's reading off a big marquee in the sky—"'Curtis Barker's five-touchdown record against Canyon Lake' ever again."

The other men at the table burst into laughter. "Hey," Curtis says, puffing up his chest. "That record stood for over twenty years. And if I would have played under these new flag football rules, I'd have averaged six touchdowns per game." He takes a long drink of beer. "Kid has a hell of an arm, though."

I head over to Gemma, the only woman in the room, perched on a tall barstool. I deliver her the bottle of Riesling triumphantly.

"Oh, honey, that's my absolute favorite. How on earth did you remember?"

"I had help," I say. "From Kim."

Gemma raises an eyebrow, slips down from her stool. She takes the bottle over to the wet bar and starts digging through drawers for an opener.

"Kim?" Ethan asks.

I go to the corner window farthest from the poker table, slide it open to let in some fresh air. I lean against the sill. Ethan comes over to me.

"She found me in the cellar."

"What happened?"

"Nothing. It was fine. She just . . . She's pretty pissed about this trip, Ethan. I don't want to take Sophie to Europe if Kim isn't comfortable with it. I mean, what did she say when you first asked her? She was fine with it?"

"She does this kind of thing, Dani." He puts his hands on my shoulders, rubs up and down my arms. "It's not your problem to worry about, okay? I'll talk to her. I'll get her on board. Don't let Kim ruin our trip."

I catch eyes with Gemma over by the wet bar. She's gotten the wine open, found the glasses too, and is taking a sip now.

"What about you?" he asks. I look at him. He has that half-tilt smile, a sparkle in his dark eyes. "Europe. Remember how much fun we had?"

"Of course," I say, tentative. "It's just . . ." I lower my voice so the men at the poker table won't hear. "I wish you had talked to me before you decided all this."

"I know this is a lot. But Sophie will be off to college before I know it. I want to make these memories as a family while we can. And, look, I promise, I'll take care of everything. We can bring Órlaith. This doesn't have to be a headache." I'm nodding along, because of course he's right. He squeezes the tops of my shoulders. "The truth is, I've had this trip planned for a while, since before . . ."

"Oh," I say, a sinking feeling in the pit of my stomach. Since before my incident. My eyes flick to the poker table. Curtis has his head half turned, ear to us, but then he sets his cards back on the table, places a bet. The other men are absorbed in the game. I think of the girl I was when Ethan met me, the girl he fell in love with. A carefree twenty-four-year-old who threw a few sundresses into a carry-on and flaked on her shifts at the coffee shop to flitter off to Paris at a moment's notice, because *Come on, it's Paris!* He had planned this trip for that girl. But that girl became a mother—tired and frazzled and needing a lot more than a carry-on.

"I thought about canceling," he says. "I did. But, then I started thinking, maybe this is what you need. What *we* need, you know?" He wraps his arms around my waist, pulls me to him. "Let's get away from this house, huh? Just reset."

That thought alone—an escape—melts my shoulder blades down my back. He kisses my hair, my cheek. The tight ball of worry inside me unfurls.

"All right, lovebirds," Gemma says. She's feet away now, two glasses of wine in her hands.

"Yeah, you two make me sick," Jaci's husband, Greg, says from the poker table. "You're the expert here, Curtis. Are married people supposed to be that happy?"

"I plead the fifth," Curtis says.

"Ha, ha," Gemma says dryly, holding one of the glasses out to me. "This smoke is giving me a headache." She tips her head toward the door. I take the offered glass and nod, follow her outside.

Though it's humid, the air feels fresh after the carriage house, the wind welcome now. There is an alcove here, a pair of lounge chairs tucked away from the pool and the party, covered partially by a screen of overgrown live oaks, ball moss hanging from their branches. *Fairy nests,* my papaw used to call them.

"He's right, you know?" Gemma takes a seat in one of the chairs. "Don't you let Kim spoil anything for you, sweetheart. Because she'll try."

I sit down beside her.

"She blamed me for her losing her license." She stretches out her legs, kicks off her nude pumps. "Did you know that?"

"Blamed you? How?"

She shrugs. "She'll blame anyone but herself, I guess." She sips her wine, stares off, lost in a memory. She shakes her head. "I loved that girl. I would have stuck by her through anything. The anger. Her blaming me. I could have dealt with that. But." She looks at me. Her teased hair is high on her head, not a single strand out of place, not even in this wind. She clicks her tongue, takes a sip of wine. "All right, honey, look. I'm going to tell you something, but I don't want it to change the way you think about me, you hear? Before I met Curtis, my life wasn't quite so, well, charmed, okay? I went through my fair share of struggles. Anyway, back in my cheer days, I . . ." She smooths the already smooth hair beside her temples. "I posed for some photographs. To make a little extra money, make ends meet. It's not something I'm proud of. The opposite. I'm mortified, to be honest."

Gemma, with her immovable hair, her pageant queen posture, her Pinterest-perfect family portraits, the twins in matching blue plaid shirts, the caption *Pray big, because God is good.*

I reach out my hand to take hold of hers. "Of course that doesn't change how I think of you, Gemma."

She squeezes my hand like a *Thank you.* "I had told Kim, because at the time, I told Kim everything. Even the website where the photos were posted. I had tried getting them taken down, talked to a lawyer, but I worried a lawsuit would only draw attention. At the time, I was sick to my stomach about it. I was losing my hair in quarter-sized circles from the stress. Kim was my support system. But, after it all went down, I guess she wanted to get back at me. She dug up those old photos. And she sent them to everyone on her contact list, which was just about everyone on *my* contact list—friends and family, people I go to church with, people I see at the grocery store, people who know my parents."

"Oh, Gemma. That's awful." And it is. It's an awful thing to have happened to Gemma. But, more than that, it's an awful thing that Kim did. And if she could do that to someone she loved, what would she do to someone she doesn't even like? What might she do to me?

Gemma raises her eyebrows, eyes lifted for a moment, then she clicks her tongue again and shrugs. "The worst part was realizing what she was capable of. She's unpredictable. That's why I'm telling you this, honey. Stay away from Kim. She's dangerous."

I nod. I think of Kim's dilated pupils in the dim shadows of the cellar, of the sharp little blade in her hand, the unstable anger of that single word—*Bullshit*. The trees above us shiver. The sounds of splashing, of laughing, of the DJ's pounding speakers.

Then there's another sound, a commotion of some kind. A thud, a gasp, a hush followed by a flurry of voices, someone's high-pitched "Oh my God, are you okay?"

I look to Gemma. Her expression mirrors my own puzzlement, and we both stand, Gemma stepping back into her shoes, and we rush toward the party to see what's happened.

39

Kim

I spot Ted, still outside, sitting at one of the patio tables near the pool with another woman. She's thin, wearing a spaghetti-strapped dress, her pointy shoulder blades like bird wings trying to escape. The way she tilts her head so that her high ponytail swings to the side—I realize it's Gwyneth, Ethan's assistant. God, I really dislike that woman. I'm about to make a quick one-eighty when Ted catches sight of me, smiles, raises a hand to wave. Gwyneth turns to look, a pinched smile making her thin lips appear even thinner. I smile back, flutter my fingers. When I reach the table, Ted triumphantly lifts the glass of white wine he must have ordered for me while I was gone. It's drippy with condensation, which had pooled on the glass-topped table. "I was wondering where you'd disappeared to." His eyes linger on my breasts. "Do you know Kim?" he asks Gwyneth. "She's a veterinarian."

"Of course. Hey, girl. It's been a while." She eyes the glass of wine, looks at me.

I take the empty seat, pick up the glass. "Cheers," I say, locking eyes with Gwyneth. She taps her glass against mine, and we drink.

"We were talking about this wind," Ted says. "What would you say this is? Twenty? Twenty-five miles per hour?" He's leaned back in his chair, completely at ease. He kicks one leg out, so that his calf grazes against mine.

"Congratulations, by the way," Gwyneth says to me, bypassing Ted's thrilling wind-speed line of conversation.

Ted is watching me. I raise an eyebrow, unsure what she's referring to.

"I didn't realize you'd gotten your license back already. That's fantastic."

I let out a hollow laugh. I lean forward, touch the tips of my fingers to

Ted's forearm. "I bet you've seen some windy places, huh, Ted? He was in the Army. Did he tell you that? He's been everywhere."

He hesitates, looks from Gwyneth to me and back. "Kuwait is pretty windy." He starts on his list again, this time ranking locations by their weather. I can feel the shift, though—his posture has stiffened, his leg is pulled back to his chair.

I realize, too, that I'm drinking my wine so quickly that my glass is empty again. The air is thick with the weight of Gwyneth's words. The back of my neck burns hot. "Sorry," I say, standing up quickly, too quickly, I realize—I've cut Ted off in the middle of a sentence. "I just need, um, I'll be right back." I start to walk away, toward I don't know where. The bar? The house? I feel a hand on my arm. It's Gwyneth.

"Did I say the wrong thing back there?"

"You're fine. I just need some air." Which makes no sense, because we're outside. "Really. It's fine." I'm looking at her as I walk away, and my foot catches on the leg of a lounge chair. I trip, the bad kind, where you think, *Oh God, I'm falling,* but you can't do anything to catch yourself, and then I'm sprawled on the patio, my legs splayed, my skirt hiked up to expose my nude-colored Spanx. "Oh my God, are you okay?" People around me are reaching down to help me up.

Through the clamor of the crowd, I see Sophie. Every ounce of embarrassment I feel is reflected on her face. We lock eyes. She shakes her head and turns away, pushing past her friends.

Fuck. Fuck. I shove a helping hand away from me and push myself up. "I'm fine. Just—I'm fine." I don't make eye contact with anyone as I move up and into and through the house. I find myself climbing the spiral staircase again, clutching the banister this time, the whole way up.

I want to be away. Just for a minute. Finally, I find myself on the balcony. I fumble with the latch on my crossbody purse. I pull out a cigarette. There is a tremor to my fingers, I realize. My palms sting from the fall. I rest my elbow on the balcony railing to steady my arm as I light the cigarette. I inhale. The smoke fills my lungs, then I let it out slowly.

Fucking Gwyneth Porter. *Hey, girl. It's been a while.* What a fake bitch.

I take a few more long, slow drags. The balcony stretches wide, suspended over the cliff's edge. I let my eyes unfocus, watch the wind rustling cedars far below, listen to the scraping of tree branches like cricket legs.

What if I am the ghost in this house?

All those emotions I felt that were too big for my body—the hope when we first moved in. The laughter. The anger. The terror that time Sophie slipped face-first while running full speed in her socks, and for a moment she lay motionless on the tile while blood pooled around her head. Thankfully, she'd only split her chin, needing just two stitches. You can still see the scar if you know where to look. Maybe places hold scars too, retain the faint traces of the things that happened there. If you know where to look.

I flick the ash from my cigarette over the railing, watch it dissipate in the breeze.

I didn't realize you'd gotten your license back already. That's fantastic.

It's strange when you look back on the big events of your life and you see all the little things that led up to them, see how stupid and unaware you were, like driving blindly around a sharp curve.

———

I had just started trail-running. This was years ago, back when Ethan and I were still married. I'd been trying to lose a good ten or fifteen pounds for a while, and, in all honesty, I needed to change up my whole routine. Maybe if I woke up early, hit the trails at 5 A.M.; maybe the quiet morning hours with early light through trees and fresh air in my lungs; maybe the stress relief that came from pounding my sneakers against a packed dirt road; maybe if my muscles were exhausted by the end of a long day—maybe then I could skip the glass of wine at night.

But the trail-running only lasted two weeks before I caught my foot on a root and fell hard on my shoulder, fracturing my collarbone. The doctor prescribed Percocet along with ice and rest.

It hurt something awful, but the medication helped, until I went to take my next dose and the bottle was empty.

The prescription was only for a few days, Ethan said.

I swear I had a couple more. The pain was like a toothache that radiated through my shoulder, caused a stiffness in my neck, and when I couldn't possibly find a comfortable way to sleep, I wrote a prescription for tramadol for Joey, our Shetland sheepdog.

I don't think that's a good idea, Ethan said.

It hurts. Or are you going to tell me how I feel? I snapped.

I had just needed a few more pills. If only I had thrown the rest of the bottle away.

———

I stub my cigarette out on the glass of the balcony railing, flick the butt over the side toward the open cliff. I slide out another and light it. I stroll to the center of the balcony, look out over the pool and the party.

I can see Sophie. My head is swimming. The cigarettes have heightened my buzz. My vision blurs. But, still, even from here, I can see that Sophie is worked up, that she's venting, and no doubt, she's venting about me. But that's not what gets my hot anger burning. She's venting to Dani. Dani, who is nodding, who is pulling *my* daughter into a hug, rubbing her back.

I used to spend hours—literally, hours—sitting on the floor, my hand through the bars of Sophie's crib, rubbing her back while she slept. She'd be in a dead sleep, heavy as a sack of dog food, lips parted and a trickle of drool, but if I dared to stop rubbing her back, if I tried to so much as lift my hand, her little eyes would snap open. So I stayed.

Now Dani thinks she can just swoop in and steal everything that is mine?

I don't think so.

40

Dani

Poor Sophie.

She was so upset. *I'm not going to be able to go to Europe,* she said. *It's too long. It's too far. I can't leave her alone.* Like she was the mother, instead of the other way around.

Honey, I told her. *She just tripped. Everyone trips.* I promised to look for Neosporin and Band-Aids, check on Kim to make sure she didn't scrape up anything more than her pride.

The other kids were getting ready for the pool. I found a way to steer the conversation to that, to her black string bikini, to sunlight on water.

I really am going to try to find some Band-Aids and check on Kim, wherever she is.

The door to the butler's pantry is slightly ajar. I pull it open, and the door swings soundlessly on well-oiled hinges. Which, I guess, is why she doesn't hear me. MaryBeth is inside my pantry. Her short, round frame, back slightly hunched as she peers into a lower shelf, her biscuit-colored hair half pulled back with a barrette, her midi-length dress covered in sweet pink and yellow blossoms. She has one of my cabinets open, revealing a row of clear plastic containers—flour, sugar, brown sugar, baking powder—a spinning spice rack, and jar upon jar of sprinkles in every color: edible glitter, metallic drageés, chocolate jimmies.

She picks up one of the jars, flips open the lid with her thumb. She tips the jar. Neon pink balls the size of pearl earrings roll into the palm of her hand. They are the same ones I used on the second tier of Sophie's cake, bright pops against the lime green buttercream. MaryBeth lowers her face to suck the sprinkles from her cupped palm. She replaces the container on the shelf. I'm so shocked that I forget to speak. She must feel my presence, though, because she turns.

"Oh," she says, then she giggles, her giggle shivering her body, pink pricking her cheeks. Is she wondering how much I saw? "I was looking for the bathroom. But, well, obviously, this isn't the bathroom." Another giggle. "I couldn't help taking a peek at your baking stuff." Her smile crinkles the bridge of her nose. "Sorry." She glances back at the open cabinet.

Hair itches the back of my neck as if a bug were crawling on it. "It's fine," I say. It is weird, though. It's a weird thing to do.

"It's just like your Instagram. I mean, *just* like it." She steps toward me, her face all big smile and creased eyes and shiny apple cheeks. "You see people online and they look so pretty, but you think, it's probably all angles and lighting and filters. Or their kitchen is spotless, but what does it really look like on a random Tuesday afternoon? You can't compare your behind-the-scenes to someone else's highlight reel, right? That's what they say."

"Yeah," I say. "Of course."

She's close to me now, looking up at me. "But you're perfect. You really are."

I release an awkward laugh. "You haven't seen me on a random Tuesday."

Her smile is fixed. "Anyway," she says, back to giggling. "I guess I better find that bathroom."

As she leaves, I am frozen in place, a coldness in the pit of my belly.

It's that word again. *Perfect.*

41

Mikayla

By the time I come back to the group, Sophie is in the pool. Emma is rubbing suntan lotion on Ava's back. The guys are horsing around. Braydon does a cannonball so he almost lands right on Tyler, splashing water onto Sophie and Emma and Ava in the process.

"Ugh. Not my hair," Emma whines, patting her buns gently to assess the damage.

Sophie swims to the edge when she sees me, folds her arms on the tiled ledge.

"Where's your bathing suit?" she asks.

I perch on the end of the lounge chair closest to her. "I think I'm going to sit this one out."

"Are you okay? You look kind of pale."

"It was that tequila shot."

She nods, her expression sympathetic. I can't believe she doesn't see it, that it isn't seared across my forehead like when Dad brands the cattle.

Braydon sneaks up behind Sophie, grabs her around the waist. She squeals with mock horror as he spins her farther into the pool.

"Who's up for a game of chicken?" Tyler asks.

"Me, me," Ava says as she dips a foot into the water. "Oh, come on. Y'all are such liars. It's literally freezing. Mikayla's the only smart one."

She looks to me, and I smile weakly.

"Where's Mason?" Braydon says.

I sit on my hands to hide that they're shaking.

I wish I had gone inside and changed. I wish I was only worried about how I looked in a bathing suit, about getting my hair wet.

I wish I could stop doing bad things.

42

Dani

I'm chatting again with Kristin and Jaci and Liz, and they're telling me about the last book that Liz chose for book club.

"I'm sorry," Liz says, snorting a laugh into her drink. "I heard it was a good romance. My sister-in-law said she couldn't put it down."

"I thought: romance, you know?" Kristin says. "It would be horseback riding and debutante balls, meaningful glances and fingertips grazing. That kind of thing."

"Oh, there were fingertips, all right," Jaci says. "Inserting."

Liz reddens. "I didn't even know men liked that. Do men like that?"

I'm laughing, sipping white wine. But I feel it: the fullness of my breasts, straining against the red chiffon of my dress. I'm not nursing today, because I'm drinking. With my arms crossed, I discreetly press the heel of my hand to my cleavage. It's hard as a brick. I should have gone off to pump whenever Órlaith took Charlotte up for her nap.

And just thinking of Charlotte—of her dark nursery and the calming whir of the sound machine and her placid, milk-drunk face, mouth slack, one orbed cheek red from where it presses hot against my skin—sends tingles through my breasts. And oh no, I can feel the milk let down. I'm wearing bamboo nursing pads, but they might not hold, and I excuse myself to the powder room beside the butler's pantry to hand-express into the sink, just temper the flood so I can make it upstairs to my pump.

I lock the door behind me, not bothering to turn on the light. I reach into the plunging neckline, my breasts heavy and sore. I press both nipples, compress, release, feel the simultaneous ache and relief as milk spurts into the sink. I look up at myself in the mirror, and I see it. Each capital letter an angry slash. I reach out to flip on the light.

Across the full length of the mirror, the words are scrawled in deep red lipstick:

CRAZY BITCH

My mouth drops open to scream, but no sound comes out.

43

The Night of the Party

It's past one in the morning. The lead detective continues pulling guests into the downstairs office, a makeshift interrogation room. Isabel Martinez, a mother of one of the cheerleaders, sits in the chair opposite him, Ethan Matthews' sleek walnut desk between them. The detective's felt hat sits atop the desk. He asks where she was when the body fell. If she might have any unique insights into what happened. Mascara raccoons her eyes. "God," she says in barely more than a whisper, "that poor child."

She thinks of the times she looked up into the windows of this house. How they all couldn't wait to get in. They had come out of curiosity. For sparkling gowns and sparkling wine. To gossip and siphon secrets. To be entertained.

Isabel answers the inquiries to the best of her recollection, but something is clawing at the back of her brain. The story she was told as a child, the one she passed down to her own daughter, the warnings to behave. Otherwise, *she* would come for you. *She* would take you away. A story repeated over generations—a mother's love turned to grief turned to madness—diminished into a tale meant to scare disobedient children, a game for teens to whisper over Ouija boards. What none of them realized was that in keeping the story alive, they had kept *her* alive.

Now, as she is asked and answers questions, it dawns on Isabel.

Tonight, they were guests in *her* house.

The Mother was their host.

44

Dani

The Day of the Party

I scrub the mirror in frantic circles, the red lipstick smearing, creating a bigger mess, obscuring my reflection with its crimson cloud. My breasts leak. My breath is quick. A wave of panic consumes me. My heartbeat whooshes in my ears. *Shit.* Who's been in here? Everyone. Everyone has been in here. It's the guest bathroom. Anyone could have done this. And, oh God, anyone could have seen this. I refold the towel, rub in parallel and perpendicular lines.

I scrub until my breath comes in ragged pants. I clutch the edge of the sink. The walls squeeze inward.

I look back up. A film of stubborn lipstick still clings to the mirror like bloody beeswax, shading the room's reflection a ghastly red.

The knob twists, but the lock holds.

"Someone's in here," I call out, hoping I don't sound as hysterical as I feel.

Shit.

I reach into my purse. My hands are shaking as I take out my phone. I unlock it, press my sister's name. It rings a few times, but she picks up before her voicemail does.

"Becca," I say in a breathless whisper. "It's real."

"Dani? Where are you?" Her voice is swallowed by claps and cheers. She's at Aubrey's track meet. With two teenagers, both her and Jason's full-time jobs, and her involvement with the school board, the HOA, and the church, Becca's calendar is a Tetris board of obligations. I can hear the sounds fading, hear the puff of her breath, as if she's climbing down the bleachers. I imagine her ducking behind the stands, near the chain-link fence in a shadowed gap between the crowds at the concessions and the crowds in line for the bathroom, one finger plugged into the ear opposite her phone to hear me better.

"Isn't Sophie's party today?" *I can miss Aubrey's meet,* she told me. *Jason can take her.* I heard her flipping her calendar then. *Oh, hmm. Well, we could probably move that around.* I could picture her sliding the nail of her ring finger over her bottom teeth, a problem-solving habit she's had ever since I can remember. *No, no,* I told her. *Y'all don't have to come. It's just a birthday party.* We'd be having plenty more get-togethers in the future. Ethan's family wouldn't be coming to the party, and neither would Kim's parents, I explained. *I think it would be weird if my family came. It's mainly for Sophie's friends.*

I could come for you, though, she said. *I mean, a big party? Are you sure you're ready for that?*

You sound like Mom, I laughed. *I'll be fine.*

But now, her absence leaves me feeling hollow and alone.

"They're here in the house." I keep my voice as low as possible, a hiss, really.

"What are you talking about?"

"The person. The stalker. Whoever was watching me, watching Charlotte. They're here, Becca. They're in my house."

"Isn't the party today?" she asks again.

She knows the party is today. She knows the track meet conflicted. It's a clever way to ask if I'm nuts. "Yes," I say. "That's how they got in. But—they've been sending me messages."

"Where is Ethan?"

"Ethan won't understand."

Someone knocks on the door.

"Just a minute," I call out, my voice upticking so that I sound downright cheerful to my own ears. I wet the hand towel, continue to clean the mirror while I talk. "Shit."

"Who are you talking to?"

"I should have taken a picture." The message. I should have documented it—more evidence.

"Dani, you're scaring me. What's going on?"

Another knock.

"Becca, I have to go. I love you."

"Wait, Dan—"

I hang up. I throw the towel beneath the cabinet, check my reflection, swipe beneath my eyes. I check my breasts. The nursing pads are soaked, the inside of my bra cups slightly damp, but the milk hasn't seeped to the dress yet, and I think the flow has paused for the moment.

I take a breath.

I open the door.

45

Mikayla

"Mikayla's babysitting," Tyler yells out, like he's tattling on me. He's talking about the drink in my hand, a melting once-nonalcoholic frozen margarita that Braydon dumped a shot of tequila into, stirred with his finger. I'm still perched on the edge of the lounge chair, arms wrapped around my middle, while the rest of them float lazily in the pool. Emma and Tyler bob atop pool noodles, Ava rests her arms on the edge of Braydon's float, her perky round butt popping just up and out of the water, and Sophie lies simply on her back, the only girl who isn't afraid to get her hair wet. It fans around her like a spill of liquid gold.

I make a point of taking a sip while they're all looking. But the truth is I'm afraid to drink more. I can't trust myself.

Late afternoon—sunset still hours away—the air is preheated enough to cook a pizza, my eyes bleached, sore from squinting.

Braydon mentions jumping from the balcony again, repeating it like he's building up the courage to actually do it. "Really, dude, you don't think I could clear the patio?"

"It would be epic," Tyler says.

Mason comes back, in his swim trunks now. I try not to look at him, but his collared shirt is now off, draped over his shoulder. The V of his waist diving into his trunks. He tosses it onto a lawn chair and hops into the pool.

"Dude," Tyler yells. "What is that?"

"What?" Mason says, but he covers his neck with a hand. "It's from the game. My shoulder pads."

"No way that's from football. That's a hickey," Braydon says, propping himself onto his elbows on the float.

"Oh my God, let me see." Ava swims over, pulls his hand away.

I watch Sophie. She hasn't moved. She is still and serene behind her sunglasses, the white-hot sun bathing the skin above the water's surface: her upturned palms, her shoulders, the rounded mounds of her breasts, the tops of her long legs. It's as if she hasn't heard them or doesn't care.

Still bobbing up and down on her pool noodle, Emma has gone wide-eyed. "Mason, who gave that to you?" she asks. "Sophie, are you hearing this?"

Sophie rotates her body, swims to the edge of the pool. She doesn't say anything, though.

Then, before anything more can be said, Gabby's voice calls over the crowd, her loud, singsongy, attention-snatching voice: "Hey, bitches, I'm baaack." Her fire-engine red bikini is cut so high up on her hips that all I think is that she must be completely bald down there. It's like that swimsuit Kendall Jenner wore that one time—okay, maybe not quite that bad, but yeah. I can feel Sophie taking in her swimsuit as well, Gabby's exposed brown skin, glistening like she's been oiled. She reaches the pool, kneels and uncovers the stash of liquor, splashes some vodka in her watermelon drink.

"Nice," Tyler says, reaching out a hand to high-five Mason, but Mason turns away, leaves him hanging.

"Oh my God," Ava says. "Gabby, seriously?"

Gabby sits on the edge of the pool, slides her body down into the water. "What'd I miss?"

Sophie lets out a humorless laugh, just a breath, really. She remains neutral, eyes covered by dark lenses, forearms folded on the tile. But I can see the warm red tops of her ears. She's trying not to cry.

Out of the corner of my eye, I see Emma and Ava exchange looks.

Sophie pulls herself gracefully out of the pool. "I'm getting another drink."

"Bring back food," Tyler calls out.

She's already disappearing into the crowd, weaving through the dance floor, where the adults, getting drunker and drunker as the day goes on, are doing embarrassing things—thank God my parents didn't come.

I get up to follow Sophie. I don't care about these other girls.

No matter what I've done, no matter what a shitty friend I've been, a shitty person, really—it's Sophie I care about. It's Sophie I can't imagine living without.

46

Kim

Of all the true crime shows and books and podcasts I guzzle down, my favorite story is probably the case of Betty Broderick.

Betty was the perfect wife to Dan. She gave him four children and was the main provider for the family while he attended law school—Harvard Law School, mind you—and built his career. And once he did, once he started making big money, he left Betty for his twenty-one-year-old blond assistant. I would say that Dan wasn't very original, but he took it a step further. He gaslighted Betty. He made her seem crazy, made her feel crazy, and then she started to act crazy—leaving hundreds of profane voicemails, driving her car into their front door, breaking into their house and smearing pie on his expensive wardrobe. Betty played right into their hands, Dan and his child bride. So Dan antagonized her further. And Betty finally snapped. She took a key from their teenage daughter, let herself into their La Jolla mansion in the middle of the night, and shot them both dead.

Betty still gets fan mail in prison. Women wearing *Free Betty Broderick* T-shirts write her love letters, shared experiences, reasons they understand what she did, understand who she is.

Netflix just did another TV adaptation of the Betty Broderick story. I read the comments on Twitter. *Men need to think twice before they mistreat a woman, think about how pissed off we can get. Betty Broderick should be a warning for them.*

———

There doesn't seem to be anyone up here. I sway slightly, eyes unfocused. That's the mirror I chose on the wall. My console table with the silk floral arrangement Ethan's mother made for us. My old bedroom, my library, my loft.

I hear the *shhhhh* of a fan or white noise machine. It's coming from the guest bedroom, what must now be their nursery.

I stand outside the door.

I'm thinking of Betty Broderick and how a person can only be pushed so far.

47

Dani

Vera stands outside the bathroom door.

"Darling," she says, "you look like you've seen a ghost."

"Oh." I laugh.

But she reaches out a hand to touch my cheek with the backs of her fingers, like a mother taking a temperature. Her hand is tepid, her skin thin and soft as paper handled again and again.

"I'm fine. I'm just a little flushed. I haven't had this much to drink since before I was pregnant."

I must look more than a little flushed, though, because Vera isn't taking my excuse. "Let's get you sitting down."

I want to refuse, to escape, to think things over, figure out what to do about the intruder in my home. And I still need desperately to pump. But my legs feel weak beneath me, so I let Vera steer me to the nearby sofa. She sets me on the corner of the L, takes the seat just beside me.

Everywhere I look, there are people, faces I know and faces I don't, people around the dining table, over by the fireplace, under the stairs, out on the patio, clumps of conversation, snatches of laughter, uniformed waiters snaking between. I am aware of the unlocked doors.

Where is Charlotte?

Upstairs. Asleep.

My heart pulses like a frightened bird caught in my rib cage.

I must really look a mess, because I notice a nearby group of women sneaking glances. I catch eyes with Gwyneth. She mouths *You okay?* her face a miming of sympathy.

I've always gotten along fine with Gwyneth. She's easy enough to talk to—an endless well of nutrition tips and yoga poses and hair trends and juicy gossip. But I've never really trusted her. She's the kind of woman who will skip over when you show up at a social event, hug your neck, and whisper the latest dirt—Karen, the bookkeeper for the practice, is getting gastric bypass surgery. But then, she'll turn around just as quick, hissing your own secrets into Karen's ear.

Plus, I'm pretty sure she has the hots for my husband.

———

Ethan and I had been dating a few weeks when I showed up at his practice one day with a single strawberry cupcake in a cardboard box.

Mr. Matthews is in with a patient, Gwyneth said, sitting at her desk, fingers poised over her keyboard.

Can I just leave this for him? The box was wrapped with a red ribbon, his name swirled onto a craft paper note.

Gwyneth looked me up and down. *And you are?*

I hadn't known how to respond. Ethan and I hadn't talked labels yet. *A friend.*

She took the box, set it on the bookshelf behind her, and continued typing on her computer. She hadn't been particularly rude, but she hadn't been friendly, and I'd left the practice feeling silly and self-conscious.

When I spoke to Ethan later that day, after he'd gotten off work for the evening, he didn't mention the cupcake. At first, my feelings were hurt. Maybe it had been childish, presumptuous to bring a gift to his office. Maybe that wasn't something people in grown-up relationships did.

But he had sent me flowers, gifts. He had never been shy about his affection toward me. He didn't play games. It's what I liked about him.

So, eventually, toward the end of our conversation, I simply asked if he had enjoyed the cupcake. He'd never received it. He explained that Gwyneth was always so busy, the only receptionist for the six psychiatrists in their practice, and it must have slipped her mind. He'd ask her about it tomorrow. But he thought it was sweet that I'd gone through all the trouble.

It made sense. I'm sure that's what happened. But there was a part of me that wondered—that female instinct that sends up warning signs about another woman.

I never brought it up again.

———

I nod at her now, and we exchange smiles. She turns back to her group, takes a sip of her drink. I watch her lean in, say something quickly. I watch the woman beside her flick her eyes to Vera and me.

I pull my shoulders back, force myself to at least appear composed.

Suddenly, MaryBeth is sitting beside me, scooching close in that overly familiar way of hers, so that our thighs are flush. "Hey, girl." Her syrupy voice hot on my neck. "Did you see what I wrote?"

I rear back from her, the skin on my arms quilling with fear. "What?"

Her smile is as wide as ever, her cheeks shiny with the strain of her cheerfulness. "On Insta?"

"Oh," I say. "No. I haven't—um, have you two met?" My phone rings in my purse. It's probably Becca. I reach inside and hit the button to silence it. I'll call her back later.

"We have," MaryBeth says, smiling at Vera. "Vera is amazing. She knows everyone in Bulverde, recommended a landscaper." She shakes the phone in her hand, where I guess she's stored the landscaper's number. "Ernesto and I are wanting some rock work out front. Kind of like what y'all have."

"Vera's a lifesaver," I agree. "We didn't plan on having a nanny," I explain to MaryBeth. "So when we ended up needing one, we weren't prepared. The thought of having a total stranger watching your infant, well, it's terrifying. Luckily, in swooped Vera, who recommended her dear old friend."

Vera is sitting with her hands folded neatly in her lap. She is smiling, but her eyebrows are knit together. "Oh," Vera says. "I don't know that I'd say that. Órlaith seems to be a wonderful nanny, sweetheart, and we've become good friends. We have a lot in common. But, I didn't meet Órlaith until after you'd hired her."

Cool dread snakes through my scalp like water, slides down my spine. My eyes drift up and over Vera's head, lock onto Órlaith, who stands alone near the edge of the room, small, unassuming, a shadow of a woman.

48

Órlaith

"Best watch your step there," I say.

The girls don't realize it's them I'm talking to. They don't register that I even exist, I'd wager. They've migrated back to the dance floor, drinks in hand, and by the way they're swaying, leaning into one another, I'd guess there's something stronger than fizzy-drink in their glasses. They're in incy-wincy bikinis now, feet bare.

"The stones are wet," I say, pushing on.

The blonde with the two buns atop her head turns to me, raises her eyebrows. "Sorry?" she says.

"The stones." I point to their feet. "They're slick as seals. You could fall, break your neck." All three of the girls are looking at me now. I was right, of course, about the patio getting wet, what with the boys cannonballing into the pool and the girls gliding back and forth from the bar, so I tell them all about the poor young one, Maeve, who was married to my brother-in-law, who tripped trying to kick a ball and hit her pretty nineteen-year-old head on the pavement, and died of a brain injury later that night.

The girls are exchanging glances. I can see they're trying to suppress their smiles, like. I can see they believe in their own invincibility.

Silly old woman, they think. But they're polite enough girls.

"Thanks, ma'am," the one with short, wavy hair says.

The pretty girl in the red bikini ducks her head to hide a snort of laughter, tugs the two others away toward the pool.

"We'll be careful," the blonde says over her shoulder, and the line sends the trio into a fit of giggles.

They won't be, of course. They never are.

We tell our children to be careful in so many ways. *Watch your step* and *Don't climb too high; Don't touch that* or *Don't put that in your mouth; Never talk to strangers* and *Always eat your vegetables; Please brush your teeth* and *For heaven's sake, look both ways; Hold my hand; Call as soon as you get there*—infinite ways to say the one thing we really mean: *Please survive.*

No matter. I've said my piece, sure, done my part. I fade back into the party, float unnoticed through the crowd, up the stairs to the upper patio. I watch the girls below, crouching in the center of that outdoor tent, splashing spirits into their drinks, barely hiding their actions beneath a beach towel.

I am near the open glass door, hovering between the party inside and the party outside.

In the living room, I see Mrs. Matthews on the white leather sofa with Vera.

I didn't see Dani during the first few days of my employment. I didn't meet her until she emerged from her bedroom, glassy-eyed and rat's-nested hair.

But that wasn't the first time I laid eyes on her. Far from it.

———

In downtown Bulverde is the Hatch Cafe & Bakery, a quaint blue clapboard building with a porch swing and a Little Free Library out front, serving coffee and pastries and great big sandwiches on freshly baked bread, knickknacks on the shelves and paintings on the wall all for sale like an antiques shop—a field of bluebonnets on canvas, a rooster-printed watering can, a sign that reads *I remember the days when I prayed for the things I have now.* That day, sure, I had popped in to escape the heat, was just enjoying a sweet iced tea and lemon tart at the corner table, minding my own business, when the bell jingled and the door swung open, and in stepped this couple—Mr. and Mrs. Matthews—a *chance encounter,* you could say. Dani came through the door mid-laugh, one hand on Mr. Matthews' forearm as he steered her inside, the other hand on her swollen belly.

I watched them as they ordered, as Mr. Matthews added a chocolate croissant—*Don't get in the way of a pregnant woman and her cravings,* he joked—as they sat together on the long wooden bench, both on the same side of the table, like, their bodies leaned into each other. It was clear by the way they looked at each other, by the way they spoke, their words edged in laughter—they were in love.

I physically ached at the sight of it, at the remembrance of that much hope—her pregnant belly at the center of their curved bodies, nothing but potential.

Yet, I could see it, sure—I, and I alone—could see the dark cloud hovering over them, could see the curse of black days ahead.

———

Now, Dani looks up and locks eyes with me. Her face is sheet-white. She looks ill, poor pet.

It's all right, though. It will be all right.

Because I'm here now, here to protect her, to protect them all.

49

Mikayla

I find her on the balcony. It didn't take long—somehow I knew she'd end up here, curled in her mom's old reading chair, an oversized round wicker chair with a thick cushion and a million throw pillows, too big for one person, but not quite made for two. She hugs her knees. "Oh, Mik," she says when she sees me. Tears roll down her face, and she doesn't even bother to wipe them away, doesn't hide them from me. I crawl into the chair beside her, pull her into me, bury my face in her wet, chlorine-scented hair, and for a good long while, I just let her cry.

The wind is whistling warm through the tunnel of the balcony.

"I hate Gabby," she says, finally, between snotty sobs. She sits up, untangling herself from me and crisscrossing her legs. She wipes her nose with the heel of her hand, looks at me with puffed and swollen eyes. "How much do I look like shit?"

"You never look like shit."

She laughs, wipes her nose again. "It's my birthday."

"I know."

I listen to her talk. Talk about how Mason looked at her when he first arrived, and did I notice?

"Of course. Sophie, that dress. I mean, come on."

I listen as she picks apart the interactions we've picked apart a thousand times—the time they met up at Hatch and he had already ordered a soy milk latte for her and one of their awesome almond croissants, and that meant he had paid attention, had remembered her order exactly, and that had to mean something, right? The time they made out in his truck, him sliding his hand up her top to cup her breast over her bra, her on his lap, rocking back and forth, their mouths never leaving each other's, until she was so hot she really thought maybe they'd do it, and should she have? Would that have made the difference?

"Screw him," I say. "He's a player. You said that from the beginning."

She leans back so she can look at me straight on.

"I just mean you're better than him, Soph."

"You just don't get it."

I hate when she does this. This is literally all we have talked about for weeks, since their breakup, for almost a year, really, since they started dating, and I had to listen to all of Sophie's rainbows and butterflies. I had to force myself to smile and say all the right lines. So, yeah, I think I fully *get it*.

"You've never been in love," she says.

My heart screams in protest, my chest a vice. I skate my eyes away from hers, look past her shoulder instead, out over the balcony and the cliff and nothing but sky, because I'm afraid of what she might see in my eyes, what she might figure out. I am terrified for a moment, balancing on this precipice.

"No offense, but having a crush isn't the same thing." She doesn't sound like herself when she says it. Her voice, the words—they're kind of mean. Maybe it's because she's mad and she's sad and she's had four or five drinks, but still. What the hell?

"What?"

She rolls her eyes—like, actually rolls them—and I feel the blood draining from my face. She stands, walks to the glass railing, and turns back to me. Sophie is silhouetted by the sun. From where I sit, it halos her head, making her hard to look at. "Come on, Mik, I'm not stupid."

I don't say anything. I can't. I don't understand.

"That night I told you Mason was a player—I was just trying to protect you."

"Protect me?" My head churns. Clouds whisk across the sky, spinning shadows over the balcony. Sophie remembers that party, that conversation. "You knew I liked him?"

"Everyone likes Mason."

I feel like she's slapped me. "Why are you so pissed about the hickey then? If he's just fair game?"

She scoffs, crosses her arms. "This is what I'm talking about. It's not the same. At all. I had a relationship with Mason. An actual, real-life relationship. You had a crush. It was imaginary. It was in your head. You do this all the time. You build up these things that don't exist. You get obsessed."

I am sitting on the edge of the chair now, fingers gripping the cushion, staring up at Sophie, dumbfounded by her venom.

The blackness inside me swirls.

She keeps going. "Mason said one nice thing to you. I could just tell you were doing it again. *I think I just had a moment,*" she says, clasping her hands under her chin, eyes mooning—this last part an embarrassing impersonation of me.

My voice is small, maybe inaudible, when I repeat, "You knew I liked him?" Because this is the part I can't get past. The whole time she knew. She just didn't care.

She was the one who deserved him. Not dull, freckled, frizzled Mikayla, but golden Sophie.

I always knew that was our dynamic, at least since high school started, since I joined FFA and she became a cheerleader. I just didn't know that Sophie knew it too. I thought she loved me.

My hands hold tight to the chair. The sun is blinding from this angle, light bouncing off the glass of the balcony, the glass of every cliffside window. Far, far away, voices and music and someone's loud laugh.

But Sophie and I are alone together on the balcony, completely and absolutely.

50

Órlaith

"I just had the strangest conversation with Dani," Vera tells me. She has found me in the kitchen, slicing a banana to prep for Charlotte's dinner. She should be up from her final nap soon, and we've been trying to introduce some finger foods along with the purees and rice cereals.

"Did you now?" I ask, not looking up from the knife. You have to be careful, mind you, getting distracted while you cut fruits and vegetables. "I knew a lady, Cara Murphy, used to do my mam's hair, who cut off the tip of her finger while slicing carrots once. It rolled right off the counter and onto the floor. She and her husband, what was his name? Sean, I think. They searched on hands and knees for the darn thing, so it could be reattached, but they could never find it. Wondered if the dog might have gotten to it first."

Vera winces. "That's why they say to curl your fingers under, when you're cutting onions or what have you." She makes a clawed hand to demonstrate. I nod in agreement. "Anyway," she says. "I was talking to Dani, and she seems to think that you and I have been friends for ages."

I set the knife down and begin to arrange the bananas into one of the cubbies of Charlotte's sectioned plate, made to look like the face of a panda bear. "I like to think we are pretty close," I say.

Vera laughs, puts a hand to my shoulder. "Of course we are, dear. But Dani seems to think that I recommended you for the job."

I turn, tilt my head in confusion. "Where in heavens would she have gotten an idea like that?"

"I don't know. That's what I mean. I told her that you and I hadn't even met until after you started on as their nanny."

"That's true," I say.

It isn't, of course.

————

The day I met Vera, I was driving aimlessly through the neighborhood. I'd tracked down the address but couldn't find the place, all the houses so far apart, metal numbers posted on big slabs of rock at the end of long drives. I slowed down beside an older woman out for a stroll, leaning on a walking stick, a wide-brimmed khaki hat shielding her face, a pair of giant black sunglasses, the kind you pop over prescription lenses. She was introducing herself before I had the window rolled down, telling me her full name and how she'd been living in this neighborhood since before it even was a neighborhood.

Do you know where I might find a family called Matthews? I asked.

In all honesty, it was her own assumption—*You must be the new nanny.* Sure, all I did was fail to contradict her.

So, you see, it wasn't me at all, it wasn't *my* actions. I was merely a vessel. No. Fate, that was. The Holy Spirit's intervention.

Who was I to turn from God's will?

You wouldn't happen to have Mr. Matthews' mobile number, now would you? I seem to have saved it wrong in my phone. Sure, I'm all thumbs with these things. Oh, aren't you a saint? Thank you. Yes, there it is. That should be a nine. I had a six.

————

"I'm just a little worried about her," Vera is saying now, quietly, even if we are alone in the kitchen. "Ethan thinks she's getting better, bless his heart, but she seems all out of sorts to me."

So Vera told Dani that she hadn't known me, hadn't met me until I started working here. That must have been quite a shock. Sure, she'll be after sacking me now, I suppose.

I cannot allow that. Not yet.

I set the knife in the sink, rinse my hands, dry them on a tea towel.

"Sorry, Vera." I hurry from the room. "I need to get the baby."

51

Dani

I need to sort things out. I've finally escaped upstairs, and since I didn't hear any noise from Charlotte's room, I've slipped into my dim bedroom, alone, with only the whirring sound of my breast pump inhaling and exhaling.

What is Órlaith up to? Why is she here?

I hate pumping—the mechanical, unnatural pull, my nipples, sore from rubbing the plastic attachments, irritated to three times their size. It reminds me of those horrifying days after the incident, my mind muddled from the medication, memories and dreams indistinguishable as the layers of wet silt and sand along the creek bed where Papaw used to take me to scavenge for crawdads and tadpoles, ant-lion hills and arrowheads.

I think of deep red lipstick on the mirror—*Crazy bitch*—violent in its anger, in its recklessness, making it that much more frightening than a note slipped beneath my doormat.

My body still trembles. The fear-fluttering of my nervous system feels a little like excitement, feels like the crank-crank-crank of the roller coaster as it crests the sheer descent.

I'm remembering their well-meaning words:

Becca's: *Don't worry. It's totally normal. I used to imagine the most horrible things when I first had Aubrey.*

Mom's: *Sweetheart, just calm down. Stop trying to do everything yourself.*

Ethan's talk of hormones, and Curtis's clinical definitions.

They were all wrong.

And I was right.

Is it possible to feel a calming sense of relief in this state of terror?

By now, I should be used to holding two opposing truths at once. Motherhood is full of impossible dualities.

In those first few days, especially—my organs literally in the wrong places, wearing a diaper, squishy and blood-filled. More exhausted than I knew was possible, I pulled myself from sleep at midnight, at 2 A.M., 4 A.M., then again at 4:45, just for fun, as though pulling myself, hand-over-hand on a rope, from the molasses pool of a dreamless sleep. And in that broken, depleted state, I cared for another human. I fed her from my body.

I was fragile and indestructible.

And it doesn't stop. This existence of two truths at once.

Each new milestone—a social smile, a giggle, a roll onto the tummy— inflates my heart with joy, while destroying me with grief for the newborn that is slipping away, the baby she will never be again.

And of course, motherhood's biggest paradox—that in creating life, I also created death.

Because no matter how much I push the thought from my mind, tell myself that it will be in a hundred years, after a lifetime of golden sunrises and interlaced fingers and laughs that ache the belly and dew-streaked grass between toes, that she will have "a good long life"—this beautiful creature I created will one day die. It is inevitable.

It's too painful, and it's too beautiful, and it is happening every single moment of motherhood.

Both bottles are full now, my breasts empty, my nipples tender. I turn off the machine. I take the bottles and the pumping equipment into our attached bathroom. I dump the milk in the sink, rinse everything and set it on a towel to dry.

Back out in the hall, I see Órlaith's obnoxiously large purse—it could swallow the half of her. It slumps beside the console table, mouth parted open. She is forever conjuring tissues, burp cloths, and Advil from this purse. A Mary Poppins bag.

I go to the purse, plunge my arm elbow deep into it. I need an ID, a passport, a bottle of prescription pills. Is Órlaith even her real name?

I hear the jingle and feel the cold metal of keys, touch the soft rubber of Charlotte's pacifier. My fingers grip something encased in thin tissues, as if she's saved a half-eaten pear. Through the sheer paper, I can make out a smear of red. I dip my other arm into the bag and open the bundle.

A cold chill comes over me. Buried in my nanny's purse, beside her ChapStick and my daughter's pacifier, is a dead bird. A cardinal. The plumage is a red as vibrant as lacquered nail polish, as a spill of fresh blood. I almost expect it to breathe, to shudder to life. I turn it over in the tissue, like a ruby in the cup of my palms. On the other side, there is a crack through its burnt orange beak. The eye is open, glossy as a black button. A single ant crawls through the feathers of its throat.

I convulse with disgust, shove it back to the bottom of the bag. I think I hear footsteps on the stairs behind me, and I hastily close the purse. When I stand, there is no one, just the thudding of my pulse in my temples.

I go to wash my hands, catch the hour on my silver wristwatch. It's 5 P.M., way past the time Charlotte usually wakes from her nap. I head to the nursery.

Órlaith. Something is very, very strange about this woman.

52

Mikayla

I descend the staircase, trying to forget the shock in Sophie's eyes.

I hate when I lose control.

It's like when you play a video game and trip a movie cutscene. One minute you're moving your character forward, jumping, picking things up, making choices—and the next, you're simply watching the most important moments happen.

From the stairs, I can see out over the whole party, over the long open living room and through the back glass to the patio and, below, the pool and the yard, an ever-replenishing line for drinks at the bar, Gabby and Emma and Ava lounging in their bikinis, Mr. Matthews entertaining a group of women. I reach the bottom step and start to make my way into the crowd, until I spot Mason, coming in through the open sliding glass doors. I take a quick right and head for the kitchen, which I so hope is empty, and it is. I breathe a sigh of relief. But then I hear him.

"Hey, Mikayla, wait up." Mason half-jogs the last few feet to meet me. "What're you up to?"

I shrug. "Just need a break or something."

"I feel ya. This party is kind of crazy. Everyone is drinking a shit ton, like, in front of the parents, but it's like the parents are all too drunk to notice." His swim trunks are damp. He's thrown on a white T-shirt.

"Yeah." I try not to look at the mark on his neck.

"You're the only sane one," he says, mouth spreading into that incandescent grin of his. And it's suddenly exactly like that homecoming pasture party, the two of us alone, tucked just out of sight—*There's always some girl crying about something. It's, like, the unwritten rule of parties,* he said then, the implication that I was different, special, that I *wasn't like other girls.*

I slip my hands into the pockets of my dress, so he won't see them shaking.

He's looking at my lips, the way he did in the bed of that stranger's pickup a year and a half ago. What if we could rewind? Go back to that night? Could we do it differently? Or are the movie cutscenes already written and recorded, and in between, we just pretend we have choices?

"I'm kind of busy right now," I blurt out, because I just can't do this anymore. "I'll see you out there."

"Oh." For a minute, he looks taken aback, like it's the first time in his whole life that someone didn't make room for Mason Fuller. "Yeah," he says, casual, a shrug of his shoulder. "Cool, see ya."

I turn and walk through the kitchen toward the farthest island. I don't check behind me, but I can feel that he's left the room. I look to the window, to that big wall of glass, so clean it almost isn't there at all. I trace the fall, down the cliffside, the cedars and the buzzards hovering and a car or two passing along FM 1863 below. I look up too, catch the underside of the balcony.

I don't think of Sophie's face, stunned.

I don't even hear him when he enters the kitchen, not until he's right behind me, until he says, "Excuse me, darling," his voice cool as rainwater. I turn my head and see that it's Mr. Barker. He puts his hand to the small of my back as he slides past.

"That your boyfriend?" He pulls open a drawer beside the sink, shuffles items around, pulls open the next drawer.

"What?"

He tips his head toward where Mason just left, where he must have passed him.

"Oh. Um. No."

He finds what he's looking for, a lighter. He's close enough that I can smell him—cigar smoke and cologne, real cologne, not Axe body spray like the boys at school wear, and something else . . . whiskey? He drums his fingers on the marble. I don't think he recognizes me. My hair, my makeup, this dress. But he's always over here, always popping by the house. He was here that night, the last night Sophie and I stayed over.

"I bet you have the boys lined up."

My mouth is dry, and I don't know what to say, but I can feel my cheeks getting pink, can feel that he's watching, that he's smiling at the effect his words have on me.

"Curtis." The voice is sharp enough to make us both turn. Mr. Matthews stands at the open entrance.

"Found it," Curtis says, waving the lighter as he strides across the kitchen. He walks past Mr. Matthews, back out and into the party.

But Mr. Matthews lingers a moment, looks me in the eyes. "You all right?"

I nod. A lie.

He turns to go, but then seems to think of something, turns back. "You haven't seen Sophie, have you?"

I swallow. I shake my head.

Another lie.

Then we hear it, a bloodcurdling scream.

53

Kim

I'm at the bar, but I don't remember how I got here. I'm hanging on to the shoulder of another woman, or maybe she's hanging on to me, as we laugh and overshare.

"I got Botox," she says. "Is it obvious?"

I squint at her face, swipe a finger across this stranger's forehead. She is as hot as a fever. My heavy hair sticks to the back of my neck. Sweat slips down my cleavage.

"My husband hates it." She scrunches her face. Her forehead miraculously doesn't move. I wiggle my own brows, thinking about the way the skin there folds up like blinds. "He says I don't need it, that I'm beautiful the way I am, that I should just age gracefully."

"Screw your husband," I say, and we crumple into a fit of giggles, our heads close, our breath mixed, the kind of intimacy that only comes with alcohol. "Men say things like that, then leave you for a twenty-something. That's what mine did."

The story sounds better this way.

"Screw him too," my new bestie says. "Who needs men?"

"Exactly."

"Two margaritas," the bartender says, setting our drinks on the counter. He's a young guy, tall and skinny with facial hair that's barely more than stubble. He's not my type, but he is a certain kind of cute.

I lean over the bar, rest my breasts on the surface. "Where's that tip jar, sweetheart?" I ask, my voice throaty and seductive. I give him a wink as I slide a few bills into the glass he indicates. He smiles politely.

Through my drooping eyelids, the backyard is all swirling Monet brushstrokes—blue sky and blue pool, a rainbow of cocktail dresses and cocktail glasses, grass unnaturally green for Texas—and movement, and everything is music, the bass from the speakers, and also the bodies, the buzzing of my skin, the conversation and the laughter.

My new friend is showing me her watch, a gift from her husband. "Fifteen years of marriage, and he still doesn't know I hate yellow gold."

It's after 5 P.M. and the sun bakes everything, reflects off the pool and every bright veneer.

When I dream of returning to this house, the great iron gates are locked to me. I find myself within its walls anyway. Being drunk is like that. You time-travel, wake up standing in a room you don't remember walking into.

I spot Ted on the other side of the pool, near the carriage house. He's on the phone, just ending a call, it seems.

"Be right back," I tell my drinking buddy, without any such intention. I'm already unsure what she looks like.

Making my way toward Ted, I focus on the patio tiles, careful not to catch my toe on an uneven edge. I focus on putting one foot in front of the other, on navigating around the pool and between the tables and chairs and big sun umbrellas.

"Hey," I say, and I cup the palm of my free hand at the nape of his neck, slide my long fingernails up to caress the back of his mostly bald head. I am leaning full into him, my mouth a Cheshire grin.

He laughs. "You having a good time?"

I take a long sip of my margarita. "Oh, I can show you a good time." I pull his head down, press myself up to kiss him, my tongue prying his lips open, exploring. My eyes are closed. He smells of sweat and Texas sun, and I'm thinking of the look of pure desire in his eyes hours before, the way he seemed hungry for me, and I want so much to be desired, to be consumed and enjoyed. It's been too long.

He pulls away.

"Whoa, Kim," he says. "I'm married."

"I won't tell," I purr, slide my body against his.

He rubs my arm. "Maybe you've had enough to drink, huh? Why don't I get you a water." There is a touch of laughter to his words.

Oh, hell no. Not when every single person here has drunk just as much as me. Not when he has been the one feeding me drinks. And what the hell were all those little touches? Those long, lingering looks?

I look up at him. I let the heat of my shame burn into something cleaner. I pull his head down for one more kiss, sink my teeth into his bottom lip.

He shoves me away. "What the fuck?" He wipes his mouth, checks his fingers for blood.

Regret fills my body like sand.

"You're fucking crazy," Ted says.

I stand unsteady on the spot. I feel eyes on me. Hear whispered words.

The house breathes over us, the wind sighing clouds across its windowed wall.

How did I get here?

I'm jolted from my humiliation by a stomach-turning scream, raw and filled with fear. It's long and painful, like a wounded animal. But it's not an animal. It's coming from inside the house. They turn—all the partygoers—they turn as one.

The screaming doesn't stop.

54

Dani

I don't hear anything behind the nursery room door. Nothing at all. She should have been up thirty minutes ago.

I turn the knob slowly, push the door open. The light from the hallway falls into the room, illuminates the crib in the corner. I can see the outline of Charlotte's unmoving form.

I hate to wake a sleeping baby, but she's already overshot her nap by so long. If I let her sleep any longer, bedtime will be a nightmare. I cross the room to the balcony, the long sliding glass door. I pull back the heavy blackout curtain. I try never to look at the balcony, though it's hard, so many rooms of this house lead out here, and it hangs over the pool, the underside of it visible from the floor-to-ceiling windows downstairs, the living room, the dining room, the kitchen. It's inescapable. I check the lock, once, twice. Pull the door to be sure. Twist the lock one more time.

I haven't been on the balcony again since that night. I can't. It makes my palms sweat, my heart race. The flash of a memory—the memory of leaning over that glass railing, dangerously far, wind pulling my hair, the taste of bile in my mouth. I shake my head to clear it like an Etch A Sketch.

I pull the curtain fully open to let the late afternoon light stream into the room. I turn. "Hello, sleepyhead," I say in a soft voice.

Charlotte stays motionless. I tilt my head. "Time to get up." But there is something odd about the way she's lying. So still. I'm across the room. Her crib is in the dimly lit corner, and I'm looking at her through the bars.

I take a few steps forward. And my heart picks up speed. I close the distance quickly. I reach down to pick up Charlotte, but it isn't her at all. It's Polly the Dolly, the yarn doll that Órlaith gave her earlier today, translucent-colored eyes, drooping and uneven, pointed blankly toward the ceiling.

I dumbly spin my eyes around the room. My thoughts are bumper cars, careening into one another at reckless speed. The note. *Crazy bitch.* Red lipstick on the mirror. Kim's spit of words in the cellar. *What would you do if someone tried to take your daughter?* MaryBeth in my pantry. And Órlaith. *I'm not sure how much longer I'll need the help,* I told her today. And, for a moment, the flash of her eyes.

Where is Charlotte? Where is my daughter?

55

Órlaith

The scream rips through the party like a knife. We all turn to the spiral staircase. Dani flies down, high-heeled feet a blur, so fast I fear she might miss a step, might come tumbling down before our eyes.

"She's gone!" she is screaming. Again and again. "She's gone!"

"What are you talking about, darling?" It's Gemma Barker, stepping out of the crowd, face stricken, abandoning her glass of white wine on a passing shelf as she makes her way to the stairs.

"Charlotte," Dani says, her face pure terror, her voice like scrapes of wind. She has reached the bottom of the stairs, her arms out, clawing at Gemma for balance. She is like an animal, hungry and wild.

"Mrs. Matthews," I say, but she can't hear me from across the room. No one hears me, it seems. Not even those within an arm's reach pay me any mind.

The partygoers are clamoring to see, to understand, heads bobbing up to look over one another, heads dipped low to whisper frantic questions.

"Sweetheart," Gemma soothes again. "What are you talking about?"

"Charlotte is gone." She is nearly sobbing now. "Call 911." Then again to the entire room, "Someone call 911."

A few cell phone screens light around the room.

Gemma tries again, two hands holding Dani steady, voice as warm as hot chocolate. "What happened?"

"Charlotte's crib is empty. Someone took my baby. Why the hell are you all just standing around?"

Then Mr. Matthews appears from the kitchen. He quickly takes in the whole of the situation—the frozen party guests, the silenced conversations, his panicked young wife at the bottom of the stairs.

"Oh, honey, honey." Gemma is rubbing her hands up and down Dani's shoulders now. "She's okay. She's all right. Órlaith has her."

Gemma turns in my direction then, searching through the party for me. Everyone seems to turn their gaze along with her, all eyes on me, the crowd parting. I am back near the fireplace, bouncing Charlotte on a hip.

Dani spots me as well, but it doesn't have the calming effect Gemma was after. Her eyes are savage. "You," she says, like a curse. She starts toward me, shouldering her way through her friends and guests. "Give her to me," she says, and as soon as she is close enough, she snatches for the baby.

"Isn't that the nanny?" I hear someone say.

"I'm so sorry, Mrs. Matthews," I say. "She woke from her nap maybe fifteen minutes ago. I never intended to give you a scare. I feel terrible, sure. I'm so sorry."

"Give her to me," Dani repeats, but her energy is all wrong, like, wound tight as a bedspring, her fingers pinching Charlotte's upper arms as she rips her away from me. She wants to clutch her child to her chest, wants to nuzzle Charlotte's head into the hollow of her own neck, because this will put the world right again, this *here-ness* of her child, the physical reality of her. But Charlotte is having none of it. She is frightened by her mother's screams. Dani is a possessed thing, so unlike her usual gentle demeanor. And before she can turn the infant in her arms, Charlotte goes rigid in that way babies do, back arched and limbs straight, one tensed muscle, the back of her skull colliding with Dani's face, a painful crack ringing the air.

"Hey, hey." Mr. Matthews has pushed through the crowd as well. He grabs his wife by the shoulders. "Are you all right? Let me see."

He takes the baby from her arms, hands her back to me. Charlotte is an angry cat, but I sway her, I shh-shh-shh until she calms, curls back into me, body shuddering with dramatic, gulping breaths.

Mr. Matthews gently pulls away the hand Dani is using to cover her nose. Blood pours from her nostrils, onto her lips. She's leaning over so as not to make a mess of her dress, drops of red bursting onto white tile. Someone nearby gasps. Dani looks at the blood in her hand. "Oh, God," she says, and for a moment I fear she'll faint. Her eyes flick back to mine, all the fight drained from her. "I'm sorry," she says, barely more than a whisper. "Oh my God." Then, weakly, to the room in general: "I'm so sorry."

"Let's get you cleaned up," Mr. Matthews says, whisking her away to the half-bath.

56

Mikayla

Dani is acting like a total psycho. That's what everyone's thinking, gathered around, watching as she freaks out that the nanny has the baby. Like . . . isn't that what a nanny is supposed to do? The music has stopped. Everyone must have heard her screaming her head off. They are gathered at the open glass to see the commotion inside.

Sophie is on the other side of the room, just outside the open back door. We catch eyes and in that brief look, we have a whole conversation, before I remember how pissed I am at her.

You're the one who's delusional, I said up on the balcony, still sitting, still gripping the chair cushion, the words coming between clenched teeth, low enough that they might be stolen by the wind. But Sophie heard them. And so I hurled the next part with purpose. *Mason doesn't want you.*

Sophie opened her mouth like a goldfish, like she was going to say something, defend herself, but I wasn't finished. I stood up. The dizzying height of the balcony and the tilting sunlight and all my emotions electrifying my blood made me feel outside myself, an observer.

You stupid bitch.

Her mouth was still open, a look of shock on her face. We had never fought. Not really. Not like this, angry words and angry voices, and I wanted to shove her, my anger and my hurt like a fist balled tight around my heart. But I turned and walked away.

Now, Sophie is across the room, and her stepmom is having a meltdown, and we're sharing the exact same memory: *That night.* The last time we both slept over here.

It was late, really late, like two in the morning. Through the wall, I heard her screaming. I couldn't make out the words, but she sounded frantic, hysterical.

Sophie sat up in bed. I could just barely make out her shape in the dark, the moonlight shading the room blue, highlighting the features of Sophie's wide-eyed face as she looked at me. Dani's voice pierced straight through the wall. She was in the hallway, just outside our room now.

Is that Dani? Sophie said.

I think so, I said.

Are they fighting?

Sophie slid from her bed, padded softly over to the wall, pressed her ear to listen.

Maybe we should give them privacy, I said.

Sophie put a finger to her lips, then beckoned me over. So I went. I pressed my ear to the wall as well.

I know what I saw, Dani shrieked.

Then Mr. Matthews, much harder to hear, but it sounded like, *Let me help you.*

The sound of the baby crying.

Dani, farther down the hall, closer to their bedroom: *We're leaving. Now. We have to get out of this house.*

Don't, Mr. Matthews said.

Then something, a thump. A door swinging hard into a wall. A scuffle of noise.

Sophie opened the door then. The hallway was dark and empty. Their bedroom door open to an even blacker darkness. The baby wailing.

Dad? Sophie said, voice timid. For a moment, there was nothing. No response. Just the darkness and the baby howling and howling. I think we both held our breath. But after a moment, Mr. Matthews appeared from the blackness. He closed the bedroom door behind him.

Dad? Sophie said again.

Are you girls awake? he asked.

Um . . . Sophie said. *What the heck? Is Dani okay?*

She'll be fine. She's just st—st—. He let out a frustrated breath. *She's dealing with a lot with the baby. Just, get some sleep. It'll be fine.*

But in the morning, we didn't see Dani, and Mr. Matthews didn't give us any more explanation.

———

Now, Mr. Matthews sweeps Dani away to the bathroom and closes them both inside.

57

Kim

I'm at the bar, sipping water slowly, listening to the conversations around me, listening to people teeter on that familiar razor's edge: well-intentioned concern—*Poor Dani, I hope she's all right. I remember what a mess I was when I first had kids . . . the hormones, no sleep at all. That's a form of torture, you know*—and pure, indulgent gossip—*I heard it's a little more than your average baby blues. That's why they have a nanny, you know?*

Ethan doesn't trust her to be alone with the baby.

This town loves its gossip, loves its stories. It won't be long until the conversation turns to the house, to *The Mother*, how she's already unraveling another life.

Not surprisingly, I'm feeling a self-satisfied thrill at this turn of events, the fact that Dani is the one causing a scene and not me, the fact that Ethan's life isn't quite as perfect as it would appear.

And, if there really is something wrong with Dani, well, then, maybe they'll just have to cancel their little trip to Europe.

And, yet, a niggling, nagging thought, like a mosquito on the brain, as I watched Dani, her eyes wild, the shifting looks and whispered words in the room, Ethan's quick action. *You know this,* says the thought, *you've been here before.* I look to the house. It looms foreboding.

I'm close enough to hear a group of women talking around a patio table, Gwyneth Porter leading the charge, undermining Dani now, instead of me. Just beneath the surface of my selfishness, defiance boils. I'm not like these people. I don't like these people. And I can't help but feel for Dani.

"Oh trust me," Gwyneth says, "it's taken a toll on Ethan. I know. I'm the one who sees him every day. That poor man. Hasn't he had to deal with enough crazy?"

She's not looking in my direction, but I'd be willing to bet she knows I'm within earshot. If I confront her now, it will be all, *Did I say the wrong thing back there? Are you all right? Do you want me to get you an Uber home?*

Once, years ago, I stopped by the house in the middle of a workday, swinging by between surgeries. I'd forgotten Sophie's dance costume, left it hanging in the laundry room. And I ran into Gwyneth, alone in my kitchen.

Hey, hon, just picking up a file for Ethan, she said. She had the file sitting on the kitchen counter as proof.

Later that night, when I brought it up to Ethan, he confirmed it.

I don't like thinking about her in the house when we're not here. I think she was snooping.

Ethan laughed, put an arm around me. *So what if she was?* he said. *You're telling me you've never peeked into someone's medicine cabinet?*

Back then, Gwyneth had her own key to the house. I wonder if she still does.

58

Dani

I'm back in this bathroom, wiping the blood from my nose with my hands, watching the pink-tinted water circle the drain. Ethan hands me a tissue.

There's not as much blood now. It's already stopped flowing. I twist the tissue, stick it up my nostril to get the rest.

"Are you okay?" he asks.

I turn to him, wringing the tissue between my fingers, tearing it apart. "No," I say.

"Hey," he says softly. He reaches for my arm, but I turn.

I'm pacing the bathroom, where there isn't much room to pace. A step, turn, a step. There is so much packed just under my breastbone, my insides a furnace. Ethan stands in front of the door. "They're here," I say in a near whisper.

"Who?"

"You know who," I snap. I take a breath in, exhale through pursed lips. "I'm not imagining things. I'm not—" *Crazy,* I want to say, but I can't make the word come out.

"Dani, Charlotte is fine. No one took her. Our nanny's job is to—"

"Our nanny had a dead bird in her fucking purse."

"What?" He says it with alarm, but it's for the wrong reasons. He isn't alarmed that Órlaith has a dead animal in her purse. He is alarmed that I am saying this. He is worried that I am losing my mind. It's my fault. I've kept him in the dark. I need to explain calmly, clearly. My thoughts overlap. My hands still shake with the fear of thinking Charlotte was stolen. From the embarrassment of screaming.

But, I *have* a reason.

"There was a message. Right here." I point to the mirror, which is sparkling clean, and why didn't I take a picture? Why doesn't my husband just believe me? Is that so much to ask?

"What are you talking about?"

"'Crazy bitch.'" My volume is ratcheting up. "That's what it said. In fucking lipstick. Someone in this house, in *our house,* wrote that about me." I jab my finger accusatorially toward the door.

"Shh," he says, glancing over his shoulder. "I'm listening."

I cover my face with my fingers, try to breathe. "The towel," I say, remembering, crouching down, fumbling with the childproof lock I installed on the cabinet door back when I was still pregnant—so prepared, so ready. I pull out the damp white hand towel, covered in red lipstick. I hold it out to him. He stares down at it.

"Let's go upstairs," he says. "We can talk about what you think happened."

"What I *think*?"

He takes the towel gently from my hands. His voice is very calm, very steady. "So, someone wrote on the mirror in lipstick?"

"Yes."

"With this lipstick?" He indicates the towel in his hands.

I nod again.

He levels his eyes with my own. "It's just that this shade"—he holds up the towel again, but doesn't break eye contact with me—"it looks a lot like the color you're wearing."

I turn to the mirror. He's right, of course. My lips are still stained with the exact same deep berry red.

59

Mikayla

He had to sedate her, Sophie told me later on the phone, a few days after the sleepover when we'd heard Dani freaking out in the hallway.

What? I sat up in bed. I could see my reflection in the vanity over my dresser, my hair plaited back in a frizzy French braid.

Dad. He had to sedate Dani that night. I think that's the thump we heard. He had to hold her down, inject her with some medication, like at a mental institution. She was seeing things. Straight hallucinations. She was going for the baby.

I felt my very essence slip out of me.

What do you mean? I asked. *Going for the baby?* I could still hear the sounds of Dani's screams from that night. I heard them in my dreams.

I don't know. Dad says she'll be fine. It's temporary, like something to do with the hormones or whatever. But, Mik, it's kind of freaky.

My mouth was dry. I didn't want to know the answer. But Sophie was expecting a reaction. *What did she see?* I forced it out, barely recognizing my own voice.

Dad says it wasn't real, but . . .

She paused. The line was so quiet for so long that I checked my screen, made sure the call was still going, that I hadn't hung up on her with my cheek or something. *Soph?*

Yeah.

What did she see?

When she finally answered, a cold zipper ran up the length of my spine.

It was The Mother, Sophie said. The Mother *wanted Charlotte.*

60

Dani

The door clicks closed, and my husband and I are alone in our dim bedroom. Late afternoon sun through the floor-to-ceiling window paints the room in watercolored light.

"The lipstick on the mirror," I tell him. "It wasn't the first message."

A troubled frown forms between his eyebrows.

"A few days ago, I found a note on the front porch."

Ethan's face contorts between perplexed and concerned.

There's no use in explaining. I cross the room, go to the closet, past sweaters and dresses and purses, around the ottoman, to the farthest row of shoes. I kneel down and reach into the plain black pump tucked back on the bottom shelf. My fingertips brush paper, and I pull out the folded letter.

Ethan has followed me. I hand him the note. I study his face as he unfolds the paper. I watch his eyes trace the words—*You don't deserve your perfect life, you crazy bitch*—and I see it, before he has the time to compose himself, to logic his way to a reasonable explanation, I see the genuine shock on my husband's face. A ripple of thrill runs through me. *See? I was right.*

A muscle in his jaw flexes. He takes a breath through his nose. "What is this?"

"I told you."

He looks to me, as if searching my face. "But who?" He looks down to the note again, shakes his head. "This doesn't make sense."

I have that feeling again, my heart a trapped bird, fluttering with panic, but also eagerness. Because the secrets have been stripped away. I am vulnerable, but we are together. And maybe we can solve this.

"I don't know," I say. "I've been trying to figure it out. Órlaith has been lying to us."

"Órlaith?"

"She isn't who she says she is. Vera doesn't know her."

"I saw them talking today."

"No, I know." I want him to catch up. "But she didn't recommend Órlaith for the position. She didn't know her before we hired her. And then MaryBeth . . . I don't know. Something is just off."

"Who?"

I wave the question away. "She's this woman who follows me."

"She's been following you?" His eyes are wide.

"Online," I explain.

"Dani." He reaches for my shoulder, an attempt to try and settle me down.

But I've started pacing in front of him again, my mind flipping through memories from the day, the party.

"Dani, just stop it." The words are quick and sharp, carrying a frustration I never hear in his voice.

I turn to him. He closes his eyes. He breathes. I cross my arms over my chest, instinctively closing back in. He opens his eyes again, and when he speaks, his voice is as level as always. "Why didn't you tell me about this?" He holds up the note.

I open my mouth, but . . . I lift my shoulders in a kind of shrug, shake my head.

"You promised," he says. And in his eyes, there isn't frustration or anger. There's hurt.

"I just—you were so excited about the party. I was just going to wait—"

"That doesn't make sense," he says. "You find a note like this, and you . . . hide it in the closet?"

"I told you." My throat is clogged with tears, but I'm not sure what kind of tears they are. "Months ago. I told you someone was watching me. Someone was at the window. Inside the house. I told you that things were moved, missing."

"It wasn't real. Dani, you have to know that. You have to remember that." The last sentence lifts like a question. He puts a hand to his head, massages his fingers over his forehead. "I need to talk to Curtis." He refolds the note, slides it into his pocket.

"Don't tell Curtis."

But he's talking more to himself than to me now, taking the door that leads into the connecting bathroom. "Maybe we pulled back on the meds too quickly?" I follow him as he crosses to my vanity, pulls open a drawer. "You've been taking these, haven't you?"

I nod, but he isn't looking at me.

He's unscrewing the caps, tipping the contents into his palm so he can count the pills. He takes one, hands it to me. "Take one of these. I, um, I have to go back to the party. Sophie hasn't even blown out her candles yet . . ." I can see the calculations behind his eyes as I take the pill from his hand. "I'll tell everyone you aren't feeling well. You just lie down. I'll try to wrap things up . . . Will you be okay up here?"

I see his eyes scanning the room. A razor in a cup beside the sink. His belt draped over a chair. The door to the balcony. An ordinary room contains unlimited dangers. I know that as a mother. Ethan knows that as a psychiatrist. I remember him telling me about the patients in the state psych ward where he used to intern, the things they took from them—headphones, underwire bras, the drawstrings from hoodies and sweatpants. I know he is thinking also of his first fiancée. The girl he couldn't save.

"No," I say, "don't tell them that. I'll be fine. I am fine. You're right. There's a whole party downstairs. Sophie needs to have her party. And I want to see the cake cut. I worked hard on it." I laugh an awkward breath. "We can handle this tomorrow." I smile. "Give me a minute, and I'll be right behind you." I look at the small white pill in my palm before tossing it in my mouth. I turn to the mirror, run fingers under my eyes, brush my hair over my shoulders and smooth the curls with my palms.

I meet his eyes in the reflection, see the way he is watching me with such concern. He stands behind me, puts his hands on my shoulders. He leans down, closes his eyes, and inhales. "It'll be okay," he says, and I'm not sure which of us he is trying harder to convince.

When he leaves, when I hear the door click shut behind him, I reach a finger into my mouth, swipe the pill from beneath my tongue, and wash it down the sink.

61

Órlaith

I round the top of the stairs just in time to see Mr. Matthews leaving the bedroom. I hold Charlotte solidly on my hip, and with my free hand, I grip the stair rail, taking the final steps carefully. I feel a cool presence pass through me that sends a shudder down my spine.

―――――――

In all my searchings, I came across an archived article, "Historic Vogel's Peak House of Local Lore Finds New Owners."

I found it in the *Front Porch News*, a small paper in Bulverde. Apparently, they call this area the "front porch" of the Hill Country. The article, over a decade old, told of a young couple who had taken a risk and bought a dilapidated Victorian mansion, were undertaking the renovations themselves. It included a photograph of Ethan and Kimberly Matthews, smiles bright and eyes hope-filled, before their new home—a great limestone castle, reclaimed by wilderness, creeping vines, and invading tree branches.

Built by German immigrants, Wilhelm and Ada Vogel, the house had towered vacant over the small Texas town for well over a hundred years by then. As the vines and cobwebs spread through it, so did its legend through Bulverde. The legend of young Ada, poor pet, only twenty-four years old when she befell a "sad accident while recovering from a bout of nervous depression." According to the 1896 obituary reproduced within the article, she'd never fully recovered from the illness that claimed her infant daughter just ten months previous. Mr. Vogel had moved away, had long since gone to his own grave, but Ada had seemingly done neither, at least if the reports were to be believed.

Locals shared tales of ghostly sightings, silvery hair between branches, and frightening lamentations in the night.

When asked about the potential haunting, Kimberly Matthews was quoted, "No, we aren't worried." She was described as laughing. "I'm more afraid of the work. We have big plans for this house." A photograph showed Kimberly in overalls and work boots, curly hair tied up, atop a ladder, grinning. Around her, the walls were torn down to beams, the floor ripped up, the guts of the home exposed.

I marveled, when I first read the article, that someone would be so bold. It demands quite the ego to take a sledgehammer to a thin place. Even more so to slice it in two, to welcome, arms open, whatever waits inside.

———

Mr. Matthews hasn't realized I'm here, and I watch him pause outside the door, still holding the knob, taking a breath, no doubt affixing the mask he'll need to face his party guests.

He turns. "Oh, Órlaith."

"How is she? I feel dreadful. This was my fault."

"No. No, of course not. Don't worry. It was just a misunderstanding . . . This is a stressful day . . ."

I look over his shoulder toward the door, lift Charlotte higher on my hip, my fingers clutching her shoulder, instinctively, as though we might need, at any moment, to run. "Mrs. Matthews didn't say anything?" I ask, aware of the thin ice I am stepping out on. I can almost hear it, the faint cracking beneath us, the whole of the world crumbling to pieces. I am thinking of the look in her eyes when she spotted me across the living room. *You,* she said, an accusation.

"About what?" he asks.

"About sacking me. She was just so angry. And earlier this morning, she mentioned . . ." I trail off, let him wait, and when he raises an eyebrow, I continue. "Well, but, sure now, didn't she mention that you might not be needing a nanny much longer?"

"No." He dismisses the idea with a shake of his head. "No, please don't worry about anything. My wife . . . well, Dani . . . she's just . . . she isn't well. I think you know that."

"Believe me, Mr. Matthews." I look him straight in the eyes. "I understand better than most a mother's love—it's a feral thing, sure."

"Hmm," is all he says. One side of his mouth lifts in a smile that doesn't reach his eyes. He nods. He touches a hand to his daughter's cheek, tickles fingers at the crease of her neck, making her fold away from him with belly-deep giggles. I wrap both hands around her and sway, feel the rumble of her laughter against my chest.

"No," Mr. Matthews says again softly. "No, Órlaith, I think it's safe to say you'll be in our lives for a long, long time."

Which, of course, is exactly what I was aiming at.

62

Kim

I'm still at the bar when I hear Gwyneth interrupt her friend mid-sentence.

"Sorry," she says, "excuse me."

I spin on my barstool, drink in hand, to watch Gwyneth zip up one of the outdoor staircases to the upper patio and toward—oh, of course. Ethan is coming back outside, and there is loyal Gwyneth, faithful as a labradoodle, only hoping he finally needs her. It appears that he doesn't, though. He claps her on the shoulder like you'd clap an old buddy, then shouts something across the patio, and I see Curtis turn to him.

"Can you believe this bitch?" I say, though it comes out slurrier than I'd like, to the woman on the barstool next to me. We were talking a moment ago, commiserating about shitty divorces and shitty ex-husbands. *Sometimes I regret it,* she told me, swirling white wine around her glass. *Don't you?*

The divorce? Hell no. But for a moment, I had to imagine life without the whole aching mess of loss, had to imagine that this was my house again, my party. That my daughter wasn't going to Europe without me. That everyone I loved didn't pity me.

She laughed. *Just sometimes I think, I don't know, about when the boys were toddlers, and John would dance with them around the kitchen island to the Beach Boys. And I think, it wasn't so bad, you know? But then.* She shook her head, looked into her wine. *I was so unhappy for so long.*

Part of me knew exactly what she meant. The other part of me was incredibly jealous of her ability to nurse a drink. She chatted and swirled the wine around the glass. She adjusted her grip and ran a finger along the rim, but never seemed to take a sip. How was that possible? How did people do that?

"What was that?" she asks me now, turning from the conversation she's having with the woman on her other side.

I point toward Gwyneth, who is already making her way back down the stairs. One of my eyes winks closed involuntarily to stop the double vision. "This bitch," I repeat.

She breathes a laugh. I can feel her exchange looks with her friend.

"Pathetic, you know?" I say. "Really, I feel sorry for her. Thinks he's so fucking perfect. *You* get it. Just like your, what's his name, John? With his Beach Boys? Give me a break, right?"

"We're going inside to get some food," she says. "Want me to bring you anything?"

I grab my drink, wave her off as I slide myself down from the barstool. With my free hand I twist my dress back into place as I walk, tugging at the Spanx folding around my waist. *No rolling or bunching, my ass.* I should keep my mouth shut. I can take a kick when I'm down as good as anyone, but seeing Gwyneth do it to Dani, I don't know. I just can't help myself.

I meet up with her just as she's reaching the bottom step.

"Heeey, hon," I say, drawing out each word.

"Kim." Her laugh is a little wary. "You havin' fun?" Her eyes flick to the glass in my hand.

"Gwyneth," I say. Then again, because it's such a decadent name, like her mom thought maybe she'd be a princess or something. "Gwyneth. How long have we known each other? Why don't we hang out."

She laughs again. She shakes her head. "You're right. We should get lunch sometime."

"Exactly." The wind has blown a cloud in front of the sun, and for now, we are in the momentary relief of shadow. "We should be swapping war stories. I mean, you? You really got the shit end of the stick, huh? You were supposed to be next in line."

Gwyneth smiles, her eyes darting around the party behind me. Her features are sharp. The smile creases the skin around her mouth and eyes. "I don't know what—"

"Do you still have a key? Still come over anytime you want, pretend like all this is yours?" I watch a flicker of the muscles in her forehead. "That must be tough. Kind of like playing with Barbie's Dreamhouse and all the accessories, but none of the toys are yours. You're a real-life Midge with no Ken."

Her eyes spark with anger. Her mouth opens.

I put a hand on her arm. "I sympathize with you, Gwyneth. They aren't mine anymore either."

Her voice is high and sharp as she starts, "I don't—I just—I don't know how many drinks you've had or what the hell you think—"

But I'm not really listening. Because behind Gwyneth, I notice the teens. One of the boys—the class clown; I'm pretty sure his name starts with a "T"—is standing over Sophie, talking to her. She's looking at him through sunglasses. She nods. He reaches into the pocket of his swim trunks, pulls out something small enough to fit inside a closed fist, hands it to her.

"Sorry, honey," I say to Gwyneth, who's still going off on whatever the hell she was talking about. "Let's get that lunch sometime."

"Are you kidding me?" I hear her say, voice tremulous, as I walk away.

I am thinking clearly enough to put my drink down on a passing patio table so that I'm empty-handed when I reach the teens. I can't have them judging me while I lecture them.

"Sophie," I say.

All their faces turn to me, and I look at them, one by one. Trevor—*that's* his name—glances momentarily at a conspicuous pile of beach towels. You don't have to be Poirot to guess what's hiding beneath them.

"Hi, Miss Kim," Gabby says sweetly, her smile gleaming.

"Hi, sweetheart," I say, then, "Sophie, can I talk to you?"

Sophie raises her eyebrows at her friends but swings her legs over the side of the lounge chair and follows me out of earshot of the others. I walk purposefully, shoulders pulled back. When I turn to my daughter, I make sure both eyes are wide open. I speak slowly and clearly, hoping it comes across as stern.

"What did that boy hand you?"

She pulls a face, a bit over-the-top, to show she has no idea what I'm talking about. "Who?"

"Trevor . . ."

"Tyler, Mom." Like it should be totally obvious.

"Okay. Tyler."

"What about him?" Her arms are crossed over her chest, her face unreadable behind her shades.

"Sunglasses," I say.

"Excuse me?"

"Sunglasses," I repeat.

She lifts her glasses onto her head. She's already rolling her eyes. I search her face. I can still see all of her toddler features. Where did the time go? "Sweetheart, I just want to be sure you're making good choices."

"Jesus, Mom, am I supposed to take this conversation seriously? Really? Coming from you?"

A current of anger jolts through me because, damnit, I'm still her mother. "I saw Tyler hand you something. What was it?"

She scoffs that annoyed-teenager scoff. "I don't know. Gum?"

I tilt my head at her, because she isn't chewing gum.

"I don't know what you're trying to accuse me of, but if you are asking if I'm doing drugs or something, just don't. Because I promise you I would never be *that* stupid." She nearly spits the words at me, like they taste vile in her mouth. Her eyes drill straight to the core of me. I have no response, and she doesn't wait for one anyway, as she brushes past me and back to her friends.

I don't turn to watch her, but I can hear the teens laughing. All around me, people are talking.

Addict.

That's what they think of me. These people who used to be my friends—sure, who cares? But also my daughter, my brother, my own parents. I am reduced to a single day, a single moment, and there's nothing I can do to change it.

———

We were supposed to go shopping at La Cantera, an upscale outdoor mall near Six Flags—Gemma, Sophie, and I. Gemma needed a swimsuit cover-up, I was on the lookout for bright sandals, Sophie was twelve and really into Pokémon GO. A trip to La Cantera was something we did often, a way to waste a nice-weather Saturday. Pedicures at the resort spa, hit up the kiosk that sold to-go cucumber margaritas so Gemma and I could "sip and shop," lunch at the Sweet Paris Crêperie.

That was the plan. I had texted Gemma the night before to confirm: *We still on for tomorrow?*

She had responded quickly with: *Pick y'all up at 10!*

I had a lot on my mind. I remember kissing Sophie good night, setting an alarm, plugging my phone in. I remember bringing up a bottle of wine, sitting on my big chair out on the balcony with a throw blanket and a worn copy of *Wuthering Heights*—I reread it every few years because it's a different book every time. Some stories are like that. They live and breathe. I remember dozing off to Heathcliff's appeal to be haunted—*Be with me always—take any form—drive me mad!*

I closed the book. I stood and stretched and let the wind cool the back of my neck. I told myself to go to bed.

The rest comes in flashes, like a dream you can't quite remember: Late-morning light flooding the bedroom. Gemma's hands on my shoulders. *Kim? Oh, God, Kim!* The taste of vomit. Dried clumps of it on my cheek, in my hair, on my bedsheets. The gut-wrenching sound of Sophie's *Mommy?!* People in the room. Too many people. The realization that my robe was open, my left breast flopping out to expose stretch-marked skin. The averted eyes of the young paramedic with his cleft chin and his chocolate brown hair. The blue and red lights of the ambulance spinning against the gingerbread trim of the house. Gemma, watching from the porch, holding Sophie koala-style, as though she were a much younger child.

Then the hospital. Ethan's hand warm on mine. Sheets stiff and scratchy. The bright whiteness like forks to my eyes. The doctor's curt explanation, his words an enigma.

It wasn't until later that they untangled themselves, that they became real, that their meaning sunk in.

Tramadol is a highly addictive opioid analgesic, a controlled substance. When I overdosed, Gemma called the ambulance. She brought the empty pill bottle to show the doctor. The pills were in my system, the prescription signed and filled by me, but the label was for a dog. I lost my veterinary license.

I lost everything.

Gemma still thinks I hate her for it.

Now I run a kennel out of my piece-of-shit house, advertise myself as a *Retired veterinarian with a passion for pets.*

———

To my left, the teens are hyena-whooping. To my right, Gwyneth furiously whispers in another woman's ear. All around me, chatter, chatter, chatter, the clinking of glasses, the tapping of high heels on the bluestone. I look to the upper patio, spot Ethan and Curtis and Gemma. Up to that seamless expanse of glass, the white glow of the house on display, the crown molding I cleaned and repaired with plaster and painted the color of an egg, the immense chandelier I chose, each glass globe shipped from Europe in a separate box. The house is a stage. This is a viewing.

Farther up, so my neck is kinked to look at it—the balcony, that smooth edge mirroring the sky. Except. I tilt my head. The sun breaks free from its cloud, turns the balcony to a slick slice of light. And there it is. A crack.

I can't help but grin.

63

Dani

How do you know if you're going crazy? You can't, right? That's the thing.

I couldn't have scrawled the message on the mirror. I couldn't have written the note.

Because I don't remember doing those things.

But how much can you trust a memory?

I'm still in the bathroom. My nose a few inches from the mirror, I study my reflection. There is a spot on my right cheekbone that appeared during pregnancy, like a birthmark, only it marked someone else's birth instead of my own.

I remember an open pantry door, a flicked light, a smell of perfume, a downturned photograph, a figure on the front lawn, a face at the window. I *remember* those things because they happened. Because they were real.

I open the drawer of my vanity, roll the pill bottles with a finger so I can read the labels.

I remember those early newborn days, even if the details of them are fuzzy, the edges of everything blurred with exhaustion, with the monotony of feedings and diaper changes, with the big brushstrokes of joy, of my baby, of indentations on chubby fingers and gas-bubble smiles and milk-drunk contentment and wide-open eyes that took in the whole world.

What I can't remember is the incident.

I go back to the closet. I push aside some of Ethan's suit jackets to find his leather briefcase. I'm not supposed to open this—patient files are confidential. But I'm not interested in those. I flip open the case, reach into the outer pocket, feel pens and a phone charger. I open the main flap, push aside paperwork, find a few loose paper clips at the bottom. I unzip the inner pocket and find a small zippered case. Inside there are capped hypodermic needles and a few vials of medication.

A Google search on my phone tells me that midazolam, a short-acting drug with rapid onset, is used intravenously to produce loss of consciousness and to relieve anxiety, as in seizures, acute agitation, and before surgical procedures. When midazolam is used before surgery, the patient will not remember some of the details about the procedure. They call it "useful amnesia."

Hazy details: Waking in the dark. The weight of the balcony door, its soundless glide. A figure crouched in shadow, like when you see the shape of a sweater slung over a chair in the dark, but your mind can't unpuzzle what you are looking at, can't sort the innocuous from the monster.

"Knock, knock," I hear someone say as the bedroom door opens.

I'm still hidden in the closet, thank God. My hands shake as I put the needles and the medication back, zip the pouch. I shove the briefcase under the armchair.

By the time I get to the closet door, Curtis is already halfway inside my bedroom.

"How you feeling, kiddo? Just came to check on you."

He has his glasses on, the same ones he wears during our sessions. The light reflects across the lenses so I can't see his eyes. But I can feel the weight of his judgment all the same.

He is the doctor now. I am his subject.

64

Órlaith

Charlotte and I are in the nursery once again, the party just the muffled sounds of conversation below, of thudding music outside. In here, we are snug as a bug. Charlotte is on her belly on the primary-colored rug in the center of the room, lifting her upper body with curious baby push-ups. I pull a basket of toys to the rug's edge, place a rubber giraffe just out of her reach. She is so close to crawling.

Charlotte's a bright child, but she gets frustrated easily. She zeroes in on the thing she wants, thrusts a pudgy arm out, falls a half an inch short, and starts to grunt. It's a short warning, sure. Soon, it'll be a wail. I squeak the toy, and her eyes go wide, a smile playing at her lips. Charlotte is the type of child who feels emotions fully—big tears and bigger smiles.

I wonder where she gets it, exactly—Mr. and Mrs. Matthews are both sort of reserved with their feelings, today notwithstanding. Does Charlotte have her grandmother's temperament? Did she inherit from an aunt or a great-great-grandfather the urge to speak her mind, to feel first and sort it later? Or is it just a Charlotte-ism, something she brought with her into the world?

When my daughter was an infant, there was the usual decoding of her features, her personality—she had my husband's nose, my own blue eyes, was the bulb of her grandfather when she concentrated, jaw set with determination, and my siblings liked to say her streak of feistiness came from our side.

The thing that knocked me dead sideways, though, was that she was this accumulation of us, yes, but she was also entirely herself.

It'll amaze you each time, my own mam said. I remember she was sitting in her rocker, finishing the embroidery on Polly the Dolly's eyelashes. She had made a yarn doll for each of her own seven children and all of her fifteen grandchildren. *Each one is someone brand-new.*

Maybe that's what I love so much about babies—their purity. I mean that word by its true definition. Not that they are sweet and kind and without sin—though, but sure, they are all those things too. What I mean is they are pure, as in pure gold, pure water, free of adulteration, free of anything that is not innate to themselves.

I think, perhaps, the main job of a parent is to simply preserve, to give our children a safe, loving place to be themselves, to grow more and more into themselves.

Charlotte's fingers brush the rubber giraffe. She stretches her body, her arm, her fingers, grasps a hoof and tugs the toy to her mouth, triumphant. I pull a soft blue bunny from the basket, place it a little farther out of reach. Charlotte sets her eyes on the rabbit. In one motion, she gets a knee beneath her and shoves. Then, just like that, she's off, scooting herself forward, crawling. A milestone.

I should scurry down the hall and fetch Mrs. Matthews, like.

But I don't. Instead, I watch in wonder. I savor the moment, because for now, it's all mine. For now, Charlotte is all mine.

There is no word for a mother who has lost her only child—nothing like *orphan* or *widow.*

It's no surprise that so many ghost stories are of failed mothers—the Irish *Banshee*, who some say is a woman died in childbirth; the Japanese *Ubume*, who, should you meet her on a dark road, will hand you her swaddled infant, the poor soul turning to a bundle of stone in your arms; the Mexican *La Llorona*, who drowned her own children and now lures living ones to the water's edge; this local ghost, the one they call *The Mother.*

We are all a sort of ghost, aren't we?

But I have been a ghost for decades now, and I think it may finally be time for finishing business left unfinished.

65

Mikayla

It was a Saturday near the end of the school year. Sophie was at cheer practice, and I had spent the morning collecting eggs from the coop, chain-breaking my goat, and taking care of lunch so Mom could vacuum the house. I was helping Kylie wash her hands when my cell rang, Sophie's name flashing on the screen. That should have been warning enough—we almost always text. But I was distracted, cleaning peanut butter off Kylie's forearm and wiping all the water from around the sink so Mom wouldn't have a total meltdown.

Mik! Her voice an excited whisper, a bit of an echo, like she was hidden in a closet or a car.

Where are you?

I'm on a date! A real one. He bought me lunch and everything.

What? With who?

Mason Fuller.

My heart dropped through my center. Time stopped, and it seemed like I was silent for way too long, but it was probably only a few seconds. Finally, I said, *I didn't know you liked him.*

Mik, she said with a laugh, like I was just so dumb. *It's Mason freakin' Fuller. Everyone likes him.* Then she squealed—a quiet squeal because she was hiding in the bathroom stall of Verde Bistro, and I had to play the rest of the conversation like it was the most exciting news I'd ever heard in my whole stupid life, and all the while this crazy panic was rising in my chest, causing tears to pool in my eyes.

Now I know the truth—during that conversation, Sophie knew that *I* liked him.

And every conversation after, the two of us beneath the covers of my bed, her telling me about the way he kissed her earlobe or his hand sliding up her top or the sweet thing he'd said. All that time, she knew.

———

My arm is looped through Gabby's. We're hanging on to each other, laughing, stumbling back to the group. Gabby found me at the bar, splashed something into my empty glass from a water bottle—flavored vodka, I think—and we took a shot together before ordering more mocktails and spiking them from the bottle as well.

The guys—Mason and Braydon and Tyler—are jumping from the rockwork now. Our moms used to yell at us if we ever climbed onto those rocks, pretending to be mermaids who lived under a waterfall. *You'll crack your head open,* Kim used to say, watching us from a lounge chair, her plastic wineglass in hand and a book lying open and face down on her lap. *Is that what you want?*

But the grown-ups haven't been paying attention for hours now. No one yells at the guys to stop. Braydon does a backflip off the top rock. I'm not even sure the pool is deep enough for that, but he comes up fine, shaking the water from his hair so it sprinkles onto the girls.

They've lined all the lounge chairs in a row—Emma and Ava and Sophie—the late sun slanting onto them like a spotlight. Sophie appears to be watching the guys, her sunglasses shielding her eyes, but I know she's seen me, and I know she'll be pissed that I'm all buddy-buddy with Gabby.

So I play it up big, just to twist the knife. I lean into Gabby. "Oh my God," I say, "you're hilarious," just as we reach the others, and together we collapse, giggling, onto the chair next to Emma, farthest from Sophie. Gabby's drink sloshes onto her bare foot.

"Where's mine?" Emma asks.

Gabby lifts a slim brown shoulder. "Oops," she says, then looks at me and laughs.

"She seems kind of high-maintenance," Ava is saying. We've stumbled in mid-conversation.

"No," Sophie says, "she's cool."

"Who are you talking about?" Gabby asks.

"Dani."

"Oh, yeah, that girl is . . ." Gabby twirls a *cuckoo* finger beside her temple.

"Sophie's stepmom? She's freakin' hot, man," Braydon chimes in from the rocks.

Tyler has swum to the edge. "They say that, you know? Like there's a crazy-hot scale. The hotter a chick is, the crazier she can be."

"You're an idiot, Tyler," Ava says.

"Yeah. I don't think that's how mental illness works," Sophie says.

"She's mentally ill?" Emma asks.

"What?" Sophie snaps. "No. I just meant, like, in general." She lifts her sunglasses to glare at Tyler. "That's offensive."

Tyler puts up two hands in surrender. He looks to Gabby. "Hey, where's my drink?"

"Get your own drinks."

Tyler's eyes flick to mine. He shrugs. He plugs his nose, dunks his head into the water, and kicks off the wall, swimming back to the other guys.

Gabby reaches down into one of the bags piled by the foot of the chairs, and pulls out something small, hidden in her closed palm. She and I are sitting on the same chair, her knees tilted toward me. There's a look in her eyes, mischievous, as always. Her lips curve in a grin, like a cat about to play with her food. She sidles up closer, so her bare thigh is pressed to me, so her breath is hot on my collarbone when she whispers, "Here," and opens her hand. "Take these."

I look down to see two orange and white capsules in her palm.

"What are they?"

"Just some of Tyler's Adderall. It's no big deal. Everyone else has already had some."

She waits. I scan Emma and Ava and Sophie, chilling behind their sunglasses. Tyler and Braydon diving from rocks too slippery into a pool too shallow. Mason doing backstroke laps, the hard cut muscles of his torso as he slices through the water.

Gabby shakes the pills in her hand.

"I don't know," I say. "I don't . . . I mean . . . I haven't . . ."

"Just to get you out of your own head."

Get me out of my own head?

She peeks over her shoulder, as if checking that no one can hear us. "By the way. Earlier, Tyler told me that he thinks you look really hot today."

I look at her, and she is so close to my face, her dark eyes hooded with the alcohol and, I guess, the pills. She tucks my hair back, her finger tracing the top of my ear. "I mean," she purrs, eyes flicking down and up my body, "he isn't wrong."

I watch Tyler do a cannonball from the rocks. I inhale sharply as I see his head miss the limestone by just inches.

Gabby watches my face as I watch Tyler come up for air. She leans back only slightly. "I just think maybe it would be good for you, you know? Getting out of your head, I mean."

It does sound nice. I've been trapped in an endless loop of memories. I wish things could be simple again.

"But whatever," she says. "Why don't you keep these. Decide later."

I realize she's reaching for my pocket, that she's going to slip the pills inside, and I panic. I grab her wrist too quick and too hard. "No." Her eyes flick to mine. "It's cool," I say. She opens her hand. I take the pills and toss them back, swallow them with a gulp of my drink, which burns on the way down.

"Nice." She presses her shoulder to mine, looks out on the water. "So. Do you like him?"

Gabby is always so touchy-feely. And Dani's dress feels tight and hot, especially with everyone else in swimsuits. I look to Tyler, who is kind of cute, even if he is a doofus sometimes, but I imagine kissing him, imagine him sticking his clumsy tongue in my mouth. I think one of those pills is stuck in my throat. There's a grown-up couple grinding on the dance floor. I can see Kim watching us, but pretending not to, sipping on yet another drink.

And Mr. Matthews has just come back outside. He is standing on the upper patio, scanning the backyard. He spots Sophie. He does this thumbs-up-thumbs-down motion that he's done since we were little, checking on us as we climbed the jungle gym amid a sea of kids at the Bulverde Community Park. Sophie rolls her eyes, but she sends him a thumbs-up in response. It's so weird, because every once in a while, Mr. Matthews is just a big dork like everyone's dad. And the whole swirling mess of it all makes me want to puke.

Gabby nudges me with her elbow, still wanting an answer.

"I have a boyfriend," I say, but I guess I say it loud enough for everyone to hear.

Ava lifts her sunglasses, leans forward. "What? Who?"

"Oh, um. He doesn't go to our school."

"Tell us everything," Emma says.

From the corner of my eye, I can see that Mason has stopped swimming his laps. I can see that he's shaking water from his ear.

Crap, crap, why did I say that I have a boyfriend? What is wrong with me?

"Yeah," Gabby says. She smiles, biting onto her bottom lip, eyes sliding over to Emma and Ava. "Tell us about this *boyfriend* who *doesn't go to our school.* I bet he's a total snack." She doesn't put air quotes around the words, but they hang there anyway—a slippery accusation. She doesn't believe me, of course. Why would she? A red heat scorches up the sides of my neck, flames my cheeks.

"I'm bored," Sophie announces, swinging her long legs over the side of the chair, standing up and stretching her arms over her head, putting her body on full display. The guys certainly take notice. "Let's play a game of chicken. Braydon, give me a boost?"

"Totally," Braydon says, swimming over to the edge, where Sophie has sat down, dipped her legs into the water.

"I wanna play," Emma says, hopping up too, claiming Mason.

Gabby makes a beeline for Tyler so that she isn't the odd woman out.

"Oh, boo," Ava says.

"Get the drinks," Emma laughs.

"Well, I'm up next," Ava says, a pout to her voice, hands on her hips, but the girls are already climbing onto the boys' shoulders, giggling and slipping. "Come on," she says to me. "Help me carry everything." She cuts through the dance floor to the bar, confident I'll follow her, which I do.

And—*poof!*—the attention is off me. Gabby has lost the scent of blood, at least for the moment.

Sophie did that on purpose. She did that for me.

———

That day last spring when Sophie called from the Verde Bistro bathroom, when my heart felt like someone had stomped on it with a boot, because not only was Mason off the market, he was off limits forever—you can't date your BFF's ex—Mom found me crying into my pillow. She sat on the edge of the bed, stroked my hair.

Of course, Dad had to be passing by my bedroom door at that exact moment.

What's wrong this time?

George, a reprimand in Mom's voice. Then a stage whisper: *I think it's a boy.*

Well, he's an idiot, Dad said. *Any boy who doesn't like you isn't worth a second thought. You got that?*

Then he left. And I know he meant well, but it was just, like, Jesus, he had literally no idea.

Mom tried too. *Oh, sweetheart, I know this feels so big right now, but I promise, when you grow up, you won't even remember this boy.*

Her words hollowed me.

Because this did feel so big right now, and right now was where I was, and there was no one in the whole world I could talk to who would understand, because Sophie was the person I talked to about everything.

Why don't we order pizza? my mom said, like that was enough. *Find a movie?* She tucked hair behind my ear. *I just want you to be happy, honey.*

So I forced myself to smile, told her that sounded great.

Then I went for a walk down to the park near the front of the neighborhood next to the bank of mailboxes. The playground was empty—it was so freakin' hot even though summer hadn't even started—and I was glad. I could sit on the swings alone, drag my tennis shoes through the sandy dirt.

That's what I was doing—blinking away tears and thinking about how it was definitely the worst day of my whole life so far.

Life can be like that sometimes. When you're busy looking at your own feet, the world is still turning.

And sometimes stars are aligning.

66

Dani

"Ethan didn't have to send you up here to check on me," I say with a laugh that I hope sounds breezy.

Curtis steps back, inviting me into the bedroom with him. His hands are full with two glasses. "Gemma would kill me if I came without bearing gifts." He offers me the flute of champagne. In his other hand is a crystal tumbler of whiskey.

It's as though the time line splits . . . or has already split. One life laid over another. One person over another.

Curtis: The friend. Nights after work around a fire pit on the outside patio of some downtown bar, Curtis and Ethan taking turns buying rounds, making sure the women are never left on empty, our faces flush from the fire and the drinks and the laughter.

And Curtis: The therapist. He knows me too deeply. Knows my darkest moments. *Intrusive thoughts. Completely normal,* he assured me. *For anyone, but especially a newly postpartum mother.* Even the worst ones, though? The time I brought Charlotte out onto the balcony and couldn't trust my own arms. The time I took Charlotte on her first walk, stroller wheels in the grassy gravel shoulder because there are no sidewalks, a neighbor passing in a white pickup—the sudden image of the stroller crushed by the truck's grille, my daughter's fragile body crumpled. I didn't *want* to push my child in front of a truck. The image simply appeared, unintentional and unwelcome, like a movie still, frozen on the screen of my mind.

Curtis is a professional. He has a poker face. He showed no shock or disgust.

But my thoughts *are* shocking and disgusting.

"Parties can be stressful," Curtis says. "Triggering."

I take a sip of the champagne. "I'm just embarrassed about making such a big scene. I want Sophie to have a good time."

He narrows his eyes. He has Paul Newman eyes, handsome squints, like he's looking into the sun. "Ethan said you had the feeling that someone was watching you. Do you think this is similar to the feeling you had as a child—that something was in the closet, someone was under the bed? Or, as an adult, the way you check a door you already know is locked? Or is this different? Do you think this is real?"

He leans onto the foot of the bed, crosses one leg over the other. I am looking at his spotless alligator skin boots with the pointed toes. I am aware that we are in the bedroom. It is dim. It feels intimate. He could have sat in one of the armchairs, but he chose the bed. He swirls the whiskey in the glass. The amber liquid spins around and around. Suddenly, it's like remembering something through an opaque window. I can't reach the memory, but the feeling associated with it returns just the same—a clenching of my gut, that female instinct that says, *You're in danger.*

"You told me once," Curtis says, "that you distrust happiness. You worry that if you are too happy, it means something bad is about to happen."

He's talking about the time I told him that my parents planned the perfect family weekend, watching the Longhorn Cattle Drive at the Fort Worth Stockyards, a trip to the toy store for a pink teddy bear as big as I was, who got his own seat at the movie theater, where Becca and I were each allowed to pick our own box of candy, and Mom not getting annoyed when I grabbed the hem of her lavender blouse with a chocolate-smeared palm, then IHOP—pancakes for dinner—and even ice cream on the way home. It was like my parents had been charmed, bewitched, had forgotten how to say *no,* and as I drifted off sleepily in the backseat, belly full and the teddy's soft ear on my cheek, I saw my father reach his hand from the driver's seat, grab my mother's, saw their fingers interlace, and everything felt safe as a bird's nest.

They had wanted to give us one last perfect family weekend before they told us about the divorce.

"Do you think," he asks, "maybe you worry that you don't deserve to be so happy? To have such a perfect life?"

I snap my head up at his words. Ethan must have shown him the note. He's implying that I wrote it myself. He is trying to guide me toward that revelation.

But I couldn't have. I would remember doing that. Wouldn't I?

That instinctual warning has turned into a siren, and Curtis is still churning that whiskey around and around. Why does it feel familiar? Why does it slosh uneasily in my stomach? Curtis was here the day of the incident. He stopped by to bring me a prescription that I hadn't yet decided on taking. Ethan poured him a drink, invited him to stay for dinner. *Please do. Don't worry about it. We made plenty.* He left after dessert. But he was here for part of that evening.

"The medication you gave me—can it affect my memories?"

He cocks his head, raises an eyebrow. "Why would you ask that?"

Before I can answer, my phone rings, making me jump. I cross to Ethan's dresser, where my black clutch sits. I pull out my cell and check the screen.

"It's my mom. I need to take this."

"Of course." He stands from the bed. He takes his glasses off, folds them into his jacket pocket. "I'll see you downstairs. Soon?"

I give him a polite nod and a smile. I turn away, but I listen for the click of the door closing behind him. I slide my finger across the screen, put the phone to my ear.

"Hey."

"Dani?" My mother's voice on the line makes me want to weep, want to curl up into her. "I talked with Becca earlier. She's worried sick. I just got off the phone with Ethan. What on earth—"

"Mama," I say, in a hot whisper. "Something's not right. Someone's here. In the house. Someone is—"

"Oh, Dani," and her voice is filled with so much sadness it stops me short. "I thought we were past this. I thought this was over. Becca was right. You sound just like you did before."

"But, Mama, you don't understand. Someone is—"

"It isn't real, baby."

I feel it all, cool as water, as ice in my veins.

"It isn't real," my mother says again. I'm a little girl, glowing star stickers on the ceiling and Mama stroking my hair. *It isn't real, baby girl. It was only a nightmare.* "No one is watching you," she says now. "No one is sending you messages. You're sick. You have to trust me."

I am frozen. Turned from the bedroom door, I can see my reflection in the mirror over my dresser, hunched, phone clutched to my ear, eyes wild and pupils wide. I am near the sliding glass door. There is the glass balcony railing, and beyond, I can see the shadow that the house casts across the ranches below.

As soon as the sun begins its descent each day, the shadow begins to slip down the cliffside. People in town talk about it, the way it stretches out like a ghostly hand, fingers reaching for the highway, spreading over the pastures.

At the precise moment when day wanes into early evening, the shadow transforms. It is like one of those Victorian silhouettes. Those shadow portraits. The house with its asymmetrical shape, its spiral tower, its sloping dormers. For that brief moment—blink and she's gone—the shadow becomes the portrait of a woman, her gown bustled, her hair gathered atop her head, leaning over a bassinet to check on her sleeping child. It is *The Mother*'s shadow. That's what the people of Bulverde say.

I can see her now.

"Dani?" my mother says. And when I don't respond right away, she repeats herself.

"Yeah," I say.

"You have to remember, sweetheart."

"Yeah," I say again, because I do remember. I think all along, *I remembered*. I just didn't want to.

67

Kim

"This house is unreal," I hear a woman behind me say. "I can just picture watching every sunset from right here."

I order another drink—a glass of cabernet, my one true love. The sky is dimming now. Light sweeps sideways, stretches shadows long. Soon the timer will activate the outdoor lights—carriage lanterns on the house, Edison lights woven overhead, the soft blue glow from underwater. I know because I chose every one of them. I used to love to sit out here with this view and this breeze, with a bottle of wine and a book. What could be better? What else could I have possibly wanted?

———

There were family photographs on the shelves of the den in the east wing that I moved whenever I dusted. One of the photos was of me as a little girl, around ten years old, atop a horse. My grandfather held the reins. We were both smiling, faces washed in sunlight. Every time I saw that picture, I felt so sad for that girl, like if I could only go back. If I could only warn her.

Somehow, she had been erased. When I looked in the mirror, she wasn't there anymore, and I didn't like the person who had replaced her. I woke up most mornings hungover, a sinking uncertainty in my gut. I checked my phone, skimmed through texts I'd sent and comments I'd posted online to make sure I hadn't said something the night before that I'd now regret. I walked on eggshells around Ethan until I was sure I didn't owe him an apology.

Then one day, I had lunch with one of my vet techs at a Mexican restaurant near the practice. A next-door apartment complex faced the patio where we sat, and as I ate chips and salsa, I caught sight of a woman on the balcony of her apartment, a small wrought-iron table, a cup of coffee, scrolling her phone.

I imagined myself there, transposed, and suddenly it was all I wanted, all I needed—to get away from this house. That's what had happened. The house with its tap-tap-tappings, its wind against glass, its mazelike corridors and ever-changing reflections against so many windows. The house had changed me.

I went back to that apartment complex, parked my car, strolled the courtyard lined with red bougainvillea. I sat there for thirty minutes one time. For an hour the next. I pretended that I lived there. Once, I struck up a conversation with an older man who was taking his terrier for a walk, told him I lived in Building Five.

Once, I wandered into the main office, and when the manager asked if she could help me, I told her I was looking for a two-bedroom, but not for a few more months. I took some floor plans, folded them up, and hid them beneath the fast-food napkins and old receipts in the center console of my SUV. The next time, I took a tour.

It was only a fantasy, though, a crazy game I played.

Until it wasn't. Until I paid a deposit and signed a contract and made a plan.

———

My eyes travel up to the balcony. I pick out the window to the master bedroom, where Dani hides away now. I think of the look on her face— uncertainty, self-doubt, her mind unspooling like cotton thread. It feels too much like déjà vu.

Me and my foolish fantasy apartment. I should have known that it was never going to be that easy to escape.

68

Órlaith

I've deleted the video from my phone of Charlotte's first time crawling. Later tonight or whenever it happens that Dani sees her daughter crawling, I'll just let her believe it is the first time. Some secrets are like lies, but some lies are like kindnesses. You don't live as long as I have without learning a few things. One is that the world isn't black-and-white. It's gray as an Irish soft day, when the air is a mist so fine my da used to say you'd get yourself soaking wet without ever noticing a single raindrop.

The Matthewses have everything top-notch, like this baby monitor. One screen but three cameras, placed in rooms where Charlotte often sleeps or plays—the nursery, the master bedroom, and the downstairs guest.

I heard them by accident, didn't even realize the monitor was on, but now, I'm earwigging shamelessly, Charlotte still on the rug, spent from her marathon, like. Curtis and Gemma Barker have shut themselves off from the party in the spare room downstairs, talking fast and hushed.

"She's completely delusional. The anxiety, the paranoia, the hallucinations." Curtis ticks symptoms off with his fingers. "It's classic postpartum psychosis. Ethan knows that. Clearly, she hasn't been taking her medication. She needs to be hospitalized immediately."

Gemma crosses her arms around herself. "Have you told him that?"

"He doesn't respect my opinion as a psychiatrist. He never has. If something happens to her or Charlotte, it'll be my fuckup." Curtis lets out a sound of disgust and swallows some whiskey. "He doesn't want to separate her from Charlotte. He says it'll kill her. Dad always thought Ethan was this brilliant psychiatrist. But he's blind to what's happening in his own house."

Gemma tightens her lips. "He never got Kim the help she needed either."

"And look what a fucking mess she is."

"Curtis," she says softly.

"Ethan cares more about showing off this goddamn house than the safety of his wife and child. Thank God Dad isn't around for this." He tosses back the whiskey, slams the empty glass on the dresser.

I do a Google search for *postpartum psychosis* on my phone. *A woman suffering from postpartum psychosis experiences a break from reality. Senses are affected. She can see, hear, and feel things that aren't real. Research suggests there is approximately a 5% suicide rate and a 4% infanticide rate associated with the illness. This is because, in her psychotic state, the delusions make sense to her. They feel very real to her. Immediate treatment is essential.*

Holy Mary, Mother of God. I make a quick sign of the cross. Poor Dani. And Mr. Matthews appears to be just at his wit's end about how to help her, doesn't he?

A marriage is a funny thing. One would think that to build a life together, a real one and a long one, would necessitate utter honesty, a stripping away of all veneer, the years like paint thinner. In the end, my Colm slipping away to Alzheimer's, me helping to lift him from the toilet when his legs were no longer strong enough beneath him. What was left then that I didn't know? Where was the barrier between us by then?

And, yet, sometimes I think it might be the opposite. That a marriage, a good one, requires secrets. Things left unsaid, grievances quieted, dissimilar opinions smoothed away, dreams released. That to love one person forever, you must lie, at least a little bit, either to them or to yourself.

My Colm and I were together for forty-three years. I knew the way he took his tea, the sound his shoes made as he shuffled in from the porch, which of the wool throw blankets was his favorite, the volume he liked the television to be set to, what he'd say every time it rained, and how many beers he'd had down at the pub just by how hard he pressed a kiss to my cheek. I could pick him out by the sound of his cough through a solid wall. I could tell you just what he thought of Father's homily every Sunday without him needing to say a word.

And when my Colm passed, after the removal and the funeral mass, after I buried him beside our daughter's grave, after I tried my best to stay in that house, but couldn't stand the company of two ghosts now, after I decided to pack it all up, while I was sorting through Colm's belongings, that's when I found his secret. Found the envelope hidden in his toolbox in the outdoor shed, a place I'd never look in a million years, a place I hadn't looked before.

That's when I found the letter that made my whole world a lie.

69

Dani

The lipstick on the mirror. The note on the doorstep.

This isn't the first time I've done things I can't remember.

The day Sophie and Mikayla slept over, Ethan had been marinating a flank steak for twenty-four hours. I had cleaned the house, changed the sheets on Sophie's bed, prepared a black-bread dough for dinner rolls, and found a new peach tartlet recipe for dessert. Sophie arrived with a big bag of presents for her new little sister, including an impractical cupcake of a dress in a newborn size that Charlotte had probably outgrown already, and I made a mental note to post a pic to Instagram ASAP.

The memories from that day, from that night especially, slip from sight like minnows when I try to look at them too directly.

Brushing the rolls with an egg wash, sprinkling them with oats. The sounds of Sophie playing peekaboo with Charlotte. Mikayla asking if we needed any help. Ethan tending the grill, swirling a crystal tumbler of whiskey around and around. Curtis at the door. Arranging peach slices, a single sprig of mint. Charlotte cluster-feeding beneath a nursing cover. Ethan staying up for a last drink and cigar by the pool. Nursing Charlotte again in bed, pillows propped behind my back and under my elbow.

And later—waking in the dead of night. Charlotte crying. Or was she asleep? Ethan beside me in bed, his back to me, a lump of covers. Did he groan?

The sound I do remember is the moaning. The wind. That wind, always moaning and groaning, shrieking and whistling through the balcony, through the trees, against the windows. That night, it sounded human.

The truth is I haven't really tried to look directly at these memories. I haven't wanted to remember.

The heavy pull of the door. The wind whip cold, and the night dark—just the glow from the pool below, the twinkling of a few houses down on the hills, and a thousand stars above. A figure crouched in shadow. As I tried to comprehend what I was looking at, what I was seeing, a face turned to me, white and luminescent as the moon, frightened and frightening.

And I remember thinking, *Oh, it's been you. You were the figure on my lawn. You were the one shifting furniture and flicking lights and leaving the scent of old perfume. Of course, it was you.*

I tie my hair back with a satin scrunchie to avoid any creases, carefully pin back the shorter face-framing strands. I wash my face with cool water. I reapply my makeup—concealer over the shadows beneath my eyes, two coats of mascara on my lashes, a new shade of lipstick, a pretty pink this time.

It wasn't until a few days after the incident that I woke in my bed. Ethan had already hired Órlaith, and they had been feeding Charlotte with breast milk I had pumped and stored earlier when my supply was overflowing. Ethan explained what had happened that night, gently, tenderly, his hand over mine on top of our crisp white duvet. As he spoke, the memories surfaced in the murky waters of my mind. Leaning over the glass wall, dangerously far, wind pulling my hair, the taste of bile in my mouth.

Sometimes the brain blocks out a memory to protect itself, Curtis told me. I haven't tried to remember the incident. I haven't wanted to. *It isn't necessary for your treatment,* Curtis said. *Don't go back there. Focus on the future.*

———

I woke to the sound of the wind, well after one in the morning. I snatched Charlotte from her bassinet. The glass door was silent as I slid it open, the winter air cold as I stepped onto the balcony, as I carried my child to the very end. The crouched figure. The turned face. I believed some delusion, one that had been building for weeks. I believed that I encountered *The Mother* out there, that she had been the presence in the house, that she wanted Charlotte. Leaning over the glass wall, dangerously far.

I had left the balcony door open, thank God, because that's what woke Ethan, the cold December wind, what sent him hurtling toward us. When he found me, I already had Charlotte over the railing, dangling her tiny body over the cavernous hole of the cliffside, a hundred-foot drop, holding her out like an offering.

I didn't *want* to throw my child over the balcony. The impulse had simply appeared, unintentional and unwelcome, and, yet, in that state, completely logical. An act of kindness. Of compensation. A debt was owed. A child was owed. And I didn't deserve her. She was too perfect.

Now, I let my hair down, touch up the curls. I use a hand mirror to inspect my reflection from all angles. I cross the room to the bedroom door. I take one last steadying breath before turning the knob.

"Ah, there's your mammy now." Órlaith is already in the hallway, and as she approaches, she holds my daughter out to me.

I take Charlotte, feel the weight of her, solid and right. "Órlaith," I start, hesitantly, "I'm sorry—"

She puts up a hand to stop me. "There'll be none of that now." Then she turns and starts down the staircase ahead of us.

I pause to kiss Charlotte's head, to feel her soft, fine hair against my nose. I have the same thought—the same marrow-deep feeling—that I had when the nurses first placed Charlotte in my arms, sticky and white with vernix, angry-faced, and miraculous: that motherhood is terrifying.

I settle her on my hip and start down the stairs behind Órlaith. Around the spiral, and the entire party rushes into view, guests lifting their heads to see who is coming. I smile brightly at each face. I raise my free hand to wave to Gemma, who, in return, raises a pair of wine-glasses in my direction.

The world is full of every kind of danger.

But it seems, somehow, that *I* am the most dangerous thing in Charlotte's life.

And I'll do anything to keep my child safe.

70

Kim

Dani has come back downstairs, and somehow, she's more radiant than ever, like she just popped out of the party real quick to freshen her makeup. She has the baby on her hip, her head thrown back in a laugh at something Gemma has said.

A waiter, a young man with a splash of acne across his forehead, arrives with a glass of cab. I shake my head. "Do you have ginger ale?" I ask.

"Ginger beer all right?"

The word *beer* makes my stomach flip. "Sprite?"

He nods and walks away.

"I'll be needing to get the baby to bed soon enough, like," the woman next to me says in a thick Irish accent. I turn. It's the nanny.

"Oh, yeah," I say slowly, my mind working like mud now, my tongue thick in my mouth. "What time is it?"

"Quarter past seven."

We're in the living room. I'm not sure exactly when I wandered in here or why. Did I go to the bathroom? Yeah. That's what it was. I didn't throw up, but there was a moment when I knelt in front of the bowl, when I felt thick saliva pooling in the hollows of my cheeks. I splashed the back of my neck with water, holding up my heavy curtain of curls with the other hand. I caught my reflection for a moment, and I looked like shit, mascara and eyeliner running.

"This party just keeps going," I say. I lean back against the wall, look out over the sea of faces that are blurring into one. I have that slight feeling of everything spinning.

"Isn't that the truth of it, sure? All these people, they've been drinking since early afternoon. God knows how they plan on getting home. Fair play to you for ordering a fizzy drink. I hope you'll be careful, like. Give it a second thought before you get behind the wheel of a car. It's best to order a taxi, if you ask me. Of course, no one ever seems to. Ask me, I mean."

I'm trying to focus across the room, decide if someone is in the bathroom in case I need to make a dash for it. The bathroom door is closed. "No way in hell I'm leaving my car here." I imagine showing up at Ethan's door tomorrow afternoon, admitting I was too drunk to get myself home. I'd rather drive straight off the cliff now.

"If you need a ride, love, you just let me know. I'm more than happy to drive you home. There's nothing worse than drink driving, sure. Wouldn't you agree?"

"Mmhmm." I probably won't throw up. I have a pretty steel stomach. I used to never get a hangover—even after nights out with the girls or evenings by the pool when Ethan and I would get lost in conversation, pouring one glass of wine after another, one bottle after another—Ethan used to joke that it was my superpower. Age has caught up with me, though.

"People don't think about the consequences of their actions. All the things we do, all the decisions we make, they matter. Big or small, our actions matter. Every action has a reaction. Every cause has an effect."

I place her words one after the other in my mind like a puzzle in the newspaper, like they can be unscrambled into a message with a meaning. "I'm not sure I know what you mean," I say to the Irish nanny. Across the room, the bathroom door opens. There isn't a line. My stomach gurgles, but I feel okay.

"You should be held responsible," the nanny says, "for the things you cause to happen."

I feel the burn of acid in the back of my throat. The bathroom door is still open.

"I'm sorry," I say, and rush away from her.

Mikayla

I am standing alone, near a trash can between the bar and the pool. The others are still playing chicken, or some version of it, the guys dunking the girls, all splashing and shrieking and laughter.

I am watching *him*.

Watching the perfect line of his jaw as he speaks, the movements of his strong hands in the midst of a story. I *will* him to look at me, and, as if by magic, he does. Of course he does, because it's like our souls are tied by an invisible cord—where he goes, I go; what I think, he thinks. And for a moment, his lips curve in a smile I've memorized by heart. No matter how wrong it is, it is also heartbreakingly right. It is the kind of beautiful that makes you ache from the inside out, like that new deep space photograph from the James-whatever telescope, each speck of light a galaxy, countless and unimaginable—it makes you feel so very small, and yet a part of something infinite.

"Mikayla!" It's Tyler, calling from the edge of the pool. "We're going to play volleyball. Wanna keep score?"

I nod, and when I look back, he has already turned away. The moment has passed, and he is putting an arm around Dani's shoulder. He is tapping Charlotte on the nose.

I reach into the pocket of my borrowed dress, and my fingers find the cool metal tube. My heart pounds as I pull out the berry red lipstick that I stole from Dani's closet earlier today. I throw it in the trash can, watch it slip beneath paper napkins and plastic toothpicks, out of sight and gone.

72

The Morning After the Party

It's nearly 5 A.M. when Gemma Barker enters through the Emergency Room doors of North Central Baptist Hospital. The party guests have finally been dismissed. The great house on top of the cliff is empty, its rooms dark, even as the Hill Country horizon brightens with morning.

It's 5:08 by the time she has navigated through the labyrinthine halls, up two different elevators, asking twice for directions, to 3C, the pediatric floor. She is still in her party clothes, though she switched out the teetering heels for a pair of old tennis shoes she found in the backseat of her car.

She reaches the desk, explains, a little breathlessly, who she is and who she is here to see. The nurse's face is one of practiced empathy. She takes Gemma by the elbow to the patient's room. "She's asleep," the nurse explains. "She had to be sedated." She points out a lounge with a Keurig and bottled water in the fridge. She shows Gemma the call button, tells her to ring if she needs anything at all, and if anything changes.

Once the nurse leaves—the rattle of the privacy curtain and then the clicking of the door—Gemma pulls a chair to the bedside. She sits, watches Sophie's steady heart rate and oxygen levels. She folds her hands in her lap. She says a silent prayer that is more of a jumble of emotions than a coherent thought, hopes that whoever is listening knows how to untangle her meaning. She waits.

Mikayla

The Night of the Party

The sun dips close to the horizon now, gilding the treetops. The nanny takes Charlotte from Dani's arms.

"Say good night to Mammy," she says.

I've left the others to score their own volleyball game. I am by the open back door, sipping a Dr Pepper and watching.

"Should we do the cake soon?" Mr. Matthews asks. He is tracing fingers across Dani's bare shoulders.

"Hmm?" she says, absentmindedly. And, like, are you kidding me? How is she not entirely in this moment? How can she just ignore the burn of his fingertips on her skin? I would never take him for granted like that. She doesn't deserve him, doesn't deserve any of this.

"The cake," he says.

"Oh. Of course."

"Great. I'll start steering everyone inside."

Earlier, I saw them in the window of the carriage house, right beside the glass, like she was putting it on display, like she was deliberately trying to hurt me. Dani's face tipped up to his, eyes closed, lips parted. Mr. Matthews kissing her, pulling her perfect body tight against his. And I just completely lost it. I couldn't breathe, the whole world tunneling down to a dark pinprick. Somehow, I made it to the bathroom. I wanted to scream, to crawl out of my own body, and there was nothing but that roiling sickness inside me, nothing but the lipstick in my pocket, the mirror, and my own stupid reflection.

I didn't plan on falling for my best friend's dad, obviously. But, for real, what could I do? I mean, listen to any song, watch any movie, read any book. Love is the most powerful force in the universe. All those stupid galaxies spinning like pinpoints of light, gravity so strong it collides planets, collapses stars to form black holes that suck up whole worlds like a pulled bathtub drain? That's baby stuff compared to love.

After Sophie called to tell me she was on a date with Mason, I sat on those swings, so absorbed in my own misery that I didn't notice the car pull up, didn't even hear him the first time he called out to me.

Hey, Mr. Matthews said again, *you okay?*

I guess I didn't look okay. He sat on the swing beside me, the chains squeaking.

You want to talk about it?

I shook my head, looked back to my dirt-covered shoes, my neck blazing with embarrassment. I felt pathetic.

But Mr. Matthews never made anyone feel pathetic. He just nodded. He probably had a million adult things to do—his car parked over by the mailboxes, a stack of bills still in one hand—but he sat on that swing like he had all the time in the world.

And finally, because the silence was total cringe, and because I knew he was being polite and that I was wasting his day, and also, a little, because—obviously—I *did* want to talk about it, to someone besides my parents, at least, who just wanted to convince me that I shouldn't be upset about something I was totally devastated over, I said, in a kind of under-my-breath-not-looking-at-him mumble, *The guy I like just started dating someone else.*

Oof, he said. *That's hard. I mean, that's the worst.*

And I almost smiled, because it was hard, and it was the worst.

Look, he said, checking his watch. *I've got groceries. In this heat, the eggs will be hard-boiled if I leave them in the car any longer. But Dani should be home soon, and she's been prepping this dough for croissants since yesterday. She always makes too much. You interested?*

I thought of my mom, of her plans for pizza and a movie. But that would be hours from now. In her mind, I was already over the whole thing, and she had moved on to Swiffering the hard floors and wiping the counters and lugging Dad's laundry basket full of bulky canvas clothes from the bedroom to the mudroom and back.

I helped Mr. Matthews unload the groceries, setting aside the Brie and jam Dani needed for her croissants. Two sheet pans were stacked on wire racks in the oversized fridge, the raw dough rolled and arranged in three rows of four.

They're "proving," Mr. Matthews said, like it was a borrowed word. *It's a whole process, apparently. She rolls the dough, adds butter, folds, rolls again. She tells me there are eighty-one layers. How crazy is that?*

Where is Dani?

Prenatal yoga. She's been going every weekend. It's supposed to help with the labor. He grabbed two Topo Chicos from the fridge, popped the tops, and handed me one. *Want to see what I've been doing with my Saturdays?*

I followed him to his study. As I stepped through the doorway, I thought, *I've never been in here,* which was weird, because, obviously, I'd been over to the house, like, a billion times—I had my own key. It was basically my second home.

One wall was floor-to-ceiling bookshelves. The windows looked out over the side yard. In the middle of the room was a heavy wooden desk, a leather swivel chair. There was a burgundy leather sofa against another wall, a pair of matching chairs. And everywhere—on the sofa and the chairs and the desk and the floor—were boxes stuffed with files and papers.

I'm writing a book, he told me.

But it wasn't like a *book*-book, you know? Not like the girl-gone-missing mysteries my mom read for book club or even the fly-fishing memoir collections my dad always had sitting on his nightstand, getting through a page or two before he was snoring, reading glasses at the end of his nose, the book face down on his chest.

Mr. Matthews was writing an academic book that I guess only other psychiatrists and college professors would read.

Have you heard of confirmation bias? he asked.

I shook my head.

It's the tendency people have to seek out information that confirms a preexisting belief.

Like my dad getting his news from just one website?

A smile spread across his face, creases by his eyes. He tapped his nose, something he'd always done, a way to say, *Bingo!* He was always teaching us something, always treating us like we were smart enough, mature enough to understand. His praise made me glow, set my skin humming.

He stepped behind the desk, shuffled some papers. *It's natural,* he said. *Some people do it more than others. Some jump to conclusions, while others like to sift the evidence. But we all do it. We all have blind spots, I guess you could say. Hell, speaking of blind spots, we do it with our eyes too. I mean, we do this on a biological level—our eyes are only capable of perceiving so much. The retina is simply a sheet of cells at the back of the eye—rods and cones, you know? And the eye sends this raw data—light waves and colors—to our brain. It's our brain that constructs the visual world. Our brain that decides what we see and what we ignore.*

There was something about the way he was talking. He was so passionate. And he was watching me, watching my face while we spoke, like he wanted me to get it, and I thought that maybe I did. I stepped toward the desk too, toward the side, so just kind of the corner was between us. *So is that what you're writing about? How our eyes, like, trick us?*

He shook his head. *I'm not a neuroscientist. I'm more interested in the way confirmation bias affects memory recall. We construct these narratives, see? Stories about who we are, our relationships with the people in our lives, the mistakes we made, the achievements we earned. We don't remember things the way they really happened. We recall the details that fit the narrative.*

Like when you remember a road trip, I said, thinking about a specific one—me and the Matthewses driving down to the beach in Port Aransas, three hours there and three hours back, two nights in a blue house right on the water. *And the memory is just junk food and singing to the radio and that one time everyone was laughing so hard our stomachs hurt. But, obviously, there must have been more. There must have been just boring hours of staring out the window, or checking the time, or trying to stretch our legs.*

Exactly, he said. *I knew you'd get it.* That smile, like he was proud.

And I felt warm all over and honey gold.

But I have to sort through all this. He swept a hand over the papers spread across his desk, stretched his arm out to indicate all the boxes. *Research and patient files.*

I looked to his desk, to a plain cream-colored file folder opened right in front of me. I ran a finger over the thick black bar that obscured random words throughout the page.

They've been redacted, he said, coming around the desk and standing behind me, looking over my shoulder. I could feel the heat off him. *See?* He pointed, lifting his arm so it brushed against mine. *The patients' names, their personal information, have been blacked out. Otherwise, I couldn't let you in here.* He laughed a little.

I turned to look back and up at him. He was looking at the file, but then his eyes met mine. And for a moment—for *that* moment—we were so close our breaths mixed. My heart, a hummingbird. I could feel the pulse in my neck. And then—and then—

We heard the front door open. Dani's voice, *Hey, babe. Please tell me you made it to H-E-B.*

Mr. Matthews took a step back. *Of course,* he yelled out.

Then Dani was in the office doorway, yoga mat rolled under her arm, hair pulled back in a ponytail, her skin post-workout glowing, and she wore a cute yoga outfit that pulled tight over her new pregnant bump. *Oh, hey, sweetheart,* she said to me. *Is Sophie here?*

No, Mr. Matthews said. He put a hand to my shoulder. *Mikayla just stopped by. I told her to stay for a croissant.*

Dani smiled. *The dough takes, literally, forever, but then it's only fifteen, maybe twenty minutes in the oven. Can you wait that long?*

I nodded.

Good. Let me just pop into some fresh clothes while the oven preheats.

———

"Ms. Matthews?" It's the party planner, the woman in the white blouse and black pants who brought us our first mocktails, who I've seen bustling around all day. "Mr. Matthews wanted to offer champagne with the cake. I told my staff to set aside ten bottles, but, well, I guess champagne has been popular today, and, um, it seems we're down to only three."

"Oh," Dani says. "Oh, that's fine. We have plenty in the cellar. I'll grab a few bottles."

"Wonderful. Let's do eight, if you can spare it. Just to be safe." She turns, gestures toward the bartender, who nods. She starts to walk away.

"I can help," I say, stepping through the door.

Dani turns to me then. She smiles. Her lips are a soft pink now, I notice. "Mikayla. Hi, sweetheart."

———

I came back the next Saturday. I waited until I saw Dani's car pull out of the drive, on her way to yoga.

Hey, Mr. Matthews said when he answered the door, a slight furrow to his brows. *Sophie isn't home.*

I knew that, though. Cheer practice, then she and Mason were going to Main Event for bowling and laser tag.

I thought I could help you sort through all those files, I said.

He smiled. For a week, I had thought about his smile as I fell asleep each night, closed my eyes and pictured his face on the backs of my eyelids. *You don't want to spend your Saturday with a box of files.*

I thought it was really interesting what you were talking about—confirmation bias—I read some more about it, I said. *Just Wikipedia or whatever.*

Yeah? he said. He waited for just a beat longer, then shrugged, let the door fall open. *If you want to, I won't refuse the help. I'm buried up to my neck in here.*

He had me sort the records into piles and showed me how to scan them into the computer so they could be keyword-searched.

But mostly we talked. That Saturday and the next and the next, and all the while, I collected moments like flecks of gold in a pan.

The time he reached for a box on the top shelf of the closet, his gray T-shirt riding up to expose a strip of hard abdomen that sent a strange flutter to the depth of me.

The time he said I was *incredibly perceptive*, that he'd always known I was, and I realized that he saw me, like, really saw me, and I saw him, and I loved him, and I think some part of me had always loved him, back to when he took me to Disneyland when I was nine years old, probably before that, even, like maybe our souls had been doing this dance across lifetimes.

The time he noticed my necklace—a bronze and silver sunflower pendant that my memaw gave me for my thirteenth birthday. *That's pretty,* he said, touching the flower, so his fingers grazed my collarbone, and I felt—not *sparks,* which sounds so surface-level, like pretty pops of light; no, this was below the surface, this was the deep magnetic pull of desire, and I knew it wasn't just me. I knew he felt it too.

———

"You don't need to help," Dani says. "Go have fun."

"I don't mind," I say. "You can't carry eight bottles of champagne by yourself."

She considers this. "Well, thanks," she says. She turns, heads toward the door that leads down into the cellar.

I follow close behind.

———

When Mr. Matthews noticed my necklace, we were standing in the kitchen, taking a break from scanning files to get a cold drink from the fridge. I leaned back against the counter, him standing in front of me. *That's pretty.* He touched the sunflower, his fingertips gliding along the sensitive skin of my neck, my collarbone. His eyes slid up to my lips. And I felt it, I swear I felt it, deep and urgent and mutual. I pushed off the counter, up onto my toes, and I kissed him.

I felt the roughness of his unshaven face against my chin, the softness of his lips against mine.

Then he stepped back.

I opened my eyes.

Hey, he said. *It's okay. That's okay.*

Every feeling drained from me like blood. I wanted to die. I wanted to be dead in that moment.

74

Órlaith

Charlotte is asleep, and I'm just heading down the spiral staircase when I am hit again with that sudden loss of balance. My knees buckle beneath me, and I clutch at the railing, lower myself to sit on a top step. A veil of shadow falls over my eyes.

I feel her hand again on my shoulder.

The whoosh, whoosh of my blood sounds like rabid whispers.

I reach for my shoulder, like. There is nothing there, of course, and yet I feel the pressure, feel her curl her fingertips like claws that grip me.

Then, like the pulling of a cord, she is gone, the curtain is lifted, sight and sound restored. I am left panting, catching my breath. I gather the baby's bottle and blanket from the step beside me, use the railing to haul myself up to standing. I hold tight and make sure I'm steady before I begin again.

I head toward the kitchen to wash the bottle. Already at the sink, though, the ex-wife is slumped, filling a large plastic tumbler from the faucet and draining it greedily, water sliding down her cheeks and into her hair. She's in a right state.

"Ah, fuck," she says low to herself, then she spots me out the corner of her eye, sets the empty cup on the counter, wipes her mouth with the back of her hand. "Sorry. Jesus, I'm a disaster."

I cross the expansive kitchen to her. She leans back against the counter to give me room to rinse the bottle. "You'll have to do more than drink to shock an Irish woman."

She laughs, then her face crumples like an old napkin. She looks every bit her age right now. "It's just, ugh." She lets out a moan of dis-

Mikayla, he said, stooping to look me in the eyes. *Listen to me. It's okay. But, you probably don't need to be coming around here when Dani isn't home. Okay?*

I heard the beep of Dani locking her car then. I looked to the time on the digital clock on the oven. How had it gotten so late already?

He was looking at me, his eyes full of concern, waiting for something, so I nodded.

Hey, babe, he called out, striding out of the kitchen to meet her at the door. I stood there, mortified beyond belief. I could hear him explaining me before she saw me. *I told her Sophie wasn't home, but I think we're both hoping you might try that maple bacon scone recipe you've been talking about.*

———

The stairway that leads down to the cellar is dark, and it takes Dani a moment to find the switch. Even then, the light is dim, just an amber-covered sconce mounted near the foot of the stairs. The steps are uneven stone. Dani, in her stilettos, begins the descent.

I close the door behind us, muffle the party.

And now, we are alone.

gust. "I promised, you know? Promised myself. Promised Sophie. God, I'm a piece of shit."

I set the bottle downward on the drying mat. "Sure, that's no way to be talking about yourself."

"I'm a veterinarian, you know? It's harder than being a doctor. My patients can't tell me what's hurting them. I have to figure it out on my own. I can diagnose all kinds of animals. Lizards to horses. I'm good at it." Her mouth twists in a wry smile. She closes her eyes, squeezes them shut. "But I can't figure out what the fuck is wrong with me."

"Oh, pet." I pat her arm. She keeps her eyes closed.

"I lost my career. This house. My daughter."

I set the teat and the rest of the bottle's pieces on the mat as well, turn off the tap. "Your daughter is in the other room," I say.

"No. I mean—"

"I know what you meant." Something about my tone, I suppose, shuts her right up. She squints, like she's trying to assess me now through the fog of her drunk. I rip a paper towel from a roll near the sink, hand it to her. "What you need is an Irish cure. A piece of dry toast and a full pot of tea so strong it's almost stewed."

I get to work, filling the kettle on the stove, rustling through the cupboards for the china teapot that I brought with me when I started working for the Matthewses because, for heaven's sake, they didn't have their own.

Kim is wiping the napkin under her eyes, where her mascara has bled into dark shadows, settled into the fine lines. She dabs her face, wipes the back of her neck. "So what brought you here? To the States, I mean."

I put three bags in the pot. "We took a trip here," I say. "My family. A long time ago, when my girl was only little, seven years old. And, sure, she fell so in love with the silly place. I think it was mainly the trip itself—getting on a great big plane, crossing oceans, finding new people and places. Didn't it make the world expansive? Didn't she want to peek into every corner? She was always that way. Curious. She said that one day, when she grew up, she'd come back here." I gather supplies as I talk—sugar in a covered dish beside the coffee maker, milk from the fridge. I spoon two scoops of sugar into the bottom of her cup without asking how she takes it—I've found Americans don't really know how they take their tea, and, sure, Kim doesn't really know what's best for her right now anyway.

"Did she?" Kim asks. "Is that what brought you here? Following your daughter? I get that."

"Yes," I say, and I leave it at that.

Kim turns her back to me to refill her water cup from the sink.

When the kettle starts whistling, I pour the water into the pot, and we wait for it to steep.

You'd think I would have known somehow. That my daughter was going to die. There would have been an omen, a sign, mother's intuition. I think often of the last day I had with my girl, her beside me on the sofa, leaning into my shoulder, laughing.

I can still feel the vibration of that laugh. It echoes on my bones.

On the kitchen island, I set a plate with a piece of dry toast, the steeping teapot, and the single cup. I pull up a barstool. "If you'll indulge an old woman for a moment," I say. After all, isn't this what tea is for? For talking? And Kim needs a good talking-to right now.

Kim takes a seat as well. She looks to the tea set. "Aren't you going to have a cup?"

I shake my head. "You need the whole pot, pet. Now eat your toast." She does as she's told. "You see, in life, there are things outside your control. Do you know what I mean, like? I'll tell you about this family—a husband, his wife, their son, I think maybe five or six, he was, and their baby daughter, even the dog. Sure, weren't they after going on a camping trip into the Oregon woods? This was, oh heavens, 1960 . . . No, it was the seventies. 1974, was it? Well, anyway, they disappeared. The whole lot of them. Only the dog was found, wandering into the town. Not a trace. Not until nearly a year later. The father's body was found tied to a tree, and miles away, the mother and both the little ones in a cave. All of them dead. Murdered. The case was never solved." I cross myself. The poor souls.

"Jesus," Kim says.

"I'm only saying the world isn't fair. I know that all too well. But the things that are within your control? You need to be responsible for them, you need to be accountable. Do you see what I'm saying, love?"

I pour the tea into her cup, steam rising, hot tea flecking onto the skin of my thumb. I take the spoon, stir until the sugar has dissolved. I pour the milk. *Be patient,* I say to the voice that whispers. *Be patient,* I say to the hand that clutches my shoulder.

I slide the cup to Kim, watch her take a sip. She smiles a kind of thanks, but sure, I can see she's thinking over my words. Good.

Because I meant what I said. The world isn't fair.

But God is. *For God will call all our deals to judgment, all that is hidden, be it good or evil.*

One way or another, we will all be held accountable.

75

Mikayla

After I tried to kiss Mr. Matthews, I was so embarrassed I could have slid straight from my skin like a snake. I thought I never wanted to see him again, that I'd never be able to look him in the eyes.

But, also, I missed him. I missed our Saturday afternoons together. The way he made me feel seen. He talked to me like I was a real person, not a kid, told me about his week, asked for my advice. He listened too. Once I was complaining about how Kylie was always coming in my room and stealing my stuff—she liked anything shiny and small: a ring, a necklace, an FFA pin—and I'd have to go track it down, find where she'd hidden it in her dollhouse or her Hello Kitty purse or whatever. A few weeks later, we were going through the patient files in a comfortable silence—I had never known silence could be comfortable. It was Mr. Matthews who taught me that. *It's nice,* he said once, *when you feel close enough to another person that you don't mind the quiet moments, that you can simply be together.*

And in that comfortable silence, he hopped up from his chair to get something from the closet. *Oh, I almost forgot.*

He handed me a box wrapped in burgundy-colored paper.

For me? I said.

He nodded, watching my hands, and I could tell he was eager for me to open the gift.

I unfolded the paper carefully. It was a jewelry box, cherrywood, four gold legs, an inlay in the top of two doves encircled by a heart-shaped ribbon.

I found it at an antique store near the practice, and I figured this would solve your problem. Perfect for keeping out thieving little sisters, he said, pointing to the key, that smile tugging at his lips. *Do you like it?*

Of course I liked it. Of course it was perfect. Just like him. Just like us.

———

The cellar is dark and chilly. Sophie and I used to play down here sometimes, pretend it was the forbidden wing of a beast's castle or use it as the perfect spot during hide-and-seek. I'd always get a little freaked out, though. It's so quiet down here, underground. Like no one would hear you scream.

Dani is looking up bottles of champagne on her phone and making stupid small talk.

"So, y'all are having fun?" she asks.

"Totally," I say.

She's setting bottles on the island.

I'm looking through the drawer. There is a silver spoon with a long, thin handle. There is a wooden dowel–type thing that I think Mr. Matthews uses to smash up berries in the bottom of a glass. There is a corkscrew with a small, sharp blade that folds out from the top.

———

At first, I just planned to walk by the house. I watched from the trees. I just wanted to see him, to catch a glimpse of him out in the backyard or smoking a cigar by the pool. Soon, I was peering through windows, watching him pour a drink or look over papers at his desk.

And, at first, that was enough.

But I had my own key. I'd always had a key. Sophie had a key to my house too. We grew up together. This was practically my house. It had been my house long before it had ever been Dani's.

So I let myself in. Mostly when no one was home—Ethan at work and Dani out shopping or at an OB appointment or, after Charlotte was born, on one of her walks around the neighborhood or a quick trip to pick up groceries.

I just needed to feel close to him, to sit in his office chair, to lie in his bed, close my eyes and inhale the mixture of cologne and sweat on his pillowcase. I pretended it was our house. Once, I rummaged in the closet, put on one of Dani's silk robes, spritzed myself with her perfume, and wandered the rooms of the house. Sometimes, I took things, just little things—a pair of cuff links from the top of his dresser, a pencil with teeth marks from his desk, a tube of hand cream from Dani's nightstand that I imagined Mr. Matthews had bought for her because he liked the scent. I slathered the lotion into my own hands, into the pulse points of my neck. I kept all my treasures in the jewelry box he gave me and hid it in the back of my closet. Kept the box locked, the key on a chain around my neck.

———

"What about you?" I ask.

"Hmm?" Dani says, setting a sixth bottle on the island.

"Are you having fun?"

"Oh." She kind of laughs. Dani is so stinking pretty, the kind of pretty that is just easy and light as a bubble. "Who doesn't love a party?" she says.

And it's like everything is fine, like everything is normal.

I know she saw my message on the mirror. I saw her go into the bathroom after me. I know she got my note the other day. I saw the color leave her face as she read it.

More than that, I know she saw me.

That night, Dani saw me out on the balcony.

But now, I don't know, it's like she doesn't remember or something.

———

It was late, really late, like two in the morning, when I crept back down the hall and into Sophie's room. Thank God she was still asleep. I slipped back into bed beside her, pulled the covers up to my chin. I pretended to be asleep. I tried to not even breathe. Through the wall, I heard Dani screaming.

Sophie sat up. My heart was a jackhammer. What if she hadn't been fully asleep a second ago? What if she knew I'd been out of the room?

But she didn't seem to know. *Is that Dani?* Sophie said.

I think so, I said.

Are they fighting?

Dani's voice through the wall, frantic, hysterical. The sound of the baby crying.

I shrugged. But it was a lie. Because, of course, I knew. I knew why Dani was screaming.

I know what I saw, Dani shrieked. *We're leaving. Now. We have to get out of this house.*

She was screaming because of me, because I had taken it way, way too far, because she had seen me for the monster that I am.

76

Kim

That Irish woman is strange, to say the least, and her tea is sickly sweet. But I think it might be working. I feel . . . not sober, obviously, but—less wasted, maybe? My head is pounding, though, and my stomach does not feel right. What I need right now is a cigarette.

I slip upstairs and out through the door in the loft to the balcony. I'm already reaching into my purse as I step out, but I stop short, startled, when I realize I'm not the only one who has had this idea.

Gemma is on the balcony as well, an unlit cigarette between two fingers, the other hand digging in her handbag.

"Need a light?" I hold a red BIC out to her.

She looks up. I see the emotions skip across her features. Then she sighs and smiles a smile that isn't really a smile at all. She takes the lighter from my hand. She lights up and hands it back to me.

Gemma isn't a smoker, not really, not regularly. But she keeps one emergency cigarette in each of her purses, just in case. She only smokes if she's feeling stressed.

I still know these things about her.

I light my cigarette. I scan the pool, the lawn, the bar. I spot Curtis, who is, of course, flirting with one of the waitresses. A young black girl, maybe early twenties. He's touching her arm while he talks. She's laughing. Some things never change.

Gemma follows my gaze, then looks away, leans her forearms onto the glass railing. She flicks the end of the cigarette out and into the wind.

Gemma never understood why I wanted to leave Ethan. I never understood how she could stay with Curtis.

Except that she comes from a long line of Southern Baptist women who stand by their men. And, of course, there's the money. Gemma grew up without any. She'd trade just about anything for security.

"Have you talked to that nanny Ethan hired?" I ask.

"Órlaith?" Gemma asks.

And I feel a loosening in my chest. I realize that I've been afraid she wouldn't respond. That she would simply refuse to speak to me, even out here alone in the dark.

"Yeah." I take a long drag on the cigarette. We both look out over a dark sky striped with darker clouds. "She made me a pot of tea and told me the most horrific story I've ever heard."

Gemma lets out a bubble of surprised laughter. "God, I know." She turns so she's facing me, leaning back against the railing. "She cornered me earlier, told me this horrible story about a little girl who was killed by a hit-and-run while her family was on vacation overseas. They never found the driver. It was awful."

"At least yours only had one dead kid," I say.

"Who tells stories like that? To strangers? At a party?"

We're both laughing now. And how many times have we laughed together just like this? The sound of her laugh. The way her nose crinkles at the bridge.

"I miss this," I say.

"Yeah," she says. There is a flatness to the single word, an unreadability. She looks to her feet, taps at something invisible with the toe of her shoe. She takes a long inhale on her cigarette, tips her head back to release a stream of smoke into the air. "I should be getting back." She flicks the butt off the side of the house. "I think Ethan's trying to gather everybody for, you know, candles and cake and all that."

She's about to leave.

"Gemma."

She stops.

"I never got to explain," I say, "I never got to . . ."

She turns back to me. She chews her bottom lip. I can see a shimmer to her eyes before she blinks them hard, crosses her arms. "Okay."

"Okay?"

"Go ahead."

I've imagined this conversation a thousand times, and now I'm unprepared, my stomach sick and my palms sweaty. "It's just Ethan, you know, he—"

"Oh my God. I don't care about Ethan," she snaps. "Are you serious? I don't care what Ethan did. I care what you did, Kim. I mean look at you. Look at your life. Not everything can be Ethan's fault."

Gemma turns and walks away, shutting the door behind her, leaving me alone on the balcony.

I look out over the party, look down. What is it? Thirty? Forty feet to the bluestone below?

My stomach doesn't feel right. I'm dizzy, and my heart is rapid and erratic. I grip the railing. I try to focus on one unmoving spot, a poolside umbrella.

The words of the Irish woman float back to me now.

You should be held responsible.

77

Mikayla

I find Ethan near the carriage house.

"Yeah, see ya in there," he says to a couple headed toward the house.

He turns, sees me. "Mikayla," he says. "We're going to do cake soon. I'm trying to get everyone moving that way."

The sun has nearly set now, the sky a dark denim shade, just a kiss of light near the horizon, and all the yard in shadow, so that we are hidden together in this alcove. We are safe.

I step up to him, wrap my arms around his neck. I close my eyes and tip my head back, tip my face to his, and I wait for him to kiss me.

He doesn't, though. He steps away from me, deeper into the alcove. "Mikayla." His voice is sharp. "I thought we t—t—" His eyes shift behind me. "We went over this," he says slowly.

"No one can see us," I assure him. "Everyone is going inside. We're alone."

"This can't happen, Mikayla." He waves a hand vaguely between our two bodies. "You know that. You're a smart girl."

I want him to pull me close, to kiss the top of my head, to tell me it will all be all right, that we will be together. But he doesn't, and I feel that swirling rage deep inside me. "She doesn't deserve you." Doesn't he know that? Can't he see that? "She's a crazy bitch."

His eyes snap to mine, wide as saucers. "What did you say?"

"I—"

He grabs my shoulders hard. "Mikayla, tell me the truth. Did you send a letter to Dani?"

I don't say anything. He searches my face, eyes flicking over me so quickly that I want to flinch. He lets me go.

"Oh my God," he says, under his breath. He runs a hand hard over his jaw. I can see him thinking, I can see the worry on his face, in the clenching of every muscle.

"Ethan," I say, small, reaching out a hand, but he jerks his arm out of my reach.

"No," he says.

I'm shaking my head, because this can't be happening. This doesn't make sense. Mr. Matthews loves me. "What about us?"

"There is no us," he snaps. "It's in your head." His words are an echo of Sophie's earlier tonight, up on the balcony. *You had a crush. It was imaginary. You get obsessed.*

He tries to walk past me, back to the party, but I grab his arm, desperate. I want him to want me, to be in love with me, like I thought he was.

He rounds, looming over me, and in the shadowy light, his face looks hard. "Stay away from my family. I mean it." He jerks his arm free from my grip, then he is gone.

78

Dani

Charlotte is asleep upstairs. For now, she is safe. Safe from me. And that's what matters.

I am standing in the great room, near the long dining table, waiting for the cake-cutting to start. Ethan has been ushering people this way, and the room is filling like sand in a timer, all the people from every corner of the party condensed into one hot space.

Through the crowd, I make eye contact with Kim. She locks onto me, starts heading my way. I turn to avoid her, bump into Jaci and Liz.

"This party is a blast," Liz says.

"I can't remember the last time I had this much to drink," Jaci says.

"I'm glad y'all are having fun," I say. When I look back over my shoulder, Kim still has me in her sights. "We're doing cake soon," I say to Jaci and Liz, but they're already moving past me.

"Dani."

It's Kim's voice behind me. I take a breath, prepare myself for her verbal abuse, before affixing a smile and turning to face her.

"Kim, perfect timing. Sophie's about to blow out her candles."

She narrows her eyes at me, searches my face. "You don't have to pretend, you know?"

I keep smiling. I don't have the energy for Kim's bullshit games right now.

"To be happy. You don't have to pretend to be happy. Listen." She grabs my upper arm, leans in. She smells like cigarettes and sweat. She's drunk. "I remember what it's like, living here, in this house." Her gaze flicks up to the ceiling, to the high corners of the room. "It can make you doubt yourself." Her fingers tighten and her eyes return to mine. "Don't believe it."

A chill runs through me.

For a moment, we just look at each other. "You're doing a good job. With Charlotte. With everything. I should have thanked you for making that cake."

I'd be less stunned if she slapped me. "I loved making the cake," I say. I can hear the false cheer in my voice, and I hate it, but the party presses from all sides. I can't risk being vulnerable. Not now. Not here.

"Okay, well," I pull my arm away. "I think Sophie is changing back into her, um, my, well, *that* dress. For pictures and stuff. So, yeah, it should be fun."

I turn and walk away before she has a chance to say any more. I take a few deep breaths, and then MaryBeth is right on top of me.

"We have an emergency," she says, breathlessly.

"Emergency?"

"The cake. Someone must have knocked into it."

I look to the cake on the end of the long dining room table. She's right. A small chunk has been taken out from the second tier, like maybe someone standing nearby turned quickly and clipped a corner with her purse.

"It's fine. I can touch it up."

"You can? Oh my gosh, you are so cool under pressure."

I head to the pantry, grab my decorating tools, and return to the cake, where MaryBeth is waiting, talking the ear off the man beside her, a guy in his mid-forties, short and solid, dark hair peppered with gray at the temples.

When I lay my supplies out on the table, she squeals. "Is it okay if I record you? Is that weird? Just, ah, to see you at work! How cool is that?"

The man beside her laughs, says, "Babe, calm down. You'll scare her away."

I look up at him. He has a well-maintained mustache and a big smile that rivals MaryBeth's.

"Y'all haven't met yet, have you?" MaryBeth says. "Dani, this is my Ernesto."

Ernesto sticks out his hand to introduce himself.

"I've heard a lot about you," I say, taking his hand. His grip is strong.

"Trust me, I've heard an earful too. Sorry about my wife. She comes on a little strong."

MaryBeth slaps him on the shoulder.

"What?" he says with a shrug. "I'm not complaining. It's my favorite thing about her." He winks. They both laugh. I imagine that together, they spend a lot of time laughing.

I'm glad to know her husband actually exists, though I'm not completely convinced she didn't ding the cake herself just for the chance to watch me fix it. As I work, MaryBeth asks me about tools and techniques and what I think makes the perfect sponge.

I learned to bake from my grandfather. Some of my first memories are of standing on a chair pulled up to the counter, watching Papaw's hands work dough. The first thing I ever baked myself, with his direction, was a peach turnover for the annual Parker County Peach Festival.

It isn't only MaryBeth and Ernesto watching. The room is full to bursting now.

Ethan joins us, introduces himself to MaryBeth and Ernesto. He comes up behind me, hands on my shoulders. "You doing okay?" he asks.

"Mmhmm." I'm concentrating on replacing a scalloped row of highlighter yellow sprinkles. But when I glance to his face, his expression is so intense that I immediately stop what I'm doing. "Are *you* okay?"

"Can I just say y'all are so perfect together?" MaryBeth says. "How did you meet again?"

"Oh, um." I tear my eyes from Ethan's taut expression. "I was working at a coffee shop."

Under MaryBeth and Ernesto's attention, I watch Ethan hide away that expression of concern, flip on the charisma. "The coffee maker at my practice crapped out on us," he says, starting the story the way he always does. He puts an arm around me. I set down the tweezers in my hand and lean into him.

I have always loved a *How We Met* story.

"I wasn't even supposed to be working that day," I say. "My friend Marissa called me with a hangover and asked if I could cover her shift."

It's this that I love—the near miss of it all.

My grandparents were married for sixty-three years, an incomprehensible amount of time. *It was a church dance,* Papaw would say, *and your grandmother didn't even want to go.* It was her friend Carol Ann who dragged her to the party. Even then, they almost missed each other, *did* miss each other, in fact. Papaw was already behind the wheel of his truck when he realized that he had forgotten his jacket and had to go back inside, and that's when he saw *the most beautiful girl* he'd ever seen in his life, and asked her to dance. Whenever he said this part, he took her hand, kissing the knuckles, knotted from arthritis like the lumps on the crepe myrtles beside the front door. She couldn't even remove her wedding ring anymore, something I found terribly romantic.

And every time I heard the story, I was on the edge of my seat. If Carol Ann hadn't wanted to go, if Nanny hadn't let herself be dragged, if Papaw hadn't forgotten his jacket, if he hadn't asked her to dance . . .

My existence, Becca's existence, my mother's, my aunts' and uncles' and cousins', shimmered like mere possibilities at every turn.

"That is so romantic," MaryBeth says in a dreamy swoon, then, "Ernesto and I met online." Her mouth is a little frown.

Ernesto shrugs. "She signs up for a dating website, then is disappointed when it works."

I reach for the box of toothpicks, but they aren't there. I spread out the tools, the scraper and the palette knife, push aside piping bags and sprinkles.

"What are you looking for?" Ethan asks.

"Just toothpicks. I swear I brought them out here."

"You know," MaryBeth says, "I do that all the time. Ernesto says I'd lose my head if it weren't attached to my shoulders." She giggles. "The best thing to do is retrace your steps. Let's start in the pantry." She heads toward the pantry, and I start to follow.

"I'm going to check on Sophie. You okay?" Ethan asks.

"Yeah, I'll find them." I lean in to peck him on the lips absentmindedly, but he cups my face in both hands, kisses me tenderly. When I open my eyes, I'm staring into the dark warmth of his. "Are you okay?" he asks again.

There is a heavy sinking inside of me, because, no, I am not okay, but he is pleading with me, so I nod my head.

He kisses my forehead, and so low, he says, "I promise. I can fix everything. I will."

Then he smiles and heads off into the party, and I follow after Mary-Beth. She is prattling on about a time she retraced her steps, starting with the moment she woke up in the morning. "And wouldn't you know it, but my wedding ring was inside the copy machine, right there in the gosh darn paper tray. Can you believe that? I mean really. I never would have thought to look there."

We do find my toothpicks. They are sitting on top of the mini fridge. I must have grabbed them from the drawer where I always keep them, then set them on top of the fridge while I pulled out the piping bags of frosting.

"Works every time," MaryBeth says with another giggle.

I can still feel Ethan's kiss to my forehead, hear the warm reassurance of his tone. He wants so badly to protect me, to be the protector, the fixer. But he can't fix this.

No. I have to do it. I have to remember, *truly* remember, for myself. And MaryBeth may have a point, because I've never retraced my steps. Not since that night.

It's time to go out onto the balcony.

79

Mikayla

There is no us, he said. *It's in your head.*

I am on the balcony, just outside the door to the nursery, where the baby sleeps now. I try to picture her. I wonder if they still wrap her in that blanket like a caterpillar in a cocoon, bind her arms like she's in a mini-straitjacket.

I look out over the yard and the pool, watch people drift inside for cake and candles. Sophie and Gabby and the girls are gone, in the poolside lounge, I think, changing back into their dresses. The boys are still by the pool, tugging T-shirts back on to wear with their damp swim trunks. I think of how they kept talking about jumping from here to the pool. It's too far, I think. You'd definitely go splat against the stones.

I step up onto the chair, so the balcony railing is pelvis-high. I bend at the waist and lean out. My stomach does that funny floaty flip, like when you ride a roller coaster, like your body is afraid, but it's also kind of fun.

The look on Mr. Matthews' face.

I guess Dani must have told him about the note, about the lipstick.

And now he knows what I've done, and he must think that I'm crazy. Maybe I am.

"What in heavens? You get down from there this minute, you crazy girl."

The voice startles me, almost makes me lose my balance for a second, and I turn to see the nanny. I didn't hear her come out onto the balcony. I step down from the chair, a flush of embarrassment hot on my cheeks.

She's reaching for my arm, helping me down.

"I'm okay," I say.

"Oh, you're okay, are you? Well, isn't that good to hear, Miss Invincible? You young ones, never looking past your arm, I swear to sweet suffering Jesus. And this silly balcony. Sure, who puts a glass wall on a balcony? Tempting the fates, if I ever heard of it. Look right here at this crack."

I look to where she's pointing, and she's right. A star-shaped chip, like when a rock hits your windshield, a splinter off the side as fine as a strand of hair.

"Right where you were leaning over, like. A bird hit it. I found him dead earlier on the patio below. Completely mental to lean over this railing. What if it had split in two? Sent you tumbling to your death? You have a mammy, don't you?"

I nod, but before I can even answer, she's yelling at me again.

"She's at home, no doubt, waiting and worrying the way all mammies do and expecting you to come through those doors tonight. So get out of here. Go downstairs. They're having cake, and I don't want to be seeing any troublemaking from you."

So, I do what she tells me, and when I come down the stairs, everyone is there, the whole party, crammed into the great open room, around the dining table, where Sophie sits at the head. I shoulder through the crowd, come up just beside the cake.

"Are we ready?" Dani asks, holding a long lighter.

Ethan is there, his hand on the small of Dani's back. I can tell that he has felt my presence, but he doesn't look my way.

Mr. Matthews is such a good man. He isn't the kind of man who would leave his wife. I remember how devastated he was when Kim left. How he felt he had failed.

Even now my skin burns where he touched me. The spot on my collarbone where my necklace sits. The weight of the jewelry box key is a constant reminder of him. I think of the slow drag of his eyes up to my lips. The way they lingered there. The way our bodies burned for each other. Mr. Matthews wants me. Just as much as I want him. He wants to be with me.

But Dani and her stupid baby are in our way.

80

Kim

I'm holding my hair back so that I can tip my head under the faucet, let the water run directly into my dry mouth. I've just vomited up what has got to be the last of everything in my stomach.

I try to open the door quietly, hoping I can slip back into the party without being noticed, but no such luck.

"Here she is." It's Vera, our old neighbor, and everyone at the party is looking at me. "Oh, dear. You look peaked. Are you all right?"

If everyone could just give me the benefit of the doubt—I had to take a quick pee or check my lipstick—but no, of course, I can see through the crowd and down the long quartz dining table to Sophie at the end. I can see that she knows that her mom had to put a pause on her "Happy Birthday" song and Sweet Sixteen candles so she could puke in the bathroom. She looks . . . not disgusted . . . not disappointed . . . What is that look on my daughter's face? Then I realize, with a sinking feeling, that it is the absence of an emotion. She is completely and utterly unsurprised.

"Are we ready?" Dani asks, then she clicks the long lighter on, slowly lights each candle, and when all sixteen are lit, someone turns off the light. The candles and the cake and my daughter in her champagne-colored dress glitter in the dark window's reflection as the whole town sings in unison.

———

Last year, my parents had their fiftieth wedding anniversary. We threw them a big party—well, my brother did, mostly. He was the one to book the private room, pick the menu, invite the guests. Michael is good at planning. Anything tedious and robotic is right up his alley. It was nice at first, a DJ playing the Supremes and Mom and Dad dancing to Nat King Cole and seeing cousins I hadn't seen in years. But after a while, it was just so many old friends and family asking the same questions. *How's the vet practice? How's Ethan? Oh no. I hadn't heard. Janet didn't tell me. Y'all seemed so perfect.*

There was an open bar, and at some point I thought it was a good idea to give a speech, and during that speech I told a joke—something about Aunt Darleen and a stick up her ass—that apparently wasn't as funny to everyone else as it was to me, and Michael took the microphone away, and I bumped into the table and spilled red wine onto Mom's butter yellow party dress, and I could just feel it. Everyone exchanging looks, filing it away to gossip about later. Everyone judging me, when they had no right.

I went outside for fresh air and a cigarette. Michael followed me.

Don't, I told him.

I didn't say anything, he said.

I don't want to hear it, okay? You have no idea what I've been through. I had everything. And now look. You know, Ethan—

Jesus, Kim, really? Ethan isn't here. He didn't make you drink too much or piss off Aunt Darleen or tip the table over. That was you.

I inhaled my cigarette and refused to look at him, and finally he went back inside. Proud of my own stubbornness—that's what my dad has always said about me. But Michael was right then, and Gemma was right tonight. I don't have anything left to be proud of.

———

"And many more," Ethan sings out in a baritone.

I watch Sophie close her eyes, make a silent wish, and blow. We are all plunged into absolute darkness.

I slip out the back door.

I take the steps down, and I am alone on the lower patio, the house dark through the windows, the glow from the pool, the sky full of stars, and the black cliffside. I pull out my phone, unlock the screen, scroll through my contacts. I don't let myself hesitate. I hit call, press the phone to my ear.

I guess I should have known I'd call the number one day. Otherwise, why would I have kept it all these years? Who knows if it's even any good anymore?

I listen to it ring once, twice, three times, then the click of an answer.

"Hi, Kim." The voice on the other end is bright and clear. "I always hoped you'd call."

Órlaith

I can see that the tea is taking its effects on Kim, in the way she ran to the jacks a moment ago, in the red-rimmed look of her eyes now.

The lights come back on. The party planner slices into the cake, reveals the surprise of its blood red center.

Everyone is meant to be together now, meant to be in this room. I should leave things be for now.

But I can't.

Dani

The lights are off. Everyone is singing "Happy Birthday" in the darkness. I use this moment to flee. I'm halfway up the stairs by the time Sophie blows out her candles. The lights cut back on just as I enter my room. I close the door behind me, lean back against it. I hear someone say the cake is too pretty to cut. They will no doubt be looking for me to receive the compliment. But I've vanished—a ghost.

I lie on my bed, party dress and stilettos still on. This is where it all started. I've gone back to the beginning. The room is dark. The sky behind the glass is inky black. I close my eyes. I force myself to remember.

The wind moans against the windows, like it did that night.

I remember brushing the rolls with an egg wash. Sophie playing peekaboo. Curtis handing me the pill bottle. Mikayla helping Ethan at the grill. Something about the way she was looking at him, a tingle of warning in the back of my mind, Ethan swirling that glass of whiskey. Charlotte cluster-feeding while we played Taboo. Charlotte feeding again in bed.

There was always this—someone touching me, needing me, pulling me, pulling milk from my body, a body that was still sore and loose. Had my organs even found their way back to their regular positions yet? I was so tired all the time.

It was the baby, of course, waking every few hours, nursing around the clock, and sometimes not nursing, not latching well, just crying and crying unless I bounced and paced.

But it was also my own uneasiness. The presence—things missing and shifting, the figure on the lawn, the face at the window—all of it making me feel insane, but also all of it feeling entirely real.

Earlier that day, while we were getting things ready in the kitchen, Ethan had come up behind me, squeezed my shoulders with his strong hands, and kissed my neck.

I flicked my shoulder, the way a horse's muscles shudder to rid a fly. *Sophie and Mikayla are coming,* I said. I checked the monitor. Charlotte was asleep in her bassinet in the downstairs guest room.

They aren't here yet. Ethan's voice was flirtatious. His lips were on my neck again, trailing up to my earlobe.

It made me furious. *I'm exhausted. There are a million things to do before the girls get here, and who knows when Charlotte will be up again?*

Hey. He ran reassuring hands up and down my arms. *It's going to be fine. It's not a big deal. And those?* He looked to the lump of black-bread dough I was kneading on the floured counter. *Those are going to be awesome.*

He kissed me on the forehead and went to cut tomatoes for the salad.

He was right, of course. It was fine. It wasn't a big deal. Just Sophie and Mikayla over for dinner like a thousand times before.

But, by the end of the night, I was so tired that I kept nodding off while Charlotte nursed. I had to keep shaking myself awake, until Charlotte finished, her sleeping mouth unlatching from my nipple with a pop. I transferred her to the bassinet beside the bed and fell into a heavy sleep.

And then . . .

And then, what?

Then there are only chipped fragments of memory, like a broken mirror.

I woke.

So, now, I retrace my steps. I sit up in the dark room. The bed I'm sitting on is made, but that night, I turned and saw the shadowed form of Ethan beneath the covers.

The bassinet is gone, moved to the attic, because Charlotte sleeps in her crib in the nursery now. But that night, it was beside me, within arm's reach. I leaned in to peer at her in the dark, and . . . did I see her? Did I snatch her sleeping from her bed?

I can't remember.

I just remember the wind, the strange sound of the wind that night, almost human, and I went to the glass, pushed back the curtain, peered outside.

So I do that now. I rewind. I hit play.

That night, I unlatched the lock. I slid open the door. I stepped outside.

My heart hammers, and my breath comes quick, but I flick the latch. I tug the door, and just like that night, it glides along the track, silent against the roar of the wind.

I look at my hands now, assure myself that they are empty, that Charlotte is safe in her bed, before I step across the threshold.

I am on the balcony now. There is only a half-wall of invisible glass between me and the drop of the dark cliff. The wind is stronger up here—it always is—and it pulls my hair like fingers. It whips my dress around my thighs.

I cling to the wall of the house. I breathe in furious, shallow pants, so that I feel lightheaded. I can't see that glass wall in the dark, the light playing tricks. There is only the drop. One jagged shard of memory—leaning out over that glass wall and the cold wind clutching my hair.

No, no, no. I can't do this. I am paralyzed with fear—the fear of falling. The fear of knowing.

Another shard slices my brain, a picture as clear as a paused movie screen. Charlotte dangled over the edge, nothing but dark air beneath her. My stomach flips.

I think of her Moro reflex in those early days. The way any trigger—a loud noise, the sensation of drifting into sleep—could startle her, send her arms and legs flying out, then curling back. Born with the fear of falling. Born with the need to be swaddled, held womblike to remind her that she is safe.

And who am I if I can't keep her safe?

I breathe. I feel the sensations of my surroundings. The window at my back, against my palms. The cool wind on my skin. My dress fluttering against my shins.

I breathe. I reach out and touch the glass balcony railing. I start walking.

And MaryBeth might have been right about retracing steps, because my feet are moving along the same path they did that night, past the door that leads into our bedroom, past the door that leads to the open loft, past the door into Sophie's room, all the way to the far end, outside the nursery, where a pair of chairs and a side table sit.

As I get closer, as I see the shape of the farthest chair, I remember the shadowed figure, the one I couldn't unpuzzle, limbs at odd angles, the outline of a monster. And in the moonlight, a face turned to me, frightened and frightening. In all my slipshod remembering from these last few horrible months, this face was featureless.

But now—

But now—the features click into place, and I remember.

It wasn't *The Mother* that I found up here.

It was Mikayla.

Sweet, timid Mikayla, and now, just like I did then, I think, *Oh, of course, it was you.* Mikayla, who helped my husband tend the grill that evening, who looked at him with stars in her eyes. Mikayla, who dropped by multiple times when only Ethan was home, even after he tried gently to dissuade her. *I think she's feeling abandoned by Sophie,* he told me. *But, come on. I can't be hanging out with a teenage girl.* He even asked me to stay home from prenatal yoga, but I didn't take it seriously. *She's sweet,* I said. *She loves you like a dad.*

Of course, it was Mikayla who turned down the photograph of us on the River Walk, peered through Ethan's study window, sprayed my perfume and stole my hand cream. Mikayla who, oh my God, was in my closet just today, playing with my makeup, with my lipstick.

And, oh, I remember it all like a torrential flood. My throat seizes with panic, because that night, when I found Mikayla here on the balcony, she wasn't alone.

83

Mikayla

Sophie and everyone else—they're all eating red velvet cake and clinking glasses of sparkling cider and laughing at someone's dumb joke, because everything is still easy for them, still simple.

Sophie has even forgiven Gabby for making out with Mason. *Don't be salty,* Gabby said. *You said you were over him. Remember?*

But I don't belong in that world.

I open the door silently, slip into the dark room.

———

The night we slept over, Sophie was all goo-goo-gaga over Charlotte.
Isn't she just the cutest?

Even I admit she was cute, with these impossibly huge eyes like a Disney character, all warm chocolate brown, just like Ethan's. Dani asked if I wanted to hold her, and, I mean, what are you supposed to say? You look like a psychopath if you say no. She made me sit in a chair and reminded me like a dozen times to support her neck, and Charlotte got red-faced, and Dani said, *Uh-oh, I think maybe someone's pooping,* but in this voice like it was adorable.

I know it's kind of messed up to hate a baby, but I couldn't help it.

It was the first time I'd seen Mr. Matthews—like, face-to-face talked to him—since I had tried to kiss him. I was sick to my stomach the whole week before, but then Mr. Matthews was just Mr. Matthews, an open door and a big smile, and *Hey, Mikayla,* like there was nothing to be embarrassed about at all.

I brought him a clean plate for the steak while he grilled, and we were alone together in the backyard. He was telling me a funny story, sipping his whiskey, and I was laughing, and he said, *It hasn't felt right without y'all these last few weeks. We need to get back to our routine.* And I knew he meant Sophie staying every Wednesday night and every other weekend, but the way he looked at me when he said *get back to our routine,* the way his fingers brushed mine as he took the plate, I knew he really meant *our* routine, that he was talking about us, the secret us—our Saturday afternoons, his fingertips on my collarbone, my lips on his lips—and I burned all over.

So, yeah, when Dani plopped her stupid baby in my arms, I kind of hated her.

And when I couldn't sleep that night, after hours of tossing and turning and hearing the steady rhythm of Sophie's breathing, I got up and snuck into the hallway.

It was like when I had let myself into the house, when I had taken the cuff links and the hand cream—I hadn't planned it, not really. I couldn't help myself. I just wanted to see him, you know? It felt like we were tied together, that invisible thread taut. I had already snuck around the house so much by then, and I'd never been caught, so it didn't seem that crazy, as I stood outside their bedroom door, not a single sound coming from inside so that I knew they were sleeping, to just turn the knob, just push the door open a hair, and slip inside. I just wanted to see what he looked like sleeping, hear what he sounded like. And, really, what would they do if they woke up and saw me there? I could remember a time not really that long ago when I had done just that, woken from a nightmare while sleeping over at Sophie's, and I'd come to this exact bedroom and woken Kim and told her I wanted to call my mom, and she had pulled me into one of her big, soft hugs, smelling like she always does of Bath & Body Works body spray and that crunchy mousse she uses in her wild curly hair. So, yeah, maybe I would just tell them I had a nightmare.

The bedroom was dark. There was Dani. There was the baby. And there was the wind outside, calling.

I hadn't planned it. Not really.

84

Kim

The house is lit again from within. I watch the catering staff disassemble the cake, pass out slices with flutes of champagne, and my tongue feels dry with want. I turn from the party, look out over the dark cliffside instead.

"You saved my number too?" I say on the phone.

"I had a feeling." It's Anita Lewis, the sponsor Ma found for me three years ago.

There is a long pause in which neither of us speaks. My throat is tight, my tongue thick. I press the phone to my ear, hard. Finally, I swallow. "Um," I say, and I'm surprised to find my voice crack. I realize that I've never done something quite so terrifying. It's like I'm standing at the window of a plane, about to skydive, just free-fall through the air and hope that my parachute works.

"I think, maybe, I need to stop drinking," I say.

"That's good," Anita says.

85

Dani

On the balcony, I have to grip the glass wall to keep my legs from going weak beneath me.

Because I remember it all now with crystal clarity. I remember Mikayla turning to me. Remember the way all the color drained from her face, leaving her white as a ghost, her long copper hair streaming in the wind like a scarf.

What the hell is going on? I said back then.

And, when I spoke, *he* turned to me as well.

———

Ethan hadn't been in bed beside me. I had woken, looked hastily toward his side, seen a lump of covers and assumed he was there. It was Charlotte I cared about in that moment. I had leaned over the bassinet, put my hand to Charlotte's chest and waited, holding my own breath until I felt the rise and fall of hers. I had heard something mixed with the sounds of the wind—a moaning that sounded almost human, and I had slid open the balcony door to see what it was.

No, Ethan hadn't been in bed beside me, because he had been here, on the far end of the balcony, sitting on the farthest chair. Mikayla straddled his lap in her big T-shirt and flannel pajama shorts. His mouth was on her neck, one hand slid high up her thigh, fingertips under the hem of her pajama shorts, grabbing a handful of her ass. The other hand was around her wrist, guiding her hand below the waistband of his sweatpants.

What the fuck is going on? I flicked on the outdoor light, and for a moment, they were frozen in that horrible tableau that couldn't be real.

Dani, Ethan said, standing, untangling himself from the girl. *It's not—sn—*

I think he was going to say, *It's not what it looks like,* such a trite cliché that I could have laughed, but the words stuck in his throat. That's what I had thought was my husband's biggest weakness—the tripping tangle of consonants.

In the corner of the balcony, Mikayla wrapped her arms tightly around herself. Her wide eyes flicked wildly between Ethan and me—a trapped animal.

Ethan took two long breaths through his nose. Then he regained control. I saw it on his face, an almost imperceptible shift, a ripple across a placid lake. When he spoke, his words were as smooth as a melody. *Mikayla,* he said. *Go inside, sweetheart. It's late.*

Mikayla shot one last terrified look at me before scurrying off, through the closest balcony door, and into the empty nursery.

I held tightly to the railing, my legs heavy, like in a dream.

How's Charlotte? he asked. *Is she asleep?*

The question—his tone—it was so ordinary that it made me dizzy, physically sick, so I had to turn to the cliff's drop, lean over the banister, and dry-heave into the cold night air. That's where the jagged piece of memory comes from—that's why I was leaning out over the balcony railing.

Ethan put a hand to my shoulder, like he was comforting me, and I wheeled around on him, wiping the back of my hand across my mouth. *Get the fuck away from me.*

The look in his eyes—it was hurt, fucking hurt, like *I* had wounded *him,* and I wanted to rake my nails across his face.

She's a little girl, I said. *What the fuck were you doing with that little girl?*

Lower your voice, he said.

The words set my whole brain on fire.

Are you fucking kidding me? My voice was a scrape against my throat, spit flying from my mouth.

We can talk about what you think you saw, but right now, you are acting irrational. My daughter is inside. You need to be considerate of that.

I just stared at him. This couldn't be real, couldn't be happening, couldn't be my husband, who was sweet and calm, who never forgot to take the trash to the curb on Thursday nights, who brought me coffee in bed, who flew me to Paris and then proposed in Barcelona.

And yet . . . embedded deep in the fibers of my muscles, there was a part of me that absolutely could believe. Because how many times had Ethan subtly shifted my perception, skillful as a surgeon? The time I had ditched my friend Marissa's birthday party because Ethan had invited me to a get-together at a friend's house on the same night— poker and drinks. He had known about Marissa's party, but still he had been insistent in that sugar-glazed, neck-kissing way of his: *Come on. She won't care. I want to show you off.* It had been early—post-Paris but pre-Barcelona—and I was still drunk on the newness of us.

When I showed up, dressed for a cocktail party, it was just a group of guys in someone's garage converted into a kind of sports-themed den. The guys were nice enough, saying hello, offering me a beer from a cooler, but once the poker game started—I couldn't join, because they were weeks into a tournament they played for serious money—no one paid me any attention at all, not a single word, for hours. Just talk of football and poker, cigar smoke filling the box of a room, and when Marissa texted me a blur-of-sparkle photo of her and two more of my old coworkers from the coffee shop—*Jolly Rancher Shots! Bet you wish you were here!*—I couldn't help tearing up.

Our first fight in the car afterward.

Why did you even bring me there?

You're an adult, he'd said, eyes on the road. *If you didn't want to come, you shouldn't have.*

You didn't even talk to me. No one did.

I'm sorry you weren't the center of attention.

Fucking asshole, I said, tears stinging my eyes, because I felt like I didn't even know him.

But he wouldn't let me leave that night, said I'd had too much to drink, and in the morning, he brought me a cup of coffee and an English muffin spread with butter and blackberry jam. He kissed my forehead and said, *Don't worry about last night.* Like *he* was forgiving *me.* And maybe I had overreacted. Maybe too many beers and too much time alone in my head had made me bitchy. I had called him an asshole, after all, and maybe I should just be grateful he wasn't mad, that we could just enjoy the farmers market at the Pearl instead of spend the day arguing.

I had believed his version over my own.

That time, and the next, and the next.

But this was so very, very different. The wind bit cold against my skin, but I flamed hot with adrenaline.

I know what I saw. I didn't want to give him any more chances to explain, to lie, so I went back into the house, into the dark nursery, the moon and the balcony light sending long shadows at strange angles over toys and bookshelves.

I heard his footsteps behind me as I went out into the hallway, but I didn't look back.

Dani, don't do this.

Fuck you, I shrieked. I actually shrieked, my voice high and shrill. My blood rushed fast and hot through my chest, in my ears, stinging my cheeks. As we passed Sophie's bedroom, he grabbed hold of my arm.

I know what I saw, I repeated, a mantra. I could hear Charlotte then, crying down the hall.

Let me help you, Ethan said, like he was reading a script, committing to a part.

I took a step toward him. His hand was a vice on my elbow, and he loomed over me. He felt larger in the dark. I tipped my face up to his. *We're leaving,* I said. *Now. We have to get out of this house.*

We? he said, so low it was a growl.

I ripped my arm free and went to the bedroom. I scooped up Charlotte, pressed her angry little body close to me, and the smell of her made my chest hurt. Ethan followed me into the room. I didn't look at him. I thought he'd try to continue the conversation, try to convince me that I didn't see what I definitely saw, but he moved past me without a word into the closet. I shushed and bounced Charlotte. She was rooting, expecting me to feed her, but I couldn't, not in that moment. I laid her back in the bassinet, started to grab a few things we'd need—a muslin burp cloth laid over a chair, an extra Velcro swaddler from the bottom drawer of my nightstand.

I felt Ethan's hand on my shoulder. I tried to flick it off.

I don't want to hear it, I said.

But he wrapped his arms around me anyway, pulled me close, my back tight against his chest. Did he really think he could do this? Try his *Let's not fight* bullshit that he's always done as a way to sidestep an apology, a way to avoid the conversation altogether?

Don't worry, he whispered, his lips on my ear in the same way they always are when we make love, and it made me shiver with disgust. *I can fix this. I'm going to fix this.*

I tried to shove him off, but his grip only tightened, like a restraint. *Shhh,* he said. The baby was wailing.

I felt a jolt of terror run through me, and I bucked against him, succeeded in shoving him hard against the wall, so hard that the framed photos shook.

Then a pain in my upper arm, the hot slice of a needle sliding into my skin.

I thought, *Charlotte,* before my world went black.

———

Now, I can hear the party still going down below, the sounds of laughter and conversations overlapping.

Then a voice behind me. "Hey, babe."

I turn.

Ethan stands on the balcony, in his dark suit, two flutes of champagne in his hands. "What are you doing up here?"

86

Mikayla

That night, the bedroom was dark. There was Dani. There was the baby. And there was the wind outside, calling.

But Mr. Matthews' side of the bed was empty. And it felt like a sign. Of course he was up too. Of course he couldn't sleep either.

I went looking for him. Downstairs, his study was dark. So was the kitchen and the living room. Outside, the pool light glowed, but he wasn't there either. It was chilly—December—and I was only wearing a big T-shirt and pajama shorts. Then I heard a whistle. I looked up and saw him sitting on the balcony, the glow of a cigar and the glint of whiskey in a glass. He tipped his head, as if to say, *Come up here.* So I did.

I hadn't planned it. Not really. And even though I had wanted him to kiss me, to touch me, even though I had imagined it so many times alone in my bed, when it happened, it was different somehow. But I had wanted so badly to make him happy.

———

"What are you doing in here?" Sophie asks, turning on the light in Mr. Matthews' empty study.

"I don't know," I said.

"You've been weird all day. What's up?"

I shrug. There is no way I can ever tell her, no way I can ever tell anyone.

"I'm sorry I was a bitch earlier," Sophie says. She has her arms crossed over herself. She curls one foot around the other.

"I'm sorry too," I say, because I am. I'm really, really sorry. I just can't say why.

She comes to me, bumps me with her hip. "Come hang out with us. Stop being such a creep." She says it with a smile. I follow her back to the party, and she gets me a slice of cake.

———

In the morning, Mr. Matthews caught me in the hallway while Sophie took a shower. *You okay?* he asked.

I could hear Sophie's shower running through the wall. And just down the hall, the closed door to Dani's bedroom. Could she hear us?

We can't tell anyone about what happened last night, he said. The idea made me want to vomit. Sophie knowing what I'd done? My mom? My dad? What would they think of me? My whole life would be over.

He touched my chin, tipped my face up to his. And even though I was so full of panic and this swirling sickness, my heart still fluttered at his attention. *People wouldn't understand,* he said. He ran the pad of his thumb over my chin, searched my eyes.

I nodded. They wouldn't understand. Because even if it was wrong— and it *was* wrong; I could feel the wrongness like a sick animal scratching at my organs—we loved each other. You didn't do the things we'd done unless you loved each other. He wouldn't look at me the way he was looking at me unless he loved me.

What about Dani? I said.

She's not well. I think you saw that.

I wasn't sure what he meant at first. But . . . maybe? All her terrible shrieking the night before? And now what was she doing? What was she waiting for?

I'll take care of it, he promised. *Don't worry. I'll protect you.*

———

So I went home, and I waited for my life to cave in. Every time my dad answered the phone, every time my mom knocked on my bedroom door, every time I saw Sophie at school, I held my breath. I waited. But it never happened.

I waited for him too. For him to come for me. For him to call for me. He never did.

I ran into him once. Maybe six weeks later. I was at H-E-B with my mom. We turned the corner into the bread aisle, and there he was. He smiled. He chatted with my mom about nothing really—Market Days at Bulverde Village, and did we still sell that great goat's milk lotion? As if nothing was different at all, nothing was wrong.

Then a week ago, I saw Dani for the first time since that night. Getting out of the car after school, slinging my backpack over my shoulder, I turned and saw her across the street, pushing the stroller. I froze. It was finally happening. I would finally have to pay for what I had done. But Dani just smiled and waved, and I waved back. And that was it.

It wasn't fair. It wasn't fair that she could just pretend like nothing had happened.

She had seen us. Hadn't she?

So I had written her a note, dropped it on her front step. Because she was the crazy one. Not me.

87

Kim

When I was ten years old, my grandfather gave me an old mare with the understanding that she was my sole responsibility. Everything from feeding and grooming to stall-cleaning and tack maintenance. The saddle alone weighed nearly as much as I did. I fell in love with animals, but more important, it taught me from an early age what I was capable of. It taught me independence.

As a young woman, I wore that independence like a badge. I moved out and got my own apartment as soon as I turned eighteen. I worked my way through college, cleaning kennels and bartending. I took a lot of pride in being self-sufficient. The people in my life—boyfriends, friends—they were there because I wanted them, not because I needed them.

Then came Ethan. I'd gotten a flat coming home from the kennels and he pulled up with his shiny tire iron and shinier smile. He was tall and handsome, so I made it easy on him and asked him to lunch in exchange for the roadside assistance. Over tacos and margaritas, I found out he was every bit as ambitious as me, further along, though, in the middle of med school with a focus in psychiatry. I was impressed. We started dating. He was the first man to really break through my wall. As much as I had thrived on doing it all on my own, there was a comfort in trusting someone, in knowing there was someone who'd help me shoulder the burden. I fell in love with the idea of having big ambitions together, achieving them together.

We were busy all the time—in class, at work, hunkered down at the library. Any free time we did have, we spent in bed, having amazing sex, and fantasizing about our upcoming life together. *I'm going to buy you a house on the hill,* Ethan said once, and the image took root. A house on the hill, each with a practice of our own, a couple of kids. What could be better? What could stop us?

Things moved fast with Ethan. We'd only been dating a few months when my lease came up. Ethan suggested I move in with him to save money. We were engaged within the year. *We never see you anymore,* whined my coworkers at the dive where I bartended. *I'm getting married, not dying,* I laughed. Ethan made a joke about how my friends took all the money they made at one bar and blew it at another. *They'll figure out what they want from life eventually.* But I'd already figured out what I wanted from life. Ethan was right—that job, that group of friends was a distraction, so I quit and took a position at a research lab on campus. Every step we took together felt like solid ground on the road to achieving our goals.

I didn't have time for wedding planning, between school and multiple jobs, plus it was all too expensive. It seemed silly to set us back so far from where we'd gotten financially for a single party. Our dreams were bigger than that. So when Ethan half-jokingly suggested we elope, I felt a rush of relief. We were giddy as we waited in line at the courthouse. My mom was so upset. I should have known she'd be hurt. I'd just gotten swept up. Ethan agreed. *You deserve a wedding. I'll give you a wedding,* he promised. Our imaginations floated back to that house on the hill, planning the party we'd throw with all of our friends and family one day. I just had to be patient. We just had to keep working.

Then I got pregnant. I'd wanted to wait until after I graduated from veterinary school. We always used condoms, but nothing is one-hundred-percent reliable. Just a slight change of plans, and when Sophie came, our daughter, the love I felt was downright painful.

Ethan was gone most of the time by then, commuting over an hour for his residency. *Take some time off,* he told me. *I'm making money now, and soon I'll be working for a practice. You can go back when Sophie's older.* But I was terrified to stop. Gemma chipped in to babysit when we couldn't afford day care so I wouldn't miss too many classes and, somehow, I graduated, and Ethan finished residency.

Finally, finally, our dreams were starting. Both of us working as doctors, not with practices of our own, not yet, but still.

We talked about moving to Houston, getting a place near my folks, who were so excited to be grandparents. But then Ethan found the Vogel mansion hours away from them in Bulverde—our house on the hill. Roy Barker offered him a position in his practice. The money was good. It made sense. And we started dreaming again, bigger this time, planning every detail of our renovations: marble counters, chandeliers, and walls of glass.

It was everything we wanted, but the renovations and motherhood and starting my career—it was all so much heavier than the weight of that old mare's saddle. I was drowning, tired and stressed all the time. The money I meant to save away for my own practice kept being poured into preschool and strollers and this damn house.

Whenever I thought maybe we were starting to get on top of things, Ethan would surprise me, like with the Calacatta marble countertops I'd fawned over in a design magazine. I wouldn't be able to hide the anger in my voice, the tears that blurred my vision. *I thought you'd be happy,* Ethan would say, and he'd look hurt, and that would make me feel like a real bitch. There was always the implication that I should be happy. Why wasn't I happy? It was all these sacrifices I was making for the family, for these big dreams that were never quite within our grasp—a thousand tiny cuts, slowly bleeding me dry.

Ethan wanted to try for another baby. The idea made me feel trapped in my own skin. At my yearly appointment, I got on birth control. I hid the pills in a box of tampons under the sink. Keeping this secret meant Ethan and I were no longer in this together. I was alone, Sophie and I in this sprawling house that every day became less of a dream and more of a nightmare.

The house was strange. It made sounds that Ethan never seemed to hear. Light shifted, time warped like rain-bloated wood. Something always needed fixing. I started drinking. Just a glass of wine at night to unwind, to ease the worry. A glass turned into a bottle. A bottle turned into a box of wine on the counter, so I couldn't keep track, so I wouldn't have to. Sometimes, I'd try to cut back. I'd go three days without a drink, and then Ethan would bring me a glass of cabernet while I relaxed with a book on the sofa. I couldn't say no. It wasn't his fault. I hadn't told him I was trying to quit, because that would mean admitting I had a problem, because that would mean needing to explain myself when I failed.

I'd always thought I was a fun drunk, but it turned out I could be vicious too. We started arguing more often. I'd wake up sick at the memories of things I had said. But the wine gave me a tiny burst of freedom. After a few glasses, I had the courage to say what was bothering me, unleash my complaints, all my bitterness spilling like poison. I felt angry all the time. Mostly, I was angry at myself.

I looked in the mirror, and I didn't like who I was anymore. I caught sight of old pictures, and I felt sorry for the girl I used to be.

Looking back, I was like that stupid frog, slipping into a warm bath that would soon boil me alive, because I gave my independence away piece by piece. Gave myself away.

Then one day, I came back from checking the mail. *I just had the weirdest conversation with Vera,* I told Ethan. Vera seemed to think that Ethan and I had gotten into an argument, that I'd stormed off in the middle of the night, wandering the neighborhood drunk in my pajamas. *Last week,* he said. *When you got mad about the laundry.* I looked at him blankly. *I'm not upset anymore. I know you had a lot to drink. I just don't like worrying about you.* I murmured an apology, let him hold me. I almost believed him.

But it had never happened. Sure, I snapped at him, but there had never been a fight, never a wandering out into the dark. I remember that evening clearly because Sophie had woken screaming from a nightmare. I'd spent a good portion of the night comforting her, before going back to an empty bed.

I knew he had lied to Vera. And if he was lying this time, then how many times had he lied before? Lied to me and about me?

So, I started paying attention.

In arguments, even when I began on firm footing, justifiably upset about something Ethan did or said—hurt my feelings, spent too much money, stayed out late with friends—the conversation would go around and around until I was screaming through tears, ready to rip my hair out. Eventually, I would do something that needed an apology—scatter a pile of papers off his desk, shatter a glass, make a scene in front of a colleague, or, worse, in front of Sophie, so she'd burst into tears—so it always ended up with me apologizing, embarrassed by my inability to control my emotions, with Ethan forgiving me. *You can't help it,* he'd say, kissing me on the head. *My hot-tempered wife.* And I'd wonder what was wrong with me, wonder how I'd become such a mess, wonder how anyone could love such a disaster of a person.

I needed to find myself again, find that little girl I used to be. I opened another bank account, slowly squirreled away money. I packed a small suitcase and tucked it into the back corner of our closet. I put a deposit down on the Stone Oak apartment.

Three nights before I had planned to leave, I sat on a barstool at the kitchen island, looking out over our view, the lights from houses below like reflected constellations. I was so close to slipping away, to uncurling a fist I'd held tightly for so long. I was lost in thought, so that when Ethan rested a hand on my shoulder, I jumped at his touch. *Are you all right?* he asked. I looked him right in the eyes and lied. *Just stressed about work,* I said. He held my stare for a moment. *Let me open a bottle. Just relax tonight. Have fun with Gemma tomorrow. Everything will be okay. You'll see.*

I took the wine up to the balcony, read in my chair, drank glass after glass until the bottle was empty.

Then I woke up in the hospital.

My misuse of the medication had been reported to the Texas Board of Veterinary Medical Examiners. My phone was filled with texts to friends and family members, saying the most awful things. In my email, those photos of Gemma, sent to everyone we knew.

When I came to, Ethan was there by my hospital bed, holding my hand, calm and patient and ready to forgive me.

What did you do, Ethan? I asked.

Because Ethan had opened that bottle of wine, poured my first glass. He'd known about Gemma's pictures too. She had made me swear to never tell a soul, but I'd told Ethan, one stupid night by the pool while we laughed about the dumb things we'd done as kids.

But the accusation would only lead to the same tiresome cycle— wasn't it enough that I had to question it at all? That I even thought my husband could be capable of such cruelty and calculation? It made more sense that I'd done this to myself, that I had gone scorched earth on the life I was about to leave, burned every bridge back to it. I'd blacked out plenty of times, done mean and ugly things I didn't remember. There was no way I was going to let him forgive me. I didn't ask for Gemma's forgiveness either. I owned this major fuckup, whether it was mine or not, because it meant my freedom.

In doing so, I lost it all—the big house, the doting husband, the best friend, my career, my reputation. Even my fantasy apartment—I couldn't afford it anymore without my license. I had to crawl home to Mom and Dad with my tail between my legs, scrape together something of a life from the rubble that was left.

And until tonight I've hated myself for it.

Until this moment. Seeing Dani, unsure and losing control, I am reminded of who I was when I lived in this house. When I was with him. It's like looking in a mirror.

Even in my current state, it's crystal clear—

It was Ethan. It's always been Ethan.

88

Dani

Ethan offers me one of the glasses of champagne.

For a moment, I'm tempted to take it. Because when I look at him now, it's just Ethan, the man I fell in love with on sun-soaked sheets, who made midnight fast-food runs when I had pregnancy cravings for McNuggets, who held my hand during contractions, stuttered when the doctor said the baby's heart rate was too fast, held me so tenderly after Charlotte was born. The way Charlotte looked in his arms, her belly to his broad chest, small as a tree frog on an oak, and because it would be so much easier, because I liked my life, because I wanted my daughter to grow up in the same house with her father, and because what was a memory really? *We don't remember things the way they really happened,* Ethan has told me. The book he was working on about confirmation bias, about the faulty nature of memory recall. *Besides, it doesn't matter what really happened. It's all in the past anyway. It doesn't exist anymore. All that matters is the story we tell ourselves.*

That was bullshit, though. Of course the truth mattered. It mattered to Mikayla. It mattered to me. It mattered because Ethan wasn't the man I thought he was. Not even close.

"I remember."

When I say it, I see a flicker of recognition pass across his face before he is able to compose it again. He knows that I know. In this instant, already gone, we are honest.

He takes a step toward me. I feel the glass at my back. Suddenly, all of my emotions are eclipsed by a single one: fear.

89

Ethan

Dani stands on the balcony, her back to me. Behind her, the black sky stretches wider than my field of vision. Shadowed cedars and live oaks and limestone bluffs form a jagged skyline. Headlights snake along the highway two hundred feet below. I like to imagine the people in those cars, imagine what they must think when they look up at this house, because they *must* look up at it. You couldn't possibly miss it, couldn't ignore it. Especially in the dark, the wall of windows full of light, rooms exposed like a stage set. We're too high up for anyone to really see inside, but you get the idea—soaring ceilings, a massive chandelier, and the shapes of the people who live up here—the suggestion of a life just out of reach.

I want to burn this image into my brain like a photograph.

"Hey, babe," I say.

Dani turns, moonlight kissing her cheekbone, the top of her shoulder. She looks to the champagne glasses in my hands.

"What are you doing out here?" I say.

Her eyes meet mine. "I remember." Her voice is flat.

A jolt of cold panic tightens the muscles of my neck, my jaw. I take a step forward. If I speak, I'll stutter. So I don't. I breathe in the crisp night air. I lift the corners of my mouth in an easy smile, hold out a glass. I loop my words into a smooth melody. "Come back downstairs. It's all five-star reviews for your cake."

Her eyes are on the champagne again. She seems to hesitate. *Please take it.* Everything is still perfect. Everything can be perfect.

She looks to me, and I can see it in her eyes.

"I remember everything."

As a kid, I felt pure terror every time I had to speak.

People talk quickly, no filter between thoughts and words. But I was born trapped in my own head. I knew exactly what I wanted to say, but my throat would close, my tongue lock to the roof of my mouth, the hinge of my jaw tighten like an overturned screw.

"How could you?" Dani's voice breaks on the question.

I pull my brows together—confusion peppered with concern. "Are you feeling all right?"

"Stop it," Dani says. "Just stop it. I'm not an idiot. And I'm not fucking crazy."

The *fuck* tears the air. I look to the pool and the patio below. Empty. No sound but the wind and the gentle lapping of the water.

I set the glasses down on the side table. "I never said *crazy*. I would never use the word *crazy*. Let's just go inside." I take another step toward her, my hand outstretched.

She recoils from me. "I. Saw. You." Each word is pointed and sharp. She flings her hand toward the chair in the corner of the balcony. "Right there, groping Mikayla like an animal."

"St—" I stop myself in time, stop myself before the muscles catch. I drop my tongue. I release the tension from my neck. I start again. "Lower your voice."

"Lower my voice?" She laughs. Dani has never laughed at me, not like that, not that ugly, dismissive laugh.

Kim used to laugh at me.

It's amazing how memories mold us. Most of my work as a psychiatrist is helping patients deal with the past—overcome trauma, unlearn habits, dig through their childhood, and pinpoint the moments when they became, the moments that formed them. But memories are not concrete things. Even the most skilled neurosurgeon couldn't locate a memory on an MRI. And, yet, memories haunt us, drive us, shape us all the same.

My mother left when I was eight. I remember the way I felt safe in her arms, the way she would wait for me to find my words as if she had all the time in the world. She was always trying on hobbies and groups of friends like changes of clothes. It was my father's fault—he didn't know how to guide her. He was a small man. He had no control over anything, always losing his temper, losing his job. When my mother started in on him, he would match her emotions, so they were both yelling, slamming doors.

I need to find myself as a person, she'd told me over the phone. Instead, she found Brian, a CPA. They got married, moved to Illinois, had two daughters. They flew me out for a week every summer, sent me Christmas and birthday presents. My mom left us because my father was weak, because he made it easy for her to leave.

It wasn't until I met Big Roy Barker that I understood what it meant to be a strong man. Roy with his big charisma and big wallet. He had control over everything, and men admired him. Women treated him the way he deserved.

Roy saw the potential in me, took me under his wing, put me in speech therapy. I identified the words that gave me the most trouble and avoided them. I practiced sentences in my mind, imagining them to be lyrics to a song. I started my sentences on an exhale, reduced the tension that I placed on certain sounds. Once I learned how to control my speech, people saw me differently, women especially. Women, I realized, were impressionable. It was easy to control how they saw me, how they saw everything. It was easy to lead them. And that's what a woman wants, really—to be led.

Downstairs, light from the back window illuminates a square onto the dark patio, the stretched shapes of our guests moving and mingling like shadow puppets.

"Dani, please, don't do this."

"Me? What about you, Ethan? What did you do?"

That's what Kim asked when she woke up in the hospital. *What did you do, Ethan?*

I'm not proud of what happened with Kim.

I should have stopped her drinking sooner. It started with us unwinding after long weekdays building our careers and long weekends building this house. She was too headstrong. When she shrugged off the idea of a second child after Sophie in favor of going back to work and taking more time away from us, I resented her for it. Our nightcaps turned into a few glasses for her, which turned into more. The alcohol made her easier to manage. But I only ever wanted her to be happy. When that apartment complex called to confirm her move-in date, I couldn't understand it. What had *she* done? How could *she* do this to us? Just give up on everything we'd built? And for what?

She wouldn't be doing this if she put her family first. I overreacted when I gave her the pills, but it's not like she hadn't taken them before. It lined up with her own destructive behaviors—the wine, the medication, the constant picking at the seams of our perfect life. That's what was making her unhappy. That's what was poisoning our family.

I didn't hold it against her. Any of it.

At the hospital, I refused to leave her side. I needed to be there—right there—when she opened her eyes. I needed her to see that I was willing to pick up the pieces of our life together. That I could be strong enough for both of us.

But I couldn't make Kim see it that way. I'd let her go too far. I'd gone too far myself, with Gemma's pictures.

I won't let the same thing happen with Dani. I won't let Dani get away.

"Say it. I want you to tell the fucking truth for once."

I step closer, and she starts to step away, but there is nowhere for her to go. Her back is to the glass, and her neck is craned to look at me. When I speak, it is so low that she will have to strain to hear it over the wind. "She kissed me. Is that what you want me to say? I stayed up late to have a cigar. She found me out here. We talked. I told you she was getting too attached. Remember? I told you that. She kissed me, and that was it. You walked in on it, and you got upset. Of course you were upset."

"Oh, she kissed you?" Under her words, there it is again, that nasty little laugh. Why can't they ever just see it my way? She's looking right in my eyes, like she's searching for something. She shakes her head. Her lip is curled in disgust. "You're still lying," she says. "That isn't all that I saw. I know what I saw."

That night was colder than this one. A dark December sky and a bite to the wind. I did stay up to have a cigar. That part is true. To sit on my balcony and look out from the top of the world. And Mikayla did find me. Her big T-shirt and shorts, her face clean and bare, and I could see it in her eyes—she was enamored with me. I love that, I love the way a woman looks when she's falling in love.

When I first met Kim, she was on the side of the road. Big blond curls and a short skirt, leaning against a sun-beaten blue sedan with a flat tire. I pulled over to help. *Well,* she said, that flirtatious tease edging her words, *aren't I lucky?* And Dani was this sweet coffee shop girl with a smile for me every time I came through the door. I heard her talking to a coworker once, stressing about making rent that month, and I knew I could fix that. So easily, I could fix that for her. I could fly her anywhere in the world. I could give her anything and everything. And I did.

She should be grateful.

But Dani changed. Since Charlotte's birth, she stiffened when I touched her. Just that day, she snapped at me for kissing her in the kitchen.

And here was Mikayla. The night was windy and dark. A separate world. She stood in front of me, just desperate to be near me, her hands folded across her chest, staring down at her bare feet. She was hurt. She wanted me to look at her, she wanted someone to see her. To see the parts others never did.

You're cold, I said. Sliding my hands up her arms over the goose bumps. She leaned closer, then looked up at me with those lovesick eyes. She reached on her tiptoes to kiss me, like in the kitchen, but this time I didn't stop her.

Dani's right. I'm not telling her the whole truth—even if I want it to be. God, I want it to be.

I didn't push Mikayla away. I'd been drinking. It was a pathetic moment of weakness, a brief instance when I'd lost control.

I would have stopped it. I would have.

But then Dani came out and she saw what she saw, and she wouldn't calm down. She was hysterical. She was going to leave. She was going to leave, and she was going to take Charlotte with her. What would this do to Sophie? We would lose everything. I just needed to cool things down. I just needed some time. I had my briefcase with my emergency kit with the syringe of midazolam. We could put a pause on things, get the girls out of the house, talk things over in the morning. Let cooler heads prevail.

But when she woke up, she didn't remember. It was exactly what I had wanted from Kim in that hospital bed. Dani was so apologetic, so grateful for me, so happy to let me put things back in order and take care of her.

If they would just let me take care of things. If they would just trust me to lead. If they would just be happy.

She looks at me now. She lets out a scoff, then turns to slip past me, back toward the house. I grab her arm. "Dani, please."

"Let go of me."

But I don't. I tighten my grip. Because she can't leave. She can't go back in that house. Not with everyone still here. "Please," I say. "Let me go inside. Let me send everyone home. We can figure this out."

"That's what you care about? Your party guests? Of course—that's what you care about." My hand is still on her arm. She leans into me, tips her face up and close to mine, and when she speaks again, there is a meanness to her. "Everyone is going to know. You realize that, don't you? Everyone is going to know what a fucking monster you are."

I tug her back. One hard pull and the two of us are against the glass.

Her eyes flash. It's fear, I realize. She's afraid of me.

I should let her go, take a step back, but I grab her tightly by both arms, because I want to pull her close, to hold her. How can she be afraid of me? How can she think that I would hurt her? I can feel the fluttering panic inside her.

Then I realize—it's so obvious that I can't possibly avoid the realization—Curtis wanted Dani committed. Órlaith can confirm that she's ill. Dani's own mother is worried about her. Her sister too. And today? Everyone at this party was a witness. They all saw her losing it.

Who would be surprised, really?

If Dani jumped.

90

Kim

"Kim, are you still there?" Anita asks on the phone.

"What do I do now?" I say.

Inside the house, the party is getting loud again, chatter and laughter overlapping.

"You've done the hardest part," Anita says. "Admitting that you have a problem, taking responsibility."

That Irish woman was right—the world isn't fair. But it's time to be accountable, time to take responsibility for the things within my control. I can't control who will forgive me, but I can take a chance on forgiving myself.

Anita and I come up with a plan to meet soon, to check in often. "Thanks. Yeah, yeah, of course, I will." I hang up the phone.

I'm thinking of heading back inside, getting a slice of cake, when a scream rips the air, the kind of scream that flares every primal instinct. It comes from the balcony just above me. Then the sound of shattered glass. That's what falls first—a shower of glass, like glitter in the night, like sparkling stars.

Dani

People are born with a fear of falling, that hardwired reflex, that total-body jolt the exact moment you fall. We fall asleep. We fall in love. We fall into traps. It's the loss of control we're afraid of.

When the glass breaks, there is nothing left to control.

In Ethan's eyes, I think I see remorse. The falling takes forever. My whole life. I think of when I first heard Charlotte's cry. *She sounds like a kitten,* I said. Ethan kissed my forehead with a laugh choked by tears. Everything is too much, too many things, always. Always, always falling. Slipping away.

Maybe I just want to see the remorse. Maybe I've only ever seen what I wanted to see.

Still, I reach for him. Too late, but I reach all the same, a hardwired reflex.

The falling takes forever, but even forever has an end.

The bluestone patio surges up.

Órlaith

I don't say anything. I don't even think anything. I just run.

No one ever notices me, sees me, hears me. *Oh, you scared me,* Dani is always saying, throwing a hand to her chest, when I come up to talk to her. It's this old-woman gait, sure, these orthopedic shoes.

So they didn't hear me just now as I came onto the balcony.

But I heard enough.

It is the mother in me that takes over. The single-minded need to protect.

I slam into him with the full force of my feeble old body, with my hands, my elbows, my right shoulder. He is a mountain of a man. It is David versus Goliath, and he is unmovable, until he isn't, until that hairline crack in the glass gives way.

Mr. Matthews makes only a grunt of surprise, like. It is Dani that screams, screams and screams and screams.

Because the glass shatters, and I feel it the moment it happens, a wall of static tension, then a release. Because a person can only be pushed so far, because once you tip over the edge, there is no undoing what's been done. For a moment our eyes meet, his hand flails out for purchase, finds nothing but dark air, and he is falling. He is gone.

93

Kim

The scream comes from the balcony two stories above me. Glass rains onto the patio in twinkling flashes of light. But before I can even crane my neck to look, something—someone—falls, lands with a nauseating crunch just in front of me.

"Oh, God." *Ethan.* I am at his side. I am on my knees, the doctor in me taking over like autopilot, shaking fingers jabbing into his neck, but I know. I know. "Oh, Ethan."

Once, a couple brought me their chocolate Lab. He'd been hit by a car. *Just a bump,* the husband said. The dog looked relatively unharmed—no mangled limbs or torn skin. *Please, please,* the wife said. But the eyes were rolled back, blood pooled in his mouth, and the sound. The throat-closing, guttural rattle.

Ethan makes that sound now. Like when he can't form the words he wants to say. And my heart splits in two.

"Mommy?" A voice behind me. I turn. There is blood on my hands. I didn't hear the shuffle of people coming outside, the whole party, and Sophie at the bottom of the steps, looking at me, looking past me.

"Oh, baby," I say, and my knees are weak, but somehow my legs lift me, carry me, and I run to her, fold her into my arms as she collapses in shock.

Órlaith

Dani is on her knees, shaking with ugly sobs, and I am holding her, stroking her hair. I am telling her what I used to tell my own girl, when she fell from the monkey bars, skinned her knee on the pavement. "I know it hurts, pet. I know it hurts. But I'm here."

You hear stories of mothers with superpowers, the ability to lift a car from their endangered child. When you have your own little one, you can feel the truth of these tales, as if the strength of your love is more important than physics. There are no mountains you couldn't move, no seas you couldn't part, no way you couldn't—wouldn't—protect your child.

But it isn't true, sure, not always, not for everyone. Every single day, a mother loses her child.

I lost my child. I couldn't save her. Couldn't lift the car.

But she led me here, led me to another young one who needed me. She must have known that I wasn't done mothering yet.

95

The Morning After the Party

Blood still darkens Kim's dress in blotches as she arrives at the pediatric ward of North Central Baptist Hospital. Sophie rests under the sedation. Gemma sits at her side.

Kim pulls the extra chair over, touches her daughter's hand.

She is exhausted. She has been answering the police's questions for hours, and soon enough Sophie will wake, and what then? How will Kim help her navigate life without a father? Navigate the trauma of what happened—her dad falling to his death at her Sweet Sixteen? A freak accident.

Because that's what the police have ruled it: an accident.

Dani Matthews was with the victim at the time, the young wife who had recently been diagnosed with a mental illness, who had been acting erratically that very day. But there was no indication of foul play, the officers reported. The nanny had witnessed the entire thing. Mr. Matthews had simply leaned against the banister and the glass had shattered. The nanny had been warning people, in fact, that the glass was cracked. One of the waiters remembered her saying so that morning before the party started. She had warned one of the teenage girls from that spot as well.

It was an accident, plain and simple.

Kim wants a drink. Who would blame her?

Her eyes flick to the clock on the wall. She has been sober for almost ten hours now. She can make it the rest of the hour. The rest of the day. Tomorrow, even. She'll do it like that. Like Anita Lewis said, *One day at a time.*

Gemma reaches out her hand, takes hold of Kim's, and squeezes hard.

The blinds are twisted open. The morning sky is a bright blue. The fluorescent lights overhead buzz, and machines beep, and nurses and patients shuffle outside. The two women's fingers are intertwined, and they don't say the things they don't know how to say, but they feel them all the same, the way an ending can feel as fresh as newly over-turned earth.

96

One Year Later

Kim

I am on my knees in the dirt, a stiff-bristled brush in one hand, scrubbing the slimy inside of the water trough. With my other hand, I push my hair back from my face. Only April, and it's already sweaty-under-your-boobs hot. The summer will probably be brutal.

Mikayla comes out of the barn, riding boots over jeans, a *Hill Country Healing* T-shirt.

"Sweetheart, will you spread out some hay? There isn't enough grass right now, and I don't want the horses to get sand colic."

Mikayla nods. Sophie comes around the corner with a wheelbarrow to help her.

After Ethan's death, Dani got the house, the material possessions, the money in the bank accounts. But Ethan had investments, and he took care of me and Soph in his will. He was always good that way, responsible, reliable.

I bought a fifteen-acre ranch just a bit farther from town, started Hill Country Healing, offering equine therapy. Recovering addicts can benefit from caring for a horse. It's hard work to feed, to groom, to do all the things that need to be done—mend fences, shovel stables. Horses are intelligent—you can see it in the dark depths of their eyes—and a relationship with them requires trust on both sides. You can't scrub the dirt patches from a mare's hindquarters, feed her apples from your palm, take her for a ride, if she doesn't trust you, if you don't trust her. That sense of responsibility, of accountability, can get you through from one day to the next.

I think Mikayla needed this too. She seemed distant, closed up, but lately, I've seen a lifting of her head, a sense of ease returning. Who knows, really, what goes on in the lives of teenagers, though?

Gemma is taking me out tonight to celebrate earning my one-year chip. She's always coming up with elaborate ways to party without booze. I think she's booked an escape room this time—*Wear something sparkly,* she texted, *tonight is flapper-themed!*—then dessert for dinner at a place called Belgian Sweets in Castle Hills, with a waffle bar and a glass case filled with chocolates that look like works of art.

I just want you to be happy, Ethan used to say to me.

I think what he really meant was, *I just want you to be easier to be around.*

I'd see news articles, online videos—about women who stay in relationships that are no good for them. Things I'd come across when trying to figure out where my happiness had gone. I'd read the comments.

I would never put up with that.

If my husband pulled this crap, he'd be out on his ass so fast.

And my gut would twist, and my hand would reach for a drink. In every way that mattered, I wasn't strong enough. Because it's never that simple. Habits form and lives entangle. Leaving doesn't mean just letting go of the man you once loved, but losing the life you built together. Not just losing your house, but losing the home you raised your child in. It's letting go of your dreams for the future, the ones you held on to so tightly, even as they pulled you out into deeper waters, where you thought you'd drown if you ever let go.

I punished myself for so long for being weak. If AA has taught me anything, it's that the only strength I need is the strength to face today.

I spray out the water trough, rinse off any remaining soap. Then I fill it again with fresh water. I keep a rag in my back pocket, and I use it now to wipe sweat from my face and the back of my neck.

The sun is high, the sky bleached white. Using my hand as a visor, I shield my eyes to watch Sophie and Mikayla, spreading hay in patches around the dry pasture.

Sophie won't ever get over her father's death. Not his absence, and certainly not the blunt, shocking way it happened. I don't know if I'll ever tell her the full truth. For now, I let Sophie hold her good memories close, like the satin-trimmed blankie she used to rub against the tip of her nose as she fell asleep—Ethan playing big bear, swinging her around and around the open living room. Ethan sitting with her in the car in the driveway for nearly two hours after she didn't get the part she wanted in the middle school play. Ethan teaching her to boogie-board in the ocean, that blue beach house in Port A, taking her far out past the shore, much farther than I wanted, but him promising to keep an eye on her, and her smile so big it was more blinding than the summer sun. I let her keep them all. Because those memories are true too. Ethan was that man too.

Molly, my Great Pyrenees mix, comes to my side, chucks her big soft head under my hand. She loves the ranch, loves snuffling her nose into every smell she can find, pestering the horses, chasing the chickens around the yard, then holding them gently in her mouth without ever biting down.

Out in the pasture, Mikayla says something I can't hear. She squints into the light, and she smiles. Sophie laughs, bumps her with her hip.

I pat Molly. She pants with her big, open-mouthed smile. And I think about how we're all recovering. Aren't we? All of us, all the time.

97

Dani

I turn on the oven light so that I can keep an eye on the crust—it needs to blind-bake until perfectly golden, to avoid a soggy bottom—while I work on the lemon curd and the Italian meringue.

"Oh good, you're making more. It's popular today." It's Sally, my best employee, bringing a tray of dishes for the sink.

"That's because it's getting hot outside."

The bell over the door tinkles. Sally pokes her head out of the kitchen. "You have visitors," she says, picking up a tray of croissants and heading back to the register.

I rinse meringue off my fingers, dry my hands on my apron front.

I downsized to a one-story four-bedroom, crammed in next to neighbors who throw monthly block parties and let their kids play soft-ball in the streets. No wine cellar, no pool, no cliffside view, no balcony. We have a swing set, though—two pink bucket seats, a blue slide. A few weeks ago, Sophie brought a group of friends over to help me set it up. Kim came along, gave me a housewarming basket—a vanilla-scented candle, a dozen eggs from her own chickens, a white sage smudge stick. *To cleanse the spirits,* she said. A joke, of course, Kim's own dark brand.

The house—the old house—is still on the market. *Give it time,* my real estate agent tells me. *It just takes the right price, the right buyer. Someone from out of town, maybe, out of state.* Because people here say the house is haunted. How could they not?

Órlaith has told me that it is a "thin place," a place where the spirits seep through. When I drive by now, I always look up. How could I not? It is dark and empty, like a dollhouse abandoned in the attic. That's what Ethan wanted, wasn't it? A dollhouse. And what were we to him? Dolls?

Pretty playthings? Except we never belonged to him. The house never belonged to him.

It belongs to her.

It is *The Mother* that people whisper about still. *The Mother* who they see move about empty rooms through reflective glass.

"There's your mammy," Órlaith says, and Charlotte totters into the kitchen behind her, beelines for the low shelf where I keep pots and pans with metal lids that she has discovered make the most wondrous racket when clanged together.

I kept Órlaith on for practical reasons—I needed the help, especially as I started up the bakery—but also because we are bonded now. By trauma. By the dark secret of what really happened that night. By love. And Órlaith is so great with Charlotte.

My beautiful Charlotte, who flies through the rooms of our new home on legs chubby as rolls of biscuit dough, who grabs handfuls of hair beside my face to pull me in and plant a wet kiss on my nose, who reminds me again and again that the universe is terrifying and wonderful. That rocks collide and make planets, make life. And you have no control, not really, because even the decisions you make are blind, because you don't know if saying yes to a church dance will lead you to the love of your life and generations of children or if you'll get killed in a hit-and-run on the way.

There is no use worrying about the what-ifs—not for the future or the past.

The only thing to do, I've learned, is to listen to that small voice inside, the one that whispers *This isn't right* or the one that shouts *Go for it, take a leap.*

It doesn't come naturally to me, but I can get good at anything with practice. It's like making bread—one terrible loaf after terrible loaf, until the weight of ingredients is second nature, the kneading of the dough a force of habit.

"Be careful," Órlaith says, tapping the knobs of my stove. "You'll be checking that these are off before you close now, won't you?"

"Of course," I say.

"Because, you know, I had a friend once . . ."

I put on a silicone mitt and open the oven door, slide the crust out.

With any bake, but especially a blind bake, you have to trust your gut to know when the pastry is exactly right, crisp without being overdone.

It doesn't come naturally to me, but I can learn to trust myself. To forgive the mistakes I didn't mean to make.

98

Órlaith

In the wild twistings and turnings of life, I have inexplicably found myself a part of a family again. I have Dani, whose laundry I sometimes fold when she stays late at the bakery, whom I cover with a blanket when she falls asleep on the sofa, who always makes sure I take my cholesterol medication and drives me anywhere in the city because I will never for the life of me get used to these busy quadruple-lane motorways.

And I have Charlotte, big-cheeked and big-toothed smiling Charlotte, whom I am blessed to rock to sleep for nap time, to push on the swings Dani bought for the back garden, or to take to the splash pad down the road. She runs to the door when she sees me, lets me brush her hair into twin ponytails, holds my hand when we cross the street. I get to watch her grow, get to be part of the watching and the looking over.

I scoop Charlotte up from the floor of the bakery kitchen now. We've come to say hello to Mammy, to grab a pair of ham and cheese kolaches to take for lunch in the park.

I am no longer haunted.

Sometimes I feel the breeze—hot here in Texas, and smelling nothing like the sea-salted soft days of home—and I close my eyes, and I wait for a presence that no longer comes. And, in those moments, I feel dead lonely, I feel the grief of loss all over again.

But, also, I know it is right. I know she is finally at rest. My sweet Katie.

After Colm died, I packed up the rooms one by one. Sifting through decades of rubbish that had accumulated, closets stuffed with old sweaters and books and boxes of papers, kitchen cabinets with mismatched teacups and a casserole dish borrowed thirty years ago and never returned.

I almost didn't bother with the outdoor shed at all, almost told Caroline Doyle down the road to just let her husband come and take the whole lot. What use did I have for some old tools? But they were my Colm's things, so I rolled up my sleeves and did what needed doing.

The shed was dark and dank, the wood swollen with the mist of a thousand days, and I had to wave the cobwebs from my sleeves and my hair, ducking my head to avoid the worst of it.

I found it in a red metal toolbox on top of the workbench, a folded letter, the stamps marked and faded, the handwriting of the address as familiar as the lines that creased my own knuckles.

Dearest Mam and Da, the letter began.

Katie had gone to college in the States. She had fallen in love with America on that first trip abroad, vowed to go back, and, when my girl set her mind to something, you could be sure she'd find a way. I was worried, of course, couldn't bear the thought of there being thousands of miles between us, but Katie called every Sunday, and she sounded so happy. At least, at first she did.

She met a boy, fell in love, madly, head over heels, the way you only can when you're nineteen. So young. Just a child, like. She sent us photos of the lad, nice-looking and hardworking. He called on the phone, asked Colm for Katie's hand. They got engaged, and Colm and I were meant to fly to the States to meet him properly, but that trip never happened.

Because one night, Katie got in her car. The roads were slick with rain, she hadn't been driving long, and in America everything is on the wrong side. The car veered over the double yellow lines, and she hit a tree, full force. She was killed instantly. That was what the American police told the Irish gardaí. It was Jack Kelly who came to tell us—Jack, who went to St. Joseph's with us, who Colm drank with at the pub, who had been over to ours for Sunday roast more than once—who came to our front door, hat in his hand, to tell us that our little girl was already gone. She'd been gone a few hours by then, and I hadn't known, hadn't had the slightest sense of it.

An accident, they ruled it. Plain and simple.

But that was a lie. And sometime after, sure, my Colm knew it was a lie, because he got a letter, and he kept that letter a secret for more than twenty years.

> Dearest Mam and Da, Please don't blame yourselves. I love you both to pieces. But I can't do this anymore. There is something wrong with me, something dark and ugly. I keep making a mess of it all. I keep pissing people off. I keep doing things I don't remember. I feel like I'm going insane. The only good thing in my life is him, but I don't want to do this to him anymore. I don't want to do this to the two of you. Everything will just be better without me. I will love you forever. Katie

I know why Colm kept the letter a secret, why he hid the letter for two decades, took the lie to his grave. He did it as a kindness to me. I held that letter, the paper soft, as though Colm had gone to it often over the years, and I felt the stabbing pain of Katie's death anew. Because it hadn't been an accident. Katie had done this on purpose. She had chosen to leave this gaping hole in the world that could never be filled because there would never be another one exactly like her.

But also another feeling consumed me as I read that letter. Another feeling inhabited me like a spirit.

I might not have known my daughter was going to die that day. I might have gone about my morning, making tea and toast and starting a load of laundry and whinging at Colm for leaving a pair of socks on the floor, with not a single inkling that my baby was already dead.

But I still had a mother's intuition—I didn't have a good feeling about the boy she was dating. *He seems to have a good head on his shoulders, like,* Colm said. And Katie seemed to think he was absolutely perfect, the sun and the moon, and she couldn't be happier. But I didn't like the way she sounded when she was with him. I felt a gap widening between us, more palpable than the miles of physical distance. She seemed less sure of herself, less true—when she had only ever been sure and true.

I could hear the stress in her voice when she called on Sundays. There were little things upsetting her, things that didn't make sense. A friend was suddenly angry with her, refused to speak to her, but she didn't know why. She misplaced things more often, made stupid mistakes, she said. *Everything is just falling apart, Mam,* she told me once.

Well, we'll be going there soon enough, Colm assured me, *then we can see for ourselves.*

When I found the letter, I decided it was time to do just that—I had nothing and no one left tying me to Ireland. It was time to make the trip to the States, time to find Ethan Matthews and see what kind of man he was for myself.

I had only wanted to see him, to get a sense of him, to ask him about Katie, about those last few days. But it didn't take long before I saw him for what he was.

It didn't take long before I knew what had to be done.

Because if there is anything a mother is good at, it's doing the dirty work, it's rolling up her sleeves and getting things done. The unseen things, the unappreciated. Because there is no glory in it. No one pats you on the back for doing the dishes. No one gives you an award for sweeping the kitchen tiles. No one wants to do these things. But some things need doing all the same.

My resolve hardened like steel. I knew that I would do it. I just wasn't sure how. Then there on the balcony, I saw my chance, my chance to right the wrong that had been done to my beautiful girl. On the balcony, I felt the hand to my shoulder, guiding me forward. I heard the fervent whispers on the wind.

It was the mother in me that took over.

Acknowledgments

The idea for *Party of Liars* hit me all at once while I was on my hands and knees under the kitchen table, scooping up peas.

Earlier in the year, I had made the decision to give up on my dream of becoming a writer. We were in a pandemic, and I had two small children home with me while I taught multiple composition courses online across two different universities. I barely had time to shower, so writing in my "free time" now seemed ludicrous. I texted my sisters and told them that my twenty-year journey of trying to become an author was over. And, for about a month, I'd convinced myself I was relieved. But then those peas fell . . . and I opened a new Word document.

So, I'll start this list of so many thank-yous with the simplest one: Lucy and Edie, thank you for being messy eaters.

To my incomparable agent, Stefanie Lieberman: You rescued me from the slush pile and believed in me before anyone else in the industry. I will never be able to thank you enough. And, of course, thank you to Molly Steinblatt and Adam Hobbins. The three of you read each draft with care. I love our phone calls. I love that you push me to be the best writer I can be. I am in awe of how ferociously you have championed this book.

Thank you to my amazing editor, Alexandra Sehulster. The day you called me will forever be one of my favorite days. Your edits are sharp, and this book is better for them. To the entire Minotaur team, thank you for your enthusiasm (and for the great title).

Phoebe Morgan, my UK editor, your email made me cry in a Jiffy Lube parking lot. Thank you to the Hodder & Stoughton team for all of those kind words. To Hayley Steed and the Janklow & Nesbit foreign rights department—Nathaniel Alcaraz-Stapleton, Maimy Suleiman, Emily Randle, Janet Covindassamy—and to all my foreign editors, thank you for bringing this book to the world.

Thank you to my film/TV agents, Orly Greenberg and Olivia Fanaro, for saying the ending was "perfect" and for making fairy tales seem possible.

To dear friends and family, who read early drafts and live-texted me their reactions—Marilyn Boswell (the best bookstore-browsing buddy), Sarah Pitarra (who has dragged me along to some seriously swanky Texas parties), Angela Pitarra Langenberg (the best at sister-in-lawing and thoughtful gift-giving), Aunt Ann, Aunt Julie, and Aunt Meghan (the scene when Kim sneaks to listen to her aunts laugh around the kitchen table was, of course, inspired by all of you)—your questions helped me, and your words of encouragement kept me going. To Susan McNamara, who helped me with the Irish details and dialect in Órlaith's sections—all remaining mistakes are my own.

To my fellow writers, too many to name, but especially to Amanda Eyre Ward, May Cobb, and Katie Gutierrez. Thank you for writing books that inspire me. Thank you for coffee shop dates and Copa nights that kept me sane and pool days with the kids that saved us from the Texas summer heat. To all the authors who blurbed this book—I fell in love with your words first.

Thank you to everyone who ever encouraged me to write, starting with my mom and dad—Kathleen Cox and Captain James T. Cox. Beside the front door of my parents' home hang three framed portraits of me and my sisters, labeled: "The Writer," "The Adventurer," and "The Artist." I am "The Writer." Mom and Dad, thank you for calling me a writer, thank you for watching the girls every week, for giving me that most valuable gift of time. Mom, thank you for being a reader, for giving me my first mystery novel, for watching *Columbo* with me and *Monk* and every British mystery we can find. Thank you for checking that the doors and windows are locked, for worrying and keeping us safe. Dad, thank you for teaching me the names of trees, for taking the girls outside, for always fixing my car, and for keeping the house stocked with wine and so much soup. But mostly, thank you for telling me to "choose greatness" and for showing me how with everything you do.

Resa, thank you for being my fairy godmother. For letting me write in your clean house while you were at work, for being among the aunts who I love to hear laughing around the table, for reading this book, and for being the most decent human being I've ever known. Thank you for holding me when I was little and pointing up into the night sky so we could say good night to the moon.

Thank you to my entire family, for being loud, for being a collection of readers and writers and artists and storytellers, for texting and calling (even though I know you hate talking on the phone, Cathy), for sharing in my joy. To my oldest friends, Gracie, Kaylee, and Erin, for sticking by me. To my Pitarra family, thank you for crude jokes and casino trips and being there when it matters. To Lynn Sinclair, for sharing your kindness and wisdom with a seventeen-year-old girl who posted the first chapter of her book to a discussion forum way back when the internet was brand-new.

To one cousin specifically: Jessica Leake. You might as well be a sister. You are always my first reader. Thank you for the nights we stayed up in middle school to dream up stories together, for the thousands of pages shared back and forth, for paving the way.

To every awesome English teacher I ever had, but especially to Christine and John McDermott. Thank you for making the creative writing department at SFA. Thank you for writing on my poem "See me after class" and then telling me you thought I had real talent. I held those words tightly in my chest for two decades.

Thank you to the Purdue MFA, to my fellow cohorts and to the faculty—Porter Shreve, Patricia Henley, Sharon Solwitz, Beth Minh Nguyen—for expanding my taste as a reader and helping me find my voice.

And to my sisters, Mady ("The Adventurer") and Annie ("The Artist"): Thank you for texting me your random thoughts at random moments, for reading every book I tell you to and then calling me immediately after, for a million nights in our pj's on the couch and adventures all over the world, for being my best friends.

To Nick, my big-hearted, fast-talking, arm-wrestling, comic-artist husband. When I first told you I was a writer, you believed me. Thank you for forcing me to take Amanda's novel-writing class. For creating space and time for me to write. For talking out plot holes and dreaming up creepy imagery. For reading multiple drafts and arguing over each and every word. Thank you for being so sure this day would come.

Again, to Lucy and Edie: Thank you for making me a mom, for showing me how painfully exponential love is, and for being so wonderfully yourselves—please always stay yourselves.

About the Author

Kelsey Cox received her MFA in fiction from Purdue University and works from home in the Texas Hill Country. You can often find her writing at the Mammen Family Public Library, chasing around her two young daughters, or watching British mysteries with her mom and aunts. On nights when bedtime goes as planned, she enjoys curling up on the sofa, a glass of wine in one hand, and a book with complicated characters and a killer twist in her lap.